The White Raven is a work of fiction. All events and dialogue, as well as all characters, with the exception of some well-known historic and public figures are products of the author's imagination and are not to be construed as real. Where true historic or public figures appear, the situations, incidents and dialogues involving those persons are entirely fictional and are not intended to depict actual events or to change the entirely fictional nature of the work. In all other respects, any resemblance of the characters to persons living or dead is entirely coincidental.

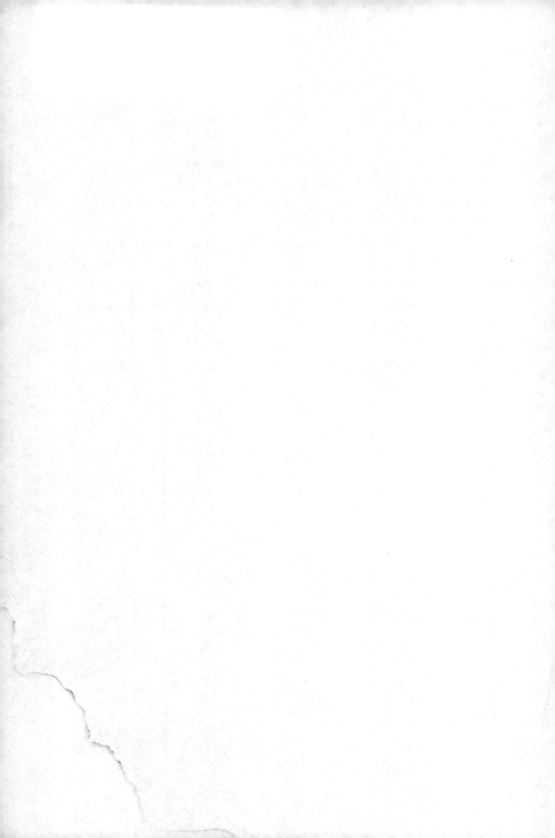

For

Autumn and Layla Jane

Other Titles by John Bushby

Shadow Soldiers

The Warszaw Express

The Rhinemaiden's Song

Prowler Ball

The Last Voyage of the Paramaribo Queen

"If any foreign minister begins to defend to the death a 'peace conference', you can be sure his government has already placed its orders for new battleships and airplanes."

Joseph Stalin

Contents

Final Orders

Cicadas whirred as hot breaths of wind rose from the scorched hillside swept under the door and raised swirls of dust in the room. In one corner a censer smoked, its lavender scent battled with centuries of life's aromas that had permeated the walls. It was not working. Advancing death hung in the air and neither the country air nor the incense could mask the odors of sickness and decay within. The lonely stone farmhouse seemed an incongruous place for a wealthy man to sit out his last years. Still, the magnificent views from the veranda of Cap d'Ail and the shimmering Mediterranean beyond must have provided some solace. Lieberman had made the journey from Warsaw by train at this man's request. He owed him that much at least. Seeing him propped up on a woven-rush chaise, a coverlet swaddling his frame had startled him when the ancient housekeeper ushered him in. Once one of the most powerful men in the world, the erstwhile Merchant of Death, Sir Basil Zaharoff was seated in a woven-rush chair, his feet propped up on an ottoman, in front of a warming fire. He had gone into seclusion the year before, and now Lieberman thought he knew why. The acrid smell of ketone had increased as he drew nearer to the old man.

Zaharoff nodded at the servant and then looked to see who had entered the room. His eyes, once honed to see through other men's deceptions, were now dulled, and he stared at his guest.

"Sir Basil? It is Karl Lieberman. You sent for me." The Latvian spoke slowly and with hesitation, not knowing if the sick man recognized him.

"Yes, yes Karl, of course. Come in. Sit here near the fire. Life is nothing but ironic. I was borne in a house like this. Now having lived a life lived of excess I find myself comforted by these humble surroundings."

Despite his infirmity the man's mind appeared to be as sharp as ever. Lieberman was relieved, for he had hoped he had not traveled all this way to listen to a maudlin apologia from a doddering old man. For nearly two decades, Zaharoff had been Lieberman's employer, sending him on forays throughout Europe, always in secret and always as part of a larger scheme. After Zaharoff had secured the rights to the Maxim gun, the world's first successful machine gun, for Vickers, Ltd., the one-time Turkish arsonist cum British peer turned his attention to aviation. He was especially interested to see how the new machines could be employed in war. Back then, Lieberman was just an enterprising young engineer, but being both Jewish and a native of one of Imperial Russia's Baltic provinces his opportunities were severely restricted by the Tsarist caste system. The wily Zaharoff saw something in the ambitious Lieberman and had put him to work. As the years went by Lieberman learned all there was to know about the developments in military aviation in Europe and at the same time became adept at spy craft and the ability to survive while being surrounded by enemies.

The White Raven

Lieberman looked about the room, so Spartan in its appointments, and wondered why here of all places? The man had a villa on Cap Ferrat, staffed by scores of servants.

"I can see it in your eyes, Lieberman, you think I must have taken leave of my senses. Why shut myself up in this farmhouse in the middle of nowhere? Well, I have come to know that I cannot trust anyone in this part of the world except old Mathilde."

"That was Mathilde, the one who showed me in?" asked Lieberman.

"Yes. Everyone thinks I am somewhere else, living out my years in regal splendor. Even my family are not sure when or where I will turn up. They have enough of my money, so I will do as I please. Well enough of that, I did not ask you here to reminisce, if that was what you were fearing," said Zaharoff.

Lieberman sighed with relief.

"Pour me some wine. There is a bottle of decent champagne in the bucket on the side table. I may be a diabetic, but I can still enjoy the bubbly, even if it may cost me a few toes."

Lieberman winced, walked to the sideboard and returned with a flute for Zaharoff.

"Not drinking, Karl?" asked Zaharoff.

"No sir. Not just yet."

"Well, you may reconsider after I tell you why you are here." Zaharoff grunted, or perhaps it was a laugh, Lieberman could not tell.

"Karl, do you remember back four years ago, in 1928 when I destroyed all my papers? Everyone said I was crazy. It caused quite a stir. But there was general relief in some quarters."

"Yes, you said that a valet or one of the servants had gotten their hands on your private journals, and so you destroyed every shred of your files."

"Yes, I did. It was, of course and as with most tales about my life, not the entire truth, but close enough. There are quite a few individuals walking around today who might not still be breathing had I not done so. Moreover, I convinced the world that I had done so in order to buy myself a few more years of life. Although anyone saying that my current situation falls under the category of 'living' must be delusional. In any event, that is not why you are here. I have a last commission for you to undertake for me."

Lieberman thought to protest, but he knew that the man would find such a comment as supercilious and at best out of touch with the facts. Zaharoff was clearly ill, and no amount of happy assurances to the contrary would change that. There is someone I need you to contact—and work with if it comes to that. She is in Germany, and I fear that she is the kind of woman who could find herself in danger, if she is not careful." Zaharoff sipped some of the champagne. "Veuve Cliquot 1922, a good vintage, especially coming so close after the war." From under the folds of his blankets, Zaharoff extracted a small brown envelope and handed it to Lieberman.

Lieberman looked at the sealed envelope Zaharoff offered him, on the outside of which his name was scrawled in a shaky hand.

"That is a little something that I kept from the flames. Karl, have you read *Mein Kampf*?"

Lieberman looked up, startled by the question. "No sir, not my cup of tea," Lieberman replied.

"No, I suppose not, but you should. Everyone should, despite the atrocious and pedantic writing; it is a warning, as clear as any as to what is going to happen in Europe. As it turns out a master of deception has hoodwinked the Germans. This man Hitler means to do what he says in those turgid pages. If he and his gang of thugs gain real power in Germany, then Europe, and then I fear that the world will be in for a very nasty period. Of course, someone might do humanity a kindness and eradicate the man before he succeeds. But his kind seems to have nine lives, like cats. In any event, you should really get a copy of it, and read it before the apocalypse descends. But now, let me tell you a story, it concerns the person mentioned in the papers inside that envelope. Perhaps you should get that drink, for it is a long story, and it is a hot afternoon. For that matter get me one too. Mathilde need not know."

For the next two hours, Lieberman sat and listened to the old man. As he had promised it was indeed a long story and one that required going back to long before the war, to when men like Zaharoff traveled in private railcars and were entertained in the finest homes of the men who once ruled the now long–dead empires. By the time the old man had finished, the Provençal sun was dipping into the west, and a fresh sea breeze had begun to rise up the slopes, filling the room with a salty tang.

"So, my dear Lieberman, I am entrusting you with not only a very deep secret, but also with a person's life, someone who is quite dear to me."

"I can understand that," said the Latvian, "but what do you want me to do with this secret? And how do you wish me to proceed? You could have given this to your friends in the British Foreign Office."

"Yes, once I could have done, but no longer. I fear that my old friend Perfidious Albion is not to be trusted any longer. I have long suspected that years ago my old enemy Felix Dzerzhinsky had found a way for the Bolsheviks to compromise both the Foreign Office as well as Britain's counterintelligence service, MI-6. No, I think you might take this to your new friends from across the ocean. The Americans may be amateurs, but I doubt that they have yet been turned by Moscow. Nonetheless, be very discrete. I do not want another innocent death on my conscience. It is black enough as it is. Perhaps when I die I will know that at the end I did some good for this sordid world. Now you must go before darkness descends. Mathilde will give you another envelope with money and the number of an account upon which you can draw, even after my death. It is not a fortune, but enough. Now be off with you. Thank you, and goodbye."

Lieberman looked at the once powerful man, his body broken by illness and age and stood to leave.

"Good-bye Sir Basil, I will take care of this matter, on that you may rest assured."

The Man in the Mosel

Summer had turned brittle and dry. The land was waiting for the autumn rains. Plane trees turned up their withering leaves in hope of a bit of moisture. Along the stream bank the leaves of the trees gave off a dry rattle in the breeze, their tips glinting in the sun like flecks of gold. Further up the slopes of the narrow valley and across the hills, patches of brown and ochre replaced summer's green. Soon these forests of the South Ardennes would fall silent, the birds would head south to Africa, and the only sound to be heard would be the thud of a local woodsman splitting logs for his winter fire.

Still, it was a fine day. In the forest, motes of dust rose and swirled in shafts of hazy sunlight that shot through the canopy of leaves. The stream, a small tributary of the Mosel, was sluggish, its current diminished from the spring torrent to just a bright ribbon that splashed around rocks and gravel bars and shimmered like molten silver in the September sun. From the slope above the stream there came the soft but steady sound of a man walking. He was stepping carefully to avoid tree roots and stones that might have caused him to tumble and, in so doing, break the wispy bamboo fly rod he carried in his right hand. A quick glance at his attire would confirm that he was just another late-season angler off to try his luck with the mountain trout. Dressed in a canvas jacket with bulging pockets that held the accessories of his sport, and with his legs encased in tan hip boots, he stepped out from the tree line and halted. Before him was a narrow, seldom used path that wound through a meadow of tall grass that led to the stream. Standing perfectly still, his body half in the shadow of the trees, he listened carefully. There were no sounds save the wind, the soft gurgle of the stream, and a few birds calling. Nothing else stirred, he was alone. When he was at last certain that he was alone and unobserved, he stepped onto the path and out into the sunlight, making his way toward the rippling water. There had been little rain in the past month and the muddy roads in the area were dusty white. In the stream, the lack of water forced the trout to school in the deeper, cooler pools.

He knew there were fish in this stream; he had been fishing here for the last three afternoons. As he had on each of the previous afternoons, he approached the water quietly and then waded out to where he could stand knee-deep in the current and began to fish. The current was cool and pressed tightly against the legs of his waders, holding him fast. To anyone passing, a man standing in the stream casting for fish simply became a fixture of the landscape—had anyone there been paying attention. At the Pensione Gastman, a small hotel that he used as his home when in this part of the world, they knew him as *fou Americain pecheur de truite*—the crazy American trout fisherman, because he fished alone and far from the popular places. To the locals, fishing was not a sport, but a way of putting food on the table. He was just another extravagant tourist, and he did nothing to dissuade his hosts of their opinion. Yet, they gave him grudging approval, because he always returned in the evening with a creel full of trout, which he shared with the innkeeper and her family.

For nearly ten minutes he stood there, at the forest's edge, listening, taking in everything around him. The riffling water, the waving grass at the far side of the bank, the way the sun cast shadows on the hillside, he took all of it in. Far off to his right, on the south bank of the little stream, he could see a small cluster of buildings made from the local gray stone. Above them rose a conical steeple covered in the same gray slate. He knew that was the German village of Wallendorf across the river. A flutter of red in that direction caught his eye. That would be the customs post on the German side of the narrow bridge, marked by the new national swastika flag. No, he would not be crossing there today, not this time.

Less than nine months had passed since Adolf Hitler had been made chancellor of Germany. Although National Socialism was tightening its grip on Germany, it was government policy to make most Americans welcome. Hitler wanted to impress the world with his plans and programs, so it was that most American visitors were left alone. Of course they were followed, that was to be expected, but as long as they expressed admiration for the new Reich, they were ignored. Still, he thought better of crossing, best to stay on the Belgian side this trip.

Stepping further out into the flow of the stream he could feel the current tug at his ankles, as if it wanted him to tumble southward. When he found the right spot, he stopped moving and watched and listened. In a moment, his patience was rewarded as a sleek trout rose from the depths and snatched a caddis fly from just above the surface of the stream. He smiled and reached into his jacket and extracted a small black metal box. On the outside, the word "Hardy's" in gold lettering was just visible. He flipped open the box and extracted a concoction of feathers and fur that was identical to the insect now lodged in the trout's belly. With a few quick motions, he tied the simulated caddis to the end of the fly line's silken tippet and cast it out over the pool. He would fish until the man he had come to meet appeared.

Werner Walthers was not a very important man in the new Germany, just an economist, but an economist with very interesting connections. Although a graduate of Leipzig University, he was not notable; he had never published any important papers; nor did he sit on any major government committees. True to form, Germans kept records of everything. Meeting minutes and reports were carefully recorded, and Werner Walthers was in charge of making sure the records were cataloged and safely filed away, an important job. So, even if he never set foot in the gilded offices of the Reich Chancellery, when it came to financial matters, he could read the reports about everything that went on in the higher echelons of the Third Reich. What was more important, in that that autumn of 1933 was that Walthers knew where the money was coming from and where it was going. And he did not like what he saw.

Walthers was a patriot, but not a zealot; not like the Nazis. He had a natural hatred for the French and felt much the same about the British. But his sister had moved to Chicago after the war. She had written to him and told him of the wonders of the "city with broad shoulders," and so he felt some synergy with the Americans. Maybe they could help with his problem. He did not want Germany to continue to suffer under the crushing weight of reparations payments, but he had read *Mein Kampf*, and he was certain that the Nazis were not the answer. Somehow, he thought, if he passed the information that he had to the Americans, maybe they could help Germany rid herself of this new scourge. So in 1930 he took a chance. He knew that American businessmen frequented the Adlon Hotel, when they were in Berlin. He made it a habit to stop at the lobby bar there, and despite the extravagant cost of their beer he met a few Americans. Finally an American businessman asked him if he would like to make a few extra marks. They would help each other, the man had said. Since then, every six months or so, he would arrange to go fishing and deliver what information he had.

The contact plan was simple, and that's the way Braham liked it. He would appear in the area as a tourist and fish the stream. At some point Walthers would cycle down the road on the German side and, appearing hot and thirsty, stop and approach the stream. Whatever information he was to pass would be placed on the stream bank. Walthers would cup his hands, dip them into the stream and take a drink. Then rising from the water, he would place the packet of information on the stream bank, remount his bicycle and continue on. Braham would continue casting his fly, then casually step over to the German side and retrieve the deposit. Any reply would be made as a matrimonial advertisement in the *Berlin Tageblatt* the following week.

After two hours Harry Braham eased his back against the broad trunk of an ancient beech tree and smoked a Gauloises, the only cigarettes he could find in this part of the world. Walthers might not be coming after all. Still, he had to see it through. Next to him was a creel full of fresh trout, covered in moss to keep them moist. He had caught the fish, but now he waited for the man he had come all this way to meet. From his perch under the beech, Braham could see the narrow dirt road that wound north from Wallendorf along the German side of the stream until it disappeared into the hills. If his man were coming, this would be his route.

From inside his jacket Braham drew out a small flask, silver and wrapped in fine calfskin. It was from Swain and Adney in Piccadilly, a parting gift from Jocelyn Cavanaugh when she left Braham to marry Sir William Bishop. Damn, she was beautiful. Why did she have to marry that cocaine-addled asshole anyway? Title, money, well, sooner or later he would see her again. Marriage was always the best camouflage. In a silent toast to the lovely lady, he unscrewed the cap and, putting the opening to his lips, tipped it back and took a long pull of single malt. Then, screwing the cap shut, he replaced it in his pocket. From his pocket he took a very small pair of field glasses and scanned the opposite shore. Nothing moved, no sign of a watcher.

With a slow release of breath he shifted his position. Despite the wads of dry grass upon which he sat, he was getting weary of the waiting. He felt as if his whole life was spent continuously waiting. Waiting for contacts, waiting for information, and waiting for the woman to come along who would erase the memory of Agata. There had been other women, and Jocelyn had been just one. God knew that he had his pick of the bright young things of Paris, Berlin and even a few Americans who had wandered to Europe looking for romance and adventure, but nothing ever developed. Either his job got in the way, or he grew bored. Beautiful as they were, none of them captured his heart the way Agata had. But she was gone, swept away on the retreating red tide of a defeated Bolshevik army.

Braham did not feel sorry for himself. He could get along in life on his own, but there were times when a pang loneliness grabbed him. Sometimes on rainy nights, the empty spot in his bed became as hospitable as a polar ice sheet, empty, cold and too frighteningly real. It was on those nights that he would get up and pace his apartment, or dress and go out into the storm and walk along the glistening cobbles until thoroughly soaked, he would return home to a hot bath and a brandy. Yet it was the life he had chosen. Women would come and go, and, as he grew older and, he hoped, wiser, perhaps one would appear who would change everything.

The afternoon was wearing on, and his man had not yet shown. He looked down at his wrist, a plain gold Piaget with an alligator strap indicated it was going on two-thirty. He would wait another hour. Moscow rules said that it was the contact who dictated the timing and location of the meeting. Harry Braham would have to wait. The afternoon was warm, and he was getting hungry. The old woman at the *pensione* had mad him some ham sandwiches, and he looked into the big pocket on the back of his fishing vest and retrieved two tiny cylinders of baguette wrapped in newspaper and a half-bottle of gewürztraminer. He pulled a battered Opinal with a corkscrew from his trouser pocket, and opened the wine. He should have sunk it in the stream when he arrived. It was warm, but still bright and dry. Ten minutes later he was no longer hungry but felt sluggish and stupid from the wine. Above him a fat brown spider, always the harbinger of autumn, was spinning an elaborate web. With precision the arachnid swung back and forth dangling from its length of silk and creating its masterpiece. Fascinated, Braham sat back and watched, mesmerized by the weaving.

He woke with a start, he had been dreaming. How long had he slept? That had never happened before during an operation. He must be getting old, and careless. But she was there in the dream, warm and alive, smiling contentedly as she had done after they made love. Agata looked at him with those blue eyes that held his soul. Maybe if he closed his eyes she would be there again. He tried, but the buzzing of insects around his face emphasized the futility of conjuring her back from the dead. She was gone, and he was alone. In the stream he heard a splash and looked to the spot along the riffle where he had been fishing. A man was standing there.

Slowly, Braham rose to his feet and picked up his gear. With creel dangling from his left side and rod in his right hand, he clanked his way toward the stream's bank. The man was facing eastward, his back toward Braham, as he made a series of short, rolling casts over the water. The man knew what he was about, thought Braham, for the fly drifted slowly over the riffles and landed almost lifelike on the surface. Instantly there came a flash. The fly had just landed on the surface when a greedy trout gulped it down. Braham was closer now and saw how the man expertly played the fish and set the hook into the trout's mouth. Another splash and the man had the fish within arm's reach and then into the net.

"Very nicely done!" Braham spoke in German.

The man turned and faced him. Braham could see that he was dressed for the stream in what would have delighted the outfitters at Abercrombie & Fitch or Orvis. A green-tweed Norfolk jacket, blue shirt with a plaid tie, and hip boots covering tan corduroy trousers topped with a flat brimmed tweed cap; the man seemed to have stepped out of a fishing outfitters catalog.

"I am sorry if I woke you," replied the man in German. He had a slightly high-pitched mellifluous voice, and his German carried the sharp tones of Berlin. "I noticed you up there under the tree and thought to take a few fish while you enjoyed your nap. Have you been fishing here long?"

Braham moved closer as he watched the man deftly remove the fly and hook from the gleaming fish before he plopped the creature into his wicker creel.

"Yes, I had good luck this morning and found that spot," pointing back over his shoulder toward where he had been resting. "Have you fished here before?"

"Me? No, I just happened to be in the area on business and thought to give it a try," the man replied.

From where he now stood, Braham could see the gleaming curved fender of a car parked along the edge of the German side of the stream. It was a Horch if he guessed correctly.

"Is that your car up there?"

"Yes, I drove up from the village," he said, using his rod to point toward Wallendorf. "A man at my hotel recommended this stretch of river to me."

"Funny part of the world here, the borders are very confused. I wonder if that fish was a German trout or a Belgian." Braham spoke in an attempt to engage the man.

The man laughed. "I suppose so. In any event, I am standing on the German side of the stream, while you appear to be on the Belgian side. Did you have any luck?"

Braham looked at the man before him. Despite the expensive fishing outfit, the man had the look of someone who seldom left his office. His wan face had the look of the bureaucrat, and his Berlin accent had a flavor of officialdom.

"Taking a vacation from the office?" Braham ventured. "Won't you be missed?"

The man did not respond at once, but reeled in his line and hooked the fly to the wire hook retained at the front of his rod's cork grip.

"Missed? No, I don't think so. I had business in the area and I decided to take the time to enjoy a few hours outdoors. I have the luxury of making my own schedule, although I might not have been able to reach this place at all."

Braham's instincts were kicking in. What was he trying to tell him?

"Why was that?" he asked jovially. "Flat tire on your Horch?"

"No. That I could have attended to. No, there was a horrific accident in the village just as I was about to leave. A man on a bicycle was struck by a large beer wagon that was attempting to turn in the village square."

"My goodness," said Braham. "Perhaps some elderly person who misjudged speed and distances?"

"Oh no. The man was a guest at the same hotel as I am. He was some kind of bureaucrat from Berlin. We met over coffee last evening, and he said he often visits the area to tour the countryside on his bicycle."

"Was he badly injured?" Braham asked forcing a note of hope into his voice.

"Well, yes I suppose so. He was crushed to death when one of the barrels rolled off the wagon and fell on him."

Braham looked at the man's face and knew that he knew, but keeping up the charade, went on, "dreadful, his family will no doubt be devastated."

"Well perhaps, but the Reich will compensate them for their loss." Then he looked at his wristwatch, "my goodness look at the time. I am afraid my schedule will not permit me any further dalliance in this lovely spot. I will leave the trout, whatever their national origin, to you."

With that the man waded through to the bank and was about to climb up to this car, but turned toward Braham instead.

"I'm sorry, how rude of me. I never introduced myself. My name is Albrecht Theurer, Doktor Albrecht Theurer to be precise."

"How nice to meet you Doktor Theurer, my name is . . ."

"Yes. I know who you are Mr. Braham. *Auf wiedersehen.* Perhaps we will meet again. Oh, before I go."

From his inside jacket pocket the German produced a small round metal can and handed it to Braham. It was the kind photographers used to hold rolls of 35-millimeter film. It was scratched and one corner slightly bent. "That is the canister of film that the departed Herr Walthers was supposed to have on his person at the time of his untimely accident. I am sure the Gestapo is still looking for it. Take it as a token of good faith. Perhaps one day you may return the favor."

Braham looked at the small can. A man had died to bring this to him.

"Undeveloped and unexposed?"

"Certainly, take it to any pharmacy and have prints made, although I dare say you would rather handle that job on your own. The information on that film may be compromised, but it is nonetheless valuable. *Bis wir uns wiedersehen, Herr Braham.*"

Merchant of Death

The April storm had its origins somewhere over the North Sea, east of the Dogger Banks, the fishing grounds of several nations. The storm swept in across the barrier isles west of Cuxhaven and then charged inland over the port cities of Hamburg and Bremerhaven, soaked the geometrically aligned fields of Saxony, and then crossed into Brandenburg, where it pelted against the windows and slates of the von Teischen estates. From the upper windows of that mass of stone and timbers, clouds appeared as gun smoke rolling out of the tree line that bordered the broad lawns. Springtime seemed to be so long in coming, thought the Countess von Teischen. She watched forlornly as the large drops splatter against the casements and run down the wall into the clipped ivy. Each gust of wind rattled the panes and sent curtains of droplets dancing across the flagged walkways below. She wished, as she stood there, to be anywhere else, be anyone else. But if she was anything at all, she was a realist, and reality, like the storm, was beating against her castle walls.

The White Raven

Gisela von Teischen was thirty-five, dazzlingly attractive, very wealthy, and miserable. She was described in various European fashion magazines as having flaxen blonde hair that rippled like corn silk in the summer breeze, offset by blue eyes the color of a Scandinavian fjord. She was taller than most other German women, at just under six feet tall, with an athletic frame that was firm and taut from hours of skiing and playing golf. She exuded a quiet confidence, but displayed no bravado. Rather she knew that she had the ability to do whatever she wanted. Yet, she also understood the world in which she lived and that the men in her world expected her to fade into the background. Her beauty permitted her to step out into the light. She was aware of her image and made the most of her looks. Her signature color was white, and nearly all her clothes, despite the season, were white, strategically offset with dashes of color, perhaps blue, indigo, crimson, or her favorite, lavender. Even her Mercedes, a 1934 super-charged cabriolet was white, with dazzlingly bright chrome trim. Berlin's most fashionable couturiers sought to have her be seen and photographed in their creations. And she obliged, as long as they were white. To the German public, she was promoted, as epitome of the new Aryan woman, a poster image of femininity for the new Reich, by Goebbels' tightly controlled press. She regularly appeared in the photos on the society pages surrounded by the glitterati of the new world order. In interviews, she joyously extolled the party line, just another woman who believed in the new order, and so she would have been, if she did not secretly hate these thugs who had stolen Germany from her and the people.

Gisela von Teischen had been born in Pomerania, the youngest of three daughters of the late Baron Ulrich von Falken whose Junker forebears had held sway in that part of the world for several centuries, first as knights of the Teutonic order, and later as officers in Frederick the Great's new armies. From childhood, young Gisela was able to keep her father wrapped around her little finger. He indulged her constantly, and when it came to marriage, he did not object to her marrying the youngest son of one of his old comrades in arms, Christian von Teischen, even if he had doubts about the soundness of her choice. It should have been a perfect match, it could have been. The young man she had chosen had a law degree from Heidelberg. He held several directorships in old-line Prussian companies; he was also an accomplished rider, held his own with the saber and looked to be just the kind of man to keep a bridle on his beloved daughter. Still, there was something that troubled the old man. The flaw was there, he just could not put a name to it.

The couple married in 1924. After a whirlwind honeymoon on the Cote d'Azur followed by a leisurely cruise through the Greek Isles aboard a family friend's yacht, the newlyweds returned to set up housekeeping in a large villa in Wansee. The honeymoon was soon officially over. Because of business commitments, Christian was obliged to work late and attend dinners in Berlin. Gisela had to divide her time between the Wansee house and the estate in Pomerania. They saw less and less of each other, and so they agreed that her husband should have a small apartment where he could retreat after an arduous day making money. That was when things began to go awry for the couple. At first, Christian would stay one night in town, and then slowly as weeks turned into months, he spent more and more evenings there.

It was impossible that Gisela would not find out about his amorous adventures, but when she did, it was not what she suspected. Gossip of all sorts was rife in the Berlin of the nineteen twenties. It was a wild time in a city caught up in all sorts of revolutions—political, economic and moral. She began to hear the stories of his debauches. Christian had eclectic tastes in sex, and his wife, lithe and attractive as she was, simply did not fill them, mostly because she lacked the one thing that he craved most—a penis. Of course, to outsiders they appeared the proper German couple, a testament to what some of Christian's other new friends espoused. They had the looks and the breeding that new Germany needed.

Christian had been too young to fight in the Great War. He had wanted to be a soldier; he liked manly things, and he wanted to be a modern Teutonic knight, resplendent in his uniform as he went into battle. He was by nature an aggressive person, and he felt stifled by the tedium of business. Yet even the endless parade of handsome male lovers that adorned his apartment could not satisfy him. Some of these men were members of a new political movement. Slowly he found his political awareness growing. He began to read the writings of the German nationalists, and soon he saw that the real problem was that the Jews in Germany had sold out the country. He became incensed, but at the same time he was frustrated. What was he to do? He wanted to take back the Germany that the Kaiser had forfeited. Then one of his lovers gave him a copy of *Mein Kampf*, and he drank in the words as if they were nectar from the gods. He had, of course, heard of Hitler and the Nazi Party, but until this moment he had not understood that the Party's purpose and his were to be intertwined. He wanted to become a Party member and wear the swastika. He wanted to march with them and reclaim Germany. He drank in the twisted rhetoric of Hitler and his cronies. Better still, these men wore uniforms acted like soldiers, and they were not allowing anyone to put them off their track.

He told Gisela nothing about his new ambitions, yet she, as a dutiful wife, was expected to go along with them. While he was off with his new friends, she was left alone in the mansion by the lake. He went off to Munich and Nuremberg to meet the leaders of this new cult of strength, this movement called National Socialism. There, they welcomed him with open arms, for nothing impressed Hitler and his cronies more than money. And the most impressive was old money, especially old Junkers money—and Christian von Steinberg had plenty of money.

When Christian began attending Party functions the dutiful Gisela was often brought along as window dressing. She found these events ghastly displays of excess and the Nazis disgusting. Most of them were middlebrow bureaucrats. The Jew-baiting, street beatings, lies, and the hatred these thugs were preaching made her sick. Worse, they boasted of their crimes while stuffing caviar in their mouths and guzzling champagne. She naively believed, like millions of other Germans, that somehow they would go away, be drowned in their own vitriol. When at last Hitler became chancellor she wept. For the first time in her life she thought of abandoning Germany, of running away, perhaps to America. But how could she, her father's estate had been eaten up by inflation and his securities were made valueless by the global depression. She needed the prosperity that the Nazis said was just around the corner to restore her fortunes. All she had was her husband's growing bank accounts and his rising influence in the Party. All the while she knew that this was too high a price to pay

She never knew when the idea first came to her. Perhaps it was at the opera while she had to sit through hours of Wagner only to be ogled by the fleshy-lipped storm troopers that surrounded Hitler and his cabinet of mediocrity. But when Christian came home, proudly wearing the midnight-black uniform of an SS Sturmbannführer, she was certain of what she had to do, and so she would set about destroying them—she would find a way; but as it turned out, the way found her.

The White Raven

It wasn't too long before neither of them had any illusions about their marriage. Mercifully, because of Christian's predilection for other men, there had been no children. Of course, for people at their social stratum, divorce was out of the question, but to make sure that she never considered it, von Teischen showered her with money and gifts and attempted to keep her in a gilded cage. Between them they made a private pact. She would appear at his side whenever required, and he would make no other demands upon her, sexual or otherwise. He could cuddle with his boyfriends all he wanted, and she would construct a private life away from prying eyes.

With their marriage merely a tableau, Gisela began traveling on her own. In 1926 she met Sir Basil Zaharoff on her first visit to Nice. She could no longer abide being cooped up in the big house. Berlin winters were depressing and she needed the fresh air of the Mediterranean. Christian was happy enough to see her go to the south of France each winter, either alone or in the company of one of her new friends from the artier, and in his opinion, decadent slice of the capital. He could then have Berlin to himself. She had read something in a magazine and had chosen Nice and the Hôtel Negresco for her seasonal retreats. After the frozen drizzle of Berlin, the pallid winter sun on the Mediterranean was a tonic that produced immediate results.

Zaharoff was enjoying the fruits of a long life when he met Gisela von Teischen. Shortly before he had destroyed his extensive files on everyone and anyone and had been very public about wishing to live out his last years in quiet luxury. He knew he was nearing the end, and although he had long since lost the raffish aplomb with which British newspaper cartoonist had stylized him, he was a charmer and always interested in a pretty face. Her face appeared to him out of a crowd at some forgettable soirée given by who-knew-who at a villa high up on the Corniche. Gisela was not one to mince words about her opinions of the world situation, even at a dinner party among strangers, and the elderly Merchant of Death was soon captivated by her vitality. He returned the favor by offering her a ride back to the Negresco later that evening and was delighted to tell her that he too was staying there. Could he offer her dinner one evening? She said she would be delighted, and the next evening, over champagne and langouste on a terrace overlooking the sea, he regaled her with tales of his early triumphs and about that master of spies, Sidney Reilly with whom he had sparred before the Great War.

She saw him often during her stays in Nice, and he became a surrogate father to her. Zaharoff had, of course, a family of his own, but something about this lovely German woman touched him deeply. It was not so much that she needed his help, he could see that she was quite independent, rather he wanted to protect her from what he saw coming.

Each winter, until his illness began to intrude, they continued to meet in Nice, he came to enjoy the sunset of his life on the Cote d'Azur and she to bask in the warm winter sun. She learned more about the world from him, and in turn told him all the Berlin, gossip. He saw the growing danger of an increasingly fascist Europe, a continent that would soon be at odds with its Soviet neighbor. He hated to see her return to the heart of that danger.

Gisela dreaded the necessity of returning to Berlin each spring and each time she wept as she boarded the train back to Germany. She was quite literally leaving the light and entering what felt like perpetual night. Each time what she saw on her arrival was worse. Black and red bunting adorned by the twisted cross of the Nazis was everywhere. People, who heretofore had been friendly and welcoming, had become suspicious and withdrawn. Out on the street, a new practice called *Berliner blicke* had become common practice. This was simply a quick look back over the shoulder as one turned a corner—just a quick glance, to see if one was being followed. Paranoia abounded, and with good reason. The *Geheime Staatspolizei*, or Gestapo, had been formed under Adolf Hitler's right-hand man Hermann Goering and they had set about making Germany safe for Nazism.

She was grateful, at least, that they would write to one another, not directly of course, for that might be dangerous. Instead they used what in espionage terms was called a cutout, a place where messages could be received and sent without directly connecting the correspondents. Zaharoff had created the world's largest private intelligence network, and he placed part of it at her disposal. It had been essential in his line of work. If she needed his help, she need only contact a particular person at a certain address, and he would make arrangements to help her.

Zaharoff had told her what he thought was coming. On a starlit evening in January of 1930, Sir Basil was entertaining several of what he called his winter friends, those individuals, who, like himself, found the tepid sun of the Mediterranean winter more palatable than the rains and snow of the north. As with most gatherings that year, the table talk turned to politics, especially the politics of Germany.

"Mark my words," he said in a low voice, "Hitler and his Brownshirt thugs are gaining power in Germany. If they ever get control of the government he will want to set right the indignations of 1919. You can feel the Teutonic drums beating even here on this placid shore."

The White Raven

"You cannot believe it will come to that Sir Basil,' cried one of his guests. Female and very French, she had a worldview that went only as far as the Rive Gauche. "What about the league of nations, surely they will put a stop to any act of hostility."

Zaharoff looked at the lady and, while appreciating her delightfully displayed cleavage, wondered how anyone could be so naïve

"Mademoiselle Langlois please do not put your faith in the League of Nations, even its most vocal proponent, President Wilson, could not convince his own country to support it. Oh, no doubt there will be some fussing and fuming in Geneva when the ultimatums begin to flower, but no more. The League is a sham, with no power to do anything. It is only a matter of time. Europe is in many respects a village, and its two biggest bullies are eyeing each other over their back fences. First, we have Mussolini strutting about. This Austrian Corporal, Hitler is trying to emulate him. Then there are the Bolsheviks; Stalin is just a greedy warlord from the Caucuses. No, mark my words, there will be another war."

Later, long after the guests had gone, Zaharoff spoke to Gisela over a glass of port. He was about to enlist her in the world's second oldest profession: she would begin to pass information and, in some cases, people, out of Germany to the relative safety provided by Zaharoff and his associates.

"You are in a position to help avoid the war that will plunge the world into another dark age," he said.

The White Raven

"How can I, what can I do? Please don't misunderstand me. I want to help. I hate them so, I hate what they represent and what they are doing. What should I do?"

Zaharoff swirled his glass, the thick liquor coating the sides with curtains of translucent purple. "Wait and watch. Memorize what you need to, but let nothing be found that could incriminate you. Should things reach a critical state in Germany, and I fear it will soon be so; I will get in touch with you. Not directly, but I have a man in Germany, a man who I trust. He is my eyes and ears there. If necessary, he will become your guardian angel. You may trust him implicitly."

"But who . . ." She was shocked. A guardian angel, who was he, and where was he?

"Gisela, do you trust me?"

"Yes, of course."

"Then trust Karl. I will tell him to make contact with you but when it is time, not before. He will take it from there. He has been with me over twenty years. Alas, if I were younger, I would come myself." Zaharoff smiled wistfully.

Gisela kissed him softly on the cheek. "I know you would."

Zaharoff coughed gently and said, "You will need a name, a code name, if we go forward."

Gisela thought for a few moments, her brow furrowed, then she smiled at him. "Well, this may sound like an affectation, but why not *Der Weiss Rabe*, The White Raven? There was a story my old Oma told me when I was a child, about a village that was beset by wolves. The people were frightened and sought a huntsman to come to kill the wolves that were eating their flocks. After a long while they found a huntsman who would help them. When all the wolves were dead, he told the villagers, a white raven would appear with the leg bone of the last wolf in its talons and then fly up to the rooftops and sing out that all was safe."

Zaharoff thought for a moment, "Yes, yes, that is good. The White Raven shall pick their bones. Hah!"

Man on a Train

Viktor Ryshkov stared through the soot-streaked train window at the passing scenery. April, or so it said on the calendar, but the fields he passed had just the first tinges of green upon them as if the political chill of the nation had some effect on the land. Ryshkov had chosen a local train, now moving slowly from town to town rattling over switch points and narrow trestles spanning rushing streams. Darkness would soon envelope him, and the orderly rows of houses and fields would sink into the murk with streets identified by regiments of streetlights, rural electricity being one of the new benefits of National Socialism. The interior of the third-class coach, worn wooden panels scarred and dented from the packages and luggage of uncounted numbers of passengers going from town to town across northern Germany, had over the years acquired a stale aroma of onions, urine, and unwashed bodies. There were only a few passengers on the narrow, slatted benches arrayed on each side of the aisle. None of them paid any attention to the man dressed like themselves in the rough clothing of a factory worker, his flat cap pulled down over his forehead. Ryshkov tried to sleep, but his constant companions; fear and anxiety, kept him awake. Ryshkov was running, running for his life.

The White Raven

He hoped just to be swallowed up by the night and disappear from sight. Ryshkov looked at his wristwatch for what must have been the hundredth time; the hands seemed to crawl across its face. In the dim light he saw that it was nearly ten o'clock. The watch was a good one, a Breitling and not something a man traveling third class would likely own, so he kept it out of sight. Swiss made, he had learned, gold with a gold face and a sweeping second hand. It was nearly new, having had only one previous owner, with an alligator band, and was probably worth a good deal. He could sell it if need be, but he would hate to do so. It was a trophy of sorts. He had taken it off the wrist of a German socialist. The man was a poseur, the scion of a wealthy Junkers family who was assuaging his guilt of inheritance by "helping" his fellow man. Of course, the man had been alive up to the time Ryshkov had encountered him, and then, in an instant he was dead. Nine grams of jacketed steel fired into the back of the neck, quickly done and without much mess. It was party politics, business as usual, but there was nothing in the operating rules of the NKVD that said he could not help himself to a little compensation, well, at least so far that no one found out. Life had been simple for Ryshkov in Berlin, delightful in fact, if he was being honest with himself. Well that was until three days ago.

What did it take for a man to betray his country, his ideology and his conscience? Now that this question had come around to him, he felt he didn't really know its answer. Perhaps not too much more than self-preservation, if recent events in his life were to tell. He had never before considered taking such a step, and yet Ryshkov knew how to coerce other men into betrayal. He had made other men, perhaps even better men than he, wince with the pain of making such a choice. At the Party's behest he had been doing such things for over fifteen years. He was a skilled aparatchik, and he knew how to apply what they called "the pressures": those small influences of money, prestige, egotism, and even the self-delusion that men accepted as justification for giving up their country's secrets. He had employed women to seduce, blackmail, and even violence to get what the Party demanded. For since 1917 it was always the Party's needs that superseded everything else in Ryshkov's life. Dzerzhinsky himself had taught him that when he recruited the teenaged Ryshkov from the rabble of the Moscow streets for the Cheka. He had been taught him well and knew that every man had his pressure points, his vulnerabilities, and it was the duty of the loyal Cheka, and then NKVD, officer to find those points in order to further the revolution.

And Ryshkov was doing just that when the NKVD's shadow fell over him. He had been in Germany for five years, starting small, but becoming more successful as time went on. Officially, his name was listed as part of the official Soviet diplomatic delegation, a trade representative, thus he was not an illegal, and if caught would be afforded some of the diplomatic niceties. He went places and saw people, traveled to political rallies, and occasionally wrote a report back to Moscow that raised his stature in the eyes of his superiors. That was his day job, for his night work he went about the business of subverting loyal Germans to be informants for the Soviet Union. With the rise of the Nazis, this became ever more important, and his work turned from the purely political to that of looking for hard facts—military intelligence.

Ryshkov did not share the heavy Slavic features that often marked his fellow countrymen. He was slim, just above average height, and a dark pencil-line moustache highlighted his narrow face. He kept his jet-black hair combed back from his face, revealing the beginnings of a widow's peak. He prided himself on his appearance. A natty dresser, any one on the street would have taken him for an actor who is inevitably cast as a villain in a forgettable B-movie. Women were attracted to him, and he had used that to his advantage as well. But on this night train to nowhere, he simply wished to blend in, invisible and alone with his fears.

He had been doing so well in Berlin. True, he was a spy, and Berlin was the heart of the capitalist German camp. It was enemy territory, but, despite the dangers, it was good duty for a loyal Chekist like Ryshkov. Berlin was so much better a place to be than Moscow, or, if one were truly unlucky, stuck in some dreary border town along the Bug or Pripet, the traditional bloodlands of Russia's western borders, checking on rumors of insurrection as one peasant tried to use the *aparat* to avenge himself on another over some village intrigue. No, Berlin, despite its Prussian regimentation, felt free. Oh, it could put on the gray mantle of austerity and despair, just like Moscow, but somehow the city seemed to edge its grayness with sparkling sequins and cast off its inhibitions in its cabarets and *nachtlokals*. He liked it here; here he felt that he was living. He liked strolling the avenues and looking in shop windows at things the people back in Russia could only dream of. He liked ordering his *schokolade mit schlagsahne—großen schlagsahne* in the cafés on wintry mornings and watch the world pass by. The nightlife was exotic, erotic and decadently excessive. Nothing in Berlin was hidden behind closed doors as it was in Moscow. No, here sex, any kind of sex, was on display and readily for sale. One had only to specify which of the lovely *mädchen* on display you wanted, and, *voila*, you paid the madam and she was yours for the specified time period. Very regular, very correct, this was Germany, after all.

The White Raven

Post-war Berlin might have been chaotic, with both the right and the left fighting it out in the streets. The strife was especially nasty up in the slums of Wedding. Yet back in Russia, the obvious failures of the state-run economy continued to take its toll. Following the slaughter of a civil war that pitted Reds and Whites against each other, the horsemen of the apocalypse were still running rampant. Retribution was the order of the day, and so the revolution was lubricated with the blood of ordinary Russians. No matter how he looked at it, being in Berlin was better. Here, the unchecked inflation that had brought about the collapse of the Weimar regime was gone. But now economic recovery seemed at hand, and, with the coming of the Nazis, unemployment would be a thing of the past for German workers. He had done his job well; his bosses were pleased with the results he had achieved. Then how could this disaster have befallen him? What god had he offended?

Until several days ago, he had been respected as one of Russia's elite army of defenders, or so the oath that he took when he had joined the Cheka all those years ago had said. Of course, Ryshkov was not his real name; who in the service kept their own names? He had used so many in his career it was hard to remember the one given him at birth. But whoever he really was, he had been recruited, schooled, and then ordained as one of the guardians of the people's revolution, bound by oath to defend it, even if it meant his own death. God knows he had seen enough men and women die for that ideal. Now it appeared that it would be his turn.

Throughout his Chekist career he had followed orders, performed his assignments to root out the enemies of the Revolution. Often that meant that he had taken lives at the behest of his bosses, the men who ran the Cheka, or whatever it had morphed into over the years. He had done so loyally and without question. When he was recruited, the organs of state security were called the Cheka and were staffed in many areas by men who had served in the Tsar's own secret police, the Okhrana. After Dzerzhinsky's death, it had morphed into the GPU, then the OGPU, now it was called the NKVD; it did not matter; it was the same *aparat*, and it served the same purpose. It was rumored that the security service made these changes in order to confuse the capitalist enemy. That might be, however, no one in Russia was fooled. Chekists were a class apart, in what was supposed to be a classless society. On the street, they stood out, maybe because they were better fed and certainly better clothed, than the masses they were supposed to protect. The mere sight of Chekists racing along Russian streets in their Pobeda cars and Stolypin vans froze the blood in the veins of ordinary citizens. For who knew for whom they might be coming next. As the vans passed, people on the street secretly made the sign of the cross, both for the lost souls on their way to the cellars of the Lubyanka as much as for themselves to be spared that fate.

Now, under the new leadership of Comrade Stalin the security service was searching for new enemies of the state. And maybe it did not have to look too far. The wily Georgian had begun to suspect those closest to him. Were they loyal to him, perhaps not? Who knew what lay in the heart of a man, even a trusted comrade? Therefore, they had better look into their own ranks before he did it for them. The service that had kept Ryshkov alive and fed had grown insatiable for new enemies to devour and in a cruel twist of fate, had begun to nibble away at the edges of his own life.

He had been in the field too long not to know something was amiss. Ryshkov felt a stab of fear, and yet everything seemed so normal. The feeling would not go away. Fear rose in him a like some long forgotten dream—a dream in which death was at his heels and gradually overtaking him, and he could not escape it. It was subtle. Something had changed, and yet his dealings with the Berlin resident the previous day had been perfectly normal. Then of course, that was what you would expect. Nothing was said, of course, but you saw it in their eyes. You knew that they were suspicious, and they wanted you to know, for with them, if you knew you were suspect, perhaps you might just slip up and implicate someone else that they had overlooked. Under this subtle pressure just what step would you take to save yourself? Where was the ticket out? Whom perhaps had they not suspected? Better still, would you be able to confuse them and offer up someone in your stead, hoping to gain time, a day, an hour, before they snatched you? The service wanted to catch you off balance, and they would hit you when you least expected it. But Ryshkov knew, as he always knew. His day would come; people did not grow old in this service. Even working as he had, far from Moscow and in the heart of the new fascist regime in Berlin, he knew.

The Berlin posting had been a plum position for Ryshkov, and despite the fascist drumbeats, he enjoyed the freedom of the city, especially the *nachtlokals* and cabarets. Had not the Red Army been dealt an ignominious defeat outside Warsaw in 1921, it was likely that Berlin and most of Germany would now be a socialist state. But who would have thought the Poles could fight so well? Clearly, not Josef Stalin, who commanded part of the Red Army's assault against Pilsudski's army, something he would let simmer in his mind for years. Lenin had blundered badly in underestimating the Poles, and now Poland was firmly set against Russia, a bulwark against its expansion to the west.

Warsaw was made difficult by the Polish secret service, so for years the Cheka had run agents in Berlin and it had become one of its largest bases of their operations. Recruitment was not difficult, what with the defeat of the Kaiser's army in 1918 and the collapse of one government after another. The place was teaming with communists, nihilists, fellow travelers of all stripes. His hardest task was to weed out the inept and find the few who could provide the kind of information that he needed. He even had a few among the Brownshirts who thought that a worker's paradise was still possible. They were pansies, most of them, and easily manipulated. But then he had struck gold, and he had Adolf Hitler and his gangs of thugs to thank for that.

Arndt Dietrich was a born flier, and he had risen to the rank of Rittmeister in the *Luftstreitkräfte,* Germany's air force during the 1914–18 war. He had served on both the eastern and western fronts, accumulating over thirty victories before the armistice. Wounded twice, he went on to fly with Pilsudski's Poles against the Bolsheviks. When his Fokker D.VII had been hit by ground fire during the Battle of the Vistula, he had sustained shrapnel wounds and was hospitalized in Warsaw. Like so many wounded men, he fell in love with his nurse. Blonde and witty, nurse Gracja Bartosz captured his heart, and, unlike so many nurses whose patients vowed adoration and undying love, she said yes and married Arndt when he asked her to. Arndt Dietrich loved Gracja more than he could bear and wanted to have a life with her full of laughter and children and long quiet nights in the peace of their home. After the fighting in two wars, in France and in Poland, that was all he yearned for. And yet, with peace, his pay from the Poles came to an abrupt end, and Arndt needed a job. He had been in an out of airplane cockpits for nearly six years. All he knew was flying, and, after a few false starts at fledgling airplane companies, he was able to put his flying skills to work as a test pilot and instructor for the Messerschmitt company.

The White Raven

In his new position Arndt Dietrich soon became more than just a veteran flight instructor. As part of the Treaty of Rapallo, the Soviet Union and the Weimar Republic signed certain secret codicils, one of which allowed Germany to build airplanes and train pilots for a new and rejuvenated air force at secret bases in Russia. Germany's army, the Reichswehr, anemic and undermanned by the rigors of the Versailles Treaty, had set up a training facility at Lipetsk outside Moscow. Manufacturers like Messerschmitt had their own operations at the base. There, Dietrich was one of several former officers who had come under the command of Herman von der Lieth-Thomsen. Improved versions of the Fokker DVII and other designs were being built, ostensibly for the Argentine Air Force. At the facility Dietrich and Gracja lived comparatively well, without the privations that the local population had to endure. But Russia was a long way from Germany, and in 1932 the couple returned home, where through his connections at Lipetsk, Dietrich secured another position training pilots on the new planes that were slowly rolling off the assembly lines at Messerschmitt.

Viktor Ryshkov found Dietrich alone on a Berlin tram one afternoon and struck up a conversation. Dietrich knew at once that the man asking him about the weather was Russian, and he had a pretty good guess that he was a Chekist. He had met enough of them at Lipetsk to know the type.

"So, Rittmeister, how are you and your lovely wife settling in here in the new Germany?" Ryshkov asked with real sincerity.

"Who are you, and what do you want?" Dietrich was unsure of what was happening politically in Germany and was alert to the constant probing of the Polpo, Berlin's political police, so he was very wary of strangers, especially Russians.

The White Raven

"Why nothing Rittmeister, only to wish you good fortune, and to let you know that you have friends back in Russia, who wish you well. Perhaps if you find the climate a bit too rough here in Berlin for you and your wife, you might give me a call, I would be glad to help." With that Ryshkov rose, tipped his hat, and got off the tram at the next corner, but not before he pressed a card into Dietrich's hand.

Dietrich tried to see where the man went as he stepped off into the crowd, but lost him in the bobbing heads. Then he looked down at the card in his hand. There was nothing on it except a scrawled telephone number. He was about to throw it away, but something stopped him, and he tucked the card into his vest pocket.

It was nearly a year before the two men met again, but by then things had changed dramatically for Arndt Dietrich. He had not noticed at first, but when he thought about it all the signs were there. The looks, the slights, the friends who began to turn down dinner invitations from Arndt and Gracja—he had thought at first it was because she was Polish. But it was not. Somehow, someone, perhaps someone in the personnel department of Messerschmitt, or maybe even the dreaded Polpo, had gotten wind of the fact that Gracja, like so many Poles, had Jewish ancestors. In German terms that meant that she was not quite Jewish, but rather a *mischling*, a crossbreed—like she was some kind of animal.

It was the increasing tempo of the racial actions against Jews by the Nazis, an activity closest to the hearts of the fascist street thugs that led Dietrich back to Ryshkov. By the spring of 1934 there were daily incidents in the streets of all German cities. Each successive incident more violent that those that had gone before. The Nazis' rabid persecution of the Jews opened the way for his betrayal, for without the outrages against the Jews, he would never have found the courage to commit what amounted to treason. It was not long before the outrages on the streets came into his home. Gracja had made no secret of the fact that she was Polish, and in their neighborhood no one paid much notice. That is until a bunch of Brownshirts took over the corner *bierstube* as their local headquarters.

Once lodged there, they began to scour the neighborhood for undesirables, which meant essentially anyone who did not fit their Aryan model of humanity. The Brownshirts found out about her. In their book she was an *untermenschen*, not much difference between her and the Jews of the city. But they also knew about her husband, so for the time being, they tread lightly. Of course, Gracja had to endure their taunts on the street: sometimes they threw things at her and called her names. Some months after his encounter with Ryshkov, Dietrich returned home to find Gracja in tears, nursing a bruise on her face; her clothes bloody. She was standing at the sink, trying to staunch the blood from a gash on her cheek. As he rushed forward toward her he saw a strange bedraggled man seated in their cozy kitchen.

"Gracja! My god. What has happened to you?" Dietrich tried to take her in his arms, but she winced with pain. "No, Arndt, please. Those thugs beat me with sticks when I tried to help Jakob here. They were going to kill him," she cried, sobbing heavily as she spoke.

"Who? Brownshirts? Nazis? The ones from the corner, was it them?"

"Yes, Arndt. There were a dozen of them. They had cornered Jakob and were beating him. I tried to make them stop. I thought that if I shouted at them they would stop, but they only turned on me. The called me the Polish *mischling* bitch! They knew who I was. Worse, they didn't care."

"You need a doctor. Let me take you to the hospital," Arndt implored.

"No, Arndt. I will be fine. I need a hot bath. Then we can talk."

"I love you Gracja. We can't live like this. You have to tell me what is going on. First off, who is he?" Dietrich asked derisively as he looked at the young man, bruised and in tattered clothes seated at the table.

Gracja looked wearily at her husband. "Arndt, please don't be cross. This is Jakob; he is the son of my father's business partner in Warsaw. He is a student. The Nazis have beaten him again and thrown him out of university. The gang on the street was chasing him. At first, I didn't even know it was Jakob. I just couldn't take any more of their violence. I had to do something."

"How did he know to come here? And, moreover, why?" Arndt Dietrich spoke as if the young man was not present in the room, yet he kept staring at the torn and bloody clothing.

"The Nazis threw him out of his lodgings, and he did not know who else to turn to. He needs to get out of Germany. Jakob's father, Israel Goldbaum, had sent him our address and told him to come to us if he needed help. Who would have known this would happen?"

Arndt finally turned to the boy, and, with a kindness that he did not feel, spoke softly, "Tell me what happened to you."

And so, Jakob Goldbaum, an engineering student at the Max Planck Institute, told his tale. The Nazis had recognized his talent, despite his un-Aryan antecedents. Of course, being Nazis and arch opportunists, they had kept him on as a lab assistant, hoping to milk from his mind all that they could before expelling him. That is, until a bunch of Brownshirt thugs intervened and accosted him on his way home, and, while holding him captive in the street, looted his tiny apartment and then beat him.

Goldbaum was young, not yet thirty, but he was no fool, and he could see what had happened in the short time since Hitler had become chancellor. More stringent racial laws were rumored to be coming, and he knew that the new German Reich would never accept him. He wanted to find a safe haven, and he was sure that the Soviet Union was the only safe place. As he went on and related all the problems he faced, Arndt Dietrich thought of his time in Russia and thought perhaps the young man was right.

Dietrich spun on his heel and went to a large desk in their front room and returned with something large wrapped in an oily rag. He placed it on the table and unwrapped the broom handle Mauser that he had kept since the war.

"I will see about these thugs!" he said with a touch of venom in his voice.

"No Arndt. That won't solve anything, and they will just come after you, and then what will happen to me? No, we must help Jakob to get away, Arndt. And then, we can make plans to leave as well. But, please, is there anything you can do? Don't you know anyone who might help him leave Germany?"

Dietrich's mind was reeling, then he remembered the man on the bus. "Perhaps."

Gracja arranged a place for Jakob to sleep in the small pantry in the rear of their house. The next day Dietrich called the number that Ryshkov had given him.

The White Raven

When Ryshkov met Dietrich, the pilot had been waiting in a doorway, trying his best to avoid being seen, as he watched a gang of Hitler Youth pummeling a Jewish peddler with paving stones and sticks. The peddler's only crimes were to have been in the wrong place at the wrong time and, worse, to be seen in public with the long side locks of a Hassidic Jew. Ryshkov appeared beside Dietrich and offered to buy him a drink in a worker's bar that stridently, if not foolishly, displayed a hammer and sickle on the wall. They would be safe there, there were no Nazi thugs hanging about. Ryshkov listened and bought another round of drinks. As Dietrich explained about young Jakob Goldbaum, Ryshkov realized that he had made a rare connection. Through Dietrich he found a German who actually wanted to go to Russia. Moreover, he was not a political refugee, but a young man who, with his engineering talents, could help the cause of socialism.

Dietrich knew there would be a price for the Russian's assistance. Ryshkov offered Dietrich a deal to get Goldbaum out of Germany. The price was simple. Dietrich need only help Ryshkov with information. Ryshkov had been watching the comings and goings of men from the aircraft design works, and he had been keeping an eye on Dietrich in particular. Ryshkov new that there was secret work going on in the office, and he had hoped it would be something to send to Moscow. Ryshkov had been tasked with finding out all about Germany's not so secret rearmament plans. What he had not expected was the treasure trove that the necessity of the young man's exodus might unlock. What Dietrich delivered, over the next several months, was pure gold. Sketches and designs for new airplanes, specifications and performance requirements, as a test pilot, all seemed to pass through Dietrich's fingers.

What Dietrich delivered was much more than the Russian could safely send out at any one time. Ryshkov knew the Russian mind when it came to secrets, anything too easily obtained was likely to be discounted the information became suspect as well as the purveyor. So, like any savvy field agent, he decided to parse out the information and feed it piecemeal to Moscow. Then too, he was simply saving the stuff for that rainy day when nothing else was available. Once they began to digest the information, Ryshkov's bosses at the Lubyanka could not get enough and urged him to press for more, but the agent remained cagey. A month went by and Dietrich sought out Ryshkov again. It was getting too risky to keep Goldbaum at the house, and he wanted to know when the blessed Soviet passport might arrive and when the boy would be on his way to the people's paradise. Soon enough, Ryshkov counseled, in the meantime, could Dietrich lay his hands on the design of the new BMW aircraft engine that was rumored to be ready for testing? Dietrich was caught in the age-old trap of the traitor, he could not go back and put everything right, the Gestapo would shoot him, and god knew what they would do to Gracja. He could only say he would try.

But then, for Ryshkov the world shifted and everything began to collapse around him. Through a trusted Moscow contact, Ryshkov received word that his sister and her family had been arrested. There had been another round of middle-class persecutions in the land of the classless society. In Berlin Ryshkov was his only identity by which he was known. The local Resident did not know anything more about him, nor should he have, for the NKVD all knowledge was compartmentalized. No one in Berlin could have known his real name, or that he was born in the Ukraine to a farming family—people that comrade Stalin labeled as Kulaks. Still, it was at that moment that he began to feel the chill. It was only a matter of days before they would arrest him.

The White Raven

Ryshkov had been born in 1898, the youngest boy of a prosperous farming family. His family was well to do and ardent Tsarists. It was a comfortable life, one that he rejected when he joined the revolution in 1917. Not more than a boy at the time, he had bigger aspirations than breeding better livestock. When he left home, he completely cut himself off from his family's bourgeois life. Once or twice over the years he had written to Olga, his older sister, using an address of convenience as a cutout. The work he did never allowed for such connections, and there was always the risk that the cutout would fail. Still, there was a list, and on it the family name, Miroshnychenko. Stalin was calling for the extermination of the Kulaks by Ryshkov's own service. Kulak families were being turned out from their homes and forced to live off the land or starve to death, victims of another Five-Year Plan. The lucky ones died quickly, some were deported and found themselves either in work camps or simply wandering the steppe in search of a scrap of food.

Moscow Center had put out a request and was now asking if there were any recent Ukrainian immigrants in Germany. They provided a list of surnames, and he saw Miroshnychenko half way down the page, and he knew what that meant for him. In the hands of NKVD interrogators, a prisoner would confess to having sex with the devil if it meant no more pain, no more torture. His father might hold out, even die before he said anything, he was an old crust of a man, but his sisters and his mother would break and talk about the boy who left the family for Moscow. They would probably even plead for his intercession in their agonies. The interrogators would make notes and someone would take time to look into what the prisoners, no doubt long dead by this time, had said. It would not be difficult. In the labyrinth of files in Dzerzhinsky Square, they would find what they needed, and soon the heavy men would come looking for him. It would take only a telegram to the embassy, and he would be in their hands.

He decided that he had no choice but to run, but to where? Who could he turn to for help, certainly not any of the capitalist governments, they would snap him up to be sure, then after they had sweated out of him all he knew and anything he could invent, they would chuck him out and let the Bolshevik dogs eat him. No, he had to find someone who played the game for the game's sake. He wandered around the city for several hours and found a small coffee shop near the KaDeWe department store. Exhausted and now afraid, he sipped his coffee and forced himself to think.

He had only a few hundred Reichsmarks in his pockets, like rubles, German money that was nearly worthless outside of the country. He carried only the Soviet passport issued to Ryshkov. He had no travel visas, and the passport was not likely to make him a welcome guest in most countries. Still, he had to make do with what he had. As for Dietrich and Goldbaum, he had to leave them to their fate, knowing that if the fascists did not do for them, the NKVD might start looking for Ryshkov's contacts and well; that would be that. As for himself, he could not go near any of his regular haunts, but the packet of data and drawings that he had held back from Moscow was tucked away in the safest place he could find, taped up under a pew in St. Mark's Lutheran Church off Tegelstrasse. Once he had the packet, he could trade it for his own security. But to whom, it was not that he could take out an ad in the personal pages of the newspaper, "secrets to sell, spy needs a ticket out of Germany." It was a nice fantasy, but one without any chance of success. Even in thinking that he could outrun the organs of state security if they wanted him, he knew that he was deluding himself, but staying alive was the only thing on his mind. He just needed to make the right connection. It took a week, but he found the person he needed.

Ryshkov had been in Berlin for almost five years, and he had made contacts throughout the city, but what he needed now was the kind of contact that he could rely upon not to sell him back to the Russians, or just as bad, to the Gestapo. He wanted a way out, not just from the city, but also from his life. He needed to start somewhere new, so he joined the refugee business, becoming one of the lines of ghosts who were looking to make the right connection to get out of the Reich.

The answer came to him at last in a caffeine buzz. He had been sleeping here and there for two days and drinking coffee in order to stay alert.

There were several people in Berlin, who, though not communists and certainly not fascists, had been useful to him in the past. These were people whose names he had scrupulously omitted from his reports to Moscow. In the NKVD you had to keep a hand out for yourself. Who knew when a purge might descend and sweep along the innocent with the guilty into the cellars of the Lubyanka? So Ryshkov left out some details in his reports from time to time. These were the names of people who had kept faith with him as a matter of honor. He knew that his very profession and especially his service did not recognize honor, but somehow even from his first day in Berlin he had felt the need to hold something back from his masters in Moscow. The service owned him, of course, but in his calculations they were not entitled to everything that he knew, so he had kept some things for himself. One of those secrets, the most guarded of all those he kept, was a woman.

The White Raven

Inga Carlson had never appeared in any of his reports. Their meetings were quite off the books and purely romantic in nature. Inga ran a small florist's shop, called *Blumenparadies*, off the Kurfürstendamm. Ryshkov had at one time, in his capacity as a trade official, needed some flowers sent to the wife of an Italian banker with whom Ryshkov was meeting and had chanced upon her shop. From the moment he laid eyes on her, he had become enchanted. Pert and blonde, she had an elfin quality so un-Russian that he could not resist. Soon he was finding excuses to be in her neighborhood. He would drop by at closing time and offer her a drink or dinner. He could not stay away. At first she refused, but his persistence paid off, and soon she relented. Within a few weeks they became lovers, the romance all the more intense because of the necessity for secrecy.

Inga, he soon found, was a social butterfly, scratching her way to the top and enthralled by the comings and goings of Berlin society. She told him that she had to put on a show in order to succeed in her business. Better still, she kept records of all the events that she catered. She used those guest lists to find new clients, and she was successful. She had a clientele drawn from among the wealthy and important of the city, and from time to time she shared what she learned from her clients with Ryshkov. Her business grew and she had several employees and a delivery van. At one point, she had moved in some of the more Bohemian circles and knew people who knew people in the arts and theater, and yet she knew many of the right people in the old Junkers class of Prussian elite. He never questioned why she chose him, perhaps she did not know herself. She was German with a Norwegian father. She ascribed to all the Nordic hocus-pocus of the new regime, but perhaps it was the way he talked to her, feeding her on the poetry of the Ukraine, who knew? So it was to her he went, the only person he could now trust.

When he told her what he needed, she immediately understood. Inga thought she might know someone. She would not tell him who it might be. Who knew when one might need a lifeline oneself? That evening she stepped out of the flower shop and went to a public telephone a block away. There she made a call to a number in Wedding. The call was answered with a non-committal, "Ja."

In a hushed voice she said, "I have something for the Raven."

There was a long silence on the other end of the line, at last the voice spoke, "Give me the number you calling from. Hang up, and we will call you back." Inga gave the number

For though Inga enjoyed Ryshkov as a lover, she had never expected their affair to go on as long as it had. He had told her from the very beginning who and what he was. In return, she had become his confessor, his fount of redemption, and now he was asking her to help him to leave her. It had never occurred to either of them to leave Berlin together. Ryshkov had once asked her to come away with him, before his work put her life in such danger. But Inga refused and said that she could not just walk away from her life. She had told him from the beginning that she was a Berliner and could exist nowhere else on earth.

Perhaps now it was time for her to move on. With the recent political changes in Germany, she had begun to meet some of the more powerful in the Nazi firmament. There was even one man who had been particularly attentive of late. He was older, an officer in the SS, with all the brash bravado that came with the evil-looking black uniform. Though she thought the man odious, well, who knew, perhaps he could be useful. She might need a protector with the Russian leaving.

When she returned from the café's public phone, he asked her if she had made contact.

"Yes, I should hear in a day or so. You will have to stay here, out of sight."

Ryshkov then pulled one of the sheets that Dietrich had provided from his pocket and gave it to her. She looked at it skeptically.

"What is this?" she asked looking at the lines and symbols on the paper.

"It is my ticket out," he said, "if you can make the right connection, and if they like it. You can tell them that I have more, if they will get me out of Germany."

The next day a note arrived addressed to her. It had been slipped in amongst the morning's mail. Inside the envelope was a single page that read: *Ten o'clock-Krenzler's.*

Inga went upstairs to where Ryshkov lay dozing in her bed. She reached under the covers and put her hand in his groin. His eyes flew open in alarm. She smiled benignly.

"I need to go meet someone. Let me have one of the drawings."

He went to the chair where he had hung his coat and removed a sheet from the sheaf. She took the page and placing it in her purse, left him to wait for her in her bedroom atop the florist shop.

"I will see what might be arranged," she said and looked at him with a sudden sadness as she went out the door.

The White Raven

For Ryshkov this was the worst part of his escape, waiting and trusting that Inga could find someone in that treasure trove of contacts of hers. He paced the room, tried to the read the paper, but gave up on it and sat smoking cigarette after cigarette. Four hours passed since she had left him, and he was well past being anxious. He had taken the first step and that led him to this tiny room. Now he was caught inside and afraid to go out. He knew it was irrational, but there it was. Then he heard her step on the stair, and then she opened the door. Inga smiled at him and nodded. "The person I spoke to is willing to meet with you on condition that the paper you gave me proves valuable. There is someone who can make sense the paper you gave me. Apparently, it may be worth something. In any event, they will need a day, maybe two, before they will let me know. In the meantime, you will have to stay here." She was all business now, no hint of romance in her voice.

"I brought you several newspapers to help pass the time."

Ryshkov grimaced at the thought of two more days before he could move, but he did not know what else to do. Only thirty hours had passed since he read the bulletin asking for émigrés with the name Miroshnychenko. Every hour that passed raised the stakes against him. The embassy might not miss him for a day or two more, he had been known to go off on various missions without a word before, unless Moscow sent word, of course. But the trains would be the first place they would look. He did not even have a change of clothes, just the suit he was wearing when he dressed the day before.

From below he could hear the sounds of the shop, the comings and goings of customers, the occasionally loud guffaw of the deliveryman as he flirted with the girls who made the arrangements, the normality was hard to bear. While Inga tended her flower business on the ground floor shop, he could only lie on the bed and try to think of alternatives if her contact did not come through.

As the tiny train rocked on through the night, he watched the towns slip by. Each one resembled the one before. Neat and tidy, almost like those model villages that model train enthusiasts built in their basements, very precise and very German. Often the train would stop at some lonely station and a few stragglers would come aboard, find a seat, and in a few moments the rhythm of the rails would put them to sleep. Ryshkov longed for sleep. His body ached, and he felt the grime of two days on trains with soot and dirt blowing through windows kept open to relieve the stifling summer heat. But he could not allow himself the luxury of closing his eyes, even for a few moments. Once he was over the border and in Holland, he could allow himself a few moments of rest, but not until then. He had to get to Paris. In Paris there was the promise of a new life waiting for him, that is, if the woman in the park was to be believed.

Two days had passed before word had come, two anxious and agonizing days. Inga stopped fucking him, and made him sleep on the floor of the closet. In her perverse way she had decided he was already dead and wanted nothing more to do with him. Early in the morning of the third day, a boy on a bicycle appeared and delivered the message. He heard voices in the kitchen below, and then Inga came up to the bedroom.

"We have to make a telephone call. We use a public phone. There is one up on the Kurfürstendamm, but we must hurry." There was no warmth in her voice, only a brisk efficiency.

The White Raven

The phone was inside a small café on the broad boulevard. They took a table and Ryshkov ordered two coffees while Inga made for the ladies room next to which was the pay telephone. The coffees had just arrived when she returned. She was nervous, and Ryshkov stretched out his hand to take hers, hoping to calm her, but she quickly withdrew it. She leaned over, close, toward him; she spoke softly, and repeated the instructions she had been given over the telephone. Then, rising abruptly, she kissed his cheek and muttered a goodbye. She was ending their relationship then and there. He could not go back to her. She was now of the past, it was the present and, hopefully, the future that now mattered. He was as much of a pawn as Dietrich had been, and whoever might or might not help him, he was theirs now. In either case, he was never to return to the shop or to her again. He was on a one-way road; there were no exits, either to hell or to salvation.

Ryshkov found the bench on the north side of the Teufelsee in the Grunewald. He did not know who to expect, yet he was not surprised to see a woman seated alone and tossing bits of stale bread to the ducks. He doubted that they were alone. Somewhere amidst the foliage there must be a watcher, a babysitter. Not so much for him but to protect her, he would think. The woman had done her best to hide her face, he tried to guess her age, but in his state of weariness, he could not tell. Despite the promise of a warm day, she was wearing a bulky coat and a wide-brimmed hat with a gauzy veil that kept most of her face in shadow. He decided that if she did not want to be recognized, he was not going to stare. He sat down and looked straight ahead at the sheet of water surrounded by the spring foliage. A moment passed, and then she spoke.

Staring straight ahead, she said, "The material that you provided looked promising. We are told that you have more, but that you are in a great hurry to get out of Germany and wish to trade the remaining material for safe passage. Is that so? Just nod if it is."

Ryshkov nodded.

"Very well," the woman went on. "We will arrange for a new passport on condition that we can make a satisfactory examination of the rest of the material. When I leave you will find a newspaper on the seat inside of which are rail tickets to Hamburg and then to Paris. Unfortunately, you will have to risk using your own passport until then. I suggest that you stay on local trains until you reach Hamburg. In any event, I think you know what to do. There are instructions there as to what to do when you get to France. In Paris, you will hand over the rest of the documents. If our experts feel they are of use to them, we will make the exchange for a valid passport in a new name and five hundred American dollars. Please memorize the instructions and destroy the paper. Do you agree? Just nod if you do." As she spoke, he tried to place just who this woman might be. Her voice had none of the guttural intonations of a Berliner; rather the woman spoke German in the high tones of someone raised in the south, Bavaria perhaps. He could not tell.

"Let me also say that if at anytime after this moment we feel that you have betrayed us or feel that you are being deceitful with us, we will take the appropriate steps to terminate your existence. Is that clear?'

Ryshkov swallowed hard and wondered who the "we" might be. The British? Perhaps it was the French or Poles? Still, he nodded as instructed. Then without speaking another word, the woman rose and walked off down the path and into the woods. On the seat there was a copy of the *Berliner Zeitung*. He picked up the paper and sauntered off in the direction from which he had come.

The woman stood behind a screen of leafy branches and watched him go. She had to make a decision, a serious one. Not about the Russian, no that had been easy enough. No, she thought, what shall I do about Inga Carlson? Trust was becoming a very rare commodity in the new Reich. The man she knew as Karl had told her that she would often find herself on what his English friends called "a slippery slope." Karl and the other man in Paris were her only lifeline. They had been doing this kind of work for most of their lives. That they had survived that long in the quagmire of European intrigue spoke volumes. She could feel her feet slipping, and knew that she would have to decide. There had been danger before, but not ever more than now. Perhaps, she thought, that the fear somehow fueled her. She enjoyed the tingling that living on the edge gave her, but that only heightened her concern about the florist. Inga was sweet, and she was becoming well known in Berlin society and to the new leadership, well at least to those who knew people in the leadership. Would she sell out her friend? Suddenly blurt out, "Oh, you know the funniest thing happened the other day. I had a friend who needed to get out of Germany and. . . ." No, perhaps not. If Inga said anything she would simply be incriminating herself. How could she say anything without revealing that she had a Russian lover, an NKVD Russian lover? No, she was safe for now, still there might come a time.

Inside her purse she kept a Beretta, a .25 caliber automatic. The classic "ladies gun," and at close range very lethal. Perhaps it was time to bring Inga's business to a close. Hmmm, she thought, it would be easy to do, fake a suicide note. Then again, maybe if she helped Inga even more than she had in the past, there might be some new opportunities. She looked at the tiny gun in the bottom of her bag, nestled against a Hermés scarf—a comforting thing to have these days.

.

Karinhall

It was just before dusk on an April evening, when the long black car emerged from the gathering murk of the Brandenburg forests. The Horch 830 automobile, carrying Captain Konrad Patzig, head of German military intelligence, swept through the gates that bordered the drive leading up to the residence of Reichsminister Hermann Göring. Dinner was to be at eight, but the Reichsminister had granted Patzig's request for a private interview before the other guests arrived.

This had been a momentous day for both men. Earlier that day Hermann Göring had made official what had been long rumored to occur when he handed control of the Gestapo to Heinrich Himmler. Himmler and his chief deputy Reinhardt Heydrich wasted no time in asserting themselves. At the reception that followed, in the main salon of the Gestapo's headquarters on Prinz Albrecht Strasse, the newly anointed princes of darkness made it clear that everything in the German government that touched on secrecy and intelligence operations now belonged to them. The Abwehr, long Germany's main intelligence organization, was squarely in their sights, and they would not long allow a competing organization to remain independent, even if it meant going up against the Army hierarchy.

The White Raven

This evening the captain and his host had urgent matters to discuss, which were fraught with personal danger. Eschewing the elaborate ceremonies that were the hallmark of the mansion's host, Göring met Patzig at the door and ushered him into a large oak-paneled library just off the main foyer. Decorated to remind one of an English country house, replete with burnished battle axes and country scenes painted by second-rate artists, the place housed thousands of leather-bound books arranged esthetically, by color. That no one in the house had ever read even one of them was no surprise. Like most things the Reichsminister managed, this too was all for show. Patzig was not in uniform, and the Reichsminister, noting that, tried to soften his guest's mood.

"Travelling incognito, are we? You said this was urgent. But first, a drink perhaps?"

Patzig knew he was being patronized, but perhaps when he told Göring what was going on, he too would be indignant. "Yes. Thank you Reichsminister. Schnapps if you have it."

Göring paced toward a large carved secretary and swung open its doors to reveal its gleaming contents. Row after row of bottles were bathed in the lights reflected from a mirrored interior. "I think we can accommodate you."

With Göring pouring a glass for himself as well, the two men settled into a pair of leather chairs that flanked a carved stone fireplace the size of a garage.

"So what was so urgent that the head of the nation's military intelligence needed to speak to me about it?"

Patzig swallowed his drink in one gulp before he began. He was fairly certain where Göring's feelings on the matter lay, but still once he opened his mouth to, he was stepping from the role of loyal officer into the quagmire of national and party politics.

"It is Himmler and Heydrich, sir. Now that they have official control of the Gestapo they are maneuvering to take all intelligence matters into their own hands. Worse, they are building a layer of insulation around the Führer so that the only intelligence he hears is what they manufacture."

Göring looked at his guest. Patzig was a highly capable officer. He had been promoted to his current position in July of '32 in order to consolidate the actions of the various military intelligence factors. His most important division was Section III, the section that dealt with counterintelligence. This was no doubt the section that Himmler and his acolyte Heydrich coveted.

"That Himmler covets your intelligence operation comes as no surprise to me. I was maneuvered into giving that bespectacled pig-farmer control of the Gestapo. It is no big secret that I loathe the pair of them. They are the necessary devils that propel any revolution. The French had their Robespierre, the Russians Trotsky and Dzerzhinsky, now we have Heine and Reine. But Captain, what has happened that you come to me? What do you expect me to do?

Patzig knew he was on shaky ground here, but he had gone this far, to stop now would make him look like a fool in Göring's eyes, and he needed help to blunt the onslaught of the SS men. "It seems that now, all operational planning by my sections, especially section III must be coordinated with Heydrich and his SD. I had the most insulting visit from one of his thugs today, a man called Kleist. Essentially, we are to undertake nothing unless either Himmler or Heydrich give us their approval. Worse, there is nothing to stop them from taking an operation that we have been working on and taking it over as their own."

"Ah. I see." Göring held up his empty glass, "Another?" He rose and went to the secretary and returned with the bottle. With their glasses refreshed, the Reichsminister went on.

"Not so easy in the world of politics is it?" asked Göring, chuckling to himself. "Well, whether you like it or not, you have your nose in the tent now, as they say. Now, you want me to tell you what to do about it. Is that it?"

"Yes, Reichsminister."

"Tell me Captain, do you enjoy your job, do you think you are good at it?"

"Yes, sir."

"Then, this is my advice to you Captain." Göring looked into the other man's eyes and saw the look that he had once observed in the mirror so many years ago when, as Rittmeister of Richtofen's Flying Circus, he had led men to their deaths over the trenches in France. These days, he did not see that man any longer. Where had he gone? Turning back to his guest, he said, gently, in an avuncular manner. "Captain, my advice to you is to do nothing."

"Nothing? Nothing? But they will become a government of their own with all their machinations. Germany is not ready."

"Captain, please hear me out. Right now, they have roles to play. The Führer is not unaware of their rapaciousness. At present they are just the kind of force that is needed in order for us to succeed. In any event, there are bigger things in the works. Ernst Röhm is a far greater danger to all of us, and especially men like you, the officer class. Germany has always been managed by a trained military. Adolf Hitler understands this, but until his leadership is made inviolable to people like Röhm, all of us must move carefully. Have I made myself clear?"

"Yes, sir." Patzig replied with more conviction in his voice than he felt.

"You know Patzig, you strike me as a quite able officer. You probably can perform admirably in command of a warship, and I know you have the bent to be an able intelligence officer, but it strikes me that you are quite out of your depth when it comes to politics. Am I right?"

Patzig paused for a long moment. Was this a trick question? Was the Reichsminister leading him on? Of course he would be happier on the bridge of a warship, any warship, than caught up on the party politics of the Nazis. He was a naval officer, meant to command men in battle and, short of that, a strategist and tactician able to manage the workings of the Abwehr. But the ins and outs of National Socialist politics were a quagmire to him. Looking directly at Göring he replied, "Regrettably sir, I must agree. I am a sailor trained for combat, not politics."

Göring looked at his guest with thinly masked pity. The man would have to go, but not just yet.

"Good. The other guests will be arriving shortly. You will enjoy them, old comrades from my days in the *Luftstreitkräfte*, and not an SS man among them."

———

Albrecht Theurer liked the man and, in a compassionate way, felt his pain. Still, there was not much that he could do to intervene in the current situation with Himmler and Heydrich.

"Albrecht, we have sunk into a morass ruled by devils."
Patzig had been drinking steadily since the evening before. Several
empty schnapps bottles stood on tables about the Abwehr chief's
office. Still, there was no sign of inebriation in his speech or
actions. "In six months, they will be the ones in charge of the
nation. Something must be done."

Theurer had been called to his superior's office early in the
morning after a night during which he himself had not slept well.
Yet, in the filmy light of dawn, his brain was already working at a
fast pace.

"Captain Patzig, might I offer a suggestion?"

"Certainly, do you have a way for us to skewer these pests
from the SS?"

"Well, perhaps," Theurer replied, his voice trailing off into
thoughtfulness.

Patzig was an officer used to crisp responses from his
subordinates and hated any semblance of vagueness, and now his
head of counterespionage was giving him vague answers.

"What the hell do you mean by that!" Patzig shouted, his
voice croaking from all the liquor.

"Well, sir, what I mean is that perhaps there is a way for
Himmler and Heydrich to skewer themselves, off course, with just
a little help."

Theurer was now being coy and Patzig the naval officer
hated that behavior more than the man's vague replies, but Patzig
the intelligence officer appreciated the subtleties of the business of
intelligence.

"What? How?" Patzig asked as he sat forward on his chair.

"Well, sir. First, I am not entirely certain of the "what and how" just yet. However I am certain that *you* should do nothing and that my job in this matter is to make sure nothing comes back to this agency."

Konrad Patzig looked across at his subordinate and blinked, not because of the morning glow from the window that haloed the man, but because Theurer had been thinking along these lines for some time. Patzig pushed down on the wooden arms of the chair in which he had been sitting and forced himself to stand. The schnapps seemed to have drained the strength from his legs; still he was able to keep himself erect. Using his most official voice, he spoke to Theurer.

"Albrecht, you have been in this business far longer than I, so I will trust your judgment. If you can succeed in this matter and keep the Abwehr and me out of it, then do so.

Theurer inclined his head in acknowledgement and left Patzig to suffer through the hangover that was just coming on.

Jardin du Luxembourg

A Gallic spring evening, and Paris, dressed for the season, was bathed in the golden glow of a lingering sunset. Winter's grimy gray mantle, soiled with the nation's angst could now be flung away and replaced with spring finery. Weary Parisians chose this night to ignore the constant thrumming of politicians preaching hate and stirring unrest amid the constant flow of bad news in the headlines. The dour cavalcade of inept and corrupt governments that followed the armistice had erased the glories of 1918. By 1934, exhaustion had set in. It was clear that millions lost in the mud of the trenches had been wasted, *une folie de la guerre*. For the average Frenchman life had not improved, it had just become a bit tawdrier. The Third Republic had failed to deliver on its promises. By 1934 suspicion and mistrust simmered and occasionally boiled over. In such an atmosphere, it took very little to set off more of the demonstrations of civil unrest that Parisians had learned to expect as daily events. The politics of the moment were chaotic at best. "*Vive la France*," shouted so often from the throngs in the streets, meant something very different to each voice that shouted it. The squabbles of the anti-Semitic right and the communists on the far left and all those factions in between were tearing the country apart. Premiers changed as frequently as the acts at the Follies Bergère. But all that was for another day, not on this night. Instead, on this May evening, it was as if God had kissed the city and sent the perfumed breezes to wash away care. As offices closed and café lights brightened, an endless parade of strollers appeared along the city's boulevards. For Paris was nothing if not an illusion, an illusion of love and beauty, a place of romance in the minds of those who visited the cafés and bistros and those who, far away, could only read of the place and dream.

And yet here it was again, a Parisian Spring, why worry about the headlines, *c'est la vive*! Long strands of light filtered through leafy branches along the Champs-Élysées, inviting people to take in the city. Like all Parisians anticipating a balmy night among the outdoor cafés, many of the strollers made a detour toward the flower-lined pathways of the Jardin du Luxembourg. There they ambled along drinking in the long twilight like an aperitif. With summer approaching, the Luxembourg Gardens, an oasis amid the city, attracted strollers from all walks of life. It was the second largest of Paris's elegant open spaces, beautifully manicured, and redolent with the scents of thousands of new blossoms. Lovers walked holding hands, lost in each other, while around them a few harried escapees from the prisons of government offices made a detour through the gardens, opting for a scenic route home to their apartments and glad to be free of their dusty confines. A few moments of refuge there among the flowers felt like a sip of Chablis, crisp and cold to complement an *al fresco* supper. Surrounded by beds of well-tended hydrangeas, liatris and anemone, this was an evening that brought hope for a better tomorrow. Ryshkov appeared among the evening strollers in a dark suit and scuffed shoes. As instructed, he was making a circuit of the shimmering basin with its cascade of fountains. Four days sitting up on slow trains, all the time watching for the hand of the *aparat* to reach out and grab him. He was exhausted.

Somehow he had made it out of Germany, unnoticed by the border guards who seemed more interested in passengers entering the country. That, he thought, would soon change. At Enschede, just over the border into Holland, he thought he saw an aparatchik at the railway station. He could not be sure, but the man had the look—feral and sniffing the air for prey, like a hyena; Ryshkov avoided him. Perhaps the man was just scanning the crowd, looking for a friend or relative on the train. Ryshkov could not take a chance, and so he lost himself in the crowd of passengers moving toward the exit. He knew about railway stations and borders, after all he had been crossing them legally and illegally for over a decade. He decided not to chance it this close to the German border but to go further west before catching another train. That meant he had to walk for hours to the next station. When he reached, Eindhoven he left the train, stole a bicycle, and rode into Belgium with a bunch of farmers. Outside Antwerp he stole a suit of clothes from the back of a funeral home where it had been sponged and set out to dry before being used to adorn a corpse. Now he was hot, out of money, and terribly hungry. Still, he remained watchful.

As he entered the gardens he passed anonymously among the lovers, oblivious to the beauty surrounding him. He did not look directly at anyone, yet he forced his tired mind to notice everything about his surroundings. He had been trained to do so; in fact, it was his very talents for observation that had made him a successful Chekist. Among the French strolling the park, he was just another citizen making his way through the early evening, unremarkable and instantly forgettable. In his shabby dead-man's suit he looked like just another of the city's downtrodden.

He had been told that the handover in the Luxembourg Gardens was to be a two-step affair. He needed to produce the documents for the contact to examine after which he would get the promised passport and money. He was desperate, and he knew that they had him at a disadvantage. He had no leverage, for once he gave up Dietrich's papers, he had nothing with which to bargain. He would then be beyond any support network, alone, penniless, and with no means of travel beyond France or stay within its borders.

He had almost given up when; at last he saw the couple seated on a bench by the Auguste Ottin fountain. So far, so good, he thought. The woman was, as promised, wearing white with a splash of lavender at her throat and had a large lavender handbag next to her on the seat. The man with her was dressed in a tan suit with a gray fedora bound with a lavender and gray hatband. Lavender had been the chosen signal color, a nod to the Moscow rules he had been taught. Use a color that would blend in with the situation, they had been taught, one that was recognizable, but not out of place. In this garden abloom with color everywhere, what would be more acceptable than lavender? They must be the contacts. If not, he was doomed.

He glanced at them briefly and kept walking. Then, as instructed, he went to the next empty bench and sat down. He quickly slipped Dietrich's sheaf of technical papers from his pocket and wedged them between the slats of the bench. Then, he exhaled slowly while he counted to sixty. Adopting a nonchalance that he did not feel, he stood and walked back in the direction from which he had come, being careful not to make eye contact with the pair.

As he turned out from the path around the fountain he chanced a quick look back. He saw that the man in the fedora had remained where he had been sitting and was watching him and also that the woman and the papers he had left on the bench had vanished.

Ryshkov was now truly in limbo, he could not go forward nor could he retrace his steps, and so for the next twenty minutes, he wandered through the park lost in thought. He was tired, and drawn. He had spent less than two weeks on the run and yet he felt as if he had been running for years. Would his potential saviors live up to the bargain? Or, would they sell him out to the Sûreté, or perhaps to the local NKVD? He could only wait and hope. When he completed his circuit of the park and at last returned to the fountain, he saw that there was now a lavender chalk mark drawn across three of the slats on the bench seat just where the couple had been seated. He let out a long breath—they had accepted his offer. Now all he needed to do was pick up the passport and the money. And there on the bench, exactly where he had left Dietrich's papers, was a brown envelope wedged between the slats. With a glance over his shoulder, Ryshkov reached for the packet and swept it into his inside jacket pocket. Then, filled with a renewed vigor, he straightened and walked off whistling softly. On the other side of the fountain, a large man in a rumpled gray suit sat reading a newspaper. As Ryshkov walked toward the park's exit, the man in the gray suit sighed, put down his newspaper and casually strolled along the path, following the Russian.

La Coupole

Harriet Bliss had long ago chosen the first of May as her official birthday. May Day, why not? It was a date of rebirth, spring was in bloom, why not her? No one, not even her closest friends in Paris, knew her real birthday, nor were they certain as to which year she might be celebrating. But then frankly it did not matter; her birthday parties were always exciting, fun-filled occasions. Harriet had long ago decided that she would select a date that signified the rebirth of life on which to celebrate her birth, and each year she made sure the celebration was memorable.

Harriet Bliss was, if not beautiful, certainly lovely in a natural way, with a willowy figure. For this evening, her auburn hair had been styled by an *au currant*, and likewise expensive, Avenue Foch salon, into a fashionable bob, longer on the left than on the right side of her oval face. She had warm eyes the color of a fine sherry backlit by a warm fire. Men adored her, and although she flirted she never gave her heart away; that had been lost on the western front in 1918. The young Marine lieutenant killed in the Argonne, and to whom she had been betrothed, took that with him.

Harriet had been forced to own to thirty-two, thinking that she had been living in Paris for nearly sixteen years, and no one would believe that she was still in her twenties. She was radiant and, on this warm May evening, she was thrilled to be celebrating with her friends at one of the city's brightest bistros, La Coupole. In a city that was awash in fine restaurants, La Coupole provided just the right amount of decadence and extravagance that any attractive single lady of thirty-two might desire for her birthday.

Harriet and her friends were regally seated at a plush banquet overlooking the tables of the restaurant's other diners. This evening there were to be ten friends at her table. The party was beginning to get a glow on, yet two of the chairs remained empty. She looked at the vacant places, frowned for an instant and then smiling broadly, turned to the man seated on her left.

Her estimable boss at the American Embassy, Raymond Kingman, had at her insistence occupied the seat of honor next to her. Kingman had held a rather nebulous job at the embassy, maintaining connections throughout Europe and answerable, not to the ambassador, but to a shadowy group in Washington. Nonetheless, he adored Harriet and thought of her as a daughter. Across from him sat Herbert Greene, the American investment banker. Both Greene and Kingman were long time friends, going back to when she first arrived in France at the end of the war. Joining them was Jerzy Krol, another long-time friend from

Warsaw and currently the Polish air attaché in Paris. He had brought along another of their Warsaw friends, Cas Gubernaut. Gubernaut, an American pilot from the war, had been one of the famous Polish Falcons who had helped to trounce the Red Army on the banks of the Vistula a decade before. Gubernaut, not a devotee of celibacy, seldom travelled alone and so had brought along his *amant du jour*, a delectable senorita he had met in Montmartre. She spoke rapidly and in some strange dialect that was neither French nor Spanish and remained untranslatable, but she seemed to answer to Inez. She smiled a lot, but her main asset, as far as the men at the table could divine, was a pair of stunning breasts that nearly leapt from her low-cut gown. Finally, it was Gubernaut who explained that she was indeed speaking Basque. Inez was from Bilbao.

Gubernaut had found her in a café one day, and she obligingly went home with him. That evening they simply smiled at her when they spoke, hoping their intonations would let her know she was welcome. She replied with some bewilderment, Gubernaut's hand on her thigh keeping her from bolting. On Harriet's right was her current flame, a young naval attaché from the embassy named Bill Forrest. Forrest had fallen under Harriet's spell soon after arriving at his post in the embassy, and although he was merely twenty-eight and had never been anywhere like the city of light before, Harriet thought him a worthwhile project—at least for the time being. She would take him for a lover until she grew tired of him, then send him on his way, all the happier for his having known her.

Karl Lieberman was one of the three people who rounded out the group. Harriet always invited him, though he never was really sure why he had become part of the coterie that surrounded her. She had known him for years, a Latvian Jew who operated on the fringes of the clandestine world. He had been a friend since the fighting around Warsaw a decade before. It was an open secret that he had once worked for Sir Basil Zaharoff, but then again, maybe he still did, who knew?

The one man who was sure to know was Harry Braham. He was late, and it was his place at the table that was still vacant. Harriet looked up, and there he was, arriving late and with a luscious brunette in tow. Carefully navigating the room, the pair was making their way toward Harriet's table. The brunette's glittering diamonds and daring décolletage flashed before his eyes as Andre, the maître d' led the pair to where Harry's friends awaited. It would seem that all of Paris was out celebrating this May Day evening, and the restaurant's tables were packed.

Harry Braham was the person who was the nexus of this little group. As a former army fighter pilot and man about town, he appeared to be the classic American expatriate of the time. Rather than going back to the States, he had remained in Europe after the end of the war, living chiefly in Paris. Herb Greene had given him a job. He was ostensibly the Paris representative of Biddle & Company, one of the private investment companies with headquarters in Philadelphia's Rittenhouse Square. As such, Braham was responsible for ferreting out investment opportunities for the firm's elite clients. His specialty was aviation and armaments, two areas of business that were thriving despite the armistice. His reputation and expertise as an ace pilot in the 1918 war gave him access to companies throughout

The White Raven

Europe. The flying fraternity was a close-knit group, eschewing, for the most part, nationalities and politics. For his clients he acted much like a marriage broker. He was able to match the needs of the companies with those of the investors. All the while, although unofficial, his real job was to help the United States get a picture of what dangers might lurk in a Europe with resurgent and competing militaries. Simply put, he was a spy. With an apartment with a decent address and an excellent tailor, he cut a fine figure. Women liked him; some even loved him—at least for a time, until his work got in the way. Though he lived in Paris and smoked Gauloises, he had not gone completely native, and drove an American car. This year it was a maroon 1932 Ford Victoria Coupe, with which he coursed through Paris at speeds that infuriated the Gendarmes. He had no family in the States and, in the sixteen years since the armistice, had only been back there for a total of nine weeks, during which he rambled about aimlessly until he could catch a boat back to France.

Harriet loved Harry in a very special way, and yet she had her own *amours*, as did he. Since 1922 they had been on-again off-again lovers. There was no jealousy between them, and as the years went by, from time to time they would find themselves in one or the other's bed, and then they would move on to someone new. She had lost her fiancé, a Marine officer, in the summer of 1918, but the grief that they shared was the loss of her friend, and his lover, Agata, during the rout of the Red Army on the Vistula.

When they finally arrived at the table, Braham introduced the woman on his arm, "This is Cynthia Waite, she's just over from the States on the *Ile de France*. And since it is her first time in Paris, I wanted to give her a taste of what Parisian night life is all about." Then, just for a moment he abandoned her to their smiles and nods and walked to Harriet and gave her a kiss, "Happy Birthday, kiddo," and handed her a small box, elegantly wrapped in silk. Cynthia Waite looked on just as bewildered as Inez and wondering exactly who these people were.

At twenty-six Cynthia Waite had decided to leave the protected environs of her parents' home near Devon on Philadelphia's main line and get a taste of Europe. She decided that she needed a bit of an adventure before settling down to marry some pinstriped Rittenhouse Square–banker and raise the requisite number of children, attend the functions of the junior league, and whatnot. She was vivacious, with a brilliant smile and green eyes that sparkled when she turned them on any unsuspecting male. Her father was a client of Biddle & Company. Greene had given Cynthia Harry's name before she left the States. And not having a shy bone in her body, immediately upon arriving she called Braham and asked him if he's show her around town. He had told her he had an event to attend that she might find amusing, and she agreed to come along. Braham had no idea what to expect, but when he picked her up at the Crillon, Braham took one look at her and was more than pleased with what he saw.

"Save it for later," he thought. Stepping back to Cynthia, who lay becalmed like a ship in mid-channel awaiting a berth, he said, "Let me introduce you properly." For the next few moments he rattled off their names and provided her a commentary of who and what they were until totally bewildered, he called for a chair and sat her down next to Inez where the two women struggled to communicate throughout the evening. "So, Harriet, are you finally going to announce which birthday this truly is?" asked Braham with a mischievous gleam in his eye.

"Of course," she smiled. "This is my thirty-second," then she paused, "as always."

Everyone laughed, even Inez, who thought it best to go along with the joke even if she had no idea as to what was being said. Cynthia smiled and tried to pick up on the conversation.

As usual, La Coupole was packed that evening. The restaurant had earned a high reputation for fine dining and offered its customers the finest seafood in the city. There were platters of Cancale oysters, Ouistreham prawns, fresh Breton *homard*, still streaming seaweed from La Manche all set out on heaping beds of shaved ice, along with the freshest catch brought in each morning from St. Malo. Along with the seafood, there were rolling carts from which waiters would cut slices of tender roast beef. There were trays laded with charcuteries accompanied by champagne-drenched sauerkraut carried by waiters as they patrolled the aisles. As a finishing touch, piles of crispy *frites* and a host of other delights were brought to the tables of smiling diners. Everything and anything to please the palates of the customers was the aim of the management. The place was also known for its selection of patés, each redolent with the rich aroma of the choicest truffles hidden at their center. Of course, the cellar provided a broad selection of wines from throughout the country along with an assortment of lagers and, for those with an added discrimination, *cidres* of the most delicate flavors. The entire experience was an ménage of flavors and aromas. Amid this cornucopia of temptations, the conversation at Harriet's table gaily went on touching on the important and the absurd.

Harriet leaned across the table and said, "Harry, you must tell us all about your new airplane. I want you to give me a ride in it. And Bill, too, if there is room." And turning to her escort she said, "You wouldn't know it to look at him, but Harry here is an ace aviator and has fought in two wars!" She then looked sheepishly at Gubernaut added, "And so too is Cas, there!"

The young naval lieutenant, who had been too young to be in America's war effort, eyed the man across the table with a mixture of respect and a touch of envy. "Is that true, sir?" he asked.

Braham looked at the young man's eager face and with an effort at self-deprecation said, "Yes, I suppose I have had a few Germans for breakfast, as they say."

"Oh don't forget the Russians, darling," teased Harriet, knowing full well he could never forget the fighting outside Warsaw. "You and Cas had plates full of them."

"So a new kite, huh? What *are* you flying these days," Cas Gubernaut asked.

With a wry smile, Braham replied, "It is a modified Pitcairn Mailwing, I had my mechanic install an extra wide seat where the mailbags normally ride, so now two passengers can fit into the front seat. It's a nice little airplane, and I have Herb here to thank for it. He keeps me in airplanes—and that is good for business. Sometimes just by giving potential investors a flight out to one of the European airplane factories helps convince them to pony up the money to invest, and that keeps a roof over my head."

Herb Greene laughed and then added, "You know Harry here is a whizz at getting people who have no idea about the potential of aviation to become serious investors in new planes, engines, and now, airlines." Greene looked down the table with an air of supreme self-satisfaction. No one said anything, after all this was a birthday party not a business meeting.

Finally, Kroll broke in, "Harry," he asked, "What do you hear from your old friend Stiffler? Lately I heard he was back in Germany and in uniform."

Harry gave a rueful smile. "I saw him last year in Berlin, just about the time that Hitler and his cronies burned down the Reichstag. He was well enough, and he seemed to be flying a lot. He is not political. He never said anything about the military, though. I know that he knows Göring, perhaps he is helping them."

Cynthia Waite looked bewildered at this turn of conversation. To her, fresh from the States, the Nazis were depicted as political Keystone Kops, just a bunch of thugs strutting across the newsreel screens. "But I thought that Herr Hitler was doing wonders for Germany. I saw in the papers that he was putting people back to work. What is wrong with that?"

At the table everyone's jaw dropped. Harry was about to intervene when Jerzy, polite as ever, explained.

The White Raven

"Mademoiselle Waite, you are newly arrived in Europe, so one may forgive your misunderstanding. When one reads the papers, we hear of the gangs of thugs in America. During your experiment with prohibition they murdered each other to gain some advantage over rival gangs. Hitler is such a thug. Although now a politician, he is leader of a gang, much like your Al Capone in Chicago. Like your Al Capone, he pays off judges and others in order to stay in business. He does this sometimes with jobs and sometimes with cash. In Capone's case, he uses money from criminal activity to boost his power. In Germany, the Nazis are using the state treasury and political power to boost their own criminal activities. In essence, Mademoiselle, they are raping the state, and soon they will begin looking elsewhere for more spoils."

"But how can they do that? Aren't there laws?"

Jerzy smiled at her naiveté. "Yes, there are. Only now they are writing their own."

Cynthia Waite looked dumfounded and was about to speak when Harriet spoke instead.

"Harry, what about Stiffler. He hasn't become a Nazi, has he?" asked Harriet. "I like Reinhardt. It would be disappointing to have to hate him over his politics."

"No, I don't think so. He has known a lot of them though. Hard to miss them, if you are a military flier. Göring loves pilots. He introduced me to a couple of the real fanatics. There was this one, Otto Kleist, dressed to the nines in his black SS uniform, who seemed to exude pure evil. Reinhardt seemed not to be fazed by the ranting and rhetoric, though. He loves flying and tries to keep to aviation and stay out of politics."

"I think I read that he is going to be part of the team that the Germans are sending to the *Challenge International de Tourisme* this August," Cas Gubernaut chimed in. "Didn't I see that in the Warsaw papers, Jerzy?"

"Yes," said the Pole, "that's why I was asking if Harry had heard from him. There will be several teams from Poland, Germany, Italy, Czechoslovakia, Italy, even the Brits are sending a team."

"So what is the contest?" Everyone turned to look at Cynthia Waite who had been listening and urgently needed to focus some of the male attention back to her.

"Since Poland is the host this year, I suppose I should explain," Krol began. "The idea is to create a kind of Olympiad of the air, while at the same time showing the general public the capabilities of civilian air travel in Europe. However, like the Olympics, we have seen a severe emphasis on national pride. Each nation will want to best the others."

"But what is it, an airshow? We have plenty of those in the States," replied Cynthia. "I went to one where a woman stood on the wing of an airplane as it flew by. It was thrilling!"

"No, this event is much more than that. For a month, beginning in August, the teams of each participating nation will fly a prescribed route around the whole of Europe. Each leg will be timed, and the pilots and airplanes must perform against specific criteria such as fuel consumption, time en route and various techniques of pilotage. Believe me, it is not an air circus," said Jerzy as he warmed to the topic.

Gubernaut added, "Americans were decidedly not invited. I am surprised to hear that the Brits are coming."

Karl Lieberman joined in, "This summer's event mademoiselle, presents an opportunity for each of these nations to try to best the other while at the same time glimpsing the technical prowess of their potential military adversaries. Many of the observers hope that the lust for victory will unmask some secret of a potential enemy and thus avoid a costly defeat in battle. I suspect that there will be as many spies along the way as there may be onlookers, maybe more."

"In the meantime, if we, as Americans, cannot participate, we can at the very least advise our clients as to which companies display technologies that might warrant investment," said Herb Greene.

Harry waved for more champagne. "Enough shop talk, let's remember whose big day this is." When everyone's glass had been topped up with bubbly he went on, "To Harriet, the loveliest thirty-two-year old in Paris!"

The dinner went on and the restaurant filled with patrons and the noise from a hundred chattering mouths swelled to a roar. Waiters scurried past the party carrying their trays of delectables. As their glasses were filled and refilled, Cynthia Waite, by then brightly drunk, thought that the evening was wonderful and hoped it would never end.

The White Raven

It was after midnight when the calvados and champagne had begun to produce their inevitable results. The dessert cart, groaning with the exhaustive selection of tartines, éclairs, petite fours and ices had come by the table twice. Harriet had foresworn a birthday cake, preferring not to chance the heat of too many candle flames, but was seduced by the pastry chef's artistry, and opted for a éclair filled with mocha cream.

"I can eat no more, it is now time for you to take me home," Harriet declared to her escort.

Somewhat befuddled by all the booze, Lieutenant Forrest stood and, weaving slightly, offered Harriet his arm. "Of course, my lady. Let me help you to a taxi, and I will see you safely home."

The other men at the table eyed the young officer with thinly veiled amusement as the couple toddled off toward the street.

"How long before she has him in bed do you think?" Gubernaut asked Braham as he watched them leave.

With a thin smile Braham replied, "Not too long, but she may have a tough time keeping him awake in order for him to do the honors."

As the party began to break up, Karl Lieberman caught Braham's attention. "Can we speak for a few moments before you take Mademoiselle Waite home?"

"Sure." Turning to Cynthia, Braham asked, "Can you give me a moment to speak with Karl?"

"Sure, chum. I'll just find the ladies and powder my nose."

Cas and Inez made their way out the door followed by Raymond and Herb, the two men going off somewhere, no doubt for a nightcap.

When they were finally alone, Karl turned to Braham. "I received a gift today, sent all the way from our friend in Berlin. I should like to show it to you. Can we meet tomorrow?"

Braham nodded, "Sure, breakfast then?"

Seeing Cynthia navigating her way back to them, Braham said, "Sure. The usual place, let's say around eleven?"

"Very well," said Lieberman, and to Cynthia Waite, "Good night Mademoiselle."

The White Raven

T he city of light had turned out the lamps and gone to bed. From where he stood on his narrow balcony overlooking the Rue Clauzel, Harry Braham could gaze up between the narrow corridors of buildings to where the course of the Milky Way formed a frothing mountain stream rolling through the heavens to the far horizon. Braham sighed, dawn would soon rinse the stars from this patch of dark and he would have to be about his work. He often liked to be awake while others slept, to watch the night die in its sleep. Here in the ninth *arrondissement*, amid the confines of the city, in the dead of night, he could sense the immensity of the world beyond. Alone amid the millions in Paris, on nights like this when shops and cafés had been shuttered, he tried to find solace, but sometimes he just felt alone. If he just vanished, who would notice, who would care? Once in a while a lone taxi would rattle down the pavement, bringing home a couple from some late-night spot, perhaps an evening at Fouquet, then home to bed, and a finale of lovemaking. He often thought of how nice that would be, how easy it could be to find someone—but he had not chosen to tonight.

He could have, he knew. She would have come if he had asked. After leaving La Coupole, Cynthia Waite seemed ready for romance, eager for it, something she could tell her Main Line friends about when she got home. As the others drifted off toward home, she put her arm in his and leaned her head on his shoulder. It was not easy to say goodnight to her. She seemed even lovelier in the glow from the streetlights, and, as they walked along the boulevard, he could feel the heat from her skin. He could have hailed a taxi at the restaurant entrance, put her in it, and brought the evening to a close, but there seemed to be a need to linger for a few minutes. Maybe it was the wine or her perfume; something from Roger and Gallet was it? Its scent of lilac with a touch of something sharper mixed in the air and added to the champagne and vodka he had drunk. Who was she anyway? He barely knew her, and, even if they only had this night, she would be a complication. She was just a kid, sexy and very appealing, but a kid nonetheless. Still, as they walked on she seemed more than willing; she gripped his arm more tightly and looked up at him.

"Where to now, Captain Braham?" she asked, using his wartime rank and kidding him slightly having heard all the war stories from Krol and Gubernaut.

"I don't know. It's a lovely night, let's walk down to the river, you need to see the bridges all lit up."

"That would be lovely," she said and gave his arm a long squeeze and wondered why he was so standoffish.

They walked along in silence for a few moments, both caught up in the nighttime magic. They were both slightly tipsy from all the drink, and she was totally intoxicated by Paris. At last he spoke.

"I hope we didn't bore you tonight. I know how hard it is to fit in with a lot of cronies talking about people one doesn't know, but I thought it might be a nice way for you to spend your first evening in the city, and well La Coupole is, well La Coupole—it's a show in itself."

She laughed. It was a champagne laugh, sparkling and effervescent. He liked it, liked her for that matter.

"No, I was captivated by all of you. You seemed to have already lived such fascinating lives. Flying in the war, fighting Bolsheviks in Poland, and all of it while I was still going to grade school."

"You make me suddenly feel quite elderly, "he laughed.

They stopped at the corner of the boulevard, and he pulled her toward him and kissed her. She seemed surprised for an instant and then kissed him back and pressed her body into his. She wanted him, wanted him badly.

"Don't you think we should get off the street," she said when she caught her breath again.

He hesitated and said, "You're right, let's find a taxi and get you home."

She stared at him in surprise; perhaps he meant to seduce her in her hotel room. Well, she wouldn't mind that at all, perhaps a champagne breakfast in the morning. But when they alighted at the Crillon, he merely saw her to the elevator and left her there. She found herself somewhere between anger and anguish.

He could not explain it, not to her nor to himself. Making love to her would have been splendid, but then what? The rituals of a relationship were not what he wanted or needed, and he sensed that she would want all of the trappings of being with someone, at least until she decided on someone else, and Braham thought that for a woman like her that would not take very long.

The White Raven

Braham was tired of being the tour guide to every name that Greene handed him. He had played the genial host too many times, and although it was part of his job, he had never warmed to it. Over the years, several of the wives of visiting clients had made it clear that they would welcome a *rencontre sexulle*, however brief. And when confronted with even the boldest advance from the most predatory of these women, he had succeeded in gently putting them off, once even alluding to an unspeakable war wound that cooled the ardor of the randy wife of a Pittsburgh steel executive.

This young woman was much the same. Rich, spoiled, and used to getting her way; Cynthia Waite was only interested in her own world. It wasn't just that her naïve worldview was shocking; he expected that from most newly arrived Americans. The oceans were wide and things that happened here in Europe were indeed distant from the tittle-tattle of Philadelphia's Main Line. But she would never last in his world, and he was tiring of being the first act in someone else's drama. No, Cynthia had come to Paris to have her own adventure, that she had met him on her first night was a plus for her. But she was just a kid after all, and besides in his real work, the work that occupied his nights, she did not fit in.

So he found a taxi and rode back to the quiet of his apartment, alone but not lonely. Maybe he would go see the Duchess Darya. She was Russian and claimed to have fled from the Bolsheviks with the clothes on her back and a dubious noble pedigree. She was dark and sensual with fingers that could relieve any care or fear. A courtesan of the first water, Darya was his refuge from relationships. With her it was business, although it hardly felt that way. She kept an apartment in the Avenue Foch, and, if she liked you, she treated you as a lover, not a client. Well, perhaps another night. He gave the cab driver his address and went home.

The White Raven

In his study, on the rough-hewn mantle, a souvenir from an ancient Norman farmhouse, that was supported by wooden airplane propellers taken from a pair of derelict SPAD XIIIs, were arranged a line of framed photographs. These were his memories, his ghost squadron he called them—the people, some living, but most now dead, who had meant something to him in his life. This melancholy feeling seemed to grip him of late, and he needed to shake it off if he was ever to get a good night's sleep again.

When he finally did slip off to sleep, he tossed and turned, unable to relax completely. Seeing Cas again that night had brought back memories of leading the tiny Polish Air Force on those long patrols over the snow-covered steppe, looking for signs of Red cavalry. In the air, it was so cold that his hand nearly froze around the throttle of the battered Fokker. In his dreams he saw the vastness of white, and in a flash the white snow was showered with red as bits of men and horses, cut through by his bullets and bombs, were tossed up into the air. Finally, as the sun's rays began to hit the windows opposite his bedroom, Braham drifted deeper into sleep.

Breakfast was a serious ritual in Braham's life, and he took his regularly at a tiny café on the Rue des Martyrs. Each morning he rose at six, dressed, and ready or not went out into the world. He was known as a regular. When he entered the tiny café the *propriétaire*, a large woman of fifty with flaming red hair and an ample bosom, had his bowl of café au lait ready along with a brioche or two, fresh from the neighboring *boulangerie*. As he lingered over his coffee, he lit another Gauloises and perused the Paris dailies. He was smoking too much again, he thought. He should quit, but then what vices would he have left? Thoughts of Cynthia Wood were still fresh in his mind, and those too seemed to gnaw at him. He was roused from his doldrums by the appearance of Karl Lieberman.

"So here you are alone again my friend," said the Latvian, who held up a hand to indicate two more bowls of coffee for the table. "What happened to that delicious young lady, ah, Miss Waite isn't it?"

"Let's just say I had a severe case of scruples and made sure she got safely to her hotel." Braham lit another cigarette.

"Safely?" I do not mean to pry Harry, but you don't seem to be your old self. Tossing away lovely young ladies like that, how very un-Parisian of you. Are you ill?"

"What did you want to tell me?" Braham paused to let the *propriétaire* pour fresh coffee into their bowls. Braham winked at her, and she winked back with an *"I'm here and ready for you boys, if you like"* smile and then she turned and, swinging her hips, she returned to the bar.

"We received a package from Berlin yesterday; it contains something you should examine. It was brought out to us by a Russian, he appears to be on the run from the NKVD. That makes it all suspicious, but this looks to be genuine, and, as far as we know, the Russian checks out. Still, with the Russians you are never quite sure."

Braham arched an eyebrow, but he knew that if Lieberman thought something was worth his time, it no doubt was. Liebermann and Braham had a relationship that went back to the waning days of the Great War. Through all those years, Lieberman had tutored Braham. It was Lieberman who took the young flying ace and taught him the realities of the spy trade that Raymond Kingman had recruited him into. Espionage, as it was practiced in

The White Raven

Europe in the wake of the First World War, was not the bold and dashing stuff that filled novels. He was no Ashenden. It was gritty stuff, ground out by little people doing small jobs and sending information onward. It was the job of the spymasters to put the pieces together, make sense of it, and then take action. But Lieberman, who had worked in the shadows of the espionage world throughout Europe, saw in Braham the makings of one who could do both: gather and understand what the crumbs of intelligence meant. Braham was Raymond Kingman's protégé and that was good enough for him. That Braham had the courage for the job Lieberman did not doubt, especially after the battles outside Warsaw in which the American had led wave after wave of airplanes in attacks on the advancing Russians.

Lieberman always claimed that though the British might have the oldest and most prestigious espionage service in the world, the most effective service was that created by Felix Dzerzhinsky. The Cheka, built on the ruins of the Tsar's Okhrana, was the largest of any secret service, with agents scattered like seeds throughout the west. There, the successful would take root and grow, some obviously and others more covertly, because world revolution, the aim of Soviet Russia, would not be swift. For was it not Lenin himself who said, after the failure of the Red Army on the Vistula: *Push out a bayonet. If it strikes fat, push deeper. If it strikes iron, pull back and wait for another day.* Even the great Lenin recognized the need for covert action to move the masses toward revolution, and so he ordered Dzerzhinsky to take action.

They had first met at a celebration bash for Braham and his squadron mates, at the Crillon, following the Armistice. It was on that same night that he had first seen Agata. On that evening Lieberman had posed as an engineer, now and again employed by Sir Basil Zaharoff of Vickers, Ltd. In truth, Lieberman served the

Merchant of Death by keeping tabs on developments in military aviation. What began as a kind of symbiotic relationship between Braham and Lieberman had evolved into friendship and trust, and over the years they had learned to help each other, and rely on each other.

"Harry, I have a story to tell you," he began.

"Is it a long story? I only ask because if it is going to be another of your tales involving multiple nationalities and names with lengthy patronymics, I am going to need a lot more coffee."

Lieberman laughed, "Not that long. It is the countess. Her network does not know her real name, so she calls herself *Der Weiss Rabe*, The White Raven. In German it is a masculine name, and like all good code names means something only to her. I have met her, several times. You should meet Countess Gisela von Teischen. Perhaps the next time she comes to Paris. She is quite beautiful, intelligent, and determined; she is also very well placed, being married to a senior SS officer. You both have something in common, not so much a death wish, but the ability to handle danger without being afraid. Interested? Hmm, I thought you would be." Lieberman lit another of his disgusting harsh Turkish cigarettes, and then he proceeded to tell Braham about the White Raven.

"Who says I'm not afraid," asked Braham when Lieberman had finished.

"I will explain after you have seen this," and from the inside pocket of his jacket, Lieberman produced the packet of plans that Ryshkov had brought from Germany.

"You never act as if you are. In any event, this is what the Russian had with him. It is the preliminary design of a new

German fighter airplane. Anyway, I assume this is an accurate copy of a design specification. They have designated it the model Bf-109. No one else has anything like it. A low-wing, all metal design with a retractable undercarriage, and it is designed to mount machineguns in the wings and a cannon that fires through the propeller shaft. The designers are hoping to exceed 400 kph with their new engine. The plans are preliminary, but there is an early variant, a training plane dubbed Bf-108, which the Germans plan to enter in the Air Olympiad. Apparently, the Germans will be ready to build a prototype of the new plane early next year. This one they are keeping very secret."

Braham looked at the documents and gave out a low whistle. "Jesus, this is way ahead of what anyone else has on the drawing boards," he said. "I've seen a photo of the 108, but from the looks of these drawings, this things is more than a variant. Are there performance specifications, too?"

"Here," said Lieberman and passed along another sheet of paper covered with items listing airspeeds and rates of climb, all the things that are meat and potatoes to aeronautical engineers.

"This is gold, Karl. You must know that. How did this Russian make contact with the, ah Raven?"

"Through another woman, a florist. One of my men in Berlin is keeping an eye on her. Funny how those things work. I told you the Raven was well placed. Well, as the wife of a senior Party official, she knows everyone in Berlin. She entertains her husband's friends, and she has a favorite florist. It turns out that her florist has been this Russian's lover for some time; a secret he hopes remains unknown to the NKVD.

The people running the purges in Moscow had his name on a list, and it was either wait to be snatched by the NKVD or make a run for it. He chose to run and went to his lover for help. So, the florist brought it to the Raven and she contacted Herschel."

"Herschel? Is your nephew still in Germany?'

"Yes, and you will appreciate this. He has a job with a Nazi art dealer in Berlin. The man thinks Herschel is a Greek. Herschel is now calling himself Konstantinos Kourkoulakis and has a genuine Greek passport. In any event, the Nazis are coercing the wealthy Jews to buy their way out of the country, so there is a fire sale on art. Since the dealer needs to contact other dealers and galleries around the world to obtain prices, the Nazis don't read or block his communications. Herschel has been using this means to communicate with me. In this case, the request for the value of a Vermeer meant he had something worthwhile for us. So, I made the deal, and this Ryshkov brought the goods.

"How long can Herschel hold out in Berlin?"

"Not much longer, I suspect. We are trying to arrange passage to Brazil for a doctor and his family. Once that is done, I think it will be time for Herschel, or Konstantinos, to vanish."

Braham laughed and shook his head. "Such a world we live in, but seriously, should you be showing me this? After all, Sir Basil has paid to set up her network, shouldn't he get the first sniff?"

Lieberman sighed and looked around the room. From an inside pocket he pulled out a box of Sobranie cigarettes and opened it. These were Balkan cigarettes, wrapped in black papers, tipped with gold foil and filled with strong Latakia tobacco. Lieberman flicked the end of a wooden match with a thumbnail and fired the tip. Instantly, to the café's aromas of coffee and pastries, was added the heavy scent of the *Srednogorie.*

Wafting the smoke with his hand, Lieberman took a moment to answer. "Things with Sir Basil are a bit complicated at the moment, he is very ill, and although still the proprietor of this enterprise, but he is beginning to slow down, visibly so. In some ways he has cut himself off from those of us in the field. You may have heard that he burned his files, well a lot of them in any event. It is inevitable I suppose, especially at his age, to want to leave a legacy of some meaning. I think he believes Hitler is the incarnation of evil and wants most of all to destroy him and his party. Most of the time Sir Basil stays in the south of France, enjoying the sun and the wine, perhaps a little too much. He is dying but cares for Gisela von Teischen. Business is not his main concern these days. Still, he will get his share of this, but you will likely appreciate it more. For myself and the others with whom I have been working, I must look to my future, perhaps I may be of more service to you and your Mr. Kingman?"

Braham looked at his old comrade and slowly nodded, "Well, I'd like to have you around."

"What will you do with these?" Lieberman asked, pointing to the drawings.

"Well, that may be a problem," Braham replied. "America is reeling from the crash of '29 and as far as new military appropriations, has its head firmly in the sand. No one is beating the drum for anything military. I wouldn't doubt that the Poles have a bigger armed force than America. Still, there are some people I can talk to. Maybe at Curtiss or Boeing, but rest assured somebody will see this. Now what about this Russian?"

Lieberman took a long drag on his cigarette, set it smoldering in the table's ashtray and then proceeded to tell Braham how the material got from Berlin to Paris.

"And this Ryshkov, what of him?"

Lieberman's coffee had grown cold; still he took a large swallow and nodded to the redhead for a refill. "The lady in Berlin vouched for him. He is NKVD and is indeed on the run from his friends at Dzerzhinsky Square. There were some feelers put out in Berlin and, I expect by this morning, most of the European stations of the Soviet security *aparat* will have got wind of him. Even with the papers we gave him, he may not make it out of Europe."

"But do you think he may be of any use to you, or us?"

"That's a hard one to answer, for all we know the NKVD already have him and, if not, how long can he last? Even if he runs, they will never let him live."

Braham took some more coffee, "Any other word from Raven? How is she keeping up?"

Lieberman sighed, "I think she lives for the work. It can't be much of a life with that pansy ass von Teischen and his Nazi cronies."

The pair left the café, and Lieberman walked with Braham back to his apartment where, using tracing paper, the American made a copy of the drawings. After Lieberman left Braham changed into a business suit. He did not want to be late for his lunch with Jerzy Krol.

At noon, the Polish diplomat pulled up in front of Braham's apartment in a midnight blue open Ford Phaeton V-8. Braham whistled when he saw the car. "How did you get your hands on this?"

"Lots of Poles live in Detroit, my friend. Do you think that you are the only one with connections? It's a beautiful day for a drive, and I know a great place for lunch."

"Then what are we waiting for?" Braham said and hopped in. Before his ass hit the seat, Krol was speeding down the cobbled street. Out past the Arc de Triumphe and across the city Krol kept the V-8 at nearly sixty.

"So who was that lovely young woman you brought to the party? She was stunning, but perhaps a trifle young for you was she not?" Krol kept his eyes on the road as he said this and Braham laughed.

"She is the daughter of one of Herb's clients, come over here to get a taste of Europe. Spoiled and rich, interested?"

"Women always interest me, especially here in Paris. My wife is in Warsaw and here, well, as you see, I am at loose ends. But she is your *amour*, right?"

"No, Jerzy she is not. I walked her to the elevator at the Crillon and went home. I am tired of being the tour guide to Herb's endless list of clients. I make you a present of her. Here, I will give you her room number, look her up. I am sure she would be delighted."

At this Jerzy took his eyes off the road for a moment to look at his friend.

"Jerzy for Christ's sake watch out!"

Krol looked up to see a massive truck laden with kegs of beer roll out of an alleyway directly in front of the car. He flicked his wrist and for a brief moment all that Braham could see were a line of sweating beer kegs pass in front of him. Then Jerzy swerved again and, amid a chorus of obscenities that fancifully described the Poles supposed ancestry, they sped away, the heavy aroma of beer still in the car.

The White Raven

For the next hour they raced along city streets and then burst out into the countryside, all the while keeping the sinuous River Seine on their left. From time to time they could see the barge traffic on the river, but most of the time the road wound through fields atop the high bluffs north of the river. Through towns and villages they left a wake of dust and shaking heads along with a few raised fists as the powerful engine roared by. For the two fliers it was almost as if they were airborne again. Laughing and making the most of the journey, they sailed past farms and villages. The occasional hayrick plodding along with only one horsepower might have slowed them down if not for Krol's deft handling of the car and rapid accelerations. They wound out through Saint-Gervais and Gasny and across the open fields that stretched toward Rouen; the Ford cut an impressive figure in bright sunlight. At last, they reached the crest of a limestone ridge and, accelerating, Krol guided the car down a narrow twisting lane toward the distant river.

The restaurant was a small family place set among trees on the north bank. The maître d', who was no doubt the owner, led them to a garden and seated them with a view of the river below. The Seine was in full spring flow, its current rapid, despite the lack of recent rain. Barge traffic, a staple of European commerce, was brisk, both up and downstream. They ordered the Côte de veau— veal smothered in mushrooms and cooked in a cream and calvados sauce—along with mountains of crisp *pommes frites*. It was a man's lunch.

"Nice place, how did you find it?" Braham asked as they were being shown to a table.

"A friend of mine brought me here last year. She and I stayed up the road at an Auberge near Monet's garden."

"And is she still in the picture?' Braham asked trying to make a pun.

Krol looked away and sighed, then changed the subject. "No. I am like you my friend. These liaisons come and go. What do you know about this air race we are hosting this summer?" asked Krol after they each had downed a glass of the crisp local rosé.

"No more than you said last night. Is it going to be a repeat of the *Challenge International de Tourisme* that was staged in thirty-two?"

"Well, it will be a challenge, but I think any pretense that the event will have a peaceful impact on aviation in Europe will fail in its early days. Both Germany and Italy are fielding teams made up of military aviators. Since it is a lead up to the Paris Air Show in November, it is likely that this will be the one chance for the various air forces of Europe to assess the other's skills."

"And, no doubt, an event that will attract the cream of Europe's espionage agents," Braham added.

"That was what I wanted to speak with you about. In my business, well, let me say in *our* business, trust is a very rare commodity. We all know that attachés like me are nothing more than spies. Oh, we operate legally, with diplomatic cover, but we are nothing more than spies for our countries. When you and I first met back in 1918, you were a brash young pilot fresh from knocking Fokkers from the sky. You were, like so many Americans, a mere amateur playing in a centuries-old game of European politics and intrigue. America saved France and Britain in 1918, and you and your friends came on to save Poland in 1922. For that service we, of course, paid you. We paid you and all the men you brought with you, whatever their nationality, but as a nation, we owed you and continue to owe you far more than we could offer in coin. As you led flight after flight of our tattered air force against Tukhachevsky's cavalry during those bloody August days, I began to look on you as a friend. So, what I am about to tell you, and ask of you, is as a friend, not as a representative of my government."

Braham looked at his old comrade and smiled ruefully, "Those were tough days. We lost some good men, but we tore a big hole in the Reds. What can I do for you?"

"Let me begin by telling you a bit more about Poland these days. The nation that calls itself Poland is not the historic Poland. I doubt if anyone could point to the map of Europe over the past thousand years and identify the real Poland. What we are now is a nation that was cobbled together in 1919. Probably it was left to a couple of geographers looking over some ancient maps. We are now a nation of Poles, Germans, Ukrainians, Jews, Czechs, Magyars, and Slavs put together by men with no particular leaning one way or another. They just drew lines on a map. As much as language and customs divide us, so does religion. Catholicism, Russian Orthodoxy, Judaism—we have them all. Anti-Semitism is as rife in Poland, as anywhere else on the European continent, and with our German neighbors ranting about Jews, it is sure to get worse. Anywhere you look on the map, you find Poland sharing an indefensible border with a potential enemy, and if Stalin and Hitler go at it, Poland will be their battleground of choice. Our only hope, slim as it may seem, is to create an alliance with the other countries that have similar problem. You have no doubt, heard of the Intermarium?"

Braham shook his head, "Only vaguely."

"Well, it is an elegant concept that Warsaw has been hoping to keep alive, but I have my doubts. Essentially, the idea is that all the countries that border Germany and the Soviet Union—Poland, Czechoslovakia, Hungary, Romania and Bulgaria would ally themselves to form a united front. A collective defense, if you will. The Intermarium would then be an armed barrier against aggression stretching from Danzig on the Baltic to Constanza on the Black Sea. Neither of our local bullies would want to fight against such an array of armies and air forces."

"I take it from the look on your face that you don't have much faith in it."

"Not a bit. It is doomed to failure, just as maintaining any unity within Poland is politically exhausting as the government caters to each special interest, when it comes to the Intermarium, the problems grow geometrically. Each nation has its own military that will not take direction from some allied command. Add to that the sheer array of weapons of various calibers and specifications. It is a mare's nest of conflicting problems with no reachable conclusion. No, even if it means failure, Poland has to go it alone and trust that both Britain and France will live up to their commitments to help us if we are attacked."

"From what I know, that seems a flimsy defense at best."

"Perhaps our best defense, Europe's best defense is to remove Hitler before he can consolidate power in Germany. It is something we have been considering."

"Is that a serious consideration?" asked Braham.

"One of many, I suppose. I am not sure, but it sounds tempting."

Kroll poured some of their host's calvados down his throat, the sharp tang of apples filling his senses. He looked at the peaceful scene before them, the slate blue of the river running between leafy banks, above them a few fair weather clouds, the scent of fresh cut hay on the breeze, and he wondered how he could be thinking of battlefields strewn with smoldering tanks and lifeless bodies. He shook his head and came back to the conversation.

"Harry, no doubt, you yourself will be attracted to some aspect of the race. Nothing would be more natural, but here is where I need your help. Poland needs first line military airplanes. We have a few designs that we can put into production, but our German neighbors are outstripping everyone in Europe, both in production and in technical advancement.

I want to ask you to do two things for me: first, as an interested observer, would you pass on to me anything, technical or even gossip that might be of interest to us?"

"Yes, of course, you know I would," Braham replied and was thinking of the drawings he had made that morning. Should he, could he, share them with the Poles?

Kroll smiled. "I thought you would. So here is the second. It is the most difficult, part: can you help us get our hands on new military airplanes—American airplanes?"

Braham should have been prepared for this request, but he was not, and his face showed his momentary shock.

"I know the Boeing P-26 is replacing Boeing P-12 this year and may be available for purchase by foreign governments. I know people at Boeing and, of course, Ray Kingman might be of help, do you want me to ask?"

Krol looked at his old friend with deadly seriousness, "You must use discretion. Too many people in business in America and Britain seem to regard Hitler as a paragon of economic recovery and are willing to do business with him at the expense of nations like Poland. I leave it to you to see what may be done."

"Jerzy, I have never done, nor would I in the future, jeopardize our friendship or your country's future. Where I can, I will tell you whatever I may learn. Yours is a country caught between two ravenous beasts. The Bolsheviks tried to gobble you up back in twenty-two, and I have no doubt that Hitler and his Nazis want to take back what was carved out of Germany at Versailles. You can count on me to do what I can."

"Krol smiled and raised his glass. Salut!"

"Monsieur, more calvados, *sil vou plais*." Braham called out.

For Harry Braham, it had been a long day. By the time that Jerzy Krol had dropped him back at his apartment it was nearly eight o'clock. Still, in light of what Karl Lieberman had brought him and what Jerzy Krol requested, he had one more person to see. He hoped that Raymond Kingman was not yet in bed.

The White Raven

Danse Macabre

Karinhall, the country residence of **Hermann Göring**, was built on a large hunting estate northeast of **Berlin**. It was tucked away in the **Schorfheide** forest between the lakes Großdöllner See and Wuckersee to the north of **Brandenburg**. The Reichsminister had chosen to entertain a large number of important people for an English-style weekend, and nearly everyone who was anyone in the Reichsminister's new administration had been invited. Most of the guests had all come by automobile, and many were expected to stay the weekend at the hall itself, others, the less important, had been accommodated at several local inns. The long drive leading up to the house resembled a used-car lot for the aristocracy. It was lined with a wide assortment Mercedes, Audi and Horch automobiles, many parked and cared for by private chauffeurs.

Christian von Teischen had given his chauffeur the day off and had chosen to drive his wife in their black Horch 780 cabriolet. When he reached the estate, he sped up the cobbled drive and jammed on the brakes just before the main entrance to the house, creating a swirl of dust that settled on the car's long gleaming hood. Von Teischen always insisted on riding with the car's top down, no matter what the weather. His wife was therefore

114

forced to tie a scarf over her blonde hair or risk its being torn to shreds in the wind, but he did not care. He preferred driving himself and abandoned chauffeurs unless on official business where they were also required as bodyguards. But on this Saturday afternoon he had no fear of anything untoward happening on the drive to Reichsminister's home. As the car slid to a stop, a pair of white-gloved SS guards snapped to attention. Christian stepped from the car while another SS guard opened the passenger door for his wife. Liveried servants descended to carry their luggage to their rooms. The afternoon had no set schedule in order to enable the ladies to rest and bathe before dinner while the men, acting as if they had not seen each other just the previous day, went off to enjoy cigars and brandy in the billiard room. Göring arranged it thus—such an English-style weekend to be enjoyed by that country's arch competitor.

Gisela von Teischen thought the idea of spending the weekend with these people horrid. The men were odious and the women insipid and vacuous. Despite that, she did feel some compassion for these women. Most of them had no real education or ambition. For the most part they were simple country girls who had married into the SS and found themselves thrust into the Nazi firmament. She thought of them much like those storied English mail-order brides sent out to India to marry officers of the colonial regiments only to find themselves totally at sea as to how to be matrons of large households or deal with the utter brutality of their mates. Some of the wives she met were merely girls, still giggling about makeup and hairstyles, while their black uniformed husbands strutted about with their arms raised in the Hitler salute and plotted the rape of European civilization. With no mentor to guide them, many of the wives sought her out and came to look upon her as a wiser sister. They asked her advice on everything from domestic arrangements to problems with their sex lives.

The White Raven

Gisela listened to their plights with care and patience, and soon she found that as they unburdened themselves to her that these women were her best sources of information. In exchange for her patience and soothing words, they poured out secret after secret. Not just tittle-tattle or gossip, they knew things that they should not have known, and in the main they had no idea how valuable such information might be. Like most men, their husbands liked to boast about themselves, especially in bed. How better to convince their little *fraus* of the importance of their husbands?

While the strutting and self-important men in the new order jockeyed for position with one another, eager to outshine their rivals, the wives were left to talk amongst themselves. They were more than happy that their wives, necessary playthings and adornments in their world, were content to have their klatches with each other, well so be it. If Gisela von Teischen deigned to help them to become better and more dutiful and pliant wives, they might contrive to ask the Führer to give her a medal.

And so it went, at dinner parties and the theater Gisela tried her best not to retch at being forced to mix with such company. She quickly learned to glean the important facts from these women as they bewailed the infidelities, cruelties and indifferences that they suffered. Rather than show anger or become indignant toward their spouses, she counseled contrition and submission. These Nazi men liked to have a sweet buttercup at home while they kept a bit of hot strudel on the side in some Berlin apartment. She told them that their husbands were such busy, important men that they should help them by lifting their burdens, emotionally and sexually. The naiveté of these women astounded Gisela, and soon they were putty in her hands, and as she molded them into good little fraus, she kept careful notes on all that they told her. It wasn't long before she had a catalog of who was doing what in the Nazi regime, but more important, she quickly knew who was stepping on whose toes to get ahead, and who was resentful of whom in the various ministries; and that information might prove vital.

Gisela, abandoned by Christian in their room, decided to while away the hours before dinner with a long hot soak in their en-suite bathtub. Cut from a block of marble and large enough to entertain several guests, she filled it with blazing hot water and lavender bath salts. If she was going to have to endure this place, she might as well get the most out of her accommodations. There was a selection of Franken wines that had been thoughtfully laid out atop a side table in the bedroom. She picked up one of the flask-shaped bottles, uncorked it, and poured a large slug of the crisp white wine into a crystal glass. Holding the glass up to the light, she watched as the bubbles on the surface created tiny prisms displaying the spectrum from red to blue. With a sigh she put the glass on the dresser, stripped off her clothes, and tossed them onto the bed.

The bathroom was filled with steamy lavender-scented clouds. She placed her wine at the edge of the tub and let her eyes adjust to the filmy reflection of her nakedness in the bathroom mirror. Her breasts were full and round with no sign yet of the inevitable sagging. With her fingers she squeezed her nipples until they became hard. She sighed as a quiver ran from deep inside her, and she closed her eyes for a moment. Looking again into the mirror she ran her hand down over her stomach. Never subjected to childbirth, it remained taught and firm. Her legs were tanned, as were her arms and shoulders. Just a touch of blonde fuzz protected her sex. With her right hand she stroked herself until the warm shudder returned. It had been so long. As far as her marriage went, she might as well have been a nun. With a long sigh she stepped into the water and let the heat seep into her legs as she lowered her body until she could rest her head at one end while being able to reach the glass of wine. As the warmth of the water and the wine coalesced, she realized just how lonely she was and began to cry as her heart sank into a Charybdis of despair.

Dinner in the great hall was something of a macabre mixture of Teutonic revelry with a frisson of Nazi excess. An immensely long table had been set to seat over forty guests; its snowy linen and polished crystal reflected the light from hundreds of candles. The golden dinner service had been a sacrifice, the price paid by a wealthy Jewish doctor for his family's exit visas. It lay like a constellation of stars on the table's surface. Around the room stood a dozen waiters, dressed in medieval costumes straight from the wardrobe rooms of UFA studios. Swastika flags were draped along the walls among which hung an assortment of battle-axes and swords commandeered for Karinhall by the Reichsminister from various museums and private collections. Gisela von Teischen was struck by the display; as always it was meant to impress—even if it was just to serve a gathering of the minor princes of the Nazi realm and their ladies.

A string quartet was playing an assortment of songs written by German composers who had earned Goebbels' seal of approval, in other words, no Jews. Other than the host, none of the Führer's inner circle was present. As a rule, they only appeared together when the great leader was present. This evening's guests were those who owed their position to the rotund Reichsminister. The entire weekend was designed for them to show their obeisance to their new lord as he carved out his portion of the Nazi realm. These men would get the scraps from his table.

As the guests mingled a company of white-jacketed stewards flitted about proffering silver trays laden with flutes of champagne. Many of the guests were young, under thirty. These younger men were the embodiment of Aryan manhood and both the male and female guests appreciated their looks.

Also among the invitees were a few minor celebrities to round out the group. A vivacious Leni Riefenstahl stood talking with a circle of smiling admirers. A rising filmmaker, and now recognized by the Nazi elite, she had caught Hitler's attention. With his support she was now slated to make a feature film of the upcoming Nuremburg Party rally in September.

Joining the party was also Renate Müller. The blonde actress was the epitome of Goebbels' ideal German woman. She owed her career to the limping propagandist. Despite being raised to stardom by the Party, she hated all of them. Her fixed smile did little to hide her disdain. UFA's press agents did their best to keep her smiling in public, but it was a difficult task.

Someone in the studio had decided a little romance might be good for business, so on her arm was Horst Sturm one of UFA's newest stars. Pure Aryan: muscular, tanned, and sporting a shock of blond hair, he had been cast in the role of the hero of Goebbels' latest series of melodramas geared to stir the hearts of the populace for the struggle ahead. Among the other guests were a few older men, many of them senior Luftwaffe officers, including Reinhard Stiffler. They were there perhaps to serve as a solid anchor to the past, what with all these newcomers about.

Off to one side was a small group of women, at its center was an ebullient little man dressed in a decidedly dated tuxedo. He was entertaining the clutch of ladies with a series of slightly risqué stories. The latest was about travel on the famous Orient Express. He had them in stitches with the story of a well-known French countess whom the Bulgarian border police suspected of being a spy; they had stopped a train to investigate her.

"Oh, my dear Doktor Theurer, you can't just leave us like that!" squealed a pert brunette with sparkling green eyes. Her husband, Gottfried Wehlmer, was an up-and-comer in the political section of the Reich Security Office, the RHSD.

Next to her, Gertrude Flicker, wife of one of the soon-to-be revived air force's newest training squadron commanders, was reveling in her new status, "Yes, you must tell us what happened to her. What happened to the countess?"

Doktor Theurer smiled at his audience, as they now seemed to be eating out of his hand. "Well, ladies," he paused and coughed, "it seemed that the Bulgarian border authorities remained suspicious of the lady, and so they called in a matron to examine her. When she did so, the matron found strange writing on the countess' derrière. When this was reported to the guards in charge, they placed the countess in a cell. Of course, she was indignant and wailed in excited French for the Chargé d'affaire to be brought at once. The Bulgarian inspector was dubious, but relented after several hours of her protests. It was only after the Chargé met privately with the countess that the matter was cleared up." The Doktor paused and took a long drink of his wine.

"Well, what happened?" gasped the brunette.

Theurer smiled and replied, "Well, the train had been held at the border, so the diplomat sent for the porter to retrieve the waste paper from the ladies' WC in the first class compartment. Glancing quickly through the rubbish, he was able to locate several strips of newspaper from the previous day's Istanbul *Daily Mail*. Damp and with smudged type the strips were passed to the matron who reexamined the countess' nether regions and pronounced that the newsprint matched what was on her skin." The Doktor paused for effect before delivering the punch line. "You see, the countess had not trusted entirely in the cleanliness of the toilet seat and had lined it with strips of newsprint to sit upon. And *voila!* The mystery was solved."

With the ladies shrieking in shocked amusement, the wily man bowed and then withdrew in order to begin circulating among the other guests. From a distance, he spotted the one person he had most hoped would be in attendance. She stood alone, tall and sleek, wearing a white floor-length sheath that showed off her slim back and was accented with a faux cape that draped from the shoulders. Like an Egyptian ibis she stood alone watching the people flow around her. The look was exquisite, and she seemed to shimmer in the candlelight. Her flaxen hair was swept back boyishly from her forehead. The Countess Gisela von Teischen stood alone, watching the chaotic scene envelope Leni Riefenstahl as the young woman gushed to her ardent admirers over the fact that she had been personally invited to fly with the Führer to the Party rally in September.

"To film him descending through the clouds, like an eagle, to fulfill our destiny. What an opportunity!" The young woman beamed to her admirers.

Theurer watched the Countess's face as she listened. Was that a slight grimace on her lips? Yes, well, perhaps. Yet it was to meet her that the doughty Doktor Theurer had left the comfortable confines of his Charlottenburg apartment. Swimming against the tide of partygoers, he set his course. Like any predator he did not reveal himself while he narrowed in for the attack. With deftness he placed himself directly in front of the lady. Smiling, he bared rows of shining teeth and spoke: "You must be Countess von Teischen, my name is Albrecht Theurer, I knew your late father, the Baron von Falken."

Gisela blinked, her mind far away from the little man who now stood directly before her. She seemed to tower over him, and he had to crane his neck up to speak to her. She smiled down at him vacantly.

"I was hoping that you might be here. I have heard so much about you. Your picture is everywhere; another admirable example of Aryan womanhood."

The White Raven

Gisela was unsure of herself, but caution kept her from making more than idle chitchat until a servant sounded the gong that called them all to table. The good Doktor bowed, guided Gisela von Teischen to her chair, which coincidently happened to be next to his.

"How fortunate, we seem to be table companions," he said brightly.

Gisela was not so sure. She wondered if it had been a coincidence or had the wily man made a switch of the place cards. His name meant nothing to her. Over the years, claiming the acquaintanceship of her father had been a common enough approach of many people. Most were looking for a small handout or, more recently, some favor that her husband might be able to provide. But somehow, she felt this man was different. He seemed to come from some realm of officialdom, and in this regime such an approach was not needed. Indeed, perhaps this was something else. Not that he was to be trusted, far from it; she sensed he was as dangerous as he was gracious. A bad combination in anyone in these troubled times.

After they took their seats he went on, "Yes, I knew your father before the war. The Baron once held several key positions in the high command back then. I believe he even worked with General von Schlieffen on evaluating potential enemy capabilities. I was sorry to hear of his passing."

"Yes, thank you, but that was a long time ago. But my dear Doktor, I am confused," she asked with a gleam in her eye, "what are you doing at this *danse macabre?*"

So, what he had heard about her was right. She was no fool and certainly not another Magda Goebbels. She was someone out of the ordinary, to speak so openly and so disparagingly about the new order. "Well, you see I have a small position in one of the government ministries, and I often write reports on various aspects of the nation's defense, and I am particularly interested in aviation. So, the Reichsminister invited me to meet some of the new heads of departments in the Air Ministry." He smiled, but she was unconvinced.

"I see," she said. "Is this your first time to one of these Karinhall extravaganzas?"

"You don't approve of all this?" he asked and waved his hand toward the dinner guests.

"It is not my place to approve or disapprove. This is like *Walpurgisnacht* and *Die Valkyrie* rolled into one, both are the epitome of German culture. Didn't you know, I am supposed to be the living example of the new German wife? That's what our dear Dr. Goebbels over there says. Blonde, Aryan, and dutifully obedient to her warrior husband, only I can't act like Fraulein Mueller over there."

"You left out motherhood. Are there no children?" he asked.

A look of deep sorrow flashed over Gisela's face before she replied, "Even the new order cannot create children out of nothing. It takes a man and a woman. And what about you? Who are you really? Are you a spy, some agent of the Gestapo attempting to get me to say something outrageous so that you can put it in a report or file it away for a rainy day."

"No, my dear Countess. Though my business is indeed information, I am not a policeman. It just seems to me that perhaps you need to be more careful. You risk being a bit injudicious as to with whom you share your contempt."

"If I have any contempt it is toward my husband and his personal retinue of flunkies, not to the state. But, as you say, perhaps, I should avoid any more wine tonight. I might say something I will regret. But you don't deny that you are acting like some sort of spy?" Then she laughed, and the tension was released.

It was a short shimmering laugh that Theurer realized would endear her to any man.

"Yes, you have caught me out." He laughed as well, as much to hide the truth as to make sure no one was paying too much attention to their conversation.

"Countess, perhaps you will allow me to call upon you sometime in the future. I feel that we may share some topics of mutual interest."

Gisela, looked at the man appraisingly. "Well perhaps we could lunch one day. I normally stop at the Adlon on Tuesdays, if that would be convenient."

"It would be my pleasure. I shall look forward to it."

"Now, if you are interested in aviation, you must meet one of the other guests here; he can tell you a great deal about airplanes and the men who fly them. Do you know Oberst Reinhard Stiffler?" Gisela asked.

"I have heard of him, but I understood that he was out of the country at present."

"No, he is here tonight. If there is anyone here who knows the aviation world, it is he. I know him very well; in fact he is about to give me flying lessons. Would you like me to introduce you?"

"Very much," replied the Doktor, more than satisfied that he had achieved two goals that evening.

The White Raven

Dzerzhinsky Square

Red banners hung around the bronze statue of the Cheka's founder floated in the warm breeze that swept down on the city from the east. Spring had come to Moscow. And as the snow and ice began to vanish, there arrived an uneasiness that people could feel, but not name. Mikhail Andropov, in his office overlooking the square, could feel it too. Like an unwelcome party guest who hangs on long after the others have left, the sense of unease remained. Most people simply went about their business, hoping that the warming air would clear away the omnipresent sense of foreboding. Andropov was not one of the proletariat. He was not a worker, but a boss, and he knew when something was wrong. As a senior member of the NKVD's foreign directorate, he saw things from a different perspective. The *aparat's* director, Genrikh Yagoda, owed his career, and therefore his life to Josef Stalin, and just now Stalin was in a struggle for leadership of the Soviet Union with Sergei Kirov. Kirov was personable, where Stalin was rigid. Kirov was in favor of relaxing the iron hand that held the reins of government, while Stalin, who personified the evil Georgian warlord, sought total and complete control. Andropov saw the feigned friendship that Stalin proffered toward Kirov and sensed the trouble that was brewing close below the surface of geniality. Andropov knew he also needed to be careful, he had known Kirov since the days of the revolution and it would not do to appear too closely connected. Among the several photographs that stood behind his desk was one of Kirov at the opening of a new Ford tractor factory in Minsk. In it, several men surrounded Kirov as he posed next to a Fordson tractor that had come right off the assembly line. Andropov was just to Kirov's left. Perhaps that needed to disappear. Reaching out, Andropov picked up the picture and removed the photo from the frame. With his desk lighter, he set fire to the corner of the photo and watched it burn in his ashtray. It did not take much to arouse Comrade Stalin's suspicions, all the more so since Stalin was nearby, just across town in the Kremlin, while Kirov remained in Leningrad attending to Party business. All was as it should be, and yet, and yet . . . Andropov was nervous. He was too long in this job not to know when the wheels were turning. Perhaps he should make himself a little less visible. Who knew when that wily Georgian would take it into his head to clean house? Now might be the right time.

Andropov looked down at the dossier on his desk and frowned. What had happened here? An operative missing, why? And why in Berlin of all places? Ryshkov was among the best that he could field. Then there was this cryptic message from Paris, just one line on a lengthy field report. An agent there had seen someone who resembled Ryshkov on the street. Coincidence? He thought not. This was looking more and more like an intelligence fiasco, and fiascos were not being tolerated here in the Lubyanka.

He needed to make inquiries; perhaps this was a good time for him to travel. Maybe he could do a little house cleaning of his own. That would make him appear to be the soldier of the revolution he was purported to be. But then this business of espionage was nothing if not illusions. Who really knew the truth about any of the information that passed into the hungry maw of the organs of state security? He looked out the window. Beyond the greasy film on the outside of the glass, a warm day was blossoming. Yes, maybe a short trip into the fascist camp could pay off, especially if he could bring back a scalp or two.

Requests to travel had always been difficult, traveling out of the country even more so. Suspicions were raised. The *aparat* was never more suspicious than with their own people. Why, they would ask, do *you* have to travel? Can't the local *aparat* handle the job? The more senior one became, the more dubious the overseers were apt to be. The mere mention of the need to travel would start wheels turning somewhere. Questions would be asked. Just who is this Andropov? Do we really know him? Yes, he has been working for us for years, but with whom was he speaking with at the Bolshoi last month? Was it a foreign journalist? What made it all the worse for him was that his job required dealing with foreigners. Losing Ryshkov from his post in Berlin was one thing, but then he had other resources in the city. The management of those resources, sources of information that he had managed to keep very private, kept him awake on nights when he should have been making love to some lovely file clerk fresh from the farm.

His frequent insomnia was due to an agent code named Oskar. He had been running Oskar as a deep penetration agent, or what in this business they called a mole, in Berlin for nearly five years. The NKVD had placed moles in most of the countries of the world. The service was masterful in finding and recruiting these helpers. They were valuable assets who kept a steady flow of information coming to Moscow on a variety of wide-ranging topics. They also served, when needed, as triggers to activate even more deeply placed agents, known as sleepers. The sleepers remained dormant; living seemingly normal lives with no contact with the service for years before their handlers roused them to wakefulness. But moles were different. They were active, digging into western institutions, as they remained carefully hidden, often in plain sight. Because of that, the information moles provided was deemed more valuable by the NKVD hierarchy and thus more trusted. Comrade Stalin never believed any intelligence that was not paid for or extracted by coercion or violence.

It took some time before the information that Oskar had provided was deemed worthwhile. For Oskar had been a volunteer, and volunteers occupied the lowest level of NKVD trust. Questions were asked about such offers of service. Were they provocateurs? Were they plants foisted on the Soviet Union by the opposition? No, they could not be trusted on their own. If, over time their information could be corroborated or, better yet, supported by another independent source, then maybe, just maybe, the mole might be true to the revolution. It had been that way with Oskar. The man had made an approach to Andropov in 1925. Andropov had at that time been working as a station chief in Berlin. In a bar in the reddest of all Berlin suburbs, Wedding, Andropov had been approached by a man who said he had information to sell.

Andropov, who back in 1925 used the work name Yuri Penkofsky, feigned indifference at the approach. In his mind this was an agent provocateur bent on ensnarling him in some plot. Probably it was some idea of the Polpo, Berlin's notorious political police. At the time Andropov agreed to nothing, but his tormentor, who wished only to be known as Oskar, would not be dissuaded. The man shrugged and walked away, but left Andropov a packet of papers that the Russian was free to use or discard. When, back in his tiny apartment, Andropov examined the documents, he saw that they were draft copies of memoranda from a number of

Weimar Republic offices. Dutifully he packed them off to Moscow, but was careful to cloud the source of the information. Who knew how the great minds in Dzerzhinsky Square might react.

A month later, he found out. An urgent request for more of the same came back to him from Moscow. They wanted more information and details as to the source of this material. Now, Andropov found himself in a real fix. He had no idea how to contact his German benefactor. If Moscow found out he had taken information offered through a chance meeting without vetting the source, they might just shoot him on sight. If they found out he did not know how to contact the source, they would certainly recall him and then shoot him. He was frantic. For two weeks, following Moscow's demand for more information, he repeatedly went back to the seedy bar and sat for hours nursing warm beer and smoking pack after pack of cigarettes, hoping to spot his man. He had just about given up when on a rainy March evening Oskar appeared at his table.

"Miss me?" Oskar asked with an impish smile.

Andropov pressed the man for information about who he was and how he got what he gave to the Russians. Oskar remained mute about himself, telling Andropov only what he wanted him to know. Once, Andropov tried to follow the man, but had to give up when Oskar entered Anhalter Bahnhof and was swallowed by the crowd. Oskar told Andropov how he would make contact. Using a letter code, Andropov would receive a note at his apartment requesting a meeting. Times and locations would vary, and they never met more than three or four times a year. When Andropov returned to Moscow in 1926, they resorted to a letter drop in Berlin. Servicing the letter drop was assigned to the Berlin station.

The White Raven

Since 1927, as National Socialism began to grip Germany, Oskar had fed Andropov inside information about the Nazi elite. Not the broad sweep of information, Andropov could have gotten that from the public press, but intimate details that only an insider could have. That made his agent doubly valuable. That also made him worth protecting, and that is what troubled Mikhail Andropov on this day. For as the importance of Oskar's information was fully appreciated within the higher levels of the Kremlin, there were others far more powerful than Andropov, who wanted to adopt Oskar as their own. Who was this man? What was his access? Andropov had been pressed to give them the leverage with which Moscow could squeeze Oskar. What Oskar provided was deemed too important for a mid-level officer like Andropov. Andropov's role soon became secondary, and he often wondered if Oskar had opened a side channel and was conversing directly with the boss himself. Still, Andropov was not absolved of the requirements of getting leverage on Oskar. Along with care and feeding of the man in Berlin, he had to find a way to compel the man to produce. Andropov then did what any hard-pressed agent controller might do; he invented a legend for his man. He put Oskar in one of the burgeoning ministries, a vague sort of bureaucratic job. Then, even though Oskar had never asked for payment, aside from reimbursement for some small expenses, Andropov put him on the payroll for five hundred marks a month, all of which Andropov withdrew in cash and deposited into an account in Zurich at Credit Suisse in the name of Yuri Penkofsky. Instead of just running an agent, Andropov took on the role of spy-novelist, embezzler and shepherd to a flock of one.

When Andropov was finally recalled to Moscow he expected a bullet, but instead found himself in an office with a window and a young secretary. His first job was to keep the information from Oskar flowing. Andropov thought he had that all worked out. Like any good operation of the sort, communications with a mole were kept very selective and restricted. The mole had to be protected at whatever cost. So, in Berlin the mole Oskar had been assigned a special operative to be his postman. The postman served as a conveyor of information. He collected the information, or "product," provided by the mole, and he passed back instructions. Mainly contact was maintained through dead-letter drops, innocuous places where documents or instructions could be left and retrieved by both the postman and the mole. In western countries it was often a safe deposit box in a bank to which both postman and mole had a key. Occasionally, and with great care and exception, the postman might actually meet the mole to exchange information or money—whatever might be needed.

The problem facing Mikhail Andropov on this spring day was that the trusted operative who served as Oskar's postman was Viktor Ryshkov. Now it was urgent for Andropov to meet Oskar once again. But, because of the value that the highest levels of the Presidium placed on Oskar's product, if it became known that Andropov's chosen postman was also the man who had vanished and was assumed to have defected, Andropov's next trip would be to the cellars below his office.

He had to get approval to travel and that was not easy. Talk of defectors seemed to taint everyone involved. No, he would keep everything routine. After all, he was a soldier of the revolution, and he needed to take the battle to the heart of fascism. He had to make his request ironclad. It had to reek of anti-fascist sentiment, but he had to be careful in that regard too, not too much invective, just put enough seasoning in the broth, and they would buy it. But there was always the issue of money. If he traveled abroad, he would need hard currency. No one in their right mind would accept Soviet Rubles. The world treated the Soviet currency like so much used toilet paper. No, he would have to tap the funds that the Party member in America and Britain provided. Earnest Jews, most of them, imbued in the class struggle, but totally ignorant of the price being paid by the average Russian for that fight.

Now, to whom should he put the request? There too, one had to be careful—best to find the most suspicious of the lot. Mmmm, ah yes, he would put the request through General Petrenko, that would do it. Petrenko was vile and arrogant, a bully who liked to intimidate underlings and grope all the attractive females on the staff. He would get the General's signature on his travel documents. But how, he could not request an audience with the man. Petrenko hated Andropov. The old devil thought him effete and roundly cursed Andropov when he saw him. No, he would have to find another way.

The solution came to him ten minutes later. It walked into his office wearing a tight skirt and a bright smile. Of course, Oksana, Oksana Malinina Dragomirova the lovely and buxom new typist who had been assigned to Petrenko's office and who now stood at attention before him.

"Comrade Colonel Andropov, excuse me, but General Petrenko requires your comments on these reports immediately."

The girl was, what, twenty-two? Lovely red hair pulled back severely from her face, full sensuous lips, and, he suspected that underneath those straining tunic buttons a wonderland of pleasures.

"Of course, Comrade, ah, Comrade Dragomirova is it not? You have just joined us, how are you getting on?"

The color drained a little from her face as he put these questions to her. Did this man know how badly the General treated the women on his staff? Did he know what the General expected the women to do? Only an hour ago the man had taken out his, his thing, his penis, and showed it to her, telling her that if she wanted to rise in the service, she would have kneel down and suck on it. My god, did he know, did everyone know?

"I am getting on quite well, comrade colonel." She gulped.

"Where are you from? I detect from your accent that you are not a Muscovite."

"No Comrade Colonel. I am from Leningrad, sir. I have just finished training, and I have been assigned here as my first post with the service."

"Leningrad. Have you met Comrade Kirov there? No, well that is fine, one day no doubt you will. One of my duties is to ensure that new members of the staff are fully indoctrinated into the ways of this section. Perhaps if you would care to stop by at the end of your day, we could talk about that. That is if you have time from your other duties." Andropov smiled reassuringly.

Oksana looked at the man and saw his smiling face, his genial gestures—what a difference from the monster Petrenko.

"Certainly sir, I would very much appreciate that."

"Well, then I look forward to seeing you here at, let us say, six this evening?"

With that the girl snapped to attention, turned and left the room. Andropov gazed appraisingly at the narrow hips and slight sway of her walk. Yes, she would do nicely he thought.

The White Raven

The trip took several days. From Moscow to Leningrad, and then a night crossing at a soft point on the Finnish border, then overland through miles of trackless forest to the suburbs of Helsinki. From there, he boarded a ferry for the two-day voyage to Stettin. He spent a night in a businessman's hotel near the station and caught a train to Berlin. Despite the claims of German efficiency, the train was six hours late by the time it finally pulled into the familiar platforms of Anhalter Station. Andropov was groggy and tired; even though he was traveling on a Finnish passport as Eirno Stakkveld, a Helsinki-based dealer in nickel ore, the customs officials at the Polish border had taken their time to examining and cross-examining him. Very likely they knew exactly who and what he was, but since his destination was Germany they let him though. However, he would be sure not to return to Moscow through Poland. He hated them, the Poles, especially since the debacle outside Warsaw back in 1920.

Yes, he thought, that was what had brought him to Berlin the last time. That girl, that French-Swiss little bitch, she was the one. What was her name, Tatiana? No, Oksana? No, that was the girl he had to fuck in order to get the authorization signed for this trip. True, fucking her wasn't a burden; it only cost him some silk stockings from one of the special goods stores, that, and, well, the promise that he would find her a better place to live. God knows she turned out to be a hot little number: liked to fuck on every surface of his apartment. She wore him out; still it had been a long drought. What was he thinking of before he came up with Oksana? Oh, yes that girl back in 1920, the one he sent to Warsaw to kill the Americans who were helping the Poles. Hmmm, yes, now he remembered, her name was Valentina Koniev, apparently, once well connected to Lenin. He was lucky that they had not decided to shoot him when the mission failed. Well, he was dead now, and so was she, swept away by the influenza or whatever carried off so many after the war.

Berlin had changed since he had last been in the city. Then he had traveled with a pair of bodyguards to make sure neither the Reds nor the Freikorps shot him. Now, he was just a salesman from a neutral country looking to meet clients. What he needed now was a hot bath and a drink; then he would try to pick up the trail of Viktor Ryshkov and see what went wrong.

Café Normandie

"You should meet him. After all, he had you in a tight spot, and he didn't call on the Gestapo to try to take you." Raymond Kingman spoke in a fatherly tone, and Harry Braham, who barely remembered his own father, often thought of the older diplomat in that way.

"Yes, I know. But why nearly nine months later do you think he wants to meet me, and in such an out of the way spot?"

"Your Doktor Albrecht Theurer is a bit of an enigma. I have done some checking on him since you first mentioned him." Kingman replied. "Apparently he is a fellow of the German Academy of Science. He has taught at Heidelberg, and was very popular there with the undergraduates. His expertise is in economics. He was part of Abteilung IIIb, of the Geheimdienst, the High Command's intelligence section, before the war. He also seems to have a flair for art, the kind of art that the Nazis now deplore, but secretly covet and steal from the Jews for their private collections. He wrote several decent papers in the 1920s about the causes of the defeat of the Central Powers. For all that, he is pragmatic and a prescient thinker, so much so that Krupp and some of the industrialists who support the Nazis think he is a genius. However, since the emergence of National Socialism he seems to have kept a very low profile. The word is that he occupies an obscure position in one of the ministries, but my guess is that with his background that he is really working for the Abwehr."

"Is he a Nazi?" Braham asked.

"Hard to know from what I have been able to learn from my contacts in Berlin. From what I can tell, he is at heart a German patriot, and if that means joining the Nazi Party these days, then I would say, yes, he is a Party member. Beyond that, who knows? Another scotch?"

"Sure, why not, but just a touch." It was getting late, and he had things to do in the morning.

Raymond Kingman walked to the sideboard, came back with a bottle of Laphroiag and topped up Braham's glass.

"How did the good Doktor get in touch?"

"It was my usual spot, you know, the Café Juliette on the Rue des Martyrs. I go there nearly every morning. Well, this morning the *propriétaire* brought me my coffee as usual, but this time she placed one of those cardboard coasters under it. That was different. It was one of those advertising Duval pastis. You know, the one with the blue printing on the white background. At first I gave it no thought, but then I saw that there was writing around the edge of the label. It was written in English and said 2 p.m. 6/22 Café Normandie, Bayeux—Theurer. Why Bayeux for Christ's sakes?"

"Maybe he wants to see the tapestry, who knows? What did Karl say?"

"I haven't told him—yet."

"But you are going to aren't you?" Kingman looked at his friend and protégé. He could see worry written on his face.

"Yes. Do you think Theurer had anything to do with Walthers' death?"

"Hard to tell, Harry, but if he did not, then why did he tell you about it in the way he did. Why not just let you stumble upon it. No, there is something more to this. In any event, take Karl along, just in case."

June 22 was one of those iffy Norman days. Sun, rain, broken clouds, sun, then rain again, followed by crystal clear skies and bright afternoon sun. Early that morning Harry Braham drove to the Tuileries and picked up Karl who was waiting there.

Lieberman looked worn out, his clothes rumpled and he hadn't shaved. Gray locomotive ash clung to his hair like an early snowfall.

"You look like hell, have you been out all night?"

"I just got back from Berlin. I have a friend who lets me ride in the engine compartment of the night express in exchange for filling in as a fireman. So, I have been shoveling coal all night."

"Did you contact the Raven?"

"Yes, she is getting a little nervous. She has more people to move out of Berlin. She is worried about Theurer putting the arm on her."

"Has he contacted her?"

"Not yet, she is waiting for him to appear at the Adlon and chat her up over lunch." Lieberman leaned back in the passenger seat and said, "wake me when you stop for gas, I need to get some sleep."

The White Raven

Braham was driving as fast as the roads would allow and kept the Ford on the south side of the Seine as they left the city. As they travelled, Lieberman relayed what he had learned from Gisela von Teischen.

"Jesus Christ! I suppose that is what he wants with me as well," Braham replied and then fell silent as his companion, thoroughly spent, began to nod off. Braham made progress on back roads most of the way, and the pair arrived in the ancient town of Bayeux late on the evening of the 21st. He and Karl put up at the equally ancient Auberge des Trois Frere, just outside of the town. Built like a castle, Braham expected chamber pots instead of indoor plumbing. To his surprise each room had an en suite bathroom with hot water. Karl was a city person, and country inns and the surrounding open lands gave him the creeps. When Braham woke the next morning, he knocked at Karl's door only to find him still dressed in the same clothes as the day before, but swathed in a comforter from the bed. On the tiny table by the window was a heaping ashtray, an empty bottle of Norman cidre, and Karl's broomstick Mauser pistol ready for use.

"If you can stir yourself, I am going downstairs for breakfast," Braham said with a shake of his head and went off in search of coffee.

The Café Normandie sat at the edge of an ancient millrace. Long disused, the buttery brown stonewalls of the mill now supported a small café. Braham took up residence at one of the outdoor tables. Though it was turning into a lazy June afternoon, there was a chill emanating from the stone, and the water sluicing through the millrace was cooling as well. A bright young woman in a red apron took his order for cidre. When in Rome, he thought. A moment later she returned and set before him a bottle of Fruits de

Bayeux Cidre, a cold glass, and a small plate upon which several slices of crusty baguette and a slab of white cheese were arrayed.

"*Merci, mademoiselle*"

"*Enchante, monsieur. Je suis appelé Giselle.*" she replied and smiled at him revealing sparkling blue eyes and a wisp of blonde hair under her white cap.

Braham had little time to enjoy the thought of her before the chair next to him scraped, and Herr Doktor Theurer was sitting next to him.

"I think I will have one of those as well," he said.

"*Giselle, si vous plait,*" Braham called to the girl and beckoned her over to their table.

After his drink arrived, Theurer took a long pull. "Very nice—a clean, tart taste, not unlike German Apfelwein."

"I'm glad you like it. Well, here I am. What can I do for you?" There was a bit of testiness in Braham's question.

"Mr. Braham, are you a student of history?"

"I don't know, I suppose I have some feeling for it. I seem to have lived through some of the violent bits of it."

"Indeed. This is a great place for learning more, you know, especially for you Anglo-Saxons. You know about the great tapestry that they keep over there." Theurer turned in his seat and pointed up the narrow lane to the part of the old cathedral that housed the famous Bayeux Tapestry, the eleventh-century rendition of the conquest of England by William the Conqueror.

"I have seen pictures of it."

"You should avail yourself of the opportunity whilst you are in this part of the world. It is very instructive, even nine hundred years later in this, the twentieth century."

"I fear you are trying to make a point Herr Doktor, perhaps you should just come out with it," Braham said.

Theurer took another drink of cidre and went on. "Yes, well, as it happens the tapestry shows how a kingdom, beset on two sides did not survive and was conquered by another, more powerful force against which it had no defense. It is a parable of sorts for our time. Mr. Braham, I am a German and a patriot. I am ashamed of what happened in 1918 and the price that my country has had to pay to other nations who might be judged equally guilty of causing the war. That said, I am also a realist. Nothing was settled at Versailles, merely postponed.

Look around you, Mr. Braham. The result of the War to End All Wars has been the development of a score of military adventures. Italy, Russia, Germany, Poland and Czechoslovakia, among others, are set on a collision course. You, yourself, advise clients as to where to put their investments in the development of military aviation and weapons. In the last century, peace was maintained because there was a balance between the major European powers. That permitted them go off and make proxy wars against natives in Africa and Asia. But with 1919 all that has changed."

Braham waved to Giselle to bring them another round. After she brought fresh bottles and cleared the empties, Theurer went on.

"Our new chancellor, Adolf Hitler, wrote his manifesto, *Mein Kampf,* with a clear view to what he saw the future as being. Have you read it?"

"I can't say that I have."

"Don't bother, unless you are either a masochist or an insomniac. It does not read well in the original, and any translation is apt to lose the vitriolic nature of the writing. Any right thinking publisher would have pulped the entire print run. The book is a mess. In short, he has written a thesis that promotes the creation of a kind of pan-Germania that encompasses most of Europe."

"And, as a German, you think that is a bad thing?" Braham was trying desperately to get to the point of the meeting.

"If it were to happen naturally, peacefully, through some kind of political evolution, well, then no. To me such a development would not be a bad thing. Europe is still seething after the tragedy of Versailles, and the existing hegemony of nations is in need of some kind of unifying force."

"But what of this alliance I keep hearing about? This Intermarium, I think it is called. Certainly, a united line of defense on Germany's eastern border would give your chancellor some pause, would it not?" Braham asked.

"Bah! Intermarium be damned! It will never happen. And do you want to know why? Why is it that a bunch of Slav and Magyar dreamers cannot derail Hitler's plans?" Theurer did not wait for Braham's reply, but went on. "Because my starry-eyed American friend, individually they have nothing to gain from such a plan. Oh, certainly an organized wall of steel would slow Hitler down, perhaps even by a decade or so. But the truth is that these mongrel states, those your President Wilson so graciously carved from the old Hapsburg Empire, are today run by politicians more venal and self-serving than those now in Berlin. Worse, some of them are already on Berlin's payroll, willing and ready to turn over to us territories that decades before were settled by German emigrants or *volksdeutsch* when the time is right. Unfortunately, it will be left to France and Britain, and perhaps the Soviet Union, who will react when that happens. Pride will trump pragmatism, and then there will be war."

"Poland certainly won't stand still while Hitler gobbles up the land on its southern border. They are already becoming itchy about the rise of National Socialism. Don't you expect that they too will react as you say?"

Theurer looked around for Giselle and, spotting her, waved her to the table. "Giselle, a *café crème, sil vous plait,* and one for my friend here as well." Then he smiled as he watched the young lady stepped back into the bar. "Ah, to be young again. But of course, I do expect them to react. However, the Poles bicker amongst themselves. Pilsudski is not the man he was a decade ago, and the other countries of the region do not trust the old man. So, without the iron fist of Pilsudski to guide them, the Intermarium will come to nothing. Still, the Poles have many friends in Western Europe and in the States. This upcoming event, the air tour of Europe, would be an ideal time to stage a pre-emptive action of some sort against the Reich."

"Are you speaking of the *Challenge International de Tourisme?*"

"I suppose I am. A lot of airplanes whizzing through the skies over Germany on dates that coincide with the upcoming Party rally, why it would be ideal to stage some sort of provocation, one that might just destabilize the new leaders in Berlin," said Theurer. "In fact," he went on, "all the nations involved are using the flights to map the aerial defenses of the other nations."

"But the challenge is a purely non-military affair. It is designed to boost tourism in the continent, not war."

"So you say, but are not all of the aviators culled from the ranks of their respective nation's military, and, if I might add, the airplanes being flown were originally designed and commissioned by the various nation's air forces despite their civilian markings."

Braham paused to allow Giselle, whose eyes captured him for a moment, to set down their café crèmes, "*Voila,*" she said with a slight nod of her head.

"*Merci, Giselle.*" Then Braham resumed, "Do you really believe this?"

"Well, it is not too far-fetched in this modern age for an airplane to swoop out of the sky and destroy an automobile or a train or drop a bomb on a stage full of dignitaries. Perhaps if there were a significant political target, it would be worth the possible repercussions. Of course, it would be most spectacular if someone were to drop a bomb on the dais at the Nuremburg Party rally. While there are many possible problems and risks with any such plan, I wonder what someone with your experience might think."

"An assassination from the air, huh? Well that would take a lot of organization. To know where and when a target was traveling and by what means would be crucial. However, as we are just discussing possibilities here, you should know that there is one major flaw with any such plan."

Theurer's head shot up, "Flaw? What flaw?"

"Simply this, my dear Doktor, I have attacked targets on the ground from the air. I have torn up cavalry charges, bombed railroad yards, shot up advancing infantry and mounted troops from the air, and there is always one problem and that is that you cannot count on getting them all. Your intended target may be wounded or perhaps come out unscathed. No, Doktor, if you want to use an airplane to kill your man, that man should be flying in another airplane. Shooting down a transport plane is a piece of cake, and, unlike planting a bomb on a plane and hoping it goes off in the air, attacking another airplane in flight and following it until it crashes to the ground is the best way to ensure a kill."

Harry Braham stirred his coffee and focused his glare at Theurer. "You didn't ask me here to discuss fairy stories. What precisely are we talking about, Doktor?"

The German took a sip of his coffee and looked up at the raft of gray clouds sweeping in under the bright blue sky.

"Look, if I thought we could simply blow the man up and that would solve our country's problems, I would do it. It is not as simple as that." Theurer stopped talking and looked around at the tables of tourists having a pleasant afternoon. No one was paying any attention to the two men talking.

"We, I mean Germany, got to where we are now because Hitler smooth-talked his way with the bankers and industrialists. All they saw were piles of Reichsmarks flowing in if they backed him. Even Franz von Papen was taken in. He thought Hitler could be controlled. The one group that has kept its distance is the army. They wanted nothing to do with the street thugs of the *Sturmabteilung*. If Hitler wants the army's backing, he has to do something about Röhm. Even so, the army doesn't want a war; they will take Hitler if they can control him. Germany can't win a two-front war, and that is what any such adventure would mean."

Braham looked dubious and lit another cigarette, watching the smoke curl up into the sky as he exhaled. "But you just said, he wrote the manifesto for war."

"If we are going to avoid another fiasco like 1914 something must be done, and done quickly. I am among a group of committed people who want to put Hitler in check until we can sort our future out. The nation cannot survive a wholesale revolution. You may call us patriots or German nationalists, call us what you will, but we cannot allow the Nazi Party to continue its control of Germany. And, lest you think we are starry-eyed idealists, let me assure you that we are nothing of the kind; neither are we socialist zealots or Bolsheviks. Simply put, we are pragmatists who understand the realpolitik of Europe.

Time is slipping by. Each day National Socialism is changing the face of the nation while moving us closer to the edge of the abyss. At this moment only some key industrialists and certain senior army officers stand in Hitler's way. If he convinces them that he is the country's only salvation, then they will hand him the nation on a platter.

"And you think that your group can pull this off? Don't you think that the Germany that put the Nazis in power would react strongly to such an event?"

Theurer nibbled at the edge of the wafer that had lain on the saucer and accompanied his coffee. "Perhaps, perhaps not; it would depend upon who was actually running the country after the event, as you call it. You see we cannot pull this off without the help of Hitler's longest standing confidant and supporter."

Braham looked at his companion and silently mouthed the word, "Göring?"

"Precisely. Adolf Hitler would have to remain, at least for a time. There is no one else who could come forward and convince him that the Führer is in danger from within. And afterwards we would need fat Herman to assist in controlling him and steering him toward a more, shall we say internationally acceptable path will take some doing. The problem is the Praetorian Guard that has encircled Hitler. It is the SS and its leaders, Himmler and Heydrich and their ilk who must go."

"And you plan to eliminate them?"

"Oh Yes. I have envisioned something akin to a failed palace coup with Heinie and Reinie caught holding the smoking gun. Hitler will be outraged, and to whom can he turn, but those loyal officers in the army and navy? There will be a public trial of the offenders followed by the necessary executions. Of course, with the perpetrators of such treasonous acts eliminated to who would the public turn? To the nation it must appear to be a great righting of wrongs. The criminals will have paid for their brutality. But with them removed, other, more reasonable people would then have to step in and then skillfully steer the ship of state on another course."

"By others, I take it that you mean you and the others in your little cabal. Is that it? It all sounds like a pipe dream to me."

"Well, a new government might decide that accommodation rather that antagonism might prove a better course for Europe. Perhaps America and the rest of the world would like that."

"Perhaps, but why tell me, I am just a businessman?"

"Really? Somehow, I doubt that. In my world speaking precisely is to be avoided at all costs, but in this case, I see that it is unavoidable. I am not speaking solely for myself in this matter. There are others who are prepared to step in and guide the country should a void at the top suddenly appear. What would add to the believability of this plan is the discovery of a link to some foreign power."

"A foreign power?" asked Braham.

"Indeed, we originally thought of Poland, but that might be a tad too difficult to prove convincingly. Then fate came my way, and I thought of you."

"Me?"

"Our group is comprised of men of policy, and yet we lack the necessary skills to carry out such an action, and you, sir, appear to be just the man who might be in a position to provide such a link. Who better than you to provide us with a known Soviet spy?"

Braham took a pull at his coffee, which had suddenly become quite cold despite the warmth of the afternoon. "Why would you think that?"

"Come, come Captain Braham. You are and have been in the espionage business for years, since your little foray in Poland more than a dozen years ago. I have done my homework, as you Americans might say. When we first met, you were waiting for a courier to bring you information about certain American corporations that are working very closely with the new government in Berlin. Now don't deny it. Unfortunately, Herr Walthers was careless and left a trail a child could follow. Somehow he was found out. The Gestapo became involved, and you know, one thing led to another, and he met with an accident on his way to meet you. It is strange, however, that when Himmler's men there examined the contents of his knapsack, there appeared to be nothing out of the ordinary inside. The Gestapo was indeed perplexed and thought perhaps they had made a mistake and went after the wrong man. Well, it does happen, you know.

I have done you a favor. It is time for you to return the favor. I know all about the man Ryshkov. He is either with you now or is where you can gain access to him. The NKVD has not found him, so you must have him hidden. I just want him produced in time for the operation to go ahead. The operation is scheduled to take place before the fifth of September, the date of the Nuremberg Party rally."

"Even if I could find this person, why would I?

"I am glad that you asked that question, Captain Braham. Frankly, I like a man who looks after his own interests. There are several inducements that I can offer."

"Call me Harry, Doktor. I feel like we have crossed the line to informality."

"Well, then Harry: first, if you will agree to proceed, I will continue to see that you are provided you with the information you desire, especially about the new rapprochement of American firms to those in power in Germany. Money and politics go hand in hand everywhere, and there are a number of American firms that are placing their bets on the new Germany. In fact, as a gesture of good faith, let me give you this." Theurer produced a thick brown envelope from his pocket and placed it on the table in front of Braham.

"What is it?"

"Well, since you have a set of drawings you might as well have the plans for the new German air force. These are copies of notes of a meeting that Göring had a week ago concerning airplane development and manufacturing."

"That's very interesting, but is this worth a man's life?"

"Perhaps this will save many men's lives, but Ryshkov is a dead man in any event. The NKVD will certainly kill him no matter how far he runs. Giving him to me might save many lives, and, who knows, your government might see the resulting Germany in a new light."

Braham took out a Gauloises, put it between his lips, then drew out his battered lighter. It was one of those heavy brass trench lighters that the army issued to officers of the AEF back in 1917. He had picked it up in a card game when he first came to France. He spun the striker wheel, a short flame burst from the end, and he touched it to the cigarette. Braham drew in a long pull of smoke and blew it out through his nostrils, all the while giving his companion a steady look.

"Well, who knows about governments, perhaps they would. Politicians are famously fickle. One day they want this and another day they decide what they wanted the day before is untenable. I deal with real people, not concepts. But you said several inducements? This, I suppose is number one?"

"Yes, well, as I said, I know all about Ryshkov and the network that helped him escape. I even know who the White Raven is."

Braham's eyes went cold, and he held the German in his gaze.

"Don't worry, I am not about tell anyone. I have my source—an unimpeachable source, I might add, who has described your man Ryshkov and the information he had in great detail. My source also happens to know who helped him leave Berlin. Please, I have no intention of shutting down this conduit. The lady in question is unknown to the Gestapo. However, they are, how do you say, "just a phone call away?'

Then of course there is the NKVD. They are looking for Ryshkov. To them he is already a dead man. His disappearance from his post in Berlin has stirred up a bit of a firestorm in Moscow. I suspect they are now urgently looking for him all over the continent. Personally, I do not like to deal with Bolsheviks. One never is sure if they will not simply shoot everyone involved. Now, what you do with that bit of information is entirely up to you, but just put it down to a friendly gesture. Now, do you think you might be able to offer assistance?"

Braham looked at the man seated across the table from him, wished that he could just pick him up, toss him into the millrace and be done with the whole business. Then he thought about Gisela von Teischen and her White Raven network. He would have to think quickly. "Perhaps I can. Give me two weeks, and I may have something for you. How shall I contact you?"

"Excellent! Hmmm, why not place an advertisement in the personal pages of in the *International Herald Tribune*? *Lost dog. Mademoiselle Picard seeks her lost Alsatian, Walter.* The paper will provide a box number for us to use. And now if you will excuse me, I have an appointment in Caen."

The Man from Finland Station

The Finnish businessman Eirno Stakkveld sat in a back corner of the bar, a copy of *Mein Kampf* on the table before him. The *Weis Hunde* was a good location for a meeting, just a cozy quiet neighborhood *bierstube* in Steglitz, just a short walk from the S-Bahn station. Although not a busy place it was located close enough to the Steglitz Rathaus that the comings and goings of strangers were unremarkable. A shabbily dressed man came through the door just after ten p.m. and stopped for a moment to survey the room. He looked like any of Berlin's citizens who had yet to enjoy the benefits of National Socialism. He squinted through the perpetual cloud of tobacco smoke, which hung from the ceiling like a curtain, until his eyes fell upon the man he had come to meet, the man who sat with a copy of Hitler's manifesto in plain sight.

Oskar was nervous. He did not like face-to-face meetings with his NKVD controllers. He had survived this long by avoiding any compromising activities with anyone from the Soviet Union, and he had been careful to erase the traces of any past associations. Still, he had begun to imagine Gestapo men on every corner, watching him. But caution in this city was essential, he, like all the others in the capital, employed the *Berlin blicke*, that quick over-the-shoulder glance to see if someone was following. Oskar was alarmed by the call for the meeting. Any meeting was out of the ordinary, and anything out of the ordinary meant something had gone wrong. Worse, the meeting was with Yuri himself, a man he had not spoken to in nearly eight years.

Oskar stood for some time in the shadow of a haberdasher's doorway and observed the comings and goings at the *Weis Hunde* from across the street. At this time of year in North Germany sunlight faded slowly and even the shadows seemed transparent. He glanced at his wristwatch, a Tissot with a sweeping second hand. He bought it on a trip to Geneva in 1930. It had an alligator band that looked to need replacing. Still it was reliable. Looking again he saw the minute hand glide to point at nine. It was time to go.

Oskar opened the door to the bar and took in the surroundings. To his right ran a long, dark wood-topped bar that bore the scars of countless cigarette burns from customers too tipsy to maneuver their smokes to the stamped metal ashtrays bearing the logos of various Berlin breweries. Several drinkers stood to the bar, while a few clustered at the wooden tables brightened with red and white checked oilcloth. Moving slowly, he made his way toward Andropov.

Oskar knew the man he knew as Yuri by sight. Still, people age in this job, and there were signs of stress on the face of the Russian. From that point onward, Andropov and Theurer kept open a tenuous line of communication between them, through cutouts and dead drops. As Oskar approached the table, Andropov put out his hand and, in near perfect German spoke: "Mein Herr, it is nice to see you again." Looking around the room Andropov saw that no one had paid the slightest attention to the greeting.

Oskar nodded in recognition and then returned to the bar. He raised a hand, and, when the bartender approached, he ordered two steins of *Schultheiss* lager and brought them back to the table. "So why do we need to meet, what is so urgent? Where is Ryshkov? With the new government things are not easy for me in this city right now."

Andropov looked around the room before he replied, "Moscow is also unsettled. I believe that Comrade Stalin has become enthralled by what he sees here in Germany. He has seen how Hitler has dealt with his own opposition and may be wishing to emulate him. As for our mutual friend, Ryshkov, he has vanished. Comrade Stalin is particularly suspicious of those in the Soviet Union who have dealings with outsiders; especially those within the security *aparat* and those of us with German connections are top on that list. If worse comes I need to have something to barter with."

Oskar looked at the Russian and felt a brief pang of sympathy. As one bureaucrat to another, he knew the uncertainties under which operations were handled by tyrants and their henchmen.

"Yes, I know about Ryshkov."

Andropov looked at the German in astonishment. "How?"

"What do you expect, I am a valuable source of information. I listen and learn and in this instance I just may be able to help you."

"Well, then perhaps we can help one another."

Oskar looked about the room to see if anyone was interested in them. Convinced that they remained as anonymous as the other patrons, he reached inside his jacket and withdrew a long envelope and placed it on the table before Andropov.

Andropov opened the flap of the envelope and withdrew several closely typed pages of onionskin paper. The language was German, and, as he ran his eyes over the words, he made out Der Weiss Rabe.

Andropov stopped and looked at his companion. "But what is this?"

Oskar's lips parted and then he smiled. "Why my dear comrade Yuri, or whatever your real name is, Der Weiss Rabe, or the White Raven, is perhaps a rumor, but I think more than that. What the term means, I am not sure. There are rumors in this city, rumors everywhere, about clandestine groups who are anti-Hitler. Some are religious, some are intellectuals, but the point is that with the coming to power of the Nazis, there are those who are working to thwart them. This name, White Raven has come up several times. How one contacts them, or if they truly exist, if it is a group or one man working alone, I am not sure. But perhaps Ryshkov sought them out. If so, he is now probably where all refugees in Europe eventually go, Paris. I am sure that even the illustrious Felix Dzerzhinsky would appreciate the irony of a red agent using a white bird to escape."

———

Eirno Stakkveld left Berlin early on the second of July from Steglitz Station, crossing westward through Germany, using local trains. Late on the third, Egon Dranvic a Serbian dealer in metal goods, crossed the Rhine at Strasbourg over the footbridge from Kehl to the Jardin des deux Rives on the French side. Dranvic had a two-week visa stamped by the French Consulate in Berlin. The French still viewed their former allies with warmth, despite the fact that it was a Serb who, by shooting Archduke Franz Ferdinand and his wife Sophie in 1914, had brought such misery to their nation. In any event, Mikhail Andropov had shed his Finnish alter ego in the men's toilet somewhere in Saxony by burning the Stakkveld passport and flushing the ashes out of the train where they had scattered over the tracks.

The Dranvic identity would serve until he could make contact with the Paris resident of the NKVD and see about what was being done to locate Ryshkov. Oskar had told him that it was apparent that agents of what had been known as the White Raven network had Ryshkov under wraps somewhere in or near Paris. Oskar seemed to know a lot about this network, and Andropov had heard a vague rumor about an anti-fascist group run by someone using that name. What troubled Andropov was that Oskar believed that the group had an American connection. That was something new. The last time Andropov had dealt with Americans, he had come up a loser. But that was fourteen years ago, in Warsaw. It was supposed to be a simple job of assassination, but that woman botched it. What was her name? Yes, now he remembered, Valentina Koniev, a friend of Lenin's of all people. Well, she was dead now and long forgotten, or so he hoped. He would be dead too, if he did not see this Ryshkov business to a successful end, so he would take no chances. Oskar's plan was ambitious, but a dead Ryshkov was the best insurance for keeping Mikhail Andropov alive.

Le Boutillier

Paris was not one of Gisela von Teischen's favorite cities, in winter it was too wet, in summer oppressively hot. She found Paris too brusque, too haughty, too full of itself, and, well, just too Parisian. She preferred Provence and the Côte d'Azur. There the sun and the air had a way of softening the auteur of the French, and, despite their horrendous language, she could indulge herself in things French without awakening her Teutonic spirit. Now, in the middle of July, and despite her feelings about the city, she sat sipping a kir in the lounge of the Hôtel Crillon and waiting. In Berlin, she had put it about that she was making the trip to take advantage of the slack summer season to have a new autumn wardrobe fitted at some of the city's houses of *haute couture*. In reality, she was feeling uneasy.

Karl Lieberman spotted the countess before she saw him. She was dressed a summery white linen suit with a narrow calf-length skirt, her blouse, a silk white and brown polka dot affair that accented her tan and white spectator shoes. She appeared to be an island of calm resting in sea of ornate furnishings. He stood, stopping for a moment, and tried to read her expression. She had a faraway look that to him bespoke of anxiety or fatigue, perhaps both.

"*Madame le countess*," he spoke in French as he approached her trying to appear as inconspicuous as possible. Then switching to German asked her if she was well.

Gisela waved a dismissive hand, "I am fine, but I am concerned about something that happened after I sent the Russian to you."

Lieberman frowned. "What has happened?"

Gisela went on to tell Lieberman about the dinner at Karinhall and the approach of Doktor Albrecht Theurer. When she was done, Lieberman gave out a low sigh. "How long do you plan to stay in Paris?"

Gisela looked up at him. "A week, perhaps ten days. Travelling to buy clothing is part of my, how do you say, cover. I plan to visit a few designers for fittings and such, why?"

"It's time that you met Harry."

Lieberman picked Gisela up at the hotel, and they took a taxi to Fouquet for drinks. If she was concerned about being seen in public with this Latvian, she did not show it. Anyone who knew her was probably either taking the summer air on the island of Scheldt or gazing out at some alpine meadow.

"Tell me about your friend Harry," she asked after they were seated and the waiter had taken their cocktail order.

Lieberman did not know where to begin, but he plunged ahead. "Well, he came to France when the Americans entered the war. He was a good pilot and shot down his limit of Germans, including a friend of yours, Reinhardt Stiffler. After the war, he was with the Americans occupying part of Germany. When that ended, he was at loose ends and had nowhere to go until the Poles offered him a contract to go there and help them build an air force to fight the Bolsheviks. I saw a good deal of him there." Lieberman looked down at the table and tossed his vodka back in one gulp, Russian-style.

"Karl, there must be more to him than that. What happened in Poland? Reinhardt mentioned that Braham saved his life. But what about women?" she asked.

Lieberman waved to the waiter for another vodka. "Yes, Harry fell in love with an American woman. She was half-Polish, from Chicago. Agata was a rare beauty, and they were happy for a time that summer. Then came Tukhachevsky's assault on Warsaw. Agata crossed the Vistula to help gather in refugee children while Harry and his fliers fought the reds. She disappeared in the chaos. As for saving Stiffler, well, yes, he did. Stiffler had crashed between the lines. And Harry dove down over the battlefield and gunned down a line of Cossacks who were advancing on him. After that Harry went a little berserk, trying to find her and flying one mission after another until there were no more Bolsheviks to kill."

Just then a voice behind Lieberman spoke, "Well you two look glum! Whose funeral is it?" Harry Braham stood beside their table and extended his hand toward Gisela von Teischen. "Countess von Teischen, I am Harry Braham, and I am delighted to meet you at long last."

"Here, have a seat," Lieberman offered and signaled for the waiter again.

"I'll have a vodka, ice cold, and bring my friends another round."

Braham sat back and popped a Gauloises from a pack and offered one to Gisela.

"Thank you, no. Karl was filling me in on your exploits in Poland, I hope you don't mind."

A flutter of a frown creased Braham's forehead and then he laughed, "Not at all, but all that seems like ancient history. We need to talk about our mutual friend the wily Doktor Theurer."

For the next hour the three of them talked. First Gisela, told of the night at Karinhall and Theurer's approach to her. Braham considered whether to share all of his conversation in Bayeux with her, but decided that they all needed to understand what lay before them.

"Do you think he is serious, about killing Hitler?" she asked, by now a little wide-eyed and showing the effects of the drinks.

"I've given that a lot of thought, and I am convinced that he has something else planned."

"Well, what?" asked Gisela, seeming to throw off the effect of the liquor.

Braham looked at Lieberman and then at Gisela. "Its hard to put into words, and I have no facts, call it a gut feeling, but I think he is using all of us for another end. Every time I talk to him or think about what he wants me to do I conjure up an image of a renaissance assassin skulking through dimly lit alleyways. The Nazi leadership is Byzantine in its makeup, and the leaders behave like the cardinals under the Borgia pope. There is a part of this that we don't know, at least that is what I think."

Braham looked at his watch, "It's late, and I have had enough vodka to bring the Rasputin back to life. Why don't we meet for lunch tomorrow, and maybe by then things will be clearer."

That night Gisela lay in her bed, alone and not sleeping, tossing back and forth, and thinking of this man she had just met. She did not trust what she felt at that moment. He was just a man, after all. She had known others—men with handsome faces, powerful men, and men with immense wealth who were willing to shower her with gifts and privilege if only she would share their beds. But this man seemed different. He had a world-weary nonchalance. He was unpretentious and serious, while at the same time playful. As the clock ticked past three she fell asleep at last.

She woke before seven, but was not rested, her mind filled with the hangover images of the strange dreams that had kept her tossing in the bed. Nowhere was safe, she held snatches of images, terrifying images of dark cloaked men surrounding her, the more she tried to re-examine these images, the fainter they became, until in the morning sun they vanished like mist rising from a stream.

She was not a happy customer that morning, short tempered and ill-mannered, something the proprietors of the salons were used to. The couturiers received icy responses from her as they presented design after design for her approval. Her mind was not at ease, and while the designs were stunning, she could not summon interest in the new creations that she tried on. She fidgeted and more than once a seamstress's pin punctured her skin. When that occurred she snapped at the woman, launching into a string of withering invectives. She knew she was being a bitch, using her status to get her way, using the accident of her birth to give her sway over these minions. For the first time, she was showing signs of nerves. Perhaps it was fatigue, or was it something else? By the time she left the salons she had agreed to buy everything they had shown her and managed to mollify the staff with a round of generous tips. "We do hope the countess will visit us again," was the chorus of the proprietors as she swept out of each establishment. It might have been false sincerity, but money did talk.

Braham was waiting for her in the lobby of the Crillon when she returned, trailed by a pair of bellboys hefting packages. She did not see him at first as she led her parade toward the elevators. He watched her pass by and, at first, had begun to signal to her, but lowered his arm to watch. He had been thinking about her since the previous evening. His problem was that he liked to be with women, he just didn't know how to live with one. Worse, Gisela von Teischen was a complication. Knowing what he did about her, and Theurer's interest in her, made protecting her a business necessity, and he had to be careful about getting involved.

He watched her as she approached the elevators; then she turned and saw him watching her. A frown and then a smile crossed her face. He saw her hand each of the bellboys a wad of Francs, and, as they ascended to her suite with their armloads of packages, she walked over to him.

"Weren't you going to say hello?" she asked suspiciously.

"I just saw you," and pointing to the crumpled sheets of the *Herald Tribune* on the chair next to him said, "I got engrossed in the paper, bad habit of mine."

"Well, here I am, you said something about lunch, I think."

"Yes, Karl will meet us there." Braham stood and, taking Gisela by the arm, turned and nearly collided with Cynthia Waite and that young naval officer friend of Harriet's, Bill something, who were coming from the direction of the dining room.

The White Raven

Cynthia's eyes flashed danger as the young man said, "Captain Braham, you remember me, Bill Forrest. You know, at Harriet's birthday party."

"Oh yes, hello Bill. Cynthia, so nice to see you, may I present Countess Gisela von Teischen."

Cynthia withdrew her talons, but was less than gracious. Harry held his breath, and the young lieutenant was too oblivious to understand the nature of a woman's ire.

"So nice to see you both again, but the countess and I must be going. *Au revoir*." Braham guided Gisela out of the hotel and into a waiting taxi.

They drove in silence for a few moments before Gisela spoke, "A former lover, that Fraulein Waite?"

Braham waited a beat and replied, "No, no indeed," and left it at that.

"Ah, a woman scorned," Gisela commented.

To which Braham replied, " Heaven has no Rage, like Love to Hatred turned, Nor Hell a Fury, like a Woman scorned. In any event, it was I who refused her entreaty. She is a bit too young, even for me."

They lunched at Le Boutillier, in one of those private rooms normally reserved for romantic assignations. Braham liked the place where once one was admitted, discretion ruled. An American expatriate owned the restaurant. He had answered Lafayette's call and come to France in 1917. An army captain, like Braham, he found that he enjoyed Paris and the swirling nightlife much too much to return to the States. The captain, a man named Foster Davies, an artillery officer, billed himself as a raconteur. It was a sobriquet that took in a lot of territory even in Paris. Davies had a sense of the dramatic, so in each of the private rooms he created a singular atmosphere. One room reminded guests of a Turkish seraglio, another of a Victorian boudoir; he had an art deco room and a room that might have passed for the interior of a Roman villa. Even with the ostentatious décor, the food at Le Boutillier was excellent.

When they arrived the waiter, impeccably dressed in a tailcoat and white tie, led them the art deco room. Decorated with polished Bakelite vases and drawings by Erté it seemed like a nightclub. In order that they would not be disturbed, Braham already had ordered the meal, a selection of summer salads, cold lobster and baked brie. He had selected a crisp rosé from his personal stock for them to drink. When she was seated Gisela exclaimed, "This place seems more like a place for a tryst than a meeting of spies. Or, perhaps the two are very much the same."

"Well, both need to be kept secret, so this seemed the best choice for us to discuss the good Doktor Theurer. By the way, the food here is excellent."

By the time they had finished the second bottle of wine, the three had concocted a plan that they hoped would satisfy Theurer and at the same time allow them time to deflect any attention from the Raven network. As they were leaving the restaurant Gisela turned to Braham, "You know, your old comrade Reinhardt Stiffler has been giving me flying lessons. I understand from Karl, that you have a new airplane. Would you take me flying and perhaps teach me something that I can do to impress Colonel Stiffler?"

The White Raven

Gisela gazed at him like a little girl asking Santa Claus for a pony, expectant and hopeful. Braham was not one to disappoint and so he agreed.

"How many hours of flying time do you have?"

"Five," she said decisively.

Braham smiled.

"Certainly, would tomorrow suit you? This fine weather we are having would make for a great day in the air. I know where we might go for lunch, if you like. Shall we say eight o'clock, I will pick you up at your hotel."

Auberge Aigles Amour

July the fourth, just as it should be, was a perfect summer morning, clear skies and not a breath of a breeze. Braham had called ahead, and the bright red Pitcairn Mailwing was parked in front of a low hangar waiting for them. On the way to the field Braham had a chance to appraise this woman who had taken a bird of prey as her image.

"How extravagant to have your own airplane. You must be quite wealthy", Gisela said with a slight mocking tone. She had not yet decided about this man.

"Wealthy? No, I just love to fly and Herb Greene keeps finding me airplanes. I suppose it is a kind of bribe to keep me hard at work. Now, Countess von Teischen, what has Reinhardt taught you?" he asked.

Gisela was dressed in tan riding pants with a cream silk blouse and knee length riding boots. She looked over at Braham as he drove and considered before she answered, "The basics, I suppose. He had a Heinkel HD 39 trainer set up for me." He had taken her through the basics, taking off, turns, climbing and descending. She was still trying to master the landing, especially when she encountered a crosswind. "I know I have a lot to learn."

He thought about that a moment. Perhaps that was true when it came to flying, but he thought that there was little else he could teach this woman.

"What will you teach me today?" Again the innocent schoolgirl approach, she was enjoying the game.

"We'll see how you handle the Mailwing. Each plane is a bit different."

She nodded, knowing that she had so much to learn.

The morning dew glistened on the grass, the propeller swirling the droplets into silvery arcs the air as they taxied the plane for takeoff. A bump or two on the grass runway, and they were airborne. Below, the suburbs of the city spread out under the summer canopy of leaves. Off to the north, the Eiffel Tower stood sentinel over the heart of the city. They glided westward at five thousand feet, the silvery ribbon of the Seine under their right wing. The Pitcairn was in its element and responded quickly to Braham's pressure on the stick and rudder pedals.

Braham began to make languid "S" curves in the air, keeping the turn and bank needle steady and never losing more than a few feet of altitude in each long sweep over the French countryside. As they moved westward, with the sun over the port wing, he let his mind drift and for those few moments allowed no thoughts but the appreciation of sky and land to occupy him.

Flying was the only time he knew real happiness. No one to tell him what to do; no one to have to please. Even being with a woman did not compare with the exultation he felt when he was in the air. Up here no one owned him, there was no one following him or waiting for him around a dark corner. He had felt free in flight, even in combat. Flying over the shattered landscape of the western front or out over the frozen steppe in search of Bolshevik cavalry, he reveled in his mastery of the air. And if there was danger lurking in the clouds, some challenger with Maltese crosses painted on a gaudy fuselage, he was not worried. This was clean combat, the outcome a finality he could understand, not the constant play-acting of political intrigue.

Flying was where he belonged and he knew it, even if he had to steal moments away from his other life. He dropped the nose and the airspeed built up, then just a bit of backpressure on the stick, and his weight was borne on a column of air as the wings of the Pitcairn did their magic. Turn, bank, climb, and dive with the stick in his hand; he controlled his environment and was master of all he saw. But then, it could never last, what went up, at some point had to come down, and when he looked over to the front cockpit and saw Gisela's white leather helmet and her blonde hair floating in the wind, he sighed and came back to the task at hand and leveled off.

"Can you hear me?" Braham shouted into the Gosport tube that connected to Gisela's leather flying helmet. "If you can, give me a thumbs-up."

Gisela acknowledged, and then he proceeded to give her a demonstration. The Mailwing was not a fast airplane, but it was agile enough, and in the hands of an air ace like Braham, it could perform outstanding feats. For the first half hour, he wrung out one maneuver after another. A Cuban eight, then an Immelmann turn, several barrel rolls, a few slow rolls, inverted flight, then snap rolls—he did them all. Gisela, strapped in the front seat, hung on and, although her stomach was often surging up into her throat, she never once became sick. Braham was not showing off, but explained each step of each maneuver to her over the Gosport tube. After he explained what he was about to do with the airplane, he would ask her to give him a thumbs-up if she understood. She never faltered. After he went through the routine, it was her turn.

"Now, Countess it is your airplane. I am taking my hands off the controls so go ahead and try the Cuban eight. Ready?"

Gisela gave him the thumbs-up, and then she deftly started the maneuver.

Braham had promised her lunch and after a morning of boring holes in the clouds had navigated them to a broad field near an ancient farm in Normandy. The stone barn and house had been turned into an inn called Auberge Aigles and was owned by Braham's old squadron chef and his family. Braham often flew up to the place and landed in their hayfield, if only to sample some of the *propriétaire*, Henri Topenot's, home made calvados. After the war, Braham had loaned Henri the money to buy the place. Whenever he came to visit, either alone or with a female companion, Henri and his wife, Helene, treated him like royalty.

When Braham swept low over the place Henri came running outside followed by a small flock of children all shouting, "Capitaine Braham, Capitaine Braham!" The children watched with eager anticipation as the biplane turned and slid down onto the grassy field. Braham had taught them to wait on the other side of the fence until he had parked the plane and the propeller had come to a halt before they ran out to surround him. From inside the cockpit, Braham extracted a small paper bag of candies and tossed it to the ground amid squeals of delight.

"*Bonjour Capitaine Braham, bonjour,*" chorused Henri and Helene.

"We've come for lunch! You got my wire?" replied Braham.

"But of course, Helene has made an excellent apple tartine; still piping hot."

Braham stepped up on to the lower wing and helped Gisela unstrap from her seat.

"May I introduce Madame le Countess."

Both Henri and Helene smiled to each other and then at the aviators. Helene, not sure what to say, gave Gisela a small curtsey.

"Please let me show you where you can freshen up," said Helene and led her off toward the main building.

Gisela had loved the morning flight. Her senses were alive—raging hard against the laws of physics that normally held her earthbound. The elation ended with the crunch of the tires on the gravel runway. It felt as if someone had just tied her heart to an anvil. Still, she had flown the plane, done the maneuvers as Braham had taught her. Her faced was flushed with excitement and despite her glee she realized that she was famished.

After lunch, when a squall line swept in from La Manche and drenched the area, Braham led Gisela to a small room upstairs, where they performed maneuvers of another sort while the rain danced on the slates over their heads. In this moment—in this place there was nothing else—there was no one else. She knew it would be like this—she knew from their very first meeting. Their passion went on, fingers and tongues finding the special places in each other, gasps of pleasure and desire that brought them to ecstasy. When they could do no more and lay entwined on the sweat-soaked sheets, Braham spoke to her in a hoarse whisper, "Why me?"

"I, I don't know exactly, maybe because you are so different from all of them, all those pretenders who surround me. Those poseurs, preening about in their uniforms, like toy soldiers. Maybe, because you treat me like a woman, a real woman, not some object. What are you, a patriot? Why should you or any American care about what happens in Europe?"

"A patriot? I don't know what that means. I have survived two wars, I would like to avoid a third."

She looked at him, searching his face for the unspoken answer. "And yet you are here, and as the saying goes, up to your neck in things that aren't your affair. Why?"

"It's a long story." And he told her, of being let loose in Europe, no home to go back to in the States. He told her of Jerzy Krol and the nascent Polish air force and of Agata and the love he had and lost. He held nothing back from her, a confessional of sorts. When at last he fell silent, she laid her head on his chest and matched her breathing to his. For a while, they must have slept.

The rain was still falling, more gently now, when he spoke again.

"You must be careful, you know, especially around those SS bastards, like your husband. They may seem foppish like Ruritainian nobility tricked out in their fancy uniforms, but most of them are simply street thugs."

"That can wait," she whispered, "another life in another world. But really Harry, you must tell me what it was like flying in the war. How did you make sure you would win in the end?"

"Ah, well I wasn't always certain, but perhaps you need a practical lesson from the *Dicta Boelcke*. As the master said, attack from behind." And with that he pulled her toward him and deftly turned her over, then, rising above her naked rear entered her from behind. "You see?"

When they were both spent, Gisela turned on to her back and smiled at the ceiling, delicious thoughts streaming through her head. "So, my dear captain Braham, what about us, am I to be just another conquest for you?"

Now it was his turn to laugh.

"I don't think so, I am no Don Juan and I don't think the word 'conquests' can be applied to my love life. But, my dear, what about your husband? You said he did not care what you did, but this—well I am sure he would object, and he is just the kind of fool who, if he found he was wearing the horns of a cuckold, would want his so-called honor avenged. I am not about to stand at ten paces and duel it out with him. Especially after the events of the other weekend, Karl tells me that he had a hand in the affair at Bad Wiessee."

"Ha!" she snorted in mock horror. "He can't stand the sight of blood. Christian is a desk soldier, his mission so fraught with danger that he was ordered to wait by the telephone for news from Munich. You are quite safe. Then, rising on one elbow, turned to look at Braham.

"You are not bad looking, you know."

"I am almost forty, an old man for my line of work." He looked down at his nakedness and thought, well, no paunch as yet, hmmm, maybe.

"You are handsome, virile, and not cowed by the evil in this world." She smiled, "as for Christian, well, he thinks only of himself and his coterie of boyfriends. I think they are all homosexuals, you know. He does not even look at me, let alone demand his rights as a husband. Yet, I must be careful not to embarrass him. He did not seem to mind that Doktor Theurer spoke to me at the dinner at Karinhall. Now, Theurer insists on having lunch with me when I return to Berlin this week."

"He must want something from you."

Gisela reached under the sheets and ran her hand down his stomach, "Well, right now, this is something I want from you."

A Stroll in the Tiergarten

The main dining room of the Adlon, Berlin's top hotel, was a sea of smart looking uniforms seated among lovely women adorned with the latest fashions. Even for a summer's day, the icy glitter of diamonds leant a touch of frost to the surroundings. Gisela von Teischen sat alone awaiting her guest. She was not pleased at being back in the capital of the Third Reich. After the past week she had spent there she was confused and longed for the anonymity of her time with Braham. In France she had not needed to *be* anyone and, for the first time in years, felt like a woman, with just the pleasures of the day to fill her time. Back in Germany, the harsh signs of the new regime were all around her, and she felt drawn back into the character that she had created for herself.

White Raven, indeed. Looking around the room at the uniforms and seeing the swastikas everywhere she felt that her work was pitifully weak. How could she possibly make any headway against the power of this Teutonic mass? She operated by helping people one by one, while the Gestapo swept hundreds into Oranienberg and Dachau. Who was she kidding? And now this overture from that gnome Theurer, Braham had warned her about him, but what could she do, ignoring him would not work. No, she

174

would have to see what the man wanted, but she would have to be very careful.

Theurer was nearly ten minutes late, and she had already sipped half of her *Frankenwein* while growing impatient. She was more nervous than she might have expected. She recognized at least three women in the room at other tables, they seemed to take no notice of her, since they were seated with men who she knew not to be their husbands. So, it would seem that the Adlon was the place in Berlin to engage in a little postprandial trysting.

"My dear Countess von Teischen, do forgive me!"

Gisela looked up to see the somewhat harried face of Doktor Theurer standing next to her table, a young waiter hovering just behind him ready to pull out his chair for the man to take his seat.

Gisela smiled up at the little man, amused at his being the one discomforted.

"Not at all Doktor, I was just enjoying some chilled wine. It takes the edge off the heat. Summer has arrived, and Berlin feels like a furnace. Would you care for a glass?" Instantly another waiter appeared with a tall flute and filled it from the bottle that was nestled in the ice bucket at Gisela's left.

"Why thank you. Whew! Well now that I have caught my breath, I can offer the reason for my delay." Theurer leaned closer to the table and she could smell his cologne, feminine and cheap. Then he whispered, "There has been another attempt on the Führer's life!"

Gisela looked at Theurer, now alarmed and frightened but not wanting to commit to any emotion. Perhaps this was another of Theurer's games. In a halting voice she asked, "Was he injured?"

"No, not in the least." Theurer had by now, fueled by a second glass the wine, regained an air of sang-froid. "It was in Dresden. There was a bomb in a car near where he was speaking. Apparently it went off prematurely. Unfortunately several passers-by were killed and more injured."

"My god! That is terrible!" Gisela gasped.

"And so you were detained?"

There are certain contingency plans in effect in the event that some ill fate should befall our leader, and so I had to maintain my post until it was clear that there was no danger. Apparently, the individual who had planted the bomb was also killed in the blast. Himmler's men are seeking out the deceased's relatives. No doubt there will be some form of retaliation. But enough talk of that. We are meant to be having a good time."

Gisela forced a smile.

"That's it; that is better. After all, I have my reputation to maintain."

"And what reputation is that?"

"Weren't you aware? I am supposed to be a very entertaining person, a man of many anecdotes, and amusing stories as you must have noticed at Karinhall."

Gisela looked up and motioned to the waiter, who had stood like a stony sentinel beside a large potted palm. "I think we should order something to eat before we talk."

"An excellent idea!"

After the waiter left with their orders, Gisela turned back to Theurer. "Before we begin, I must tell you that you were followed into the room. There is a man sitting alone at a table by the door.

He is doing his best to look everywhere but in our direction. I hope he is not someone bent on a vendetta? He seems far too shabby, like one of those private detectives one reads about. Perhaps he is a Bolshevik spy trying to find out what the restaurant puts in its sauerkraut."

Theurer turned in his seat to look at the man at the far table.

"Doktor!" hissed Gisela.

"Him? Oh, that is just Helmut. He is my regular Gestapo minder, follows me everywhere in Berlin. I'd have to worry if he wasn't there, as it would mean they are really suspicious of me and have assigned someone who is not a bungler. I wonder that Helmut can manage to find his way home on a dark night. No, so long as he is there, I have nothing to worry about. He will make notes of our meeting, and they will disappear into some file at the Alex."

"A moment ago you implied that today's attack on the Führer was not the first. Have there been others?"

"Quite a few it seems, dating all the way back to 1923 and the putsch. He has amazing luck and comes through unscathed each time. It is something to marvel at, really. Goebbels of course does not let word of these attempts get out. Instead he uses the loss of life to embolden the government's moves against anyone who is a communist or anti-Nazi. The Party's organ, the *Völkischer Beobachter* will not publish anything about such attempts. Don't you know, we are creating the new world order and everything is humming along? Who could be dissatisfied enough to attempt an assassination?"

The White Raven

When their lunch arrived Theurer steered their conversation to other, less controversial topics. Over coffee and dessert, a large slice of Berliner torte for him and strawberries for the countess, he got down to business.

"Let me be blunt. I had the sense the other evening that you were not enthralled by the new order in Germany. You need not be afraid. There are many people who, while being German patriots are not pleased by the trappings of the Nazis. No, you need not protest. I am not here to snare you in some intrigue. Perhaps when we have finished our lunch you would care to accompany me on a walk through the Tiergarten; the Adlon is a very public place."

When the coffee had been served and Theurer presented with the bill Gisela dabbed her mouth with her napkin and said, "Give me a moment to attend to myself in the ladies and I will re-join you in the lobby." With that, she rose and glided out of the dining room.

Twenty minutes later found Theurer and Gisela strolling down one of the paths that lead away from the Brandenburg Gate toward the ponds in the center of the expanse of the park. There were other strollers, mostly couples, intent on each other, whom they passed. But what did this little man know? Was she in danger? If so then she needed to think, to find a way out. Lieberman and Braham would know what to do, but they were far away. Nervous now, once or twice Gisela stole a glance behind her to see the lumbering shape of Helmut trudging along.

"We need not walk too far Countess. Helmut dislikes walking, like many ex-policemen, he has tender feet and would prefer sitting. Ah, yes let us avail ourselves of a bench and rest for a few moments. Helmut will no doubt appreciate the gesture."

The White Raven

They found a bench where the path curved slightly. The location was ideal, as it afforded a view in either direction. Theurer thoughtfully swept the seat clean with his pocket-handkerchief before inviting Gisela to sit. As he did so, Helmut trudged by, trying hard to avoid looking at them, and took a seat on the next furthest bench, some fifty yards beyond.

Theurer had seated himself to Gisela's left and turned slightly so that Helmut could not see his face as he spoke.

"Now to business. Countess, you spoke the other evening with disdain for the current regime. No, please do not go. You will see that we will need to trust one another in this enterprise. Yes, that is better, please smile as I speak, we are just casual acquaintances enjoying Berlin summer day.

Gisela swallowed hard and forced a wide smile, despite the mistrust and fear she felt towards this man. "Well what do you want me to say," she stammered. "That I hate them and hate the role that I play in their sordid melodrama?"

"So the question remains, are you willing to do what is necessary to change the direction in which Germany is going?"

Gisela kept the smile on her face although it contained no mirth. "What do you have in mind?"

"There are those of us in the ministries and the military who feel that we can force a change if we could only remove the specter of the SS and its leaders from the scene. Himmler and his acolyte Heydrich have created a wall around the Führer that is becoming impenetrable. We plan to make certain that Hitler removes them, and when he does, we, certain ministers and generals, will help Hitler see reason."

The White Raven

Gisela hesitated and then asked, "Why tell me this? What do you want?"

"Broadly speaking, there is a move afoot to change the agenda of the Nuremberg Party rally in September. Hitler must be convinced that Himmler is no better than Ernst Röhm, and that Himmler plans to assassinate him and take control of the state. If the plan succeeds, then Himmler and his crowd will be arrested and held incommunicado, while we see that the Führer is escorted to safety. He will then declare a protectorate that will run the country."

"My god! You are going to hold him prisoner?"

"Well, I wouldn't say that, exactly, but he will see that we have Germany's interests at heart. And if not, well . . . "

"Are you serious? That was a foolish question, of course you are. But who is involved besides yourself?"

"Compartmentalization, my dear Countess, everything must be kept compartmentalized. You must not know more than you need to know in order to do your part. For now that is enough. Suffice it to say that there are a number of military officers and senior government officials who feel that the country is growing stronger. We can be strong, but not foolish, and we need not race over the precipice to another war. A strong Germany is one thing, a belligerent one quite another. We cannot risk the devastation of a second Versailles."

"I understand. So, in which compartment do I reside? And really why should I not just call out to Helmut and have you arrested?"

"That is fair enough, permit me to me tell you the what and why before you hail our lugubrious shadow. For now your role involves information. The success of the plan requires that Hitler and his closest confidants be eliminated at the same time. Our Führer has become quite modern and has taken to flying around Germany to make his speeches and to meet his political allies. He prefers flying, unless bad weather forces him to go by train. We need to know when and with whom he will be flying this summer. We need precise detail on his movements around the country."

"How can I possibly know that?"

Theurer leaned closer to Gisela. "Because my dear Countess, it seems that fate has intervened. The recent action by the Führer and the SS at Bad Wiessee has increased the urgency of our project. Fortunately for us, because of his devotion to duty and his leader, your husband has been put in charge of managing the Führer's security arrangements leading up to the rally in September. You can provide us with that information."

"Even if I could, you have not answered why I should help you." She asked.

"Ah well, does the name Viktor Ryshkov mean anything to you? Yes, by the look on your face I see that it does.

Theurer looked at Gisela and taking her hand kissed it. "Well, I think it is time for us to end our show."

Theurer stood, bowed slightly to her, and smiling said, "*Auf wiedersehen countess,*" then strode off back the way they had come with the dutiful Helmut in tail.

Gisela von Teischen sat for a few moments before continuing on the path toward the Löwebrücke, where Karl Lieberman, dressed like a Berlin banker, sat reading a copy of the *Völkischer Beobachter.*

The White Raven

After she seated herself on a bench opposite him, he asked,
"How was your lunch countess?"

The White Raven

American Long Knives

"So, now that you have heard it all, what do you think?"

Harry Braham stood in front of his fireplace, one arm upon the mantel. Despite the heat of a Paris July, the windows were kept closed, to prevent eavesdroppers, but also to keep out the fetid aromas of a city slowly cooking in its own filth. For the previous week the municipal workers tasked with collecting the garbage of the city had been on a strike. Nothing as mundane as wages were at issue, rather the issue was whether the garbage collectors would be allowed an extra day off during the coming Bastille Day celebrations. A recalcitrant city administration would not give in to an equally adamant union. And so the trash piled up, the streets did not receive their nightly hosing down, and rats, emboldened by the ready supply of food, appeared everywhere. It did not help that the garbage workers paraded around the city waving red banners and singing the "Internationale" Inside Braham's apartment the air was sweetly stuffy, made tolerable by the large spray of flowers that Harriet Bliss had brought to decorate the empty fireplace grate. There were four of them along with Braham gathered in his private study: Raymond Kingman, Harriet Bliss, Karl Lieberman and Jerzy Krol. On this humid night, Braham needed their counsel.

"We know that there are elements in Germany, very senior and influential people, who would like to see Herr Hitler eliminated." Raymond Kingman spoke softly and looked into the bottom of his tumbler as if the melting ice and scotch might afford him a vision of the truth. Then he looked up. "And yet one is never too sure with whom one is dealing in this new Germany. It is all well and good that your Doktor is who he says he is, but who are the others he has involved? Are they capable of assuming power if we provide the means? I wonder?"

Jerzy Krol looked around the room and then spoke. "As a Pole, I would like nothing better than to put an end to the saber rattling and messages of hate coming out of Berlin these days. But who is to say if someone were to kill Hitler that we Poles would not get the blame and find ourselves suddenly at war."

"Clearly Hitler is consolidating power. He has set about removing all opposition and by liquidating Röhm appeasing the Reichswehr generals who hated the SA. The killings at Bad Wiessee at the beginning of July and the wholesale arrests of others in opposition to him spell that out clearly. Who is to say that this Doktor Theurer is not next on the list?" Harriet Bliss replied as she fumbled in her purse for another Lucky Strike. She pulled the cigarette from its pack and held it out for Braham to light. "I do love American cigarettes, lucky for me the embassy ships them in with the diplomatic bags."

"What about you, Karl? You haven't said much this evening. What do you think I should do?"

Karl Lieberman looked at his now empty glass and walked to the drinks table to refill it. He took the bottle from where it resided in the ice bucket, where in the summer heat the ice had turned to slush, and poured himself a large tot of vodka.

"Two things really. I think we need to consider two things. First, it is likely that this Theurer is part of a group; it is hard to imagine him working alone. Gisela von Theurer has just met with Doktor Theurer. He has asked her to help him annihilate the SS leadership. He chose her because her husband is in charge of Hitler's security planning. Also, it may be well to note that once Theurer succeeds both Gisela and her husband will be in great danger."

Harriet Bliss spoke up, "Gisela von whatever is the woman you call the White Raven? How very romantic of her! I would like to meet her. She shows a dash of panache in that world of grey and black, don't you think?"

Braham gave a short laugh. "Well, she has been successful so far. But Karl, you know her best. Why don't you fill everyone in?"

Lieberman then proceeded to tell all of them the circumstances of Basil Zaharoff's asking him to keep tabs on Gisela von Teischen and of how he kept in touch with her. "So you see, she keeps in touch. What we call a "proof of life" arrangement. We keep it routine and mundane. Each week she visits her hairdresser, and each week, instead of using her own automobile, she takes a taxi to and from the appointment. On the way home she is sure to use the same taxi and driver. The taxi driver works with me, and she gives him a message to tell me everything is as it should be with her. If there is anything I should know, she passes the information to him, and he gets it to me here in Paris. It seems that soon after the execution of Röhm, Theurer met and had lunch with her. I met her shortly afterward in the Tiergarten.

Her husband is an officer in the SS and was involved with what the Nazis are now calling "The night of the long knives." Her husband is now attached to Hitler's entourage, and the wily Doktor Theurer wants her to alert his group to details of Hitler's travel plans before they become public."

Raymond Kingman spoke, "So, you think that she will tell Theurer and that Theurer will use the information. But once they succeed what then becomes of her?"

"I am not sure, but I don't see Theurer leaving any loose ends," replied Lieberman.

"This plan is so full of holes that if it were a boat it will sink in a moment," Kingman replied. "At any point this group of amateur plotters could be discovered. I would expect the Gestapo has several of them under observation at this moment. Even if they can set the plan in motion, Harry, you and Jerzy know how difficult it is to arrange such an event. I think it is pure folly to think they will be successful."

"I agree. Frankly I think the whole thing is bunk!" Everyone turned to look at Braham, who stood with his legs astride in front of the fireplace. "This is some kind of a set up. Theurer is playing a game with me and with the countess. We need to find out who wins and who loses with Theurer's plan. If I am not mistaken, Theurer is recruiting people who are expendable. He has something else in mind, most likely that he himself will wield the power."

"Perhaps both of you are correct, but then again, perhaps not." Lieberman said thoughtfully. "This Ryshkov who brought the plans from Germany was my second point. Why is he so important to Theurer? Wouldn't any Russian do? It's clear that once Theurer has him, his days are numbered. He seems too good to be true. I think we need to know more about this man, like who gave him the plans? How and why did he have them? How did

Ryshkov, who is now holed up in a garret near the Rue Laplace, find this man? And if Ryshkov found him, has Theurer? Somebody there in Germany with access to their aviation secrets clearly does not want their plans for an air force to succeed. I think it might be well if Harry and I dropped in on Ryshkov before he disappears, or the Russians find him."

Eviction

The soft thump and hiss of the record player in the other room accompanied by the occasional slosh of water from the bathroom were the only sounds in the apartment. The record had been a piece by Debussy, not Braham's usual fare. He usually preferred something with a little pep; there was this new guy, a clarinetist called Goodman whom he liked. But Harriet liked highbrow music, and when the others left, she remained; she had found the Debussy and put it on the record player. But that was an hour or so ago. She was now in the bath, the water becoming tepid as she leaned back against Braham's chest. She sipped some champagne and closed her eyes. He was slowly soaping her breasts, and from time to time would glide his fingers down across her stomach to reach into her. Each time he did so she would let out a soft gasp of pleasure and push against his fingers. Though she was over thirty, Harriet Bliss had the body of a younger woman. Her muscles were toned from all the walking she did in the city. Her breasts, ample for her size, had not yet given into age, and with Braham's studied ministrations, her dark nipples poked through the bubbles on the water's surface.

Braham flicked his tongue along her left ear and whispered, "So what happened to your lieutenant, did you send him on his way? You know I saw him at the Crillon with Cynthia Waite."

Harriet managed a shrug at that and then reached down to put her hand over his as he pushed against her. "Oh," she began, and then gasped as she climaxed again, "Oh, he is just a boy. He talked about meeting his parents when they visit Paris this summer. It was all very flattering, but really, can you see me playing the blushing fiancé?"

"Not from where I am right now," he laughed.

"Well, I expected as much. Bill is a dear, and the Waite girl is just the right age for him. That night at my party he couldn't take his eyes off of her. If he is lucky, he will marry her and have all that lovely money of hers to play with."

Harriet Bliss pulled her legs up, "I'm getting cold. Come, take me to bed."

As she stepped from the tub, Braham eased himself out and found towels for both of them. She liked him, he knew. They had done this before. It had been a long-running, low intensity-romance. They found each other when their lives took twists and the need for someone became overwhelming. Neither of them made claims on the other; that would have ruined it. But on nights like this, when the world around them seemed too mad to endure, they would come together, make love, and in the morning laugh over breakfast, the spell broken but sealed in their hearts.

Early the next morning found Braham and Lieberman taking coffee at a café at the eastern end of Rue Laplace. Braham had left Harriet to breakfast without him, but had made sure to drop by Madame LaMotte, his concierge, on his way so that coffee and a plate of fresh brioche would be on a tray outside the bedroom when she opened her eyes. As for him, the humid morning air did not refresh, and it would require several more bowls of the café's steaming coffee to bring him around. Twenty minutes after they arrived, a young man who Lieberman simply introduced as René, joined them. As they ordered another coffee from the *propriétaire* Lieberman asked René, "Is he still up there? Any visitors?"

The young man was chain-smoking Gauloises but waited for his bowl of coffee to arrive before answering. "He hasn't left the building for two days now. At first I thought perhaps he had slipped out the back, but the concierge has a daughter, not hard to look at, by the way. Well, I have been buying drinks for her at a place around the corner each night since he arrived, and she says he is still in the room. She thinks he is afraid to come out. By the way I need fifty francs; she can really put the booze away."

Braham pulled some money from his pocket and gave it to the young man, then he shook a cigarette out of his pack, offered one to René, and lit them both. "Any reason to think that there is anyone else interested in our boy?" He said this in English, René nodded and then replied in the same language. "At first I thought not, but yesterday, Francine, that's the concierge's daughter, said they had a new lodger in the place. She didn't like him, too rough and spoke French like a mongrel. Someone from the east she thought."

"Well then, perhaps it is time we pay a call on our Russian guest." Lieberman said.

Braham reached under his coat and touched the grip of the Browning automatic in its holster. "René, just follow us in and keep a lookout for this mongrel, give a shout if he appears on the stair or near Ryshkov's door."

Lieberman did not bother to knock, but simply hit the door to Ryshkov's room with his foot and shattered the frame. The Russian was scrambling for something under his pillow when Braham pressed the cold muzzle of the Browning against the nape of his neck.

"Now, now comrade, we are your benefactors, and we came to have a chat, not do you any harm."

With Braham holding the pistol tight against the Russian's head Lieberman checked the hallway. René was standing at the end of the narrow hallway holding a short length of pipe in his right hand. Satisfied that the young man was ready and capable of watching their backs, the Latvian came back into the room and closed the door.

"So, monsieur Ryshkov, I take it that Ryshkov is not your true name, but what are aliases among friends? We decided that it was time to have a chat with you and perhaps advise you to move on before any of your NKVD playmates decide that your defection is intolerable. So let's get down to it. Who gave you the plans that you sold to us?" Lieberman was at his avuncular best at that moment: kind and genial, with no hint of malice in his voice, with Braham holding the Browning in one hand and having uncovered the Russian's Tokarev with his other, it was the classic good cop– bad cop interview.

Ryshkov relaxed a little and slid back on the bed, resting his head against the iron frame that served as a headboard. Braham kept his eyes on the Russian, hoping that he was not going to do anything foolish that would require him putting a hole in the NKVD man before they found out what they came to learn.

The White Raven

Lieberman began speaking in Russian. "So Viktor, I may call you Viktor may I not? Viktor, tell us how you came to get your hands on those plans. Tell us what we need to know, and we will help you avoid the new lodger on the ground floor, the one the concierge's daughter says speaks French with a Russian accent."

Ryshkov blanched at the mention of another lodger. Perhaps he knew the man was there, perhaps not. He looked at Lieberman and avoided glancing at the weapons in Braham's hands. He had no more options yet it was several more minutes before he answered.

"I got the plans from a man in Berlin. He was someone who had been out at the German's secret training site at Lipetsk. I was part of the NKVD detail assigned to the airfield. I got to know all the pilots there. When I was stationed in Berlin, I made sure to meet him again. His name is Arndt Dietrich."

At the mention of Dietrich, Braham's eyes went dull and in his mind he was looking far beyond the shabby room to the memory of a sunny morning in Poland. If Lieberman noticed, he did not say a word.

"So tell me about this man Dietrich," Lieberman insisted.

And so Ryshkov told his story, all of it, in great detail, even the parts about the flower shop and Inga, the woman in the Grunewald, and his train journey to Paris." As he spoke he kept his eyes on Lieberman, hoping all the while that the other man, the man with the gun, would not pull one of the triggers.

"Very well," Lieberman said when the Russian had finished. "Where is Arndt Dietrich now?"

"He was living in Berlin last that I knew."

The White Raven

Lieberman jotted down the address that Ryshkov gave them.

"Now, Viktor, if you will take a moment to get your things together, we are all going to walk out of here together, and when we get to the street, you are going to accompany one of my colleagues to a place that is a bit less well-known than this."

"May I have my pistol back?" Ryshkov asked.

"I will give it to you when we get to the street," said Braham in perfect Russian.

Ryshkov looked at Braham in bewilderment, but grabbed his meager possessions.

Braham and Lieberman remained on the sidewalk in front of Ryshkov's building and watched René and Ryshkov's taxi disappear down the avenue. Suddenly a man came rushing from the building, his hair damp. With his shoelaces untied he stumbled into the street cursing in Russian and looking up and down the empty street and toward the taxi now receding into the distance.

"So do you think it is the same Arndt Dietrich."

"Who else could it be? He was one of the pilots that Stiffler brought along. Good flyer, and he was murder on those Cossacks. I seem to remember he was in love with a Polish girl back in the twenties. Maybe Jerzy can find out something. Well if Theurer knows about the White Raven, then he is sure to know about Arndt," Braham replied.

"So, two more souls to save," mused Lieberman.

"Anyway, they say Berlin is beautiful in summer," said Braham.

"Oh, right. I can't wait to see the rows of tiny swastikas blooming in the Tiergarten."

Spy or Thief

The ancient Norman town of Honfleur sits at the mouth of the Seine. Picturesque, and a Mecca for artists of all stripes, it had once been the target of England's Henry the Fifth as he sallied into the breach once more. Now in the waning days of July 1934, it paid host not to hordes of armored knights and longbow men, but to tourists and paint daubers whose easels lined the stone jetty at the end of the boat basin. Honfleur, because of its proximity to the great seaport of Le Havre on the Seine's northern shore, had a bit more bustle than the sleepy villages tucked into the craggy coast to the west. Unlike Deauville and Dieppe there were no hotels lining the shore, just scatterings of vacation homes on hillsides sheltered under tall pines with views to the sea. Summers along this coast were all they should be, winters were for the stout of heart.

Braham had motored through the coastal towns during the years he spent in France, and he took pleasure in the ambiance that the confluence of sea and land afforded. Where else could one find a shop devoted entirely to the various varietals of cidre and cold glass of perry? As for the seafood, well one could not ask for anything fresher. One had only to stroll along the quayside and buy directly from the fishermen. Many of the restaurants in the harbor town were family-run affairs, and, though they were for the most part tiny with a handful of tables, and offered what the chef could cook, the food was excellent.

Braham had taken a table at the Deux Huîtres and sat under the broad orange awning with the outline of a seahorse on it, enjoying the sunshine, a cold glass of cidre, and the bare legs of the young women tourists who passed by. Occasionally he got an extra treat as a capricious breezed lifted their skirts to reveal tanned thighs. Ah well, to be young again, he thought. Looking about he felt comfortable. This was a cosmopolitan crowd, bent on enjoying the day, and the sight of two men casually chatting at a café might not attract much attention.

Theurer appeared from out of a narrow alley on Braham's left and sauntered toward the table like any tourist with nothing important on his mind. As he approached, Braham ran his eyes over the people behind the German. Most were behaving like vacationers, idly chatting and enjoying the food. One man, dressed in a gray striped, seersucker jacket stepped quickly from the alley and took a perch on a bar stool fifty feet away. Sûreté or Gestapo, maybe anyone, but Braham noted the man's description. The problem was, like any good tail, he was of medium height, medium build, and, in fact, any of a million men, but his eyes followed the German's progress through the tables that lined the waterfront. Seeing that Braham had spotted him, he did his best not to look in Braham's direction as Theurer pulled out a chair across from Braham and sat down.

"And did you find the distraught lady's dog?" Albrecht Theurer asked in English.

"Better than that, I have your man. Care for a drink?" Braham asked and turned toward the door of the small café where a waiter stood attentively. With a raised hand he beckoned the man.

"*Monsieur?*"

"I'll have another glass of the house cidre and bring my friend whatever he would care for."

The waiter nodded and turned toward Theurer. "*Café au lait, sil vous plait.*" When the man left to fill their orders he asked, "Why did you choose this place to meet?"

"Why, don't you like the sea?"

"I don't mind the sea; it is just a long way to come for a meeting."

"And did you come alone? Didn't bring a shadow with you?" Braham asked.

"A shadow?" Theurer seemed perplexed. "Oh, you mean a bodyguard? No, I am just a tourist on holiday."

"I thought the Reich didn't believe in holidays, except in groups where everyone keeps an eye on everyone else?"

"Oh, you know our minister of truth always spouts off 'strength through joy,' well I am attempting to have a little joy, even if it takes coming to a place like this."

Braham nodded as if he understood. For their meeting he had dressed casually and wore sunglasses against the glare from the water. The American had arranged his seat so that the sun would be behind him and squarely in his guest's eyes, while he remained in the shade of the umbrella. After a few moments, Theurer began to twist from side to side to avoid the glare from over Braham's shoulder. At last he stood and moved his chair to eliminate the worst of the glare.

"Feel better now?" asked Braham when his companion had regained his composure.

"I think I am a creature of the shadows. Sunshine makes me uncomfortable," Theurer explained.

"Like Bela Lugosi," Braham quipped.

"What?" Theurer looked confused.

"Never mind, Doktor, let's get something straight. I don't trust you; so don't confuse my willingness to work with you as anything other than expedience. Any chance to derail Hitler and his cronies is too good to pass up, besides, so far your information has been useful, but it needs to remain useful."

Theurer was about to reply, but Braham held up a warning hand, "so this is how it is going to work. Before I produce the Russian, I want all of your files on the von Teischens and anything you might have on Reinhardt Stiffler."

"Why would I keep files on those people?" Theurer's protest was weak and he knew it.

"You want the Russian, I want the files. Take it or leave it." Braham shot back.

Theurer looked pained, "But that was not part of the bargain. You can't hold me to that."

"Look, do what you want, but if you say no, when I get up from this table, I will take a stroll over the bar and talk to the gentleman who followed you out of the side alley and see what he has to say."

Theurer whirled in his seat, just a fraction of a moment too late to catch sight of his shadow.

The White Raven

Braham watched as Theurer walked away and crossed to the far side of the rectangular boat basin. From where he sat, Braham could be sure that no one had risen to follow the German. Still, someone was interested in the man, or perhaps it was Braham himself that sparked the interest. Having lost Theurer in the crowds along the other side of the basin, Braham decided that he would retrace the Theurer's route from the alley, and, leaving several franc coins on the table, he ambled toward the alley.

It took only a second to spot the watcher. The man in the gray seersucker jacket was just a fraction too slow in avoiding eye contact. Braham then turned and walked up the alley to the next cross street and turned left in front of the Banque du Commerce. He then walked down several doors and stepped behind a newspaper kiosk. Several moments later the man, who up close appeared to be graying and carrying a slight paunch, came huffing along, looking from side to side to catch sight of his quarry.

Braham thought the direct approach would be best. In any event, he could hardly slug the man in the open street. The *flics* would be on him in a minute.

"Looking for me?" Braham asked in French.

The man whirled around and stared dumfounded into Braham's face.

"You look like you could use a drink. Let's sit down at that café over there, and you can tell me all about it."

The man started to edge away, but Braham clamped his hand on the man's wrist and guided him to an empty table at a corner café. Braham ordered two cognacs and sat down so that the man would have to pass him to escape. With a sign of resignation the man took a seat. Up close his jacket showed the signs of hard use. Several gashes in the fabric had been repaired, and the cuffs and sleeves were grimy from wear.

His name, he said, was Duclerque, and he had documents to prove it; his occupation was thief.

"So why were you following that gentleman?" Braham asked. Duclerque shrugged and began to talk. He had seen the man come out of the Cheval Blanc hotel and thought he must be someone with money so he followed him. The man walked up the hill from the hotel and went into the bank, there, the Banque du Commerce. Duclerque waited on the pavement, but through the front window of the bank he could see the teller counting out notes, which the gentleman folded neatly and placed in a money clip in his pocket. When the man came out of the bank, he followed, thinking the man might return to the hotel, in which case he would try to follow him to his room and rob him. Instead, the man walked down to the harbor and met Braham.

"So you watched us?"

"Yes," Duclerque admitted. "When the man went to the far side of the boat basin, he was out of my territory. I stay on this side, where I can drop into familiar alleys if I need to get away."

"But you kept watching me?" asked Braham.

"Well, I thought maybe he had given you the money, so I took a chance." Duclerque gulped down his cognac. "So, now what are you going to do, call the *flics*?"

Braham could see the sweat stand out on the man's forehead. He was just another one of the unfortunates who drifted through the world.

"No, I'm not going to call the *flics*. I'm curious to know how you were going to rob a man in his hotel room?"

Duclerque reached into his jacket pocket and pulled out an ancient Opinal knife. It was something that every French farmer carried to cut twine or to carve up an apple.

"Have you been successful doing this?"

"Once, but the man was very drunk, so all I needed to do was push him over and take his wallet."

Braham fished in his pocket and pulled out two fifty-franc coins and tossed them to the man.

"Here, try to stay out of trouble."

Old Comrades

A rndt Dietrich had completed the tests on the new plane and was sweeping down the course of the Fulda toward Lohfelden airfield. The medieval city of Kassel was spread out below him when his airplane's engine began to overheat. The cylinder-head temperatures of the new Hirth inverted V-8 engine soared. Then, as smoke began to pour from melted gaskets, the engine seized as one of the rocker arm assemblies exploded and a push rod shot out into the sky. The prototype Fieseler, which had performed so well a moment before, staggered in the air as the propeller came to a complete stop. He felt the sudden loss of speed as plane began to sink rapidly in the humid ocean air. "*Verdamnt!*" was all he could say as he tried to keep airspeed on the plane. He was still a half-mile from the open expanse of the landing field. Dietrich was going to have to pull some airspeed out of the crippled plane in order to maintain his altitude and avoid crashing into the houses that ringed the landing area.

The designers at Fieseler had created the Fi 97 specifically for the upcoming European touring plane challenge. The low-winged monoplane, designed to carry a pilot and three passengers, was more of a prototype, from which other more robust designs might be developed, than a pre-production model. Fieseler was looking to Goering's *Reichluftfartministerium* to provide more funding for new planes that could bring jobs and profits to the Kassel-based airplane manufacturer.

With a deft touch, Dietrich set the plane into a glide; managing to keep his airspeed, just a few kilometers per hour above the biplane's stall speed. He looked ahead and saw that he was not going to make it. He needed another hundred meters or so, but the plane's descent was going to put him into a line of someone's washing blowing in the summer breeze. There was nothing else for it. He would just have to sacrifice speed for height and began to pull back on the stick. Immediately the plane began to climb, and then staggered again as the airflow over the wing dropped. He had climbed another fifty feet, and instantly he dropped the nose to pick up enough airspeed to keep from stalling. Then he did it again, porpoising the plane, they called it. Not very elegant, but it was enough to buy him the distance he needed. Just barely missing a telephone line on the avenue next to the fence at the edge of the field, he did it again, but now there was no more airspeed to be found. Dietrich and the Fieseler fell out of the sky for the last twenty-five feet and met the ground with a heavy crunch before the plane pitched on to its nose, followed by a loud snap as the wooden propeller shattered. The ground crews had seen the smoke from the failed engine as Dietrich fought to make the airfield and were buzzing with activity. As the plane came down a red fire truck was making its way toward the wreck.

Dietrich extracted himself from the cockpit, and though his head was ringing as if it were a bell, he managed to slide down and stumble across the grass where he collapsed.

"Rittmeister, Rittmeister, are you injured?" A voice from the fire crew called.

"I am fine, damn it. See to the plane, before it catches fire!"

"What happened, sir?" asked a burly man in overalls. Dietrich recognized him as one of the line mechanics, name of Brietmann, he thought. Dietrich looked at the wreck and again wondered if this was why they had reinstated him to his former military rank in the last week. Was it so they had a scapegoat if anything went wrong with the prototype biplane he was given to test?

"It's the damned engine," he yelled to one of the mechanics who had chased along with the fire crew in one of the trucks. "The inverted oil system needs to be examined. You better get your men on it and start to tear this thing apart."

Dietrich was cursing at the wreck and taking his anger out on the several mechanics who were now attempting to set the plane back on its tailwheel so it could be towed to the hangar.

"Arndt, have you got a minute?" said a voice behind Dietrich.

"What the hell!" said Dietrich and looked to see Peter Kreisberg, Fieseler's chief engineer standing by a large Horch touring car parked on the open grass. With all the commotion, he had not heard the approach of the automobile. Beside Kreisberg there stood a familiar looking man.

"I've brought you and old friend," said Kreisberg and pointed toward the man on his left.

"Why it's Harry, right? Harry Braham. You are the man who saved Reinhardt Stiffler's bacon outside of Warsaw. My God, it has been a dozen years! Harry, it is good to see you, what brings you to Kassel?"

"Just business, and to see you. I dropped by Reinhardt's office in Berlin, and he told me that you had a new plane in development for the Olympiad this summer, so I thought I'd come out to see it. In any event Peter here and the folks at Fieseler are eager to find foreign investors, and that is where I come in," said Braham. Then, looking at the pile of twisted metal, added, "At least you didn't completely wreck it."

Dietrich turned serious for a moment, "Damned oil system. I was only inverted for a few seconds today, and I could see the cylinder head temperatures rising, so I was bringing it back when, wham-bang! The damned engine threw a rod. I am glad I was close to the field."

"Arndt, what are you doing later?" asked Braham.

"Not much, I have to write this up," he said pointing to the Heinkel, the tail of which was now being hoisted onto a truck.

"How about dinner and a few drinks, I have a meeting with Peter and the Fieseler people this afternoon, but I have the evening free. I leave for Berlin in the morning?"

The restaurant was in Seidlerstrasse a block or so from the city's town hall or *Rathaus*, as the Germans called it. Braham had always been amused by that appellation, since he had always considered politicians as a type of rodent. Located below street level, the Restaurant Brüders Grimm had all the dark ambiance of one of its namesakes' tales. Corbelled ceilings with wrought iron fixtures and heavy carved wooden chairs and tables were tucked into dimly lit corners. Braham thought at any moment the witch from *Hansel und Gretel* would appear to fatten up the customers to her taste. Dark and private, it was the perfect place for him to meet with Dietrich.

The White Raven

Expecting the witch at any moment Braham was startled by what next appeared at the entrance. A pair of gray Borzois entered the dining room, their silver and leather leads held in the gloved hand of a smartly dressed woman. She wore a green hacking jacket over a mauve silk blouse and tan slacks. Her face, in profile, revealed a longish nose under dark brown eyes. Her hair, swept back from her face, revealed shapely ears to which diamond studs were affixed. Her male companion was dressed similarly, and they both seemed to resemble each other. Braham began to wonder if the couple and the dogs were somehow related. Braham, despite having lived in Europe for so very long, was nevertheless mildly surprised when he saw dogs in restaurants, no matter how well behaved. He watched with some fascination as the maître d' led the foursome to a reserved table. As they were seated, he overheard a snippet of their conversation, as the maître d' addressed the man as "Graf." Clearly, the local nobility could do as it wished at the *Restaurant Brüders Grimm.*

Arndt Dietrich arrived a few moments later. "Have I kept you waiting long?" he asked, somewhat out of breath. Dietrich spoke first in German, but throughout the evening the pair dipped in and out of several languages, Polish, German, English, and a touch of Russian.

Braham decided not to waste any time, and after they had ordered came to the point. "It's good to see you, Arndt, but this is not a social call to relive past glories," he began.

"I had thought not. Nothing lately has been going well for me. What is it that you want?"

"First, I met a man named Ryshkov in Paris."

At the mention of the Russian's name the color drained from Dietrich's face, and he reached for his glass of beer and drained it. "*Mein Gott*! Ryshkov!"

For a minute Braham thought the other man might collapse in his chair, but the test pilot got hold of him and looked at Braham. "So that is where he went. He disappeared without leaving any word. He was supposed to help me, but he just vanished." Dietrich waved to the waiter for a refill. "What did the Russian tell you?" he asked quietly.

"Enough to get you shot by the Gestapo, if they ever found out. What made you do it?"

"Where is Ryshkov, and what about the papers I gave him?"

Dietrich was making no excuses. He needed to assess his situation: like the test pilot he was, he began to look at the problem as he would an airplane that needed corrective engineering.

"Arndt, I'll come to that. Right now I have him and the documents safely tucked away. Your problem is not with me, but with the NKVD. He left Berlin because they were going to take him back to Moscow, most likely to shoot him. You know the Russians, plots and counterplots. He was caught up in one of them. When they find him, and they are bound to, they will wring him out and then probably kill him and sell you out to the Gestapo. Talk to me Arndt? Why?'

Dietrich looked about them and saw that several tables nearby were empty. But seated just beyond the couple with the dogs, there were several men and women seated at a table with a man dressed in the brown uniform of a *Gauleiter*. Dietrich flicked his eyebrow in Nazi's direction and Braham followed his gaze. "I hate

them, Harry. I hate them and what they are doing to Germany."
Then, without prompting, he poured out the story of Gracja and
Jakob and the plans for the new fighter plane."

"Where is Gracja now?" asked Harry.

"Safe enough, I got her out of Germany. She is in Warsaw.
I haven't seen her in weeks, and I dare not write too much. I am
afraid that someone might read my letters to her. I want us to be
together, but not in Germany. She is in danger here, and as for me,
I am a German and the Poles don't want me there. We need to go
far away, but we can't plan anything. I don't have any money.
Ryshkov promised me money and a passport for Jakob, but then
he disappeared. He can't help us from Paris."

"What happened to this Jakob?"

"That was even more difficult. He had no papers. One of
the truck drivers at the factory has a niece living near the Polish
border. She is married to a Pole. The man drove Jakob to the
border, and he walked across a field and into Poland. As far as I
know he is safe. But I need to do something. I want to be with
Gracja. Now, with this Olympiad coming up, there are security
men all over the airfield. I am surprised you weren't being followed
tonight. Were you?"

"No, I seem to have a golden pass from the Gestapo, for
now at least. Anyway, Reinhardt Stiffler has vouched for me. Look,
I have a proposition to make to you. Ryshkov traded the plans you
stole for a ticket out of Germany. He used a contact that might be
unreliable. Some friends are looking into that. So it comes down to
the question of how much you want to be with Gracja, and what
you would do to make sure you were safe from these men?"

Braham looked toward where the Gauleiter and his party were seated. "Look, Arndt there is a man, a member of the Abwehr, who knows all about Ryshkov and what he was carrying to Paris. He does not yet know about you, but I wouldn't count on that for very long. Between him and the NKVD connecting you to Ryshkov, it is only a matter of time. You are not safe, and if they find you, what will happen to Gracja?"

"There is no safe place for anyone as long as they are in charge of this country. They are thugs, beasts from hell, if you ask me. I would like to wring their necks. If I had my way I would shoot these vipers from the sky," said Dietrich

"Actually, Arndt that was very well put. What would you be willing to do if it meant saving Gracja and yourself?"

Dietrich looked in wonder at Braham.

"What, what do you mean? I shot men in the war, but they could shoot back, what are you saying?"

"You are a damned fine fighter pilot. But you are also a man with a tainted reputation, at least among the Nazis. But not all of them are as loyal as they seem. There are some who want to kill Hitler's henchmen and perhaps Hitler himself. After that, there is no telling what will happen and nobody will be safe. I have been asked to bring Ryshkov to Berlin as a pawn for these people. But I have a better idea."

"If you are willing to discuss the possibility, I can arrange it so that in three months time you and Gracja will be living together in someplace warm and safe, perhaps Cuba or Mexico."

"But," Dietrich stammered," even if I did this thing, help you, the others, would hunt me down and kill Gracja and me. No, I cannot condemn her."

"No, but if you do nothing, you know that you and she will never be together. Arndt, if you agree to do things my way, no one is going to die, not yet anyway. But I need you to do a bit of flying, call it an extraction, if you will. I can assure you that no one will know you had anything to do with what is going to happen."

———

Christian von Teischen rarely arrived at his office at the Reich Chancery before ten in the morning, and on this July day, he was a little tardier than usual. Although most of the officers and staff were hard at work before eight, von Teischen felt that, as a member of the Führer's personal suite, albeit just a minor functionary, he was entitled to some flexibility in how he conducted himself. In fact, how he conducted himself contributed directly to his tardiness as well as to his increasingly haggard appearance. Gone was the healthy tan gained from hours in the sun riding, skiing and playing tennis. What had replaced the healthy look of the outdoorsman was the pasty and slightly paunchy look of the nighttime debaucher. His long carouses through the brothels and male-only *nachtlokals* of the capital were taking its toll. Each morning he arrived with a splitting headache and the fetid aroma of alcohol seeping from his pores.

Climbing the stairs into the building this morning was an ordeal, and, by the time he reached his floor, sweat had beaded on his forehead. Looking down the long corridor to his office, he was alarmed to see a pair of SS Oberscharführers in their gleaming black uniforms standing at either side of the door. Von Teischen slowed in mid-stride, inhaled deeply, and did his best to assume an air of command. With his back ramrod straight, he strode down the marble-flagged corridor toward his office, his boot heels clicking with parade-ground precision. As he reached the door to his office, the guard to his left tapped on the door, and it swung open to reveal another SS man waiting inside.

"Ah, good morning Count von Teischen. My name is SS-Hauptsturmführer Kleist, Otto Kleist. I am so glad to be able to catch you before the start of your busy day. I was hoping that we might have a little chat."

Von Teischen stared open mouthed at Hauptsturmführer Kleist. Whatever words were in his mind never made their way past his lips.

As von Teischen glided toward his desk, his visitor went on. "Your lovely assistant, ah Britta, yes her correct name is Britta, she was gracious enough to provide me with coffee. There is some more here in the pot. Would you care for some?" Kleist was smiling now, obviously enjoying the discomfort that his presence had caused bon Teischen.

At last von Teischen spoke, "I am sorry Hauptsturmführer that I was not here to greet you this morning. I had business in another part of the city that delayed my arrival." The count had regained his composure and held on to it like a drowning man clutching a piece of flotsam. "I was certainly surprised by your appearance this morning. Now what can I do for you?"

"Thank you, Count. I will come to the point. I work in a special area of the SD, the Sicherheitsdienst, which means I work for Reinhard Heydrich. I believe that you know our chief."

"Yes, I have met the Obergruppenführer on several occasions."

"Well then," said Kleist heartily "you must know that he is a stickler for details, and that is what I have come to see you about. You see, in your new role of coordinator of the Führer's security, we in the SD must make sure that our leader's security is assured at every level. So you must forgive me if I ask you some questions." Kleist smiled and poured himself more coffee.

"But, but my record in the Party and in the SS is beyond reproach," von Teischen pleaded.

"Of course it is. Why everyone I have spoken with about you remarked on how calm you were on the night the Führer disposed of that SA rabble. You did an excellent job of ensuring the telephones were properly answered." Kleist was fighting the urge to use more stringent measures with this man, but he knew to be careful. The count might be a pompous ass, and he was rumored to be a pansy as well, but he had connections far above Kleist's level.

"Count von Teischen, would you allow me to show you some photographs?"

"Certainly."

Kleist stood and came over to von Teischen's desk and placed a photograph of Albrecht Theurer in front of him.

"Do you know this man?"

Von Teischen was nervous. It would not do to make a mistake with someone like Kleist, who knew what he might say to Heydrich. "I, I don't think so? Perhaps, but one sees so many people. Who is he?"

Kleist looked hard at the man behind the desk. He thought von Teischen was uncomfortable, well who wouldn't be given the circumstances, but Kleist did not think he was lying.

"That is interesting. He was a guest at one of Reichsminister Göring's receptions recently. In fact you were there yourself. I am surprised. Still, you do not remember this man?"

"Who is he?"

"His name is Doktor Albrecht Theurer. He is a bit of a mystery. In the last war, he worked in army intelligence. He now seems to pose as a bit of a bon vivant, showing up as at guest at many social events, but in truth, he is a member of the Abwehr, section III, counter intelligence. As such, he reports to Captain Patzig, the head of the Abwehr. Hmmm . . . and you say that you have never met this man?"

Von Teischen was beginning to regain his composure and snapped back, perhaps a trifle too quickly, "As I said, Hauptsturmführer, one meets a lot of people, and not all of their names are memorable."

"Quite so." Kleist then smirked in a way that sliced through von Teischen's fading façade of strength. Then he went on, "Would it surprise you to learn that your wife appears to know this man quite well?" Kleist then produced a second photograph, showing Theurer and Gisela von Teischen sitting together on a bench in the Tiergarten.

"This photograph was taken quite recently. It would appear that your wife and Doktor Theurer are in deep conversation. From their facial expressions, I concluded that this is not a casual encounter, nor a romantic one, as I believe she has made other arrangements in that department."

"Other arrangements!" Von Teischen shot back. "What do you mean by that? Are you implying that my wife is having some kind of romantic affair behind my back?"

"Behind your back or in front of it, your wife's romantic affairs, nor your own, are of no importance to me—that is unless you would like me to make them part of my investigations. No? Well, I thought not."

Von Teischen blanched and then swallowed hard, "My wife and I have led quite separate lives for some time. She has her circle of acquaintances, as do I. Socially we appear together and we know people, but they are not what I would call friends, rather people one meets at official functions."

"Now calm down." Kleist pointed at the photo. "Still, they seem to have important things to discuss."

"You do not share the same circle of friends then?"

"No, we lead separate lives. But why is this man of interest to you?"

"Does it not strike you as odd that a member of the Abwehr would be seen lunching and then strolling with your wife on a summer's day?"

"That would depend upon what was said. Do you know if my wife knows what this Doktor Theurer is?"

"No, we don't. We came to you first to see what you might know about their relationship."

"Well, I can certainly find out!" Von Teischen stretched out his right arm to reach for his telephone, but Kleist's hand shot out and grasped the count's wrist and squeezed it until the knuckles turned white.

"Please forgive me, Count. We would not want to do that just yet."

Kleist had released his grip and von Teischen was rubbing his right wrist with his left hand. "Just what the hell do you think you are doing?"

"Preventing you from making a grave error. You see, Reinhard Heydrich is very concerned about the Führer's security, and it would seem that the Abwehr's presence anywhere near our leader raises many issues. You have been entrusted with arranging the leader's travel and so we must be careful."

"But why tell me this if you do not want me to help you?" von Teischen lamented.

"I did not say that. What we want you to do is to observe your wife and keep me apprised of her movements."

"But we hardly see one another these days! How am I to do that?"

Otto Kleist stood and, placing his cap on his head, saluted the count. "I am sure that you will find a way. Take her to the theater or the symphony. The two of you are to many in this city the ideal German couple, I am told. I left you a card with my telephone number; it is on your desk. A call to that number will find me at any time, night or day. Heil Hitler!" Kleist's arm shot upward, and then he was marching out the office door, the pair of sentries in tow.

"Heil Hitler," von Teischen mumbled and then looked out the window at the clear morning sky.

Wagnerian Rhapsodies

Albrecht Theurer took great pains to ensure that he maintained a regular and highly routinized daily schedule. He knew that he was being watched. His long years of clandestine activity had schooled him to know what to watch for. Clearly someone in the Gestapo thought he was worth looking into. The man who followed him daily was easy to spot, but as a student of the business, he knew to expect other, less obtrusive shadows. It was what he would expect from any adversary, but none more so than Reinhard Heydrich. His men were the best. Heydrich had been a protégé of Wilhelm Canaris, a crafty intelligence officer in his own right, but Heydrich had grown outside of the Admiral's control— and was now a force to be reckoned with, answerable only to Himmler and Hitler. So, Theurer watched patiently to discover how it was done. A team of two had been on him for weeks, sometimes following behind, sometimes in front of him, knowing his routines and predictable routes around the city, but always watching. All the while, the obvious tail remained. Hitler's most trusted henchmen were taking no chances. After that bloody weekend in June, the SS was in the ascendance, and they were sealing up all avenues of dissent and opposition. Let them, he thought. Patzig and the Abwehr were important to the Reich and just as crafty, so Theurer made no changes to his routine, maintained his façade of dutiful Party member, and slowly lulled Heydrich's men into a stupor.

For several weeks, he had been weaving the threads of the plan that evolved from that morning in Konrad Patzig's office. Skewering Himmler and Heydrich would take some doing, but then he realized that he had the perfect stage from which to do it. The whole world would see how inept they were, and then he and, of course, Patzig could step in and show the Führer who the real guardians of the Reich were. Hitler would then have to rely on a new cadre of guardians. Theurer knew what he had to do, but he also knew that he was running out of time.

Hitler had staged the Night of the Long Knives to rid himself of Röhm and his SA thugs. That was the price he had to pay if he wanted the army's senior officers out at Zossen to support him. Hitler secretly despised the haughty Prussian elite of the army. His time in the trenches in the 1914 war had taught him that. Worse, even though the generals supported rearmament, they hated the bohemian corporal who now served as their commander in chief. Theurer needed to play that card. What he needed now was a cabal of plotters, people who could ensure the support of the army when the purge took place. So he set about creating one, knowing that he had precious little time to pull it together. He had the sense that as he set his snares, the SS was going about trying to snare him.

He decided that he needed a group of four men. Four men with influence, but who, when the time came, were equally expendable. He went about carefully selecting them, using the Abwehr files as his guide. Finding disaffected military officers was not difficult, but finding those with the backbone to carry out his plan proved arduous. The men he chose had to be important in small ways, and yet, when their eventual elimination took place, their loss needed to pose no threat to the new Germany he was going to create. He thought of them as the four horsemen of the apocalypse, each aligned with the other, but for their own aims. Rather than Pestilence, War, Famine and Death, he called them Greed, Vanity, Position, and Glory; patriotism, or allegiance to the idea of a greater Germany, were of no concern to them. He did not want zealots. Zealots were not for sale, the men he wanted had to imbue a venality that he could speak to with money or influence. The men he finally settled upon had objected to Hitler and the Nazis on personal grounds. All of them were serving officers in the Reichswehr, and all of them adhered to the outmoded codes and morays of the Prussian military elite. They were the antithesis of the street brawlers of the Party, and they ill disguised their disdain for the new masters of the Master Race.

The sordid quartet exuded the arrogance and petulance that so typified the Prussian leadership that had abandoned Germany to the Allies. That leadership had neither the stomach nor the will to do what had to be done to achieve victory. At the end of the war, the politicians and Jewish bankers colluded and were just as guilty in that respect. Once the Kaiser abdicated the entire structure of government collapsed. With anarchy building barricades on every street corner, capitulation was the only choice, and the politicians took that option. Theurer understood change was needed. But he did not see that the Allies were going to offer Germany a way to achieve it. They approached Germany with vengeance and cared nothing for what pain that would cause the nation that had been already bled dry by war. He found he had to make a choice. German nationalism could be expressed many ways, and the thugs of the Freikorps and Sturmabteilung did not have the answer, nor did Rosa Luxemburg and the Reds. No, even in those early years, he decided that he would go his own way.

Theurer had no problem keeping tabs on his cabal. The leader, he decided, would be the man he designated as Greed. As an army liaison, Oberst Kurt Schilling occupied an office in the Tirpitzufer offices of the Abwehr, just down the corridor from Theurer's. In his mid-forties and the son of a Kiel shipbuilder, he had chosen the army as a young man and rose to command a Jagdgeschwader, fighter squadron, on the Russian front. When the treaty of Brest-Litovsk was concluded in 1917, he found himself transferred to a unit based in Metz, where he was again the commander or Rittmeister of a fighter squadron. There he survived a smash up of his Fokker D.VII and spent the rest of the war convalescing in a hospital near Wansee. He left the hospital with a slight limp and an appreciation for the finer things in life. He could have returned to the family business, but Kiel was not Berlin, and in Berlin he had sampled the city's allures and wanted more. To enjoy himself in the style to which he wanted to be accustomed Schilling needed money—lots of money. When the Nazis came to power, he saw how they grabbed at everything. Why should they get everything? Wasn't he entitled to something? Then he decided he wanted his too, but without all the Nordic and racial mumbo jumbo. If he had his way, he could have it all. When Theurer approached him he was already sold.

The other three men, Vanity, Position and Glory, were cut from the same cloth. Vanity was General Bruno Hoeffer, who commanded the Twelfth Pomeranian Artillery and who prided himself on the splendid array of medals on his uniform tunic. A careful reading of his military record cast some doubt as to the validity of some of those decorations, but he had done a fine job of obfuscating his records. In the role of Position was cast Lothar

Reimer, a Prussian martinet who held the rank of general, commanded the Berlin military district, and had at his disposal all of the Feldgendarmerie in the city. He could be relied upon to seal off the capital if needed. That left Glory, and no better person than Oberst Max Premml could be found. Premml had earned the Knight's Cross for his exploits fighting the British during the Somme offensive in 1916, his sabre running red with the blood of English officers he had slain in hand-to-hand combat. For now, Theurer needed them all.

Theurer walked down the hall toward Schilling's office. Nothing out of the ordinary, Theurer's position put him in touch with many in the building, including the big man himself, Göring. There was no surveillance here, within the ministry, so he could visit whomever he liked whenever he liked.

"Good morning Herr Oberst." Theurer spotted the man emerging from his office.

"Good morning to you Doktor."

As usual, the doughty Theurer stopped for a moment and chatted. Over Schilling's shoulder Theurer spotted Senta, Schilling's pert blonde secretary, seated at her desk, the buttons on her blouse straining against the full breasts she hid underneath. Theurer knew that Schilling was having an affair with her, often screwing away afternoons on a large leather sofa in his elegant office. Schilling had spared no expense in the décor of the place. Through his family's business he had secured several mahogany panels that were to have been installed on the liner *SS Europa* and had them refitted to his walls. Several leather club chairs that had been destined for the same vessel had made their way into his possession, and with the touch of a few oils devoted to military subjects and an expanse of Persian wool on the floor, the place took on the air of a men's club rather than an office. It was the perfect place in which to conduct his plan.

———

It was billed as an evening set in a Wagnerian heaven: principal music from the composer's major works played by the Berlin Philharmonic before a packed house at Konzerthaus Berlin on Charlottenstrasse. Otto Kleist was not a devotee of orchestral music, but he appreciated the significance of the Wagner's themes to the Teutonic mysticism that the Party employed to attract the masses. Still, he had a job to do, and he had chosen this evening as a way to get a closer look at this Albrecht Theurer. His quarry was known to be a subscriber to the orchestra's performances, and the man was sure to be in attendance on this night, so Kleist thought it might be worthwhile to arrange a way to "accidentally" run into the man. He would choose his time, and perhaps during the intermission pretend some mutual acquaintanceship and see what he could make of the man.

Otto Kleist was sure that he was enough of a judge of character that he could assess the threat that this man might pose in the space of a few words. He was just smiling to himself at the thought of snaring Theurer when he saw Count and Countess von Teischen sweep into the theater's foyer. She wore a white silk sheath with a plunging neckline and a four-strand collar of pearls. As she entered, the sea of theatergoers parted with an audible gasp of recognition. The von Teischens were among several minor Party notables who had come to hear the Führer's favorite music. Christ, he thought, what if Christian von Teischen catches sight of Theurer, would he confront the man, say something? If Kleist had any expectation that von Teischen would keep the knowledge of Theurer from his wife, he was about to be disappointed.

"Count von Teischen, how good to see you again." Kleist, dressed, in his gleaming Totenkopf uniform said genially.

Von Teischen looked up as he heard his name, winced at the sight of the SS man, but then quickly regained his composure.

"Yes, Otto Kleist isn't it?" Turning to his wife, he gently took her arm and presented her to the man. "My dear, this is Hauptsturmführer Otto Kleist."

Kleist clicked his heels and nodded toward the lady.

"I am indeed pleased to meet one of the Reich's most lovely examples of German womanhood."

"How nice to meet you, Hauptsturmführer. Are you an associate of my husband's?" asked Gisela with a warm smile fixed on her face.

"Alas, no, but we do share some very serious responsibilities for the safety and security of our leader."

Before he could say another word, an annoyed look came over Gisela von Teischen's face, and she said in a stage whisper, "Oh my god, there is that tiresome Doktor Theurer. You know Christian; I told you what a pest he has been. Inviting himself to lunch and talking such nonsense to me. He is a bore. No, please don't even look at him. He has some woman on his arm. If we don't notice him, perhaps he will just go away."

As she spoke, Kleist looked up sharply to see his quarry and a lovely young lady disappear through the crowded lobby. He recognized his man and the woman who was with him. For a moment the SD man was perplexed. Maybe he had the countess wrong. He looked from her to her husband; both were looking purposefully away from Theurer. Perhaps indeed, trying to subvert their social status for his purposes had failed.

The White Raven

Theurer arrived at the opera house shortly before the commencement of the program accompanied by Gretchen Knoller. A breathtaking blonde, she was one of many women who seemed to enjoy his company while their husbands were away from Berlin, busily attending to Reich business. Gretchen's husband, a minor trade official in the foreign office who had recently been posted to Brazil, would not be coming home soon. She would add just the right touch to the charade he was going to attempt.

The lady did not object to a night out with Theurer, she enjoyed his company. For Theurer, nothing he did could be out of the ordinary, especially tonight. He had made a great pretense of being a womanizer, so this night Gretchen was a helpful prop. Later on she might prove to be something more. Theurer was very precise in his movements since meeting with Schilling in the morning. Nothing was to be out of place, no misstep that could be interpreted as fear or concern.

As the pair entered the lobby, Theurer was surprised to see Gisela von Teischen and her husband. They were standing and chatting with a cluster of people, the women in evening gowns and the men in uniforms. Theurer kept up a steady babble of conversation with the young lady as they made their way to the box on the third floor wing that had long been his regular place. But as he and his companion passed, he made sure to avert his eyes and move on. He did so, but not before he noted that one of the men, a man in an SS uniform, seemed to be watching and taking note of him.

Theurer's pulse quickened. He knew that man; he had seen him before, what was his name? Ah, yes Kleist. He was one of Heydrich's men. He had a reputation of ruthless efficiency and so not someone to ignore. That he was chatting with the von

Teischens was not a coincidence. Men could die because of such coincidences. No, Kleist was up to something, and it would fall to Theurer to see that Kleist did not learn anything that could derail his plans.

Just after the odious Kleist had been introduced, she had gazed past his shoulder to see Reinhardt Stiffler, dressed in evening clothes, speaking amiably with another man whose back was toward her. Her eyes brightened for a moment and caught Stiffler's glance. For an instant, everything around her went into suspended animation, and there were just the two of them.

"Don't you think so, my dear?" asked von Teischen.

"I, I am sorry, the noise of the crowd. What did you say?" she stammered trying to force some cordiality into her tone.

Von Teischen looked at her quizzically and tried to see where she had been looking, but there was just the throng moving toward the doors to the theater. "I was just remarking to the Hauptsturmführer here that we are so very lucky that Wagner will now be played by a pure Aryan orchestra. No more Jews in the orchestra pit, eh Hauptsturmführer?"

Gisela forced a smile, "Indeed. I think we best go to our seats before the national anthem is played. You will excuse us, Hauptsturmführer?"

Kleist clicked his heels and inclined his head in a sign of respect. "Perhaps you will join me for a glass of champagne at the intermission."

"Perhaps," Gisela replied as she took her husband's arm and the pair sailed away.

As he took his seat, Theurer made sure that he and Frau Knoller were visible to anyone in the audience who might be interested, especially Kleist, who had only a ticket for a seat on the main floor. Theurer had stood for some time in the front of the box talking to a couple in the neighboring box before taking his seat. Once seated, Kleist realized that he could not see his man, yet he did not wish to make a scene here. He would wait, as he had planned, to accost Theurer at the intermission.

Theurer took his seat and leaned forward to cast his eyes over the audience below. He had observed Kleist as the SS man took his seat and there, across the open space beyond, were the von Teischens entering their box. He thought that Kleist would stage some kind of "chance" meeting during intermission, but Theurer was taking no chances. He had things to do this evening and with Kleist lurking about he would have to put things into action. As soon as the overture ended and the music softened, he whispered in Gretchen's ear about champagne and a suite at the Adlon. She giggled, and he led her by the arm to the Taubenstrasse exit from the Konzerthaus.

Just before the intermission Otto Kleist eased out of the auditorium and stepped into the foyer. There he commandeered a small table in front of the bar near the von Teischen's box. He had a bottle of Veuve Cliquot chilling by the time the audience burst forth at intermission. Gisela von Teischen spotted the SS man the moment she passed through the doors. Grasping her husband's arm she guided him toward the table and the wine that Kleist was now pouring for the three of them.

"You must excuse me Herr Kleist, we women are always so ain, I must powder my nose." With that, she left the two men in vkward silence with Kleist glaring at her as she walked away.

Gisela had no intention of powdering anything, but was n swallowed by the crowds pushing toward the bar. She was looking for Reinhardt. She had not far to go, because he was looking for her. As she moved down the curving corridor a voice caught her attention: "Gisela!" implored Stiffler, "Gisela, over here."

Stiffler was there along with another man. "Gisela may I present my one-time nemesis and long-time comrade, Harry Braham. Harry is an American, but we don't hold that against him. Harry let me introduce Countess Gisela von Teischen."

Gisela and Braham had rehearsed this moment. Braham acknowledged the countess with a nod and, taking her hand, kissed it in the continental fashion. "I am delighted to meet you at last. In fact, this is opportune; we have a mutual acquaintance, Doktor Albrecht Theurer."

Gisela's blood turned cold at the mention of the name, and though she looked at Stiffler and smiled she shot a warning at Braham. Before she could reply, the three of them looked to see Christian von Teischen coming their way, accompanied by with Otto Kleist along with a doddering waiter with a tray of champagne glasses.

At the approach of her husband, Gisela turned and, smiling, said, "Look, Christian. Look, who I have run into, Ob Stiffler and his friend Herr Braham." Then without a momen hesitation she plunged on, "Herr Kleist, let me introduce Of Reinhardt Stiffler and his American friend Captain Harry Braham," not stopping for breath Gisela went on, "Reinh been kind enough to give me flying lessons, you know, so be able to fly solo, isn't that right?"

Braham watched Gisela knowing that she was impressed with how she was handling herself in this s menace of Kleist and the sexual energy she had shared with Braham must be causing seismic waves in her heart.

"Yes, count," said Stiffler "your wife is a natural at the controls of an airplane. I suspect that comes from learning horsemanship at an early age. Airplanes, like horses, often seem to have minds of their own."

Otto Kleist stared at Harry Braham with unconcealed contempt. "Braham? Braham? What kind of name is that? It has a certain, shall we say, biblical flavor to it."

"It is pure American, like me," Braham replied leveling his eyes at the SS officer.

Kleist nodded, "So you are an American? What brings you to Berlin? No doubt you have come for the nightlife and racy cabarets."

"Quite the contrary, Hauptsturmführer, I am here on official business," replied Braham.

Kleist nodded his head in appreciation that an American knew the intricacies of the SS rank system.

"Have you been in Berlin before, Herr Braham?" asked Kleist with no less venom in his voice.

"Yes, Harry's company has been doing business in Germany for years, and Reichsminister Göring has invited him to observe the upcoming Air Olympiad," said Stiffler.

Kleist would not let up. "So you are an aviation enthusiast, then?"

"Enthusiast, hah," interjected Stiffler, "Captain Harry Braham here shot me down over the western front back in '18;

then we flew together in Poland to drive the Reds off the banks of the Vistula. I should say he is the second best pilot in this room."

"Second best?" asked Gisela bewilderedly.

"Yes, of course, second only to me!' guffawed Stiffler.

The theater lights were dimming on and off, signaling the end of intermission.

"We must return to our seats," said Braham, "but please allow me to invite you all to lunch at the Adlon tomorrow."

Von Teischen looked at his wife and said, "I am afraid that I am engaged tomorrow, but perhaps my wife would join you gentlemen. What about you Kleist?"

"I must offer my regrets as well," said Kleist, who had no interest at all in sharing a meal with this American. Worse, this dalliance had cost him the opportunity to confront Theurer. What chance had he now?

"Well, then countess, it is up to you," said Braham coyly.

"I would be delighted," she replied.

"One o'clock, then? *Auf Wiedersehen.*"

Night Work

From his post in the shadow of a doorway, Karl Lieberman saw the man and woman emerge from the side door of Konzerthaus. Short and slightly stocky, the man who had emerged looked up and down Taubenstrasse before taking to the pavement. At the corner the man flagged down a taxi and sped off. Within seconds a car pulled up beside Lieberman, and he hopped in.

"Did you see the taxi?" he asked the driver.

"Yes, I've got him," answered Alexi Rzigalinski.

"Good, let's see where it takes them."

Lieberman was not very surprised when the taxi traveled the short distance from the Konzerthaus to the front entrance of the Adlon. When Theurer and Gretchen Knoller descended from their cab and entered the hotel, Lieberman told his driver to wait for him while he followed the pair into the hotel. Five minutes later he returned to the cab and asked Alexi Rzigalinski to pull the cab to the other side of the street to watch the entrance.

Lieberman nearly missed Theurer leaving the hotel two hours later, now alone. Lieberman had started to doze in the back seat of Alexi Rzigalinski's cab when the man emerged from the hotel and signaled for a taxi. As the taxi carrying Theurer headed away from the hotel, Alexi put his cab into gear and followed.

Albrecht Theurer's taxi dropped him off on Tiergartenstrasse. Exiting the cab, he took a moment to scan the streets. No one had followed him, just the normal street traffic, a taxi going by now and then, no one slowing to observe a middle-aged man walking down the street. Theurer wanted a cigarette, but thought better of illuminating his face with the match. No, better to get about his business tonight, then, if he were lucky, Gretchen would still be feeling the effects of the amatol he had slipped into her champagne, and they could enjoy another romp. Well, time for that later, now he had documents to secrete, seeds, as he thought of them, seeds that could grow very rapidly.

Lieberman could have guessed where his man was going. As he saw Theurer's cab slow, and then stop along Tiergartenstrasse, he told his driver to simply drive by at normal speed and then turn in at the next corner. On foot again, Lieberman walked back down the street opposite the expanse of the Tiergarten and saw that Theurer was walking away, toward the back of the block of offices occupied by the Kriegsmarine and the Abwehr. A moment later Theurer disappeared into a long alleyway between the government buildings that faced onto Tirpitzufer. When he got to the spot where his man had disappeared, Lieberman looked down the alleyway in time to see a door open and close about fifty yards down and on the right.

When he reached the door, Lieberman tried the handle, but it was locked. With a pocket flashlight, he examined the lock and saw that it was a simple device. From his pocket, Lieberman produced a set of picks, and, in less than a minute, he was inside the building. Now was the time for stealth. The empty corridors would echo his footsteps, so he pulled off his shoes and, tying the laces to his belt, he walked on in his stocking feet.

Inside, the hallways were dimly lit by wall sconces placed every fifty feet or so. From somewhere above and ahead, he heard the steady tread of a man's footsteps. If that were Theurer, he was not making any secret of his presence in the building. Lieberman knew that there was a guard at the front desk during the night, but he was not certain if anyone made rounds, checking on the offices. His answer came a moment later when he brushed the wall on his right and a chain rattled. The chain hung from the wall and held a key at its end. It was a watchman's key, used by whoever came around at regular intervals. The watchman would have a round clock-like device hanging from a leather strap on his shoulder. When he reached a specific location on his rounds, he would insert the key into this device and turn the key. There was round paper with time of day printed on it inside the device, and, when the key was turned, a punch mark would be made in the paper. If a problem was discovered after the watchman left, one only had to match the punch marks and time to know where the watchman had been on his rounds.

Lieberman now had to be doubly alert. He had no way of knowing where the night watchman might be. Did he have a routine or did he switch things up to stave off boredom. He could be back at his desk or just coming down the corridor at this moment to punch his clock. He would have to chance it. Theurer must be heading upstairs to the area where his office was. Lieberman knew the building's layout fairly well. One of his nephews, so blond that he had Aryan stamped all over him, despite being Jewish, had befriended and then slept with Theurer's secretary Hilda.

The White Raven

Hilda was in her early thirties, unmarried, and according to Lieberman's nephew, destined to stay that way. It was not that she was unattractive; she had russet blond hair and full breasts with a deep cleavage that she showed to her best advantage in open necked blouses. Hilda's problem was that once she started talking she never shut up. Stefan, Lieberman's nephew, had endured it all just to get a description of Theurer's office and to learn who occupied the other offices on his floor.

Lieberman went up the fire stairs to the second floor. This is where Hilda had indicated that Theurer had his office. Easing open the fire door, Lieberman looked down the long corridor and saw a figure walking slowly away from him. Office doors were set at regular intervals on both sides of the corridor. At intervals were placed giant urns holding potted palms that grew to reach the ceiling. Probably they had been growing there since Bismarck. Between the foliage several upholstered chairs waited for the various supplicants who came to visit the occupants of the offices. Lieberman glanced down at the paper sketch he had of the floor's layout to get his bearings. There was a square of light cast in the middle of the hallway, and the figure stopped and turned toward it. Lieberman could see that this must be the watchman. The man approached the open doorway and spoke to someone inside. That must be Theurer, he thought. Lieberman could not hear the conversation, but Theurer must have said something amusing for the watchman gave out a loud laugh and then saluted Theurer before he went back to his rounds. Lieberman had to assume that the watchman was on an hourly schedule, so he needed to move.

Just as Lieberman was about to step into the hallway, he saw Theurer come out of his office. The bureaucrat looked up and down the hallway to were the watchman had disappeared, the man's footsteps receding as he descended toward the front desk.

Theurer had a small sheaf of papers in his hand. Deciding that no one was watching in any of the offices, he swiftly walked toward where Lieberman was hiding and turned in at another office door. According to the sketch that Lieberman had, this was the office of a man named Schilling.

As he watched, the lights in the office came on. Lieberman crept forward and found a spot behind one of the massive palms from where he could observe Theurer. Like all of the offices on this floor, Schilling's was in fact two rooms. There was an outer office where, according to Hilda's information, Schilling's secretary and, it was thought, in-office lover, a woman named Senta worked. The inner office was Schilling's private domain, and it was the door to this space that Theurer was now opening. Lieberman heard the snick of the lock. Theurer must have had a key.

The lights of the inner office snapped on, and Lieberman observed Theurer walk straight to a row of file boxes. Each of the file boxes was about three inches wide, and they were arranged like a set of encyclopedias with alphabetized tabs. Lieberman watched as Theurer ran his finger along the spines of the volumes and selected the eighth one from the left. Moving quickly, Theurer placed the file on Schilling's desk and opened the cover. After a moment, he took the papers in his hand and placed them in the box and returned it to the shelf. These documents, which he had painstakingly constructed using purloined signatures and official Wehrmacht stationery, were his insurance policy.

Germans like insurance in all forms. Life, property, fire, annuities, they went with the national character to provide for the future. But Theurer had long ago sensed that there was no future for the Germany that existed in the vacuum of the Versailles Treaty. The Nazis knew this too, but for them it was a chance to turn the nation into a thieves' bazaar, an official rape of the state for the benefit of the National Socialist elite. But he knew that wouldn't work. He had chosen sides, and, although he did not believe in Marxism or the Bolshevik dialectic, he did believe that the people should have a say in their government. He thought Germans deserved something better after Versailles and who better than a man like Albrecht Theurer to start the avalanche. But even as he sowed destruction in the ranks of the SS, these documents, when found in the office of a high-ranking army officer, would do the same within the power structure at the headquarters in Zossen.

The light in the office went out, and Lieberman watched as Theurer walked back down the hall and out of the building, all the while whistling softly to himself. He just had time to get back to his room at the Adlon. Gretchen would still be under the effects of the Amatol.

Lieberman waited and, hearing nothing in the building, made his way into Schilling's office. He quickly found the documents and spread them out across the surface of Schilling's desk. In the semi-darkness he scanned what was there, and, knowing the German reliance on documentation, saw the importance of the papers before him. He would have to risk a light.

From his inside pocket Lieberman withdrew a small, short-focus camera designed by a fellow Latvian. The tiny camera was a prototype VEF (*Valsts Elektrotehniskā Fabrika*) device designed to fit in the palm of the hand. Walter Zapp, the Baltic German inventor and designer of the camera, had asked Lieberman to try it out and let them know how to improve the design. As a fellow Latvian, they had known one another since before the 1914 war and had that mechanical curiosity so endemic among the natives of the Baltics. At the moment, however, all Lieberman was concerned with was not being caught making photographs of documents in a Reich office. The camera came with a short length of cord, which, when extended to the surface of the document being photographed, ensured a crisp image.

Lieberman waited and listened, hoping that the watchman was busy elsewhere in the building. Then, at the risk of being caught, he flipped on the desk lamp and, passing each sheet under the brightest spot of illumination, extended the camera's cord and snapped away. In less than thirty seconds, he had imaged all of the papers, snapped off the light and let out his breath. He listened again, but as before heard nothing from the hallway. Satisfied that he had been unobserved, he returned the file to its place on the shelf, making sure that it was precisely aligned with its neighbors. In another thirty seconds he was out of the office and was making his way back the way he had come when he heard the slow shuffling of feet and the jangling of the watchman's keys.

Traveling Man

Viktor Ryshkov woke slowly, his head aching from whatever they had given him. Somewhere inside his skull he could hear the sound of sheep lowing and, now and again, the moan of wind coursing through distant trees. He tried to move, but found that his legs were not free, tied to the rough wooden frame of the bed on which he was laying. Slowly the world around him began to emerge. He was in, what, a warehouse, no, the smell of manure was too strong, a barn. What time it might be he could not tell for certain, but tiny pinpricks of light, from holes in the slanted slate roof high above, gave the impression of daylight. He was confused. Ryshkov tried to remember, but the last image in his brain was of being pushed into a Paris taxicab—then, nothing. Whatever they had dosed him with; it must have been powerful.

As consciousness returned, so did a gnawing in his stomach. When last had he eaten? He turned slightly, and there was a burning sensation that ran down his spine to his coccyx. The drug had not completely worn off. There, next to the bed, stood a hewn wooden chair with a metal pitcher and mug. With feeble arms he reached for the pitcher, nearly knocking it onto the floor. He tried again, snatched the handle and drew it toward him. A cautious sniff told him that the contents were just water. Ignoring the cup he tilted the pitcher toward his mouth and gulped at the liquid, spilling as much as he drank on his shirtfront.

"Feeling better, now are we?"

At the sound of the voice, Ryshkov dropped the pitcher, which hit the stone floor, ringing out like a bell. His eyes barely made out the shape of a man sitting some ten feet away. A match struck, and, in the flame, he saw a face. He knew that face, but from where?

"Monsieur Ryshkov, you may remember me. My name is René, we shared a cab together."

"Where am I? What did you do to me?" The words came out slowly and in Russian. Then Ryshkov switched to halting French and repeated his question.

"Yes, well, as to that, we are sorry about that, but we couldn't have you wandering off into the arms of the NKVD now could we?" This was a different voice in the darkness, older and more constrained. "René, help our guest to sit up, and perhaps you can have Marie bring us some of her magnificent coffee."

René went over to the bed and helped Ryshkov to sit up, placing several straw-filled pillows behind his back. He went off and, several minutes later, returned with a tray of coffee and fresh brioches.

"Ah, that is better, thank you René," said the man. "Please help yourself Monsieur. Let me begin by introducing myself, my name is Mr. Black, which you can correctly assume is not my real name, but for our purposes must suffice. I, along with René and the other gentlemen whom you met at your hotel, are your benefactors. So, please, if you will cooperate with us, you will soon find yourself on your way to a new life with a new identity."

Raymond Kingman took to his role as Mr. Black and kept his tone light and unctuous.

"How long have I been here?" protested Ryshkov.

René responded brusquely, "Several days, it does not matter."

Ryshkov was about to speak when Kingman intervened. Monsieur, we have no intention of harming you, why should we when we went to so much trouble to extract you from you former employers. Please, sit back, drink some of Marie's coffee and have a brioche, while I explain to you where things stand. We need just a bit more information from you. Help us this morning, and I guarantee that by evening you will be on your way out of France to a new life, otherwise, we may have to announce your presence here at this lovely old Norman farmstead."

Ryshkov looked from one man to the other, trying decide if they were going to kill him. But why keep him alive for days, as they had done, if they were going to do that? His head was swimming. Then the older man spoke again.

"Viktor, I will call you Viktor until we have arranged a new passport for you. Viktor, how would you like to leave France for say, South America? That would be a good distance from Moscow. Let me see. I think we might be able to arrange passage to Uruguay, with say a Greek passport. The Greeks aren't at war with anyone, least not with anyone in South America."

René brought out a flashlight from his pocket and handed it to Kingman. "Now," said the older man, "perhaps you can take a look at some photographs. We would like to know if you recognize anyone in them and, if so, what you recall about them."

Ryshkov looked up at the man, a dog seeking to please his master.

"Take your time, anything at all? Once you have done that we will take you back to a safe place in Paris, and soon you can be on your way to sunny Uruguay."

"That one, his work name is Oskar," said the Russian.

"Tell me about him."

Friends for Lunch

"Well what do you think?" Karl Lieberman stood next to Harry Braham while he told Braham about the Theurer's actions in Schilling's office. Before them were enlargements of the photographs that Lieberman had taken in Schilling's office.

"Well, Theurer was right about one thing. He is a deskman; he hasn't the guts or the clout to pull this off on his own. Still, he knows the weaknesses of all of the Party higher-ups, and if he can play on those jealousies, he just may succeed. I expect that he is putting together the means for Göring to confront Hitler with the plot by the SS. No doubt, the documents supported by Ryshkov's testimony would spell the immediate arrest of Himmler and Heydrich. Yes, Göring is the likely messenger, but I doubt that Theurer will be the one to deliver them to fat Hermann. No, it would have to be Konrad Patzig, the head of the Abwehr."

"But why put them in Schilling's office?"

"Theurer is being cautious right up to the end. If either the Gestapo or the SD is on to him, there will be nothing to find in his files. And if, somehow, they are found in Schilling's office, well, then Schilling will be in the cellars spilling his guts. In any event with Ryshkov in tow who would bother to try to prove their authenticity? Göring would have the army and the Abwehr on his side. The generals hate the SS and would love to eliminate it; then they could manipulate Hitler into doing what is more practicable for Germany and more palatable for the world. Hitler's imperiousness will be greatly diminished without his Praetorians."

Lieberman said, "But what would induce Ryshkov to go along? Surely he must know he is doomed."

"He is doomed either way. The NKVD and the SD will both want him dead. Theurer needs to move fast. He has always wanted a show just before the Nuremburg rally. According to Gisela, Christian von Teischen is to accompany Hitler to a send-off for the German participants in the Air Olympiad. The event has been scheduled for late August, before the Party rally in Nuremberg."

Lieberman looked at Braham, "You don't mean to just hand the Russian over do you? That would be pretty cold, just leading him to the gallows like that."

Braham hesitated. "Perhaps not, but I don't have time to grow a conscience, and anyway I'm not sure what our other options are at this moment. I always knew that Theurer was playing a deep game here. It is quite Machiavellian. Ryshkov remains a danger to him either way. Certainly, a confession by one Viktor Ryshkov, a known NKVD officer, as to the complicity of senior SS officers with the NKVD to topple Hitler will be telling. It will be even better if he named one of them as Heydrich himself. But I suspect that Ryshkov's appearance, in any event, is destined to be short-lived."

"And so even in death he taints all of them," said Lieberman.

"We need to discover who the messenger will be. My guess is that Theurer will want the head of the Abwehr to present the evidence to someone Hitler trusts. My bet is on Göring. We need to keep tabs on Theurer. Can your people handle that?"

"Alexi has a brother."

Gisela von Teischen arrived at the Adlon just a few moments after one o'clock. Reinhardt Stiffler and Harry Braham were seated at a table and rose to greet her. The dining room was just a trifle warm on that summer afternoon, but the sprays of fragrant blossoms set about the room made it redolent of a garden.

Gisela held out her gloved hand to Braham, who again bowed and kissed it. Turning to Stiffler she gave him a quick buss on the cheek before taking the chair that he held for her.

"I am so glad you could join us," said Braham. She nodded somewhat warily and smiled at the two men. As they took their seats, Braham added, "You know, Reinhardt, I had dinner recently with another old comrade from those Warsaw days, Karl Lieberman." As he spoke, he looked at Gisela and thought he detected a touch of color in her face.

"Karl Lieberman, yes, I remember him. Dinner? Here in Berlin?"

"No, in Paris. Germany is not much to Karl's liking these days. He used to come quite often, you know, back when he was working with Sir Basil Zaharoff. Now Karl is helping me with a few things, especially the upcoming Air Olympiad. As you know, he knows everyone worth knowing." Braham kept his gaze level; Gisela who nodded imperceptibly.

Stiffler turned to Gisela, "Sorry, if we get off into old war stories, I hope you don't mind?"

"Mind? Of course not, I am fascinated by old stories," she replied.

For the next hour and a half, as waiters came and went, filling wine glasses and bringing their orders, the two old comrades regaled the countess with tales of their flying adventures.

"Harry, as much as I would like to sit and reminisce all day, I am forced to return to duty. Perhaps we could meet for a drink tonight. In the meantime, I must excuse myself. I hate to leave you countess, but I am sure that Harry will see that you get home."

Stiffler rose, and, as he gathered his cap and gloves, he bent over and brushed Gisela's cheek with his lips. She smiled and, turning slightly, followed him out of the room with her eyes. Turning back to Braham, she presented an entirely different demeanor, all business. "I am getting nervous. That man Kleist seems to know something and worse, he seems to be very much at Christian's elbow. I seem to see him everywhere."

"Well, at least he is not here at the moment. But, you make a good point. You know, it is a lovely afternoon for a stroll. Perhaps we might drive out to the Grunewald and enjoy the day."

Gisela looked at him appraisingly and then rose. "Give me a moment to freshen up, and I will meet you in the lobby."

Braham signaled to the waiter for the bill and looked about the room. Three pairs of eyes seemed to suddenly avert themselves. He was right to be cautious; he only hoped that whoever had put their luncheon under surveillance had not yet connected all the dots.

Gisela met him in the lobby, but instead of going out the front entrance Braham guided her to the doors on the east side of the hotel. Stepping from the Adlon out on to the street, Gisela and

Braham walked down the Wilhelmstrasse to Behrenstrasse where Braham raised his hand for a taxi. From out of the stream of cars on the street a taxi appeared. Braham held the door open for Gisela, and they stepped inside.

"Good afternoon, Karl. Have any trouble?"

A startled Gisela looked up to see the familiar face of Karl Lieberman at the wheel of the cab.

"No, the Rzigalinski brothers worked it out fine. One of them is in another car following us, just in case the Gestapo was able to follow you."

"Karl, Karl, what is going on, I thought you were in Paris?' Gisela's voice was trembling with anxiety.

"Countess, hopefully so does the Gestapo. But this little sleight of hand with the cabs was the only way the three of us could speak," explained Lieberman.

"Karl is right countess. Things are beginning to happen, and you and, I am afraid, even Reinhardt, are in danger. You know that you are being followed. There were several in the dining room of the Adlon. You noticed some of them, didn't you?"

"It is Theurer, isn't it?" Gisela said flatly.

"Yes, Karl retrieved some documents last night that spell things out for us." As they drove, Braham filled her in on the meaning of the documents Lieberman had retrieved.

It was warm in the Grunewald, the July sun penetrated the canopy of leaves on the linden trees and scattered light in watery patches. Lieberman had found a place to park off one of the narrower roads. Fifty yards behind them, the Rzigalinski brothers parked and watched their backs while the three of them spoke.

"Countess, what you, or shall I say the White Raven, have achieved up to now has been done without attracting any attention to yourself. Up to now your very station in life, and your being a favorite of people like Goebbels, keeps you above suspicion. Theurer and his plans will change all that," said Braham. "Kleist appears to be taking an interest in you and where you go and who you meet. In order to save you, we have to make sure that Kleist gets Theurer with no strings attached."

"But how?"

"Theurer is planning to topple the SS, especially Himmler. Even Goebbels hates the bespectacled pig farmer, but everyone in Hitler's inner circle plays along, afraid to take any action against another for fear that the rest will gang up against the one that makes the first move. Theurer wants me to produce Ryshkov just before the Nuremburg rally. Theurer will then make sure the man's NKVD connections will be obvious to everyone. Using Ryshkov's so called testimony as to the NKVD. Theurer will then accuse Himmler and Heydrich of complicity in a Russian plot. Ryshkov, if he is still breathing, will testify at some kind of kangaroo court and, shortly thereafter be killed. Theurer has to close off that avenue, because a living Ryshkov would be too great a liability.

Once Ryshkov is dead Theurer plans to implicate your husband in the Russian's death, as evidence of the extent of the corruption and disloyalty within the SS. How else could they explain the dead Russian? A loyal SS man must have done it. Any denials from Christian would sound hollow. From what we have seen in Theurer's files he had planned this long ago. The only problem was that Theurer could not control the paranoia of Stalin and his war against the Russian middle class. Ryshkov found out what was happening in Moscow and knew that had to escape. Once the NKVD stumbled onto his Kulak heritage, he was already a dead man. Then you come into the picture. You helped him go, and Theurer found out, probably through an informer, maybe even the woman who runs the flower shop, we will never be sure. Since that moment you have been in Theurer's power. Theurer needs the Russian, unless the NKVD kills him first. The Russians want their defector liquidated."

"But what should I do now? What can I do?" Gisela asked forlornly.

"For now, you just have to go along." Braham looked into her eyes, but could not read their expression. "There is no other way. Theurer has to believe that you still believe in his plan."

"Harry, I don't know. If what you say is true, I am already as good as dead. But why are you so committed to this? Why don't you just walk away, what does an American like you care about our local nest of snakes?"

"Because, countess, deep down, I can't let the Theurer win. As you say, he is a snake. The world seems to be full of them, but that doesn't entitle them to send innocent people to the wall. Even Ryshkov, as dirty as he is in the espionage business doesn't deserve to be sacrificed for another *new world order*. Since Theurer knows about what you did for the Russian, he will sell you out in an instant, if he is cornered. If Kleist gets to him and puts the screws to him, he will sing like a bird and the bodies will pile up in the courtyard of Gestapo headquarters."

"But you could still walk away, you and Karl and those boys with the cars. Why risk so much for people that you barely know?" Her eyes were moist now, and the words caught in her throat.

"Because of that man over there," Braham pointed toward Lieberman, "and all those who have gone before, men and women who just wanted a quiet life and found themselves on the wrong end of a rifle. Because of Reinhardt and a man called Dietrich and his Polish wife and all the people who are being dragged into the maelstrom that the Nazis have created. I can't save everyone, but even one person saved from the horrors that I see each day on the streets of this country becomes a victory."

"And," he hesitated and looked into her eyes again, "because no matter what has happened between us, or what future we may have, I care about what happens to you. Karl pledged to keep you safe, and as his friend I have to honor that pledge as well. Sometimes we don't have the luxury of picking our battles, they find us. So here we are, and now we have little time to make this work for us. If your husband's new pal, Kleist, stumbles on to what Theurer is planning before we are ready to act, then everyone he has been in contact with, including you and Reinhardt, and eventually all of us, would be scooped up and tossed into the cellars. Right now I have to figure how to make this come out right."

Gisela von Teischen looked at Braham and then at the scene beyond them, the trees, their leaves fluttering in the breeze, now green, now gold, as the sunlight filtered into the forest. Why couldn't this be her reality?

Red and Black

Karl Lieberman slid into the wooden booth at the back of the Stahlarbeiter, a *bierstube* in the Berlin suburb of Wedding, where Braham had been warming a seat for the last hour.

"How are you getting about in this land of the Aryan Brotherhood?" Braham asked.

"I look like a worker, so no one bothers me, especially in this neighborhood. How about you, did you shake your Gestapo tail?"

"I didn't have to do much, once he got the gist of where I was heading, he seemed to lose interest. My bet is that he is back at the Adlon having a beer in the lobby bar."

Lieberman guffawed, and he looked around the room once more. It was filled with men dressed like him: battered jacket, worn out shoes and peaked worker's caps. He caught the barmaid's eye, and she made her way through the archipelago of tables toward them. A large red-faced woman, she was dressed in a Bavarian dirndl and equipped with massive breasts and muscular forearms, a coarse rendition of the girl on the label of the St. Pauli bottle. She waddled toward their table, "Ja?"

The White Raven

"*Zwei bier, bitte*," ordered Braham.

For a moment she looked at the two of them, wondering what sort they might be. She had served the better dressed one earlier, American she thought, from the look of his clothes, but this other one, what was he, a Pole, or maybe a Russian, Hungarian perhaps? Not German, she thought, even with the haircut and blue eyes. Well, she didn't care much, she had seen every type in this place over the years, but he should watch out that the bullyboys in the street didn't catch him out. With a toss of her head she said, "*Ja, sofort.*"

When she had gone Lieberman replied to Braham, "I, at least, have an Italian passport. It gets me by; you know how enamored Hitler and his crowd are with Mussolini and his black shirts."

"Do you speak Italian?"

Lieberman smiled and hooked a thumb over his shoulder, "Well, let's say, I know a lot more than those thugs on the street."

The beers arrived. Monster sized glasses the size of small pitchers, strong and dark and laden with the power to set fire to the soul, even if that soul was not born in the Reich. Braham raised his glass to Lieberman.

"*Prost!*" To which Lieberman nodded and swallowed a third of his beer.

"Did you see Stiffler?"

"Yes, he was at the Messerschmitt factory going over the final checks of the Me-108s that are going to be flown in the Olympiad. He is not a very happy man, Karl."

"Why? I thought that this resurgence of the air force under Göring would have pleased him."

Braham took a moment to look around the room and light another Gauloises. "Stiffler is a flier, not a politician. He is dismayed at what he sees around him. He told me that under the Nazis," Braham lowered his voice to a whisper, "he said that under the Nazis the government is really just confederation of warlords, petty gangsters. Each of these Gauleiters has the power of a minor king in his own territory. And at the top sits Hitler and his coterie of knights, Himmler, Göring, the gimp, Goebbels and each of them is trying to cut the other's throats."

"He said all that?"

"Yes, and more. He really did not hold back, he was the old Reinhardt of Warsaw days. Each Party official has his hand in the till. The worst it seems is Himmler, who is trying to make the SS into an industry and government of its own under the leadership of Hitler. I was there with him for two days, and, between giving me a tour of the facility and taking me on a demonstration flight in one of the 108s, which by the way is a very sweet airplane, we talked. If what we saw in those plans that Ryshkov delivered is an improvement on what I flew, the rest of Europe's air forces better get busy building monoplane fighters."

Now it was Lieberman's turn to become cautious. "Let's make the barmaid happy so she doesn't spend her time snooping." Lieberman raised his empty glass, and a moment latter the buxom *fraulein* was delivering another round of beer and a dish of pickles.

When she left, treating the pair to a flip of her skirt, Braham went on, "Karl, I feel like we are being had here by the Theurer. Perhaps he is just like the others, just another minor warlord looking to make his kill before he is killed. It's not that I don't agree with him about getting rid of the SS to pave a way for change, but it's just too dangerous. Right now that snake Kleist is trying to nail Theurer. Once they get Theurer in the cellars of the Alex, he will give up everyone. No, I think we have to cut our losses."

"Well, that may have to happen sooner than we think," Lieberman added. "Inga Carlson has a new admirer."

"Who?"

"You know, the florist who passed Ryshkov on to Gisela. Well, somehow she and Kleist have recently become a hot item."

"Jesus!'

"It seems that Kleist has taken to spending two afternoons a week visiting with the lady, but not to buy flowers. Alexi Rzigalinski drives by the place on his taxi runs and spotted him going inside. One afternoon he decided to park down the block and watch. Sure enough, around three in the afternoon, a black Horch pulled up and out stepped Otto Kleist. He went in, and a few minutes later Alexi sees the lovely Inga pull the curtains in the upstairs bedroom. Alexi caught the glimpse of a black sleeve and hand about her waist."

"Well, you can't blame her. If Kleist has put the fear of God into her along with his dick, her loyalty to Gisela couldn't match the girl's fear of the SS. You need to let Gisela know."

Braham looked into the depths of the glass of beer in front of him. "I think it is time to shut things down and run like hell, and if Theurer gets burned in the process, so be it. There is something else. Our Russian friend identified a photo of a Hans Dieter Krauss as being a Russian mole known as Oskar. And get this, Krauss has an office in the same building as does Theurer."

The White Raven

"Jesus!"

"You can say that again," said Braham.

"You don't think they are connected do you?"

"No, but it is likely that whatever Theurer has been up to, somehow Moscow knows something. Worse, if this Oskar knows about Theurer he is likely to know about the White Raven. Nobody is safe."

Lieberman looked at his friend, "How good is the information that Theurer has provided? Do you think he is being played by this Oskar?"

Before Braham could answer there was a loud bang outside the entrance to the *bierstube* followed by some angry shouts. A second later the door flew open and a pair of blood spattered Brownshirts stumbled in and fell on the floor. "Communists," shouted one of the men and pointed toward the street. "Communists!" he shouted again and then collapsed.

"Jesus Christ!" said Braham. "We need to get out of here, before we find ourselves on the wrong end of everything."

Braham and Lieberman jumped up and pushed their way to the rear of the place, while most of the patrons, many wearing swastika armbands and Party lapel buttons, rushed to the front entrance to do battle.

There was a narrow hall that led past a pay telephone to the toilets and beyond to a rear door. Braham gagged at the reek of urine coming from the toilets as he pushed out of the back door. With Lieberman close behind, him they found themselves in a narrow space between two buildings, and a brick wall that sectioned off a small yard. Looking down the alley, Braham saw what looked like a crowd of men surging toward the entrance to the bar. There was nothing for it but to make it over the wall.

Lieberman found a crate that would give them a two-foot boost to the top of the wall. As he stepped up to go over, he cursed, "Goddammit! There is broken glass up here cemented into the bricks."

Lieberman looked back at Braham and pointed at a narrow plank leaning next to the bar.

"Hand me that."

Braham reached back, retrieved the piece of wood, and at the same time heard the sounds of shots fired from the front of the bar. Lieberman took the plank and, with a sweeping movement, smashed the shards of glass on the top of the wall.

"Look, I will jam this into the glass and hold it as I roll over the top. You hang on to it and do the same."

In a moment Lieberman was over the top and beckoning Braham to follow. As soon as Braham had swung over the top, he dropped to the other side, holding the plank, as a bullet slammed into the other side of the wall.

"Let's go!" Braham followed Lieberman down one alley and then across another street until they found the U-Bahn station and took the next train into Stadtmitte.

As the train rocked along, the two men remained silent, much like their fellow passengers. It was late and the people on this train were the tired. They worked hard for the few marks they could earn. They were the disaffected, those who had voted for the Nazis in hope of a better life. Perhaps they felt they were going to get it, but they would learn too late at what cost. They got off the train just on the north side of the Tiergarten.

"I had thought that the SS had gotten rid of all the Reds in Berlin," said Lieberman.

"Well that crowd tonight did not seem subdued. Hitlerism may be in force in most of the country, but it appears that it has not taken hold everywhere. In any event, it would not have done for us to be part of that mob scene."

Braham turned to his friend, "Let me have the photographs. I will be leaving town for a few days. When I get back, we may have to pay an after-hours call on Dr. Theurer's office. Can you manage that?"

Lieberman gave a wry smile, "Not too much of a problem, now that I know the layout."

"Good, I'll be in touch."

From somewhere in the distance, the strains of the *Horst Wessel Liede* could be heard, and then the pair melted into the night.

"You are very late," came a sleepy voice from the bedroom. Braham had been as quiet as he could be coming into his suite at the Adlon. A few Reichsmarks to the right porter, and he had his run of the back stairs of the hotel, avoiding both the Gestapo watchers in the lobby and the hotel's staff of house detectives. Gisela von Teischen was a well-known face at the hotel, and finding her way to Braham's room had proved no difficulty.

"I might have been a lot later," he said pointing a warning finger up to the bedroom chandelier. Who knew if someone was listening, but it was an even bet that if the Gestapo or SD were taking an interest in an American visitor, they might just as well have been listening to conversations in his room. "I need to wash, I must smell of beer and cigarettes."

The White Raven

Gisela frowned and threw back the sheet. "I don't mind," she whispered. She was naked and waiting for him to join her. For a moment he stood there, looking at her in awe, his appetite whetted by the languorous movement of her hips as she reached for him.

"So," she whispered in his ear as he wrapped her in his arms, "why were you so late. You said you would be back by ten at the latest. I drank almost a whole bottle of Piper-Heidsick waiting for you."

Braham ran his tongue up the nape of her neck and kissed her earlobe, she shuddered. "Karl and I ran into some trouble and had to take the long way back."

Twenty minutes later they lay spent in each other's arms, breathing heavily as their ecstasy ebbed. Gisela propped herself up on one arm and looked at Braham. He was a puzzle to her, moreover, she marveled at the fact that she was so forward in coming to his room in this town where everyone seemed to be watching everyone else. With her hand, she began to stroke his chest.

"Harry, what am I going to do?"

"Now?" he asked.

"No, I mean, I can't just stop what I have been doing. For the last two years, since the Nazis came to power, I have been helping people. What I do makes a difference. While I play the dutiful Nazi wife, in some ways, I think I have been saving lives. This thing with Theurer and that snake Kleist cannot be allowed to undo that. Right now, there is a family, Jewish of course, the Feldstein's. I met him a long time ago, when it was fine to have Jewish acquaintances. He is, or was, at the Max Plank Institute, until they threw him out. That he is a scientist is important, but he has a wife and two children. The Nazis will drive them to death. They are as important, but as a family—a family that needs to get away from this insanity while they can. I can help them, and who knows how many others. But Theurer will bring it all crashing down, either with or without the meddling of Kleist's *Sicherheitsdienst.*"

Braham opened his eyes, looked at the ceiling, and then at her. He reached out a hand and gently pulled her toward him until his lips were just by her ear, and softly he whispered to her.

———

Otto Kleist was tiring of the game. Even his trysts with the lovely Inga did little to mollify him. He had been following the man for two weeks, and there was nothing to report. An hour or so in the cellars of Columbia House and Albrecht Theurer would be singing his guts out. That was how he would handle it, but Heydrich had ruled that method out of bounds—for now. No, the head of the SD wanted to know everything about Herr Doktor Theurer before he had him arrested, and so Kleist and his men had to sit and watch, follow and make notes. The problem was, the man had not done anything out of the ordinary.

So on this afternoon he sat in the front seat of a Horch 780, the windows rolled down to let the breeze blow through the car. He reached into his pocket to retrieve a packet of Neue Front cigarettes. Far be it for him to smoke a decadent American or one of those filthy French brands. If he were going to defy the Party's admonitions on smoking, at least he would use a brand that profited the new order. Hitler did not allow smoking in his presence, and all of his underlings who enjoyed tobacco had to do so on the sly. Kleist, dressed as he was in his black Totenkopf uniform, made it a point not to smoke in public, but here in the car, out of the sight of any passersby, he felt he was safe enough, anyway, cops the world over will tell you that ninety-nine percent of surveillance is a bore.

Kleist had followed Theurer on his rounds from office to office from the Foreign Ministry to the Bendlerblock, where the several senior military officers had their headquarters. For several hours it was business as usual for Theurer. He did take time for a lunch appointment with a young woman at the Palast-Hotel restaurant. There, Kleist had SS-Scharführer Ritter, his driver, drop him at the side entrance, and he raced to take a table in the lobby bar to keep an eye on the doktor. As it happened, Theurer, dapper as ever in a faun colored suit and brown and white shoes, spent the entire lunch with one hand below the table ostensibly squeezing the young woman's thigh. He would have to find out who she was, but Kleist's suspicions were not focused on her.

Theurer and the young woman walked out of the restaurant together and stood before the elevator bank. For a long moment Kleist suspected that they were going upstairs to engage in a bit of post-prandial romance. But just as the elevator arrived, the woman leaned forward, kissed Theurer on the cheek and stepped into the elevator cab, leaving Theurer to make his way out on to Potsdamer Platz. Kleist followed on foot and watched as the man sauntered down Elbertstrasse, seemingly without a care in the world.

Ritter had been alert and slowed to a crawl next to his boss while they watched Theurer hail a taxi. Ten minutes later Theurer was back at work, a loyal servant of the Reich. Was Kleist wrong about him? No, the man was and had long been an Abwehr officer; maybe he had tumbled to him. Kleist had enough for one day. Ritter or Wolfram could take over and watch the man this evening. He had something else in mind for the afternoon. Twenty minutes later the Horch was parked on Karlsruhestrasse near the front door of an elegant florist shop.

———

Albrecht Theurer lived with the suspicion that he was being followed and observed everywhere he went; now he was certain of it. He was too old a bunny not to have noticed the same SS officer near two of the places he had visited that morning. He recognized the man from the Konzerthaus, and, when he saw the same man sitting uncomfortably in the lobby of the Palast-Hotel, Theurer had cut short his plans for an afternoon with a lovely and extremely willing young woman, the niece of a friend who was looking for a job in the government. Well, he would have to see about her later. In the meantime, the surveillance was getting a bit tight. Less than ten days until the opening of the Party rally in Nuremberg. More troubling was that he had not spoken to his boss, Captain Patzig in several days.

The White Raven

Snake Pit

Captain Konrad Patzig could barely take in the exquisite scenery as his car descended from the Eagle's Lair. Berchtesgaden and the Tyrolean Alps spread out before him, and yet his eyes were clouded with fury and indignation. To be treated that way; to be humiliated in front of those SS vipers was not how he, a senior naval officer, was to be treated. And then to top it off, to be told off in such vile terms by the Führer himself, right before the very men he loathed—impossible! What did they expect? Did they think he would go off and swallow his pistol? No! At least fat Hermann had a good word for him at the end. He would have to trust to that, if anything.

The conference had been scheduled at Hitler's private residence lodged high above Berchtesgaden. The Führer liked to have all of his chiefs assembled under one roof in a relaxed manner to discuss politics and strategy. There was nothing relaxing about any of it. The lesser guests, like Patzig, were put up in the Wittlesbach hotel in the town. The hotel had quickly become a shrine to Nazidom and was festooned with swastika banners hanging from the eaves. The heavy Tyrolean furnishings were of an earlier age and quite in keeping with the Party's fixation on Germanic lore and nostalgia. Oil paintings of alpine scenes adorned the walls along with the obligatory photos and portraits of the Führer. Patzig and the others lodged there were made very comfortable. No one among the hotel's staff knew whether these guests were ascending stars, and currying favor with authority was as much a Nazi trait as goose-stepping and giving the outstretched arm salute, and so their every whim was catered to. Each morning the hotel guests were ferried up to the massive chalet by convoys of gleaming Benz and Horch motorcars. Party insiders, such as Göring, had their own places on the mountain, and a few special guests were afforded the Führer's hospitality and were put up in the Eagle's Nest.

Each morning the guests arrived and were walked up the stone steps flanked by immaculately uniformed SS guards standing at attention with gleaming weapons in their hands. It was an intimidating experience. Everything was done in a slightly oversized way so that the guest, if one could assume that description, were made to feel just a bit overwhelmed and intimidated. As the head of the Abwehr, Patzig was not regarded as an insider and had been excluded from the small dinner party held on the evening of the nineteenth. Hitler and his cronies ranked him as little more than an army divisional commander. So, on the morning of the twentieth, his car followed the line of more notable attendees up the long road to the house. As his car swept to a stop, a white-gloved SS guard smoothly opened his door and held it for him to exit. Patzig was in full naval uniform, deep navy blue with gold stripes on his sleeves, which contrasted with the field grey and green of the army officers who preceded him up the flight of stairs.

Patzig had been to the Eagle's Nest twice before, to deliver military-intelligence estimates prepared by his department on the readiness of the French and Czech armed forces. This was the first time that he had been asked to participate in a meeting dealing with Party politics and what the Führer might say at the impeding Party rally in Nuremberg. Patzig came prepared with a briefcase full of intelligence summaries and estimates. Patzig knew that he could expect no friends in the meeting, even among the generals who had been regular beneficiaries of the efforts of his service.

In a long, timbered ceilinged room, maps of the continent had been rolled out on a long table before a wide expanse of windows. Beyond was a wide, flagged veranda, which ended in a low wall. Beyond lay the expanse of mountains and sky. A young woman dressed in a red and white dirndl and flat-topped black hat with streamers down the back sat atop the wall. She was playing with a small dog and now and again shielded her eyes against the bright sun with her hand as she stared back at the house.

Patzig looked about but saw no chairs. Apparently no one was to take any comfort or ease during this meeting. Among the assembled guests Patzig recognized several of the generals present: Von Brauchitsch, with his close cropped hair, and Werner von Fritsch stood chatting. He was surprised to see Fritz von Papen, cadaver-like, standing alone gazing toward the horizon. There were several others, probably *Gauleiters* from the look of them, hawk faced men sporting Party pins in their lapels. Heinrich Himmler and his deputy, Reinhard Heydrich, were both standing by the head of table when Patzig walked in. Patzig was surprised to see that neither man was in uniform, preferring, it seemed, to wear suits of grey and green worsted wool. They looked like a pair of university professors off on a Tyrolean holiday rather than the masterminds of the Nazis purge of liberal thinkers, non-conformers and Jews. As Patzig approached the table, Göring, dressed like a Tyrolean native in lederhosen and knee socks, came to greet him.

"Ah, Patzig, good fellow. Good to see you again. My, and in full uniform no less. Quite impressive, I am sure that the Führer will be impressed. For myself, I try to get into the local atmosphere whenever I can. You know the others of course."

As Göring turned to wave an open hand toward the SS men, Patzig caught a glimpse of a haughty sneer on Heydrich's lips, his boss, the one-time chicken farmer from Munich, simply looked on impassively.

Göring was about to say something when one of the side doors opened and Adolf Hitler stepped into the room followed by his large Alsatian. The Führer, like most of his guests, was dressed for a country weekend in a soft gray flannel suit with only a Party badge at the lapel for decoration. The assembly immediately came to attention and rendered the obligatory Hitler salute. The dog, impervious to the pomp displayed by Hitler's men, trotted along until one of the SS aides snapped a leash to its collar and walked it out onto the broad stone veranda. As the dog exited the Chancellor and Führer of Germany looked after it fondly, like a father watching a child run outdoors to play.

"Gentlemen," he began, "in a few short days the world will be witness to the grandest of all displays of the power of the Third Reich." As Hitler began to warm to his subject, Göring turned his eyes skyward, knowing that once he got going his long-time colleague and leader would go on for some time. Göring was right, the others knew it as well, only the military men who had not spent much time with the former Austrian corporal were unprepared for the lengthy diatribe. Those who were able found a wall or piece of heavy furniture to lean upon as Hitler described the unique opportunity the Party had at this next convocation. "Fraulein Riefenstahl will be there to film the entire event, from my arrival until the last moments. The film she will create will be an inspiration to the nation and a warning to the rest of Europe that Germany has re-forged itself from the ashes of 1919."

Hitler spoke non-stop for nearly an hour. When he had at last finished, a battalion of SS stewards entered the room, bringing trays of refreshments and an assortment of Bavarian treats for the guests.

The meeting resumed as the men juggled cups of tea and coffee and responded to their leader's inquiries. "I must speak to the entire globe this time," he insisted. He introduced a man named Joachim Ribbentrop to the group. Several of the guests had met the one-time champagne salesman to whom Hitler looked for advice on foreign policy, simply on the strengths of the man's international business connection.

"Ribbentrop," announced Hitler, "is going to form a special office within the Foreign Ministry for the specific purpose of advising me and the entire Party on matters of foreign policy. It will be called the *Büro Ribbentrop*."

Hitler smiled and others in the room nodded their congratulations. Clearly not everyone knew in advance about this innovation, certainly not Heydrich, whose *Sicherheitsdienst*, or SD, was engaged in international espionage. Heydrich frowned, and it was only when Himmler nudged him that the man with death's eyes gave a weak smile of congratulations. Most surprised was Fritz von Papen. The former Vice Chancellor and newly appointed ambassador to Austria had thought that he was to have the job of Foreign Minister. Von Papen had been spared on that bloody weekend in June, but his face remained ashen when confronted by Hitler's announcement. He had been given his life, but he began to wonder at what cost.

"Which brings us to the issue of Poland," stated Hitler, who then turned to look directly at Patzig. "Patzig what are you doing about Poland?"

"*Mein Führrer*," Patzig answered evenly, "we are carefully monitoring the Polish military. We have conducted a number of over-flights to obtain photographic intelligence."

"Idiot!" exclaimed Hitler. "I am surrounded by idiots! Are you so basely ignorant of the political impacts of such actions that I must explain them to you? Do you have such little grasp of diplomacy and realpolitik to not know how to obtain information without showing your hand? Does the Abwehr not understand what we are trying to do in Germany? Are you incapable of subterfuge and stealth? Why do I get reports from every other quarter about the Abwehr's mismanagement of intelligence."

Patzig took a step backward, "But, *mein Führer.*"

Hitler held up a hand to silence the naval officer. Then he turned to the entire room and spoke in even tones. As he did so Patzig saw the glimmer of a smile creep across Heydrich's face. Göring saw it as well, and gave Patzig a warning stare.

"Let me be perfectly clear to everyone in this room. The Poles are a mongrel race, fit only for servitude. This is the truth. We will deal with them in due time. Warsaw has complained about our planes violating their territory by as much a one hundred kilometers. Until we are ready to move on the Poles, we must do everything to keep them and the other mongrelized nations; the Czechs, Rumanians, Bulgarians, and the Yugoslavs, from joining to form that Intermarium that they have long spouted about." Hitler drew in a breath, and with his left hand he smoothed his forelock back into place. He looked about the room and then right at Patzig, "The Abwehr will cease from this moment any further incursions into Poland until I, Adolf Hitler, your Führer, have ordered you to do so. Is that understood?"

A chorus of "*Jawhol mein Führer*" immediately answered him.

The meeting passed on to other topics before the break for lunch. Patzig had lost his appetite but put on a good face before the others. He suddenly thought of the 23rd Psalm, "*Thou preparest a table before me in the presence of my enemies.*" As the thought ran through his mind, he looked out over the green forests to the blue Tyrolean ridges beyond, a few still had patches of snow.

"You were not prepared for that, were you?" It was Göring standing next to him. "I told you that politics was not your strong suit. Himmler and his friend Heydrich sold you out and will continue to do so until they destroy you. Let me see about getting you an honorable transfer away from Berlin."

Patzig looked over a Göring, hope filling his eyes. "Would that be possible?"

"I will have a word with the Führer, tell him you would be better in command of a ship. How about the *Graf Spee*? It is a brand new pocket battleship, just the right command for a sea-going man like yourself."

"Yes, many thanks, Reichsminister."

"Don't mention it. By the way, there is a man on your staff, a Doktor Theurer I believe. Do you know him?"

"Yes, he has a long history with the department."

"Well, you might go carefully there. I have it in confidence that the SD is taking an interest in him. That cannot be good for anyone. Do I make myself clear?" Göring leveled his gaze at Patzig.

"Nothing could be clearer, Reichsminister."

Zurich by Dinner

Harry Braham was enjoying breakfast in the Adlon dining room when a shadow darkened his plate of eggs and bacon.

"May I join you, Captain Braham?"

Braham knew that men like Otto Kleist would not welcome a refusal. He looked at his intruder with mild disdain and sweeping the copy of the previous day's *International Herald Tribune* aside replied, "Certainly, would you care for something to eat? No, perhaps some coffee, then?"

Braham signaled to the waiter who was hovering behind Kleist like a marionette, his starched white jacket nearly virginal compared with the black uniform and death's head insignia worn by the Hauptsturmführer.

"How was your excursion to Wedding last evening? There was some unpleasantness in the streets there. Bolshevik sympathizers no doubt, but they were dealt with." Kleist leveled his gaze at Braham as he spoke.

Braham wondered how long this polite conversation would go on. "Why, I didn't notice any commotion, although I was only in the area a short while."

"And what would a man like you, a businessman, wealthy by most standards, have to do in a slum like Wedding? It seems most out of character for a man who enjoys our fine German music and our lovely women."

" Ah, well, there you have me Hauptsturmführer. I went to Wedding in the hope of finding an old comrade from the war in Poland. One of our mechanics, a man named Stefan Grabonski. I had been meaning to look him up on one of my trips here, but something always got in the way. He was a Pole married to a Berlin girl. A great man with a wrench was Stefan. I thought I could put him in the way of some work, what with this Air Olympiad coming up at the end of the month. The last address I had for him was in that part of town. So that is the mystery."

"And how did you find your old comrade," asked Kleist with a touch of sarcasm in his voice.

'Truth is, I didn't. I got to the address I had for him, number 12 Offener Strasse, but there was no one there by the name Grabonski. So I found a lone taxi cruising by and went back to the Adlon."

"You know we in the Sicherheitsdienst can find just about anyone in Germany. Would you like me to give it a try?"

Braham knew the man was fencing with him, so he decided to parry, "Well, if it's not too much trouble. It has been years since I spoke with him. If you find him, you could let him know I am at the Adlon. Oh, but I am going to Switzerland by train later today. I will be back next week. The folks at the Adlon are very kind to keep my room for me." Braham was hoping that this man would leave him alone before Gisela awoke and came looking for him.

"You must be a favorite guest Herr Braham. You seem to flow in and out of Germany like the breeze." Kleist used his best reptilian smile as he spoke; the image of a gila monster came to Braham's mind. The poisonous lizard of the Sonoran desert had the reputation of sinking its teeth into its prey and holding on until its venom had done its trick, and the unlucky victim was dead.

"Well you know Hauptsturmführer," Braham began.

"Please, Herr Braham, using my rank sounds so formal for such a cordial conversation, please, call me Otto."

"Well, then please call me Harry. As I was saying, several of your officials in the foreign ministry, especially Reichsminister Göring, are interested in foreign investments in your country. My expertise is in aviation, and, having had the dubious pleasure of being on the receiving end of attacks by your airplanes of the 1914 war, I am interested in developing ties between American investors and companies and those of Germany. Your government has made me and my colleagues very welcome."

Kleist had no option but to acknowledge this fact, for to have thrown his weight, or that of the SD, at a welcome guest of the state like Braham, would have been personally disastrous. Hitler had given specific instructions regarding foreigners, especially Americans, and it was Kleist's duty to make nice with them, no matter how he felt personally.

"Harry, may I ask you a question?"

"Certainly Otto," Braham said cheerfully and making it sound like the SD man was just another chum.

"I was wondering if you have ever come across a man called Doktor Albrecht Theurer?"

Now Braham knew he was on that slippery slope, for to deny any knowledge of Theurer could prove a disaster. Kleist might or might not know of their meetings. Braham played it right down the middle of the fairway. "Is he connected with aviation in any way? I say that because the name seems to ring a bell, but to be honest, with all the activity of this Air Olympiad coming up, I have met so many businessmen and officials, I can't be sure. Why do you ask? I hope he has not done anything nefarious, you being an SD man and all."

Braham signaled for more coffee, which appeared instantly.

"Oh, no. Please don't give it another thought. I was asking only because we in the SD have to be vigilant about the Führer's security. Doktor Theurer is often an invited guest at affairs the Führer sometimes attends, and so we need to make inquiries and keep abreast of the dealings of anyone with whom the Führer may come in contact."

"Well, I don't think I can help you. I would be happy to give you a call if I turn something up. Do you have a card?"

As Kleist reached into his tunic to retrieve a silver card case, Braham glanced up to see Gisela enter the hotel lobby from the street door. She was impeccably coiffed and dressed for the weather in a tailored white suit with a blue striped boat-neck blouse, wide brimmed hat and blue and white spectator shoes. Knowing better than to appear in the lobby from the elevators, she had used the stairs to the side exit and made her regal entrance so everyone would notice. As she passed through the lobby, the ripple of a newspaper held by one of the men seated in the lobby caught Braham's attention. SD or Gestapo he wondered.

She spotted Braham; grimaced at the sight of Kleist, and breezed past an anxious maître d' toward their table. Braham stood as she arrived and offered her a seat.

"My dear countess, good morning. What a surprise! How delightful to see you again. May I offer you breakfast? Coffee perhaps?"

Kleist scrambled to his feet and clicked his heels. "Countess von Teischen, good morning."

"Well good morning to you both. I saw you when I entered the lobby, and I must say you two looked very conspiratorial. Did I interrupt some kind of scheme?" Her playfulness was lost on Kleist, but Braham suppressed a smile.

"No, countess. I was just telling Hauptsturmführer Kleist that I am leaving later this morning for Zurich, and we were chatting about business and mutual acquaintances. By the by, he was just asking me about someone. What was the name again, Otto, Thermann, no Theurer, that was it."

"Oh him," she scoffed, "let's not spoil a lovely breakfast talking about that boorish man." She watched the pair of them to see how she should play this and went on, "I told Christian that he was the worst sort of man. I understand that he makes a habit of preying on lonely women whose husbands are off valiantly serving the Reich in far-flung places. He's despicable." She said this with just the right touch of Junker arrogance to impress Kleist.

"Yes, you mentioned Theurer when I ran into you and your husband at the Konzerthaus. Has he troubled you again?"

"No, I think he may have found greener pastures. He was very presumptive following the dinner party at Karinhall." Gisela wanted Kleist to know that she was known in the right circles, and his meddling in her affairs might not be appreciated by the Führer's inner circle.

Kleist nodded and said nothing.

"Harry, you are leaving Berlin, but no," she pouted. "I must implore you to stay. I am planning a party next week for Reinhardt and some of the fliers in the Olympiad. Please, if you must go say that you will be back."

"When is the party?" asked Braham.

"Two weeks from Friday, the twenty-fourth of August. Please say you be there?"

"Oh, yes, I think I can manage that. My trip to Zurich will take only a few days. And then I must return to Paris, but I will be there if you want me to come."

"Don't be silly, of course I, we want you to come. The house will be filled with fliers like you," she quipped.

"Then, consider me there!" Braham looked about for a waiter.

Seeing his glance, the hovering waiter swept in and refilled their cups with fresh coffee. Nervous at having the SD man, the countess and a noted American at the same table, the waiter knew his job was on the line if he failed in any way.

Gisela smiled at the man, it was her regal smile designed to make men melt, which mostly they did. She touched the man's arm and asked, "Would you be a dear and bring me a brioche and some strawberry jam."

The waiter nearly genuflected and sped away to get her order.

The White Raven

Rising, Kleist said, "I must leave you to your breakfasts. I have work to attend to. Harry, Herr Braham, please have a pleasant trip. I look forward to seeing you again when you return to Germany."

" And a hearty *Auf wiedersehen* to you, you son of a bitch," said Braham to the back of the retreating SD man. Kleist made as if for the lobby's front door but veered off at the last moment and spoke to a man in a grey felt hat. The man had been trying to remain unobtrusive by holding up a copy of the *Völkischer Beobachter* in front of his face. Braham had seen the man when he had emerged from the elevator on his way to breakfast. Now, he was certain that Herr Felthat would become a familiar figure until he left Berlin.

At eleven Braham boarded the Zurich train at Anhalter Bahnhof and noticed the grey hat again. Braham had a first-class compartment, and he watched with amusement as the SD man scrambled for a slatted wood bench in third class. It would be a long, hard day for his tail

A Friend from Warsaw

Among the nations of Europe, the Poles, after regaining statehood, operated one of the most effective intelligence services. It was known as the *Biuro Wyaniadowcze* and evolved over the years with as many as eight subdivisions organized to deal with threats to the fledgling nation's very existence. Being geographically trapped between the belligerent Russians and the avaricious Germans, Poland needed the best intelligence it could muster. As a diplomat and a member of the service's *Sekcja IIb,* the offensive intelligence division, Jerzy Krol had access to one of the best group of forgers in the world. The Polish Intelligence Service employed a cadre of forgers, many of who were alumni of Europe's most notable prisons. When Harry Braham approached him with the sheaf of Lieberman's photographs, he was suitably impressed. Braham had taken the train from Berlin to Zurich in order to meet with the Polish diplomat.

Krol was based in Paris, but it was always more comfortable to meet unnoticed in neutral Switzerland than to risk the slights of the German border officials. Krol had booked in at the Hotel Zum Storchen. Braham had taken a room at a small hotel on the other side of the Limmat and then walked to the Zwei Hunde Gasthaus where they met to talk and enjoy some of the restaurant's famous veal and *rosti* potatoes. Both men enjoyed the atmosphere. It was smoky and loud enough so that eavesdropping was impossible.

The pair settled into a narrow wooden booth with tall seatbacks that reached to a man's height. The scarred table bore the wounds of a thousand nicks and dents from years of constant use. Lover's initials and names in a dozen languages were carved into the once-smooth surface.

"Who is that man in the corner who is watching us?" Krol asked of Braham.

"He is one of Kleist's people. I picked him up yesterday in Berlin. He has been with me since breakfast. Hard on the fellow, though, apparently he had to sit up in third class all the way from Germany. I suppose Kleist was saving on train fare. In any event, I need to behave as a businessman, so I did not try to lose him."

Once a pair of tall glasses of pilsner arrived at their table they got down to business.

"Does this man Theurer really intend to use these?" asked Krol, looking from one sheet to the next, "although these are practically signed confessions from Heydrich and Himmler. If Hitler believes these documents, I doubt if either man would survive a single day. But I don't think these carry enough weight to unseat the living embodiment of the SS. If Hitler did fall for this, then maybe."

"That is a big if. I don't believe Theurer truly understands what he is dealing with in taking on the SS. They are a gang, a big government-sanctioned gang, and as deadly as the Chicago mob. The camps they operate, like Oranienberg that the Nazi's took over last year aren't health spas. I doubt if those papers will ever reach Hitler. Someone in the SS will just shoot Theurer and be done with it."

"Well, then you need not worry too much. Surely this Kleist, or someone, would be glad to do that," offered Krol.

"Perhaps," replied Braham. "I don't think the future of Germany means that much to me right now. They have created a cauldron of fear fueled by avarice. It's not up to me to change history. What does concern me is what happens to Gisela and Reinhardt. They are real people and, for the most part, good people. That Theurer has embarked upon this adventure speaks to his being a deskman. In his world, he can move the pieces on the board and the outcome is given. Like I said, he does not realize whom he is dealing with. Right now, Kleist is one step away from nabbing him, and if he gets his hands on those documents, everyone connected with Theurer is sunk." Braham lit another cigarette and exhaled a long stream of smoke.

"Well, some of what is written here is true," said Jerzy pointing at the papers in front of him.

"Yes. Reinhardt told me that the SS is building a government within the government. They behave like medieval warlords carving up territory and treasure, only in twentieth-century style; they use banks and companies paid for with money stolen from Jews and others on their list of undesirables. The icing on the cake is the statement from Ryshkov. That brings in the Bolshevik angle, and, if I am right, Theurer will want to present him, and, after he has said his lines, the poor bastard will be shot while trying to escape."

"Yes, the Gestapo does seem to lose a lot of prisoners that way."

Braham sighed, "What bothers me the most is the last sheet, the neatly typed list of names under the heading, *Ausführungsliste*, people to be executed."

"It's a long list." Krol said.

"Read on."

"Christ almighty, he has both of the von Teischens listed along with Reinhardt Stiffler. Why for God's sake?"

"The man is cleaning up his mess. If he is able to convince Göring that the proof is ironclad, he certainly doesn't want any of the people listed there to be able to say different."

"But why does he need to liquidate Gisela and Reinhardt? After all, he will have Hitler in his pocket."

"It boils down to the simple fact that he is a bureaucrat at heart, and his neat little mind says, 'leave no traces.' So, he will make sure no one is left alive. That's where you and your skillful forgers come in."

"Ah, the penny drops."

"Yes, well, this is what I need done. It was actually in talking with Kleist that I got the idea." Braham handed Krol several sheets of paper along with two passport photos, one of a man and one of a woman. Then he explained exactly what he needed his Polish friend to do.

Krol glanced at the man's photo, shrugged, and then glanced at the woman's and said, "ah."

"So, do you think it can be done, there is not much time?"

Krol picked up the photos, "The passports will not be a problem."

"And with the others?" asked Braham, pointing at the sheaf of papers on the table.

"I think we can make the alterations you suggest and get them in the right hands. We have someone inside the SD who can help."

Braham signaled for another pilsner as Krol placed the documents safely inside his suit jacket. Looking at his friend, he patted his jacket where the papers lay and asked, "What good will be accomplished by doing this?"

Braham looked about the room at the people laughing, talking and enjoying the evening. "I can't be sure. At least the passports will save two maybe three lives, as for Theurer, I think he is a dead man no matter what happens, but who knows, maybe Germany will wake up from this nightmare before it is too late."

The White Raven

Sea Room

It was 0630 and the sun full up when Captain Konrad Patzig stepped onto the open port wing of the cruiser *Leipzig* and drank in the fresh morning air. Forty miles out of Wilhelmshaven and knifing through a calm summer sea, the warship was making twenty-eight knots under a brilliant blue sky. Like the sailor he was, he swung his gaze in a full three hundred and sixty degrees to search for other vessels. He let out a sign of contentment, for all he could see was the clear morning sky reaching from horizon to horizon. This is where he belonged. Göring had been right, he should get away from the politics of Berlin and Berchtesgaden and go back where he belonged, at sea.

As he stood enjoying the sight of sea and sky, a young steward approached with a cup of coffee. Steaming hot and with just the right amount of sugar and cream added, he savored the moment, closing his eyes to enjoy the feeling of power surging through the warship's deck plates.

"Captain's compliments sir. He asked if you would like to join him for breakfast in his sea cabin." The fresh-faced steward stood before him at attention.

Patzig smiled, nothing would suit him better. "Thank you. Tell Fregattenkapitän Landers I will join him in a moment. What is your name, sailor?"

The young man beamed at being called sailor by such an exalted personage as this. "Schweiber, sir. Fritz Schweiber."

"Very well, Schweiber, I will be along in a moment."

Patzig smiled as he saw the young man trot off. He turned again toward the sea and felt relieved. Out here, there was no Himmler, no Heydrich, only the camaraderie of sea-going naval officers. After the meeting at the Eagle's Nest, he knew he had to get himself out of the way of Hitler's entourage. As soon as he reached Berlin, he contacted his old friend Gerhardt Landers. Landers had once been his subordinate on the old *Deutschland*. Being aboard ship with an old friend in command was extremely satisfying to Patzig.

For Landers, like many post-war officers who remained in the *Reichsmarine*, life in the peacetime navy had been abysmal. Many old comrades had left, seeking positions within the merchant marine or drifting off to remote parts of the world to command tramp steamers along backwater coasts. The much-vaunted high seas fleet no longer existed, its flagships reduced in the main to serving as live fire targets for the navies of the victorious allies. Landers, however, hung in during the lean years and had been rewarded recently with command of the *Leipzig*.

Leipzig was new, commissioned in 1931. She displaced over eight thousand tons and was fast. She could make over thirty-two knots if need be, carried an array of weapons including nine six-inch guns and could launch twenty torpedoes. Patzig joined the ship in Wilhelmshaven in time for a two-week sea trial. The trial was to see how well the ship could coordinate attacks using shipboard seaplanes as gunfire and target spotters. If they were successful during these trials, the *Leipzig* would return to Wilhelmshaven to have a seaplane catapult and crane installed on its afterdeck. Naval aviation was the coming thing, thought Patzig, and he was looking forward to his unofficial role as observer as much as being away from Berlin for two weeks.

Gerhardt Landers had laid on a full English breakfast for his guest. "My god Gerd, my nose cannot believe the aromas. This is quite a feast." Patzig exclaimed as he stepped into his host's sea cabin.

"Well we can't have the head of the Abwehr fed on biscuits and salt pork, you know." Landers was a large, jolly man, who enjoyed food and wine and saw to it that the ships he commanded had the best food he could obtain for the officers and men. Sailors the world over judged a ship by its food and its cook's ability to make meals enjoyable. Everyone aboard appreciated that the *Leipzig* provided its men with the best available menus. In the parlance of the sailors, the *Leipzig* was a "good feeder."

"My lord! Bacon, eggs and biscuits! My compliments to your galley, old friend." Patzig was touched by the effort.

"We even have English marmalade, if you care for some."

As they dug into their plates, a white-jacketed steward poured coffee into their cups, and then retreated out of earshot.

"So, tell me," asked Landers "What is this sudden urge to get to sea? I have to say that I am both flattered and happy to have you aboard, but why the urgency?"

Patzig sipped from his coffee cup and looked at his old shipmate. "I needed to go to ground for a bit." Then he described about his recent visit to the Eagle's Nest and the rebuke that he had at the hands of the Leader.

"Was it that bad?" Landers asked gently.

"It was Machiavellian. I felt I was in the presence of the Borgias, the Orsini and the rest of those Italian cutthroats of the Renaissance. Around the Führer they behave well enough, but you can see the hunger in their eyes, like Nosferatau, they wait to suck your blood."

"My God, no wonder you wanted to put sea miles between you and them."

"Well, I may soon be out of this job. I spoke with Göring. Despite his binging on morphine, he does make some sense. Himmler and his acolyte Heydrich want to take over all the intelligence activities. But Hitler is not so easily swayed; he has a canny ability to play his apostles off one another. In any event Göring has let it be known that I can have the *Graf Spee* if I want it. Of course this is all speculative at the moment, but I would not be surprised if I wasn't sent back to the fleet and someone, probably old Canaris, is put in my place."

"Well, nothing would please me more than to see you back on the bridge of a warship," Landers replied. "Steward, more coffee!"

Later that morning Patzig stood in the wing of the bridge as the *Leipzig*'s forward turret engaged a series of towed targets that were just visible at the horizon. From over the ship's loudspeaker system came the crackling voice of the observer in the Heinkel He-60 seaplane that circled at 5,000 feet overhead. As each geyser of seawater exploded from the falling shells, the observer would call down the score of hits and misses. Landers, for his part, was jubilant. His gunners were right on the mark, tightly bracketing the targets, flimsy bits of wood nailed to uprights on twenty-foot long rafts, with their shells.

The first round of the action concluded with *Leipzig*'s gunnery officer taking bearings from the orbiting seaplane. A few moments later Captain Landers ordered a forty-degree turn, and the cruiser swung to starboard. Now it was turn of the number two turret, just forward of the bridge, to fire. As the ship steadied the gunnery officer passed along the target bearings and the turret's guns elevated. Seconds later three flashes from the barrels burst forth followed by long tongues of flame. The shells screamed out over the placid sea, and the surface of the water around the targets roiled under the impact of falling steel.

Patzig smiled and thought, how simple this life was, and how he longed for it again. What had ever lured him away from this life? What could he have been thinking? If Göring lived up to his promise, Patzig would be able to escape from the gangsters that made up the government and go back to honest work as a sailor. But first he would have to deal with the stack of coded messages that had reached him from Berlin and remained, unanswered, in his pocket.

———

Albrecht Theurer slammed down the phone in disgust. He had been trying to reach the head of the Abwehr, Konrad Patzig, at his office, then at his home. Theurer even tried Kriegsmarine headquarters in the Bendlerblock, but no one had any information as to his whereabouts. It had been nearly a week since he had seen Patzig at Abwehr headquarters at 76 Tirpitzufer, and Theurer was beginning to worry. Someone had replaced the bright young thing that had served as his gatekeeper and secretary. She had gone on holiday they said. He did not believe it. In her stead was a dour harridan with tight gray curls on top of the body of a sumo wrestler. The woman sat like a Buddha in front of Patzig's office door, and, like the immutable prophet, remained silent on the subject of the man's whereabouts.

Several days passed, and Theurer's concern for his boss's absence had turned to worry when a snippet of a conversation caught his ear. He had been standing next to his secretary's desk when a pair of voices drifted down the hallway. All he heard was the name "Patzig" and the phrase "sea trials," followed by a laugh. He immediately stepped to the doorway and looked down the hallway just to catch a glimpse of two men descending the stairway to the main entrance. Something was amiss. First Patzig goes off to meet with Hitler, and then he seems to have vanished. Theurer paused in thought. People did disappear from view more frequently these days. It seemed to be a new benefit of the nation's embrace of National Socialism. Don't like your neighbor? Do you have a grudge against your boss? Well a quiet word with those nice men at the Alexanderplatz and your troubles will disappear. Just a rest cure in lovely Oranienberg for the offender, and things will be right as rain. If the Gestapo or SD had taken Patzig, there would have been rumblings. Now that he thought of it, since Patzig was a sailor, why not a little sea voyage to get away from the likes of Himmler and Heydrich.

It took him another several hours to put together the information he needed. If Patzig were indeed on his way out, he would have to try something else. Patzig was his link to Göring, and, without the fat man's help, Theurer's scheme would fail before it began.

On Borrowed Wings

The note from Raymond Kingman found Harry Braham at his hotel when he returned from meeting with Krol. It was written in a simple word code, but the text conveyed urgency. From what he deciphered Braham knew that he had to get to Paris the next day. It was too late for any train. He would need Jerzy's help. While the Polish diplomat sorted out the paperwork, Braham would go to France. Still, he had to get back to Berlin in time for Gisela's soiree and in all ways appear to Kleist to be the amiable American he was purported to be. Braham did not have time for trains; if he was to cross half of Europe in a few short days he needed to fly.

At the airfield outside Zurich he found what he needed. Jerzy drove him out through an area of wide pastures to where a grass runway and a few canvas-covered hangars, leftovers from the war, had been erected. A hand cranked gas pump stood sentinel under a sheet metal sign that was cut in the shape of a scallop with the word Shell painted on both sides. On the small area of gravel inside the fence was a battered Renault truck and something resembling part of an ancient Ford. Beyond a rail fence stood a metal shed with the word *Büro* painted on its side. There were no other buildings save the tent-like hangars, so Braham took the metal shack to be a combination office and line shack. A tall pole rose from the far end of the hangars with a red windsock dangling limply. It was very early in the morning, and it seemed like there was no one about. Jerzy shut off the car engine and waited while Braham walked to the door of the shack. Then he turned and looked down the flight line at the row of biplanes tied down to stakes driven into the turf. He noticed a battered brown and white SE.5A there with a for sale sign on it written in French, German, and English.

Braham turned the knob of the door to the shack and stepped in. The interior was like every line shack he had ever seen in any part of the world. On the top of a battered oak desk an inverted piston head served as an ashtray, its contents spilling out on to the scattered papers that bore the greasy fingerprints of the mechanics who had handled them. A broken wooden propeller served as an improvised hat rack and leaned into the far corner. There was an Air France calendar hanging on the wall behind the desk, with a series of crossed out dates running through the middle of July. Since it was August either the event that engendered the need for such record keeping had already occurred or the person doing the record keeping was no longer in need of doing so.

Just behind the cluttered desk was a metal swivel chair occupied by a large man with greasy hair. Braham could not tell much about him except that he was snoring. Braham rapped his knuckles on the glass of the door and said, "*Guten tag!*" followed by a louder "*Bonjour!*" The man did not stir, though his snoring skipped a beat then continued as before. A bottle of brandy tipped to one side gave Braham the idea that the man had spent the night sleeping there. Braham looked around the narrow space for something heavy that would make a louder noise. H found a torque wrench; the kind used to tighten the nuts on propeller hubs, and, raising it above his head, brought it crashing down on the edge of the piston head. The clang and shower of ashes sent the man in the chair reeling. His head shot up from the desktop and snapped back until it collided with a tall wooden file cabinet with sharp crack.

"*Mein Gott! Was ist!*" he shouted.

Braham had returned the wrench to where he had found it and stood facing a man whose facial expressions went from shock to horror to anger.

Braham stood mute while the various displays of emotion played out on the man's face, all the while taking in what he saw. Here was a well-fed man of fifty or so. Black, probably dyed, hair upon which he used some kind of ointment, perhaps brilliantine. He was dressed in a grimy white shirt and grey trousers held up with both a wide leather belt and braided leather suspenders. He sported a moustache, akin to a caterpillar, which Braham though was also dyed, that was heavily waxed, and there was spittle at the corner of his mouth. From what Braham could see, the man's hands were stained with black oil or grease, and the skin was cracked.

"*Guten tag, mein Herr,*" Braham repeated.

The man began to sputter, but Braham remained calm with the equanimity of an angel.

"I've come about the SE. out there on the flight line that is for sale." Braham spoke in German and pointed toward the flight line. "My name is Wilkins, said Braham. Used to fly one of those in the war you know. And you are?"

The man's name was Steiger, and he explained that he was only the line manager. He had some paperwork about the plane, it had been owned by a Zurich lawyer, but the man had recently died in automobile crash and his widow wanted to sell the thing.

"Is it flyable, old man?" Braham decided to keep up the affectation of being a former RAF pilot. It would make things easier later.

Jerzy Krol smoked a cigarette while he watched Braham and a fat man stroll out to the SE.5A. He saw Braham crawl up and over the machine, open the cowling and checking the oil levels, bleed water out of the sump, and, as fliers always did, kick the tires.

"Herr Steiger, how much does the widow want for the plane."

Steiger was no genius but he knew that if the widow wanted two thousand francs he could ask twenty-five hundred and keep the difference for himself.

"Twenty-five hundred Swiss Francs, Herr Wilkins," said Steiger, presenting a row of yellow teeth in a smarmy smile.

"Twenty-five hundred. Hmm, well, I would need to test fly it of course."

"Certainly, certainly," the man was almost genuflecting now.

"I see the gas float is a little low. Can we top it off, and I will just take it for a spin around the field."

At this Steiger looked dubious.

"No need to worry, Herr Steiger, my friend Doktor Metz is there in the car waiting to take me back to Zurich. We have a meeting at one of the Kantonal banks in two hours."

The White Raven

Steiger's doubts vanished and the two pulled the plane up to the fuel pump, and Steiger went about filling the plane's gas tank. Once he was done Braham climbed into the cockpit and strapped himself in. Steiger pulled the prop through several turns and then stepped away and shouted, "Contact!"

Braham switched on the magneto and echoed, "Contact!" With the throttle cracked open, Steiger pulled again on the prop, and the engine sprang to life, chuffing out bursts of exhaust into the fresh morning air. The smell of hot castor oil and gas filled Braham's nostrils, and he was elated. Pushing the throttle ahead, he taxied to the end of the grass strip and, looking again at the limp windsock, pushed the throttle full on and raced across the ground. A moment later he was airborne. Steiger watched him climb and turn away from the field. Why was he going northwest? The plane was getting smaller in the sky, and Steiger felt his stomach sink. He looked back to where Doktor Metz sat waiting for his friend, Herr Wilkins, but only the Renault and the battered Ford remained. Steiger turned and looked skyward again, but the SE.5 was but a dot heading away toward France.

Lunch Al Fresco

Braham kept the SE.5 at seven thousand feet and leaned out the fuel mixture to cut down on fuel consumption. If he were lucky, he could extend the range of the old airplane to the Royal Flying Corps' specifications of 300 miles. There were a few cumulous clouds forming in the warm morning air as he passed from the foothills of the Alps into the northern section of the Midi. Here there were slight updrafts that helped to move him along toward Paris.

The plan was simple enough as long as Jerzy did his part. When Braham had seen the for-sale sign on the side of the biplane, he told Krol to wire Kingman to meet him at the old aerodrome outside Limoges-Fourches, about twenty miles southwest of Paris. It was a seldom-used airfield where the SE.5, once parked, would not stand out from the other veteran aircraft parked there.

Serenity always came to Braham when he was flying. For nearly three hours, since departing the grass field outside Zurich, he had a front-row-seat view of the verdant French countryside. As the fields and forests passed below his wings, he marveled at the colors of the land, as the sunlight filled the narrow places between hills and warmed tiny villages. This part of France had escaped the violent destruction of the war. The people in this region did not see their homes destroyed, but nonetheless paid a heavy price in blood with the loss of an entire generation.

As he crossed the expanse of France his mind, in glorious detachment, wandered through the paths of his current problem. Down below, country roads wound through fields and woodlands, inevitably to reach a nexus at some tiny walled village. He began to think of Theurer, Gisela, Kleist and the shadowy Oskar as being on separate roads leading to a nexus of their own. Each had their own reasons for moving forward on their courses. From his perch above them Braham could see their imminent collision, and if he was smart enough, understand the likely outcomes.

If Theurer succeeded, the world would be rid of the likes of Himmler and Heydrich. But the price was Gisela and Stiffler, and who knew how many others? What Theurer offered was nothing more than a slight, mid-course correction at the expense of the lives of innocent people. And in the end Oskar and, far to the east, Stalin would still be there.

Kleist, well, if Kleist got Theurer into one of the basement cells that the SS used to beat the truth out of their guests, well, Braham had no doubt that he would give up everyone, and still people would suffer and die and, while that happened, the Bolsheviks would simply chortle to themselves.

Oskar, well, he was in the game for the long pull. The Soviets were not likely to expose him and lose such a well-placed mole, even to catch and eliminate Ryshkov. No, for that they would use a special assassination squad. Dzerzhinsky liked to use Latvians for that work. No doubt Vyacheslav Menzhinsky, Dzerzhinsky's successor, or whoever was now running the NKVD, would have drawn on other minorities, perhaps Ukrainians, to do the work.

No, it boiled down to arranging it so that Kleist and Theurer somehow cancelled each other out. That was the trick he was going to have to pull off, and soon. Gisela had seen, with Karl Lieberman's help, that another Jewish family, the Feldsteins, had made it out of Germany and were now on their way to Greece. Isaac Feldstein had been a professor of economics until a bunch of Brownshirts tossed him out of his post at Leipzig University. If the family were lucky, they would soon be out of Europe entirely and on their way to a new life far from the reaches of the Third Reich.

Braham watched the fuel float indicator just ahead of the windscreen; it seemed to be dropping as each minute ticked by. He checked and then re-checked his watch. The Michelin road map he had spread on his knee showed the confluence of roads that had to be Romilly-sur-Seine. The country town sat along the narrow banks of the river that led to Paris. From here on, the map was superfluous. Braham was familiar with the landscape around the French capital. He looked at his watch and saw that he was making good time, but with almost an hour left to go, he began to think he might have cut this jaunt a little too close and not have enough gas to make it. Looking down at the trees below he could see a slight crosswind was blowing, neither good nor bad he thought and tried to lean out the fuel mixture a bit more until the rpms began to drop, then eased the control back a fraction and hoped for the best.

Forty minutes later, he arrived overhead his destination. As he swung the plane around to make his final approach, he spotted Harriet Bliss seated in her burgundy 1932 Ford Victoria coupe, watching the sky for his arrival. With but a teacup full of gas in the tank, he greased the biplane's tires onto the grass at the tiny field at Limoges-Fourches. The summer heat rose at him from the grass, and he felt the physical let down he always experienced when landing. The engine cut out, and he rolled to a stop fifty feet from her car. Several men watched from the far side of the field as Braham climbed from the SE.5 and jogged to Harriet's car; she began driving slowly in a circle to get out on to the road back to Paris, and Braham stepped on to the Ford's running board and jumped into the passenger seat.

"How's tricks?" he asked and pulled off his goggles to plant a kiss on her cheek.

"Ooh, you are all sweaty, and you have oil on your face," she protested.

Braham reached for the rear view mirror and turned it to see his blackened cheeks and the outline of the goggles white around his eyes. "Do we have time for me to clean up and change? Raymond said in his note that it was urgent."

"Raymond is waiting for us at a restaurant in Saint-Aubens. There is a towel and a bottle of water if you want to wash up on the way. If you are hungry, I packed some brioche and coffee. They are in the hamper in the back. In the meantime, I want to get as far from that airplane as possible. Jerzy said there might be some contest about the legal ownership." Harriet looked askance at Braham. "You stole it, didn't you?"

Braham smiled at her. "You know what I love about you, Harriet?"

"No, I am almost afraid to ask."

"It's that I can never lie to you. Yes, your honor, I stole it, but by tomorrow it should be back in Zurich with no harm done."

"Let's go meet Raymond, I'm famished," Harriet declared. From the other end of the field she saw several men running toward them waving their hands. Seeing that, she spun the Vicky around and they sped off. Braham winced as they narrowly avoided colliding with the several farm carts laden with produce that meandered through the ancient countryside. Braham tried to use the towel and water to wipe off the film of oil that the SE.5's engine had sprayed on his face during flight, only to have most of the water splash over the car's front seat as Harriet bobbed and weaved like a fighter pilot through the winding course of narrow hedge-bound lanes toward Saint-Aubens. By the time they reached the intersection of roads that defined the town of Saint-Aubens, a layer fine white road dust was added to the oil that remained on his face.

Raymond Kingman was waiting for them in the garden of Auberge Lapin Blanc where they dined al fresco. With a view out over ripening fields of oats and barley, the restaurant's garden dining area was walled off from the street traffic of Saint-Aubens. A carafe of local rosé was brought to their table, and each of the friends savored the crisp wine before they started talking. It was Raymond Kingman who broke the bucolic spell.

"Do you think she will leave with you?"

Braham knew he meant Gisela, and his friend's question had put focused his thoughts on what had been troubling him all these last days. He did not know the answer to that question, and, worse, he wasn't sure he really wanted to know. Gisela von Teischen, the White Raven, was but a pinprick in the side of the Third Reich. Still, death by a thousand such pinpricks was not outside of the realm of possibility if she were to stay in Germany. If he were successful, Theurer would not have the chance to unmask her. It was a big if.

"Ray, I don't know. I don't believe that Theurer can pull off his coup against the SS. When it comes down to it, if Hitler has to choose between Himmler and his SS and some noisemaker from the Abwehr, my money would be on the men in black. He would have to have Göring and Hess on his side, and then it could just turn into a Mexican standoff. Gisela has had some success against them, I think the only thing that will make her come out is the threat of her imminent death."

Kingman looked at the pastoral setting that surrounded them and said, "I have been considering this gift of the Theurer's, if we can call it that. On the one hand Hitler has curbed the worst of his movement by eliminating the likes of Röhm. Decapitating his SS would be welcome in most quarters, but what are we left with then? Hitler as Theurer's puppet, hard to believe, and it could just be what the Bolsheviks need to re-energize the fires of revolution. Marx always thought the revolution would come in Germany. There are a lot of people, misguided as they may be, who think they can do business with Germany in the long run."

"In the long run we'll all be dead," quipped Braham.

Before Ray Kingman could respond, Harriet asked, "And what about our Russian friend? What are we to do with him?"

"Well, I am not going to hand him over to Theurer, just to be shot. Let the Russians do what they will with him. What kind of passport did we give Ryshkov?"

"I had a friend at the Uruguayan Embassy run him up one in the name of Antonio del Vasquez," replied Kingman.

"Well, then the sooner he is on a boat to Montevideo, the better," said Braham. "Now, I am really hungry. Can we order?"

Kingman then motioned for the waiter.

East with the Sun

"**S**he is absolutely gorgeous!" Harry Braham stood in the open hangar bay at Orly airport and marveled at the paint job on his plane, running his hands over the shiny surface of its fabric skin. "It looks like a work by Cezanne. Cerulean blue fuselage and sunflower yellow wings, all set off with red, white and blue roundels. What inspired you to do this?"

"It was Harriet's idea actually," said Raymond Kingman. "I have to agree with her. Herb Greene may have given you the plane, but we are sending you on a devil's errand, and the least we can do is afford you the outward appearance of diplomacy.

I have arranged with the German embassy here to have you travel as a credentialed official American observer to the Olympiad. The Heinies are just too eager for American money to turn us down. When is the party?"

"Friday, but the big send off is on Sunday. Hitler likes Sunday events that will eclipse the church-going habits of the population. He'd rather everyone worship the gods of National Socialism."

"I wish you luck, Harry. Ah, here is the lovely mastermind of this operation. Hello, Harriet."

The White Raven

"So, you like the paint job? I thought it was *très chic*! The Huns will not know what to make of you. Perhaps we should paint 'Braham's Flying Circus' under the wings."

"Well they will certainly see me coming and going," Braham replied with a laugh.

"Do you think you will have any trouble over in Hitlerland?" Harriet Bliss turned serious as she asked this.

"Well, not going in, but coming out—it will depend on what happens next Sunday."

Dawn was but an hour old when Braham pulled out the wheel chocks and climbed into his gleaming biplane. With his luggage stored in the roomy doublewide front cockpit, he cracked the throttle and pushed the electric start button. The Wright Whirlwind engine coughed and then in a cloud of blue smoke came to life. Looking side to side to make sure there were no obstructions, he inched the throttle ahead and got the plane rolling toward the edge of the airfield. Atop the hangar the windsock hung limp as he pointed the nose east and pushed the throttle full ahead.

A moment later he was aloft and clawing for altitude. Idyllic summer weather greeted him as he left the Parisian metropolis and headed out over the clawed up earth of what had been no man's land twenty years before. Villages and towns had been rebuilt, and the land was lush with regrowth, but here and there the mounds of earth thrown up by shells and the snaking corridors of trench works could be seen. With the rising sun at his eleven o'clock position, Braham was reminded of how, during the last year of the war, he had viewed the morning sun with trepidation, "Beware the Hun in the sun!" the saying went, and, even now after sixteen years, he scanned the sky around the orb for hostile wings.

The White Raven

As he flew steadily northeast Braham reviewed his options and realized there was really only one. He had to ensure that Theurer did not succeed. Theurer's plan to seize Germany by holding Hitler hostage, even for a short while, came at too high a price. He would not sacrifice people he knew to Theurer's vain attempt. No, he would have to ensure that Gisela, Reinhardt and the others remained free, even if it meant doing business with that devil Kleist.

Two hours passed and he checked his Michelin road map that he held on his knee to mark his position. He need not have bothered as the twin spires of Cologne cathedral loomed ahead. The small commercial airfield at Leverkeusen was just to the northeast of the main city. There he could refuel and present his diplomatic credentials to whatever officials needed to see them. From there, he intended to simply follow the railroad tracks that would lead him to Berlin.

The Mailwing swooped over the trees at the approach-end of the airfield, and a moment later Braham felt the thump of his tires on the lumpy grass. He slowed the plane as a staccato of pebbles hit the underside of the wing. Pulling up to the fuel pumps, he cut the engine as a young boy ran out and set a wheel chock on each side of the port wing. Without constant rush of air in his face, Braham felt the heat of the morning wash over him. His engine ticked as it began to cool, and the scent of hot oil filled his nostrils. As he unbuckled himself to climb out and deal with refueling, he heard the sound of an approaching aircraft.

A silver monoplane flew in over the same trees he had crossed moments before and bumped on to the grass. The plane was sleek, with a pointed nose, like the one in Ryshkov's drawing. On the tail was a red band, inside of which was a black swastika.

Braham now recognized it as a Me-108, one of the planes that would be competing in the Olympiad. The 108's pilot taxied up next to Braham and cut the engine. The canopy of the German plane opened and out stepped Reinhardt Stiffler, who waved enthusiastically and shouted, *"Wilkommen in Deutschland!"*

Stiffler, wearing his blue uniform, stepped over to Braham and shook his hand. "I'm to be your official escort. Let's get gassed up and then on to Berlin. There's got to be a party somewhere in town tonight!"

"I see Harriet's handiwork in this," Stiffler chuckled. "How do you like the paint job?" asked Harry.

Things seemed to be working out splendidly for Braham, having an official Luftwaffe escort speeded things along. While in Berlin, Albrecht Theurer sensed trouble and was watching as his plans slowly began to crumble. His boss, Captain Patzig, had put off meeting with him until that very morning. At ten a.m., while Braham and Stiffler were chatting and refueling their planes, Theurer was cooling his heels in Patzig's anteroom.

Theurer was not one to wait patiently, especially with so much on the line. With Patzig's new secretary glowering at him through half lenses, he fidgeted like a schoolboy waiting to see the headmaster. After twenty minutes went by, he was about to say something to the Buddha to remind her just who he was, when the buzzer on her desk sounded. She looked up and with a nod of her head pointed toward the door to Patzig's inner office.

Theurer checked his temper at the door and went into his superior's office as if nothing had been amiss. Before he could say anything, Patzig waved him to a seat in front of the oversized desk. "I'll just be a moment, Albrecht," he said, while shuffling a stack of documents on the desk in front of him. Several more minutes went by as Theurer did all he could do to not draw attention to his uneasiness.

"You wanted to see me," said Patzig, more as a statement than a question. But before Theurer could speak he added. "I trust it is not about our brothers in arms in the SS. You know I was at Berchtesgaden before my trip to Wilhelmshaven and I think I understand the Führer's mind on the matter of our relative areas of operation. He made things very clear to me. In fact, I had a long conversation with Göring about the problems of inter-service cooperation. Now what was it you wanted to discuss so urgently?"

Patzig sat back in his chair and folded his hands into a steeple while Theurer cast about for a reply. He had come prepared to be rebuffed, after days of not being able to speak to the head of the Abwehr, he expected that there was a major problem, so he presented some pap about Soviet intentions against the Reich. Patzig listened politely, knowing that he had just pulled the rug out from under his subordinate's feet. Well, Theurer was going to have to make his way in the world without Konrad Patzig's help.

Back in his office Theurer was fuming. Without Patzig as intermediary with Göring, there was no way that he would convince anyone of the existence of Himmler's and Heydrich's treachery. He had come too far to abandon his plans now, there must be a way forward, and if not, at least he would take all of them down with him. With a sigh, Theurer realized that until he could pull everything together, he needed to disappear from view, and with luck, he would just stay ahead of Kleist.

Albrecht Theurer needed to remain out of sight. He stood in the shadows across the street from his Charlottenburg apartment and watched Kleist and his men go in and ransack the place while worried residents of the adjoining apartments cowered behind their doors. They would be waiting for him at his office as well, if he were to appear at Tirpitzufer. No, he had to use his fall back location. He had always planned for this eventuality, but had never truly believed that he would need it. As the last of the Grosser Mercedes departed the street, he faded back into the shadows, made his way to the S-Bahn, and headed for the opposite end of the metropolis. He would have to make some changes to his plan.

Champagne Nights

The occasion of the Air Olympiad prompted the embassies of
each of the participating countries to put on lavish receptions
on the Thursday evening of before the send-off. Stiffler and
Braham decided to drop in on each in turn. Sleek limousines and
prosaic taxis crowded the front entries of each national outpost.
Military men of a dozen countries sported their best uniforms with
dazzling arrays of medals displayed across their torsos. In the warm
evening, with twilight lingering, diplomatic Berlin was a sea of
lights and pleasant laughter. Outside the circles of lighted
hospitality, the watchers of the Gestapo and Heydrich's SD kept to
their posts while their senior leaders mixed and mingled with the
guests. Stiffler decided that they should begin with a visit to the
establishment of Germany's traditional foe.

The French embassy had laid on cases of champagne and a
bevy of lovely young women straight from the catwalks of the
Parisian fashion houses. Apparently, these young lovelies harbored
no ill feelings toward those wearing the uniform of their former
adversary. Most of the girls were barely out of their teens, and the
older and sultrier of the assembled flock were more than able to
hold their own against any man, regardless of nationality. As fliers
mixed with models, the inevitable tall tales began, as noted by the

pairs of hands indicating friendly and enemy airplanes swooped in front of the eyes of admiring women. Braham and Stiffler decided after a half hour to move on.

At the Italian embassy Stiffler's Luftwaffe uniform guaranteed a warm welcome. While the food and drink flowed, the atmosphere in the reception room was chilled a bit by the glowering presence of Il Duce's immense portrait on the wall. Stiffler was made welcome by the unattached females in the room and had soon found himself a redhead who insisted she was the Contessa Rosa DelaVentre. The countess, exaggerating her tipsiness, wrapped a long arm around Stiffler and demanded that he escort her for the rest of the evening. Stiffler tried to demure, after all, he had a wife and family. He tried to charm his way out of it, but when it came time to go, the veritable countess remained attached to the flier, and she joined them on their way to the Polish embassy. When the taxi brought the three of them to the embassy's front entrance, it was clear the countess wanted male company. Once inside the embassy Stiffler escorted the countess toward a groaning buffet table desperately looking for one of his younger, bachelor officers. A moment later he was introducing the young Hauptman Joachim Stürken to the lady. Tall, with summer sun-bronzed skin the young man proved just what the lady had in mind. With a bow Stiffler backed away. With a short wave to Braham he left the room and headed for a taxi and home.

Jerzy Krol was standing at the top of a long curving staircase overlooking the lobby of the embassy as Braham entered. He saw his friend take a champagne flute from a passing waiter and eye several blondes who, seemingly unattached, adorned the entryway. As a trio of them, ranging in height from average to very tall, converged on the new arrival, a hand reached out and touched his shoulder.

"There's time for them later," Krol instructed. "Karl is waiting."

Jerzy Krol had been as good as his word; the documents that his craftsmen in Warsaw had created were flawless. Much of that came from the fact that the paper upon which the letters were drafted was stolen from the offices of those responsible for the printing official documents and stationery in Moscow and Berlin. For over a decade, in the depths of night, an operation of petty thievery took place in the darkened offices of European officialdom, at the behest of the Warsaw intelligence service. Painstakingly, sheet-by-sheet, faceless charwomen, mostly Polish, who went unnoticed by the bureaucrats for whom they cleaned and scrubbed, purloined the paper and passed it along to men who gave them a few kopeks or Reichsmarks for their trouble.

"Do you think these will do the job?" asked Krol as Braham examined each sheet of carefully typed and properly aged paper.

"How did you get the paper to the right color."

"It's supposed to be a secret, but I'm told they use tea and urine," replied Krol.

Braham brought the paper toward his nose. "I don't smell it."

"Then they have done their job well. What will you do with them?"

Braham looked at his friend and smiled. "This next part is tricky. Gisela is going to have to put on another performance, this time for her husband and Kleist. Karl, are you up for a little late-night stage management?"

Krol led the pair out through the back of the embassy into a formal garden and then out of the grounds through a service door to the street beyond.

"If anyone is interested in you tonight, they will be watching the front," said Krol hopefully.

Just down the street Krol kept an embassy Horch parked for times he wanted to go places without arousing the interest of the ever-present watchers from the SD or the NKVD. Poland, situated as it was between two nations of bullies, was always being spied upon, and its embassy in Berlin was a prime target. But bureaucracies worldwide worked the same way and gravitated toward the obvious, so while the watchers kept their vigil on the front door, operatives like Krol came and went by the rear.

"Where to?" Krol asked when they had slipped into the automobile.

"Jerzy, you need to keep your skirts clean on this. It wouldn't do to have you noticed around Abwehr headquarters."

Krol laughed, "Not a problem my friend. This car is owned by the Polish nation, but the number plates on it are from a SS car that was brought into a garage for repair. No one will bother us tonight."

Fifteen minutes later, the car, its lights off, pulled to a stop in the Tirpitzufer. Braham got out of the car and looked up and down the shadowy pavement. No one was about save a lone policeman walking his beat a block away. The silhouette of his peaked cap seen in the streetlights showed him ambling away. The men held their breath but the cop just melted away into the night. Karl Lieberman walked to the car from the shadows as Braham retrieved a small satchel from the rear seat.

"It is ten-thirty now, come back in a half-hour," Braham said. "If we are not here, try again fifteen minutes later, then again fifteen minutes after that. If we are not here by then, go back to the embassy and wait to hear from us."

Krol nodded and pulled away as Braham and Lieberman dropped back into the shadows. Lieberman led Braham along the same path he had used when he had followed Theurer several weeks before. Now instead of taking things from the Abwehr office, they were going to put a few things in.

"Remember, we don't want him dead," Braham told Lieberman.

As they waited in the darkness outside Theurer's office, they could hear the shuffling step of the old pensioner as he made his rounds getting closer. "You would have thought that in a place of secrets they would have tighter security," Lieberman whispered.

Braham shrugged and looked down the long hallway. The watchman inserted the key from the watch post at the end of the hall into the clock hanging from the strap around his shoulder and twisted it to register time and place, and then he shuffled forward toward where the pair had hidden in the shadow of a pillar.

"*Guten Abend, mein Herr!*" Braham said as he stepped in front of the man. Startled, the watchman grabbed at his chest as Lieberman quickly reached in front of the man and placed a chloroform soaked cloth over his mouth and nose. An instant later, the man's legs crumpled and Lieberman helped him gently slide to the floor.

"Get rid of that cloth before we get woozy too," said Braham and went about jimmying open Theurer's office door. Braham found the files on both of the Von Teischens, along with some notes on Stiffler and a few others whose names were familiar to him. These he stuffed into the small satchel that Lieberman carried and then helped himself to a few file folders marked "*Geheime*," secret, those were something that Krol did not have in his inventory. When they left the building ten minutes later, the watchman was still on the floor, breathing softly. Theurer's office was a shambles, with files pulled out and scattered over the floor. To the Gestapo officers who would arrive in the morning everything would appear as if a break-in had occurred. When Krol came by on Tirpitzufer, Braham and Lieberman scampered from the shadows and jumped into the Horch. Twenty minutes later Braham was back at the Polish embassy and Lieberman was on his way to deliver to Gisela von Teischen the doctored documents, which were now nestled inside an official Abwehr file folder.

At just after nine o'clock the next morning Countess Gisela von Teischen swept through the SS's Albrechtstrasse headquarters and charged into her husband's office. With the protests of his worried secretary in her wake, she pushed open the doors and strode inside.

"Christian! Christian, I must speak to you. Please stop what you are doing, and please pay attention to me!"

Christian von Teischen, startled from his morning routine of reviewing reports and sipping coffee, looked up from his desk to see his wife standing before him and trotting right behind her his florid-faced secretary, shrugging her shoulders uselessly as if to say what could I do she is a countess after all and your wife.

"Thank you, Fraulein Bosch, that will be all. I forgot to mention to you that the Countess might be coming by today," and, forcing a smile, shooed her away with a wave of his hand.

The White Raven

Gisela was dressed in her signature white, but there was nothing serene in her manner. Today it was a Channel suit accented by a crimson blouse with tiny white dots with a flourish of a bow at the neck. It was the kind of outfit a woman wore to an afternoon garden party, or lunch on some millionaire's yacht. My god, he thought, she was beautiful. If it were not for the fire in her eyes, von Teischen would have dismissed her actions as mere theatrics. But something about her and the pose she was striking made him hesitate.

"My dear Gisela," he spoke condescendingly in his most unctuous manner, using the same tone of voice he employed with errant subordinates to let them know how important and powerful he had become. "You seem in quite a state. What brings you here? Please sit down."

She remained standing, impervious to her husband's attempt to placate her. "Shut up, Christian, don't talk to me like that. I am not one of your flunkies. Listen to me; there is no time to lose. I came because we—you—must do something before it is too late."

With that, she produced the copy of Theurer's list of those he would liquidate when he assumed control of the government.

"Look at this and see whose names are listed there. I am trying to save both our lives, and in the meantime perhaps make you a hero."

Von Teischen looked at his wife and seeing the icy fire in her eyes decided it would be wise to hear her out.

"But what is this?" he asked, began to speak, but fell silent as he read their names on the list.

The White Raven

"That my dear is a list of those whom Herr Doktor Albrecht Theurer is planning to have liquidated once his scheme to get rid of your playmates in the SS comes to fruition. Here, read these," she said and thrust out the Abwehr folder holding the sheaf of papers that Lieberman had delivered to her late last night.

Von Teischen did as she commanded and began to pour through the stack of pages she provided. What he read there, in the letters and notes so well crafted by Krol's associates, implicated Theurer as the head of a Moscow-based plot to eliminate key members of the Reich prior to the Party rally just a few weeks away. Getting to the end of the papers, he looked at his wife and then again went through the documents.

"But what, how did you come by these?" Suspicion had crept into his voice. But she was defiant.

"You have your interests and I have mine. Our sham of a marriage serves us both, and we have put on the appropriate front that has helped you in your career. Now it is time to shore up that front. Here is what you must do."

Von Teischen seemed to hesitate, but then listened to his wife rattle off point-by-point of the next actions he must take. When she had finished, he looked at her with surprise and a new sense of admiration.

"The only way for us to survive this nasty plot is to put ourselves ahead of it. By now, Kleist will know about a break in at the Abwehr. You, my pet, will claim that you have come into possession of files from Theurer's office, which implicate Doktor Albrecht Theurer in a plot to attack the SS and the Führer. If Kleist presses you as to how you got the file, you have to assert yourself and say that you took action yourself to obtain the evidence that Kleist needed. Don't say any more. Kleist will be pleased that you brought it directly to him; after all he regards himself as your liege lord in all this. When he sees that our names and his are on the execution list, we will be in the clear. Let him take things from there."

Christian von Teischen took a deep breath and reached for the telephone on his desk. His secretary, worried that perhaps the countess had come that morning to slit her boss's throat over one of his not too-discrete-dalliances, picked up the line on the first ring.

"Fraulein Bosch, please connect me with Hauptsturmführer Otto Kleist immediately."

Christian von Teischen put his hand over the mouthpiece of the phone as he waited for Kleist and looked at his wife. Gisela had retrieved the purse, which she had flung onto one of the chairs when she stormed into the room, and turned to leave.

"I leave you to deal with your friend Kleist, while I attend to other business. Don't forget about the reception tonight," then she turned and left his office.

Von Teischen stood staring at her while on the phone a voice was shouting, "Kleist here! Who is it?"

Silken Retribution

Gisela had known all along that this day was coming, she had prayed that it would not, but now it was too late for sentimentality. She had known from the beginning that one day she would have to do something terrible in order to save her and perhaps all the others she had helped since she assumed the role of the White Raven. The White Raven was more than just Gisela von Teischen, there were men and women throughout Germany who had helped her, offered their services and accepted nothing in return but the gratitude of the hopeful souls they had led to freedom. But Theurer had come along and changed all that. Now, if he talked when Kleist got his hands on him, and she knew he would squeal like a pig going to the slaughter when the SD had him, all would be lost. He would tell Kleist that his new girlfriend, Inga Carlson had helped her. Inga could confirm who the White Raven was, and that would be that. Inga would not stay silent, how could she? Kleist would treat her like any other enemy of the state. Either way Inga was a dead woman.

Gisela could not go from Albrechtstrasse to the flower shop; the white Mercedes she had driven that morning was too recognizable. No, she would have to drive down the Ku'dam to the Mercedes showroom and leave the car, complaining about a nasty rattle from somewhere. Herr Kreizler, the manager, would fawn over her and see to it right away. There was no rattle, but for such a customer as the Countess von Teischen, they would do anything. Meanwhile she would have them call her a taxi. She had shopping to do and would return later that day to collect the car, with the rattle, no doubt, removed.

Kreizler was just as unctuous as usual and barely refrained from kissing her feet as she entered the showroom with the sleek and gleaming automobiles, destined to grace the garages and stables of Party hacks, sparkling under the interior lights. After ten minutes of bowing and scraping, Gisela asked if she might use their telephone. Of course, was the immediate reply, and she was given the privacy of Herr Kreizler's office to make her call while he went to see about her nasty rattle.

She dialed the operator and asked to be connected to Inga's private number. After three rings the line was picked up, and Gisela heard Inga Carlson answer, "Hallo?"

Gisela wasted no time in telling the florist that she needed to speak to her in person, immediately. Was she alone? She was. That was good. Could she come up to her apartment without going through the shop? Yes, through the back entrance. That was good. Inga could expect her in thirty minutes. Gisela hung up the phone and breezed out of the manager's office.

Kreizler saw her and ran up to her. "Countess, we are looking into the problem. Would you care to wait?"

"No, I have shopping to do, please call a taxi for me. I will be back later today to collect the car."

Moments later she was speeding up the thoroughfare toward the shops near KaDeWe, Berlin's iconic department store.

The White Raven

There she had the cab driver stop and, after paying the man, walked into the store as the doorman held open the plate glass door and saluted her. Once inside, she moved rapidly among the counters holding assortments of goods and accouterments for the fashionable German woman. At one counter she stopped and bought a long silk scarf, commenting to the sales lady at the counter about the bright floral print. The sales lady dutifully wrapped the item and tied the package with ribbon. The charge for the item would go, as usual to the von Teischen account. At the opposite side of the floor she exited the building and, hailing another taxi, instructed the driver to take the back way along the Kurfürstendamm. Inside the taxi, Gisela withdrew the scarf from its wrapping and, holding the length of the scarf in both hands, deftly tied a knot in the middle of the fabric, and then returned the scarf and its package to her purse. Two blocks from the flower shop, she called out to the driver to stop and, after paying him, watched him pull away while she pretended to be absorbed by the menu chalked on a board outside a small restaurant.

With quiet determination, Gisela made her way around the block to the side street where Inga said the door to the rear entrance to her apartment was located. A small card inscribed with I. Carlson was tacked to the doorframe. Gisela stepped quietly to the door and turned the knob. With a slight push, the door opened, and she found herself in a narrow space at the base of a stairway leading to the rooms above. With all the stealth she could manage, she climbed the worn carpeted steps until she reached a landing. To her left another set of stairs led down to a closed door. That was the way to the shop no doubt. On her right was another door, painted bright lavender. She knocked quietly.

"Inga, it's I," she spoke in a stage whisper.

The White Raven

A second later the door opened, and Inga let her into the tiny apartment. She was dressed for some occasion, with a bright summer dress of cream silk and orange and green embroidery.

Gisela looked at her. "You look lovely, are you going out?"

Inga blushed, "It's nothing, just a luncheon with a new friend."

"A new friend? Probably more than that, I would guess."

Inga nodded and then turned serious. "What is so urgent that you risk coming here?" asked Inga breathlessly. Something in her manner confirmed for Gisela what she most dreaded. Inga would sell her out if she thought it would save her. Gisela smiled at the woman, the same kind of smile that a doting aunt might use with an errant niece.

"I will only be a moment. I need you to look at some photographs and tell me if you recognize any of the people in them. May I place them on this table, here?"

Inga, by now confused, was relieved that this would indeed be a quick visit; then she would be off to meet the new man of her dreams, Hauptsturmführer Otto Kleist. She set about clearing a place on her tiny dining table, the same one at which Viktor Ryshkov had spent hour upon hour waiting for Inga to make the connection with the White Raven.

Gisela had come prepared with a dozen photos of prominent Berlin males that she had clipped from recent issues of *Das Welt*.

"Here, sit down, and I will put them in front of you. Give them a good look, and tell me if you know who they might be."

The White Raven

"Why do I have to sit?" Inga protested as she sat down. Looking over her shoulder she saw Gisela reach into her purse and produce a small sheaf of photos along with a brilliant scarf. "What a lovely scarf," she said, and then turned to look at the pictures now in front of her.

Gisela waited a second while Inga looked at the first picture. "Why this is Horst Eccles, the yachtsman. I met him at, . . ."

Inga made a gurgling sound from her throat as Gisela slipped the scarf over her head and tightened it garrote-style behind her. Flailing with her hands, the florist tried to loosen the ligature, but could not get any strength to her fingers. As the silken knot crushed her windpipe her feet kicked out at the chair opposite her. Gisela held on, tightening the scarf until she heard cartilage snapping. Inga Carlson went limp and sagged, the scarf holding most of her weight.

For another two minutes Gisela held on to the scarf, then she relaxed and slid the silk from Inga's throat and replaced it and the photos in her bag. She needed only a few minutes more to complete the scene for the police. From Inga's closet she retrieved a pair of silk scarves, knotted them together and made a noose. This she slipped over the dead woman's head and pulled tight. Now was the difficult part. Inga was not a big woman, but in death she was quite literally deadweight. Moving her to the center of the room took some doing.

Like most Berlin apartments, the builders had installed a large hook in the rafters close to the casement windows. This was to assist movers in arranging pulleys to raise furniture to the upper floors without using the stairs. Gisela had noted this feature upon her only previous visit and noted that Inga kept a large potted fern hanging from it. Gisela placed a chair under the hook and climbed up on it and removed the fern, placing it on the floor near the bedroom door. With all the strength that she could muster, Gisela hefted Inga's body on her shoulder and stepped up on to the chair as it creaked under the weight of both women. With her right hand she looped the loose end of the scarf over and around the hook tying it off in a double hitch. With Inga still held on her shoulder, she lowered herself back to the floor. As she did so, she let the scarves take the full weight of the dead woman. As she stepped away, she saw that the body hung down until Inga's naked feet brushed the top of the chair's seat.

Gisela looked around for the dead woman's shoes and tossed them gently toward the apartment door. Then she tipped over the chair, as one would expect to find upon encountering a suicide. From her bag she produced a short note scrawled in the regimented style taught to German schoolgirls. Gisela had written it some time ago, for just this instance. Without fanfare it said that the writer could not go on living a lie and was signed with the stylistic "I" that Inga Carlson had used with all her business correspondence. Nobody at the Kripo office at the Alexanderplatz headquarters would pay much attention.

Gisela exited the apartment as she had come, another face in the faceless army of Berlin citizens going about their day. By two o'clock she was back talking to Herr Kreizler, who, with his usual oily manner, assured her that the problem with her car had been discovered and corrected. Freshly cleaned and gleaming in the bright sunshine, the cabriolet was wheeled out to her, and by three was driving up to her house near Wansee.

She should have felt something, she thought. She had never killed anyone before. Yet she felt nothing. Well, perhaps a certain satisfaction that she had done what she had to do. There was only one more hurdle, Theurer. As she thought about him, she heard the sound of an airplane approaching and, looking up, saw the gleaming silver shape of Arndt Dietrich's Me-108 sweep over the slates of the house and set down on the long stretch of lawn. Now, she had another role to play: hostess to the Nazi swine.

Garden Party

While the Gestapo and SD scoured Berlin for Albrecht Theurer and his accomplices, Gisela von Teischen's reception for the Air Olympiad fliers went ahead as scheduled, on Friday, August twenty-fourth. That evening the von Teischen mansion north of Wansee was awash with the glow of electric lights. Throughout the grounds pathways that led to a large wooden dance floor were illuminated. Music drifted out from an orchestra that had been instructed to play only Aryan music while senior Party officials, such as Goebbels, were present. The hosts had opened their cellar to provide the two hundred–plus guests with the finest vintages. White jacketed waiters circulated with trays of champagne flutes and various canapés that flowed out of the house kitchens in a constant stream. Arndt Dietrich had landed one of the Me-108s that was to fly in the Olympiad on the long roll of lawn in front of the house, where it was now parked, its silver skin basking in the glare of a galaxy of floodlights.

As the guest's cars arrived, they passed beneath a canopy of illuminated flagpoles, each carrying the standard of one of the participating nations. Despite this display of international cooperation, there were enough swastikas visible in every direction to ensure the guests knew who their hosts were. After each long-nosed Mercedes or Horch deposited its passengers at the front of the house, the chauffeurs were directed to an area off the lawn where they could park. Long and sleek, the aggregation of motor vehicles parked there shimmered in the reflective glow of the lights, like a fleet at anchor. There was even a separate pavilion erected in which the drivers could sit and wait with beer and sausages provided by the hosts.

In the foyer of the great house the Count and Countess von Teischen greeted their guests and pointed them to the immense French doors that opened onto the veranda and the lawn beyond. Braham and Krol arrived together in an official Polish Embassy Rolls and were dropped off at the bottom of the broad front steps. As the pair made their way to the front door, it was obvious that security for the event was unusually strong. Not only had an elite SS perimeter guard carefully examined their invitations and credentials before waving the car onward, but as they ascended to the house, they saw that all the guests had to pass through a gauntlet of SS troopers. The black uniformed men stood at attention with their rifles held at order arms position in white-gloved hands. Braham knew from painful experience that the weight of the weapon seemed to increase geometrically for each minute it was held. These must be some strong men.

Gisela von Teischen glimmered in white and silver. Her long gown flowed down and floated a millimeter above the fawn gray carpeting that covered part of the polished marble floor. Her husband, chatting to each passing guest, had diplomatically chosen to wear a white dinner jacket instead of his black dress uniform.

"Countess, may I present Colonel Jerzy Krol of the Polish Air Force," Braham said as Gisela smiled and offered her hand to him. Jerzy took Gisela's extended hand and placed a diplomatic kiss on her white-gloved fingers.

"*Enchanté*, Countess, I am delighted to meet you. Thank you for your invitation."

Braham stepped back a pace and smiled at Gisela, giving her an inquiring look as if to ask: is everything all right? She returned his gaze with a winsome smile and mouthed the word, "later" as he shook her hand and felt the small square of paper that she passed to him. He quickly slipped the note into his jacket pocket as she turned to the next guest. Then the pair walked off to mix with the other guests. As they did Reinhard Stiffler appeared in the foyer. He approached the countess and she gave him a sisterly kiss on each cheek. "Darling Reinhardt, I'm so glad you could come," she said, and he moved toward her husband to shake his hand.

"So, will the Führer make an appearance tonight? There seems to be a large contingent of security here." Stiffler asked Christian von Teischen when they shook hands.

Von Teischen looked nervously around him and replied, "No, he is not one for events like this, though he plans to be at the send-off tomorrow and give a short speech."

Stiffler nodded and drifted away, noting how pre-occupied his host appeared to be. There were many uniforms in the crowd, as with the night before, all of diplomatic Berlin had been invited.

"You don't look so well tonight." Stiffler turned to see his friend Harry Braham standing with an immaculately uniformed Jerzy Krol. Braham had a broad grin on his face. "That was very adroit last night with the Contessa whozits. You handed her off like a hot potato."

"Contessa, my ass, Harry." Stiffler swallowed the last of his champagne and placed the empty flute on the tray of a passing waiter. "She was just another Italian whore out on the town and looking for man. She probably read one of those books that come in plain brown wrappers about some Italian seductress. In fact, I don't even think she was Italian, probably some gypsy from Trieste. I hope she didn't wear out the young Hauptman Stürken. Anyway, Jerzy, you are looking very smart, did you get promoted to field marshal? That is a splendid uniform."

"Very funny, I'm a half-colonel if you must know. This is what our diplomatic service likes the military attachés to wear. I feel like a Ruritainian duke in this get-up."

Braham looked around the crowd and spotted Otto Kleist, equally resplendent in his jet black Hauptsturmführer's rig, walking at the edge of the lawn and talking earnestly with Christian von Teischen. Krol asked Stiffler how he thought preparations for the great fly-off were coming. He wanted to steer the conversation away from his adventure with Braham the previous evening. Reinhardt was a friend, a trusted friend and an old comrade, but he did not need to know everything. It was safer that way.

"There's that bastard Kleist. I think I will just have a word with my new best SS friend, Otto," said Braham, and he strode off.

Braham was several yards away from Kleist when he called out, "Otto!"

Kleist stopped in mid-stride and turned to see the American approaching him.

"Ah, Captain Braham, you know Count von Teischen, of course." Von Teischen, as he was dressed for a garden party, was wearing tuxedo pumps; still, he did his best to click his heels at Braham's approach.

"Count, did you leave your lovely wife to attend to greeting the guests. Well, surrounded as she is by SS troopers, she should be very well protected. Still, I would be very jealous if my wife had that many armed men around her." Braham was doing his best to affect the tone of the fop.

"Yes, Captain Braham. I am afraid the Hauptsturmführer and I had some urgent business to attend to. If you will excuse us."

The two Germans began to turn away, but Braham's next words stopped them.

"Otto," Braham began. "You remember that you were asking me about someone when we spoke at the Adlon. It was a Doktor Theurer, I believe, Albrecht Theurer."

Kleist looked sharply at von Teischen and then back at Braham. "Yes, that is correct. We believe him to be a dangerous man. Why do you ask?"

"Dangerous, really? Well, that is a surprise."

Kleist was losing patience with the American.

"Why do you mention him? You said you did not know him when we spoke."

Braham tried his most disingenuous smile and said, "Well that is true, but you see I was recently in Paris, flew back to Berlin in a honey of an airplane, by the way. Well, you are not interested in that part. I was at a business meeting in Paris; the subject of dealing with the Soviets came up. You know there is no money there; everything is barter and who can unload some of what they have to offer. Anyway, someone mentioned Soviet aircraft and that is when my ears perked up. Next thing you know, the man I was talking to, a French industrialist named Lescroat, said that if I wanted to know anything about Soviet airplanes or the business of importing or exporting aviation products to Russia, I must talk to someone named Doktor Albrecht Theurer."

With that Braham clapped his hands and smiled at the two Germans.

Kleist looked on expectantly, waiting for Braham to continue. At last he asked Braham, "And?"

"And what?"

"Well, what about Theurer?" asked Kleist with exasperation.

Braham feigned bewilderment, "Well, that was it. This Frenchman mentioned Theurer, and, as I knew you were interested in him, I thought I would tell you as soon as I bumped into you."

"Thank you Captain Braham," Kleist replied and turned to leave, but Braham kept on.

"I know that it is probably none of my business, but for a diplomatic affair there seems to be quite a heavy presence of your security men here. Is something up?"

Kleist was tiring of this American and decided to tell him enough to shut him up. "We are concerned that this man Theurer may have planned something outlandish to interrupt the Air Olympiad and cause an incident. Since this event is being held on German soil, the Reich does not wish take any chances. Now if you will excuse us, the count and I have business to attend to. Good evening."

The White Raven

Braham turned away and remembered the slip of paper that Gisela had given him. He pulled a packet of Gauloises from his inside pocket and screwed one of the smokes between his lips. Then he took the note and his lighter from his pocket, and, while he lit the end of the cigarette, he read the note. It read "Gazebo ten p.m." Braham looked at his watch, it was barely nine now, he would have to stall for an hour. Where was the damn gazebo? He hadn't seen one so far. As he stood near one of the long buffet tables, he watched people come and go, carrying plates laden with food, to the tables that were spread out on the grass under a large canopy. As he looked over the crowd, he saw several SS troopers walking slowly along the perimeter of light that came from a series of floodlights rigged in the trees. Kleist was taking no chances. As he watched the soldiers patrol the grass verge that bordered the woods beyond, he spotted the white, Greek columns of a small structure with a round roof covered in gray slate.

Braham saw Dietrich and several of the other pilots chatting at the bar and walked over. "Arndt, how are you?"

Braham's old comrade looked at him and asked, "Will I see you tomorrow?"

"As arranged, old friend. My plane with the beautiful paint job is hard to miss."

"Ha," Dietrich replied, "painted up like a French whore, just like we did back in the old *jagdstaffel* during the war. Tried to scare the enemy with all the bright colors, as if we were not afraid of anything, too bad it didn't work."

"No worries, old friend; just be ready to go as soon as I bring your passenger. *Auf wiedersehen bis morgen.*"

The White Raven

Braham strolled away from the bar, found an empty chair at the far end of the dining area and sipped a little champagne. Several tables away, Jerzy was entertaining several bejeweled women with tales of his exploits against the Bolsheviks back in '22. Reinhardt Stiffler sat back in amusement as he listened to his rescue at the hands of Harry Braham being related in such detail by a man who at the time was miles away. Amused, Stiffler cruised off to the bar in search of schnapps. Nearby, the orchestra continued playing an ensemble of tunes appropriate for a Nazi evening.

At nine-thirty, he saw Gisela moving from table to table among her guests making her way in the general direction of the gazebo. Braham checked his watch and keeping her in his sight; he rose and ambled off toward the gazebo and out of the lighted part of the lawn.

"Cigarette?" he asked when she came up the steps to where he was sitting.

"Yes, I need something," she whispered.

He produced two Gauloises, put them to his lips and lit them both, then he handed her one.

"How gallant," she said and took a long drag.

"So what happened with Kleist? Did he buy the story?"

Gisela smiled ruefully. "Oh, if you mean did he believe what Christian told him, then he bought it all right. Christian is now storm trooper of the month in Kleist's book. So am I, it seems, at least until he gets his hands on Theurer. If the doktor is made to tell all that he knows, well then . . . well, you know."

"So Kleist hasn't found him, then?"

"No, according to Christian, half the SD and most of the Gestapo are out looking for him. They found the others though. According to Christian, two of them were "shot while trying to escape," Schilling ran from the men sent to arrest him and shot himself in front of his secretary. The fourth, Premml, was not so lucky; they have him in the cellars at Albrechtstrasse. By now he probably wishes now that he was dead. I am scared Harry. For the first time since this all began, I am really scared."

Braham reached an arm around her, she was shivering, "With any luck, I'll find him first. He still thinks I am bringing Ryshkov to Berlin."

"I hope so." Gisela tossed her cigarette down and crushed it with the sole of her silver lamé shoe.

"Gisela, tomorrow at the fly off I can get you out of Germany. No matter what happens with Theurer, you're not safe here," Braham offered.

"What are you saying Harry, that you want me to run off to some desert island with you?"

Braham had no words for her.

"I thought so. Well, if it comes to that I might, but you don't have to be responsible for me. I can handle myself. But right now, I have to go back inside. Christian is going to make a presentation to all the fliers here. Stick around; we are to have fireworks afterwards. Don't all you Americans like fireworks?"

Braham watched her go, the long gown swaying softly as she stepped over the manicured grass. He took out another cigarette and was lighting it when Stiffler and Krol appeared.

The White Raven

"We thought we should give the two of you some privacy. Christ, Harry, have you gotten yourself in deep with our hostess?" asked Stiffler.

Braham nodded in reply, and the three friends smoked in silence. A moment later the music changed and the orchestra took up the strains of *Deutschland Uber Alles*, whereupon everyone stood, and the Germans added the Hitler salute to their posture. As the music began to repeat the strains of the anthem, several things happened at once. First, there was a long scream followed by several flat, popping sounds. Braham had no doubt about who had screamed, but he just hoped the popping sounds had not been what his brain knew them to be. A moment later, the heavier report of an automatic weapon could be heard losing a burst of ten shots or so. The guests, stunned at first, were now on their feet and making for any exit they could find. Men were shouting and some women crying out. The neat order of the garden party had turned into a melee of escaping guests.

At the second sound of shots, the three men sprang to their feet and started running toward the rear of the house. Stiffler had drawn his service sidearm, and he let it dangle in his hand as he made for the lighted doorway. At the door they stopped to listen. Shouts in German could be heard up ahead. None of the three was sure what had happened, so they moved in cautiously. Inside the house a flagged corridor led into a huge summer kitchen; the lights from this room had spilled out onto the lawn, creating a pattern of bright squares on the grass. It was clear that the catering staff, upon hearing the shots, had made a hasty exit, spilling bowls of prepared food and scattering kitchen implements as they fled.

Wordlessly, the three men made their way further into the house. Somewhere up ahead they heard more shouting and recognized the voice of Otto Kleist issuing commands. Stepping carefully up a service stairway at the end of the corridor, the three found themselves in the main vestibule of the house. The air was thick with plaster dust from where a machine pistol had stitched holes in the ornate ceiling. It was clear into whom the shots had been fired.

Count Christian von Teischen lay face down on a large Berber carpet that was turning from pale gray to burgundy. Next to him, at the tips of his dead fingers, lay a Walther pistol. Across the room another man, dressed in an SS trooper's uniform, lay against the wall, clutching at his side as blood oozed onto the polished marble, the weapon that shot the holes in the ceiling at his feet. Otto Kleist stood next to the count's body, looking down at it as if he expected the man to stop fooling around and pull himself to his feet. As the trio stepped into the room, Kleist spun around; he was holding a Mauser machine pistol in his right hand, the broom handle model with the box magazine forward of the trigger. For an interminably long moment he covered them with the weapon as his facial muscles tensed and he tried to work out who these men were. He relaxed only when he recognized Stiffler's uniform, and then he lowered the Mauser. None of the three moved. They remained immobile, watching Kleist, perhaps not quite believing that he would not use the Mauser after all.

"As you can see, gentlemen, there has been a tragic occurrence. Count von Teischen has been shot. According to one of my men," Kleist said, pointing the Mauser toward the wounded man on the far side of the room. "I had left von Teischen for a few minutes guarded by corporal Giersch, while I telephoned my headquarters. I heard shouting and then a series of shots. Apparently, Theurer had arrived at the house with the catering staff. We will know more about that when my men have done with interrogating them."

"If they survive," Krol whispered.

"Where is the countess?" Braham asked as he looked around the room for her. Before Kleist could answer several more troopers, with weapons drawn, ran into the room. Behind them came an elderly man dressed in evening clothes.

"Hauptsturmführer" shouted one of the new arrivals. "Here is Doktor Winkel."

Kleist turned to the elderly man who was looking from the corpse to the wounded trooper. The SS officer spoke softly to the doctor. "Herr Doktor Winkel, you are a physician, may I assume?"

"Yes," the man said hesitantly, "But I don't treat patients. I am a researcher in tropical medical at the Max Planck Institute."

Kleist grimaced for a moment. "Well, Herr Doktor, could you please at least see to corporal Giersch there until we can get an ambulance to take him to hospital. I am afraid the count is beyond your help."

While the doctor did his best to make the wounded trooper comfortable, Kleist returned his gaze to Braham and his companions.

"Well," said Kleist, "as to the countess, it appears that Doktor Theurer has taken her. From what I got from Giersch, a man fitting Theurer's description came into the room from the same direction as you did, pushing the countess in front of him. Giersch said that the countess's hands were bound, and she was gagged. Her husband tried to stop him, and Theurer shot him and the corporal. Then he dragged the woman toward the north side of the house."

"Why did he take her?" asked Stiffler.

"Ah," replied Krol, "those questions seem to be answered by this," whereupon he held up a sheet of paper that he had been holding in his left hand. From the distance of ten feet Braham could see that it was covered with a slashing scrawl and spattered with flecks of red.

"What is it?" Braham asked pointing to the paper.

"Well, Captain Braham, it is interesting that you should ask, as you seem to now be a part of this melodrama. It is a manifesto of sorts; it demands, among other things, that Doktor Albrecht Theurer be flown out of Germany tomorrow to a neutral country." Kleist took a moment to look again at the paper. "Yes, and he demands that you, of all people in fact, be the person to fly him away to safety. He will call here with instructions in the morning."

"Me? Why me?" asked Braham.

Kleist looked further at the document, "Well it says that you will do this or he will kill the Countess von Teischen. He must assume that you have some feelings for the lady."

Before Braham could speak another of the SS guard detachment ran in, blood gushing from a wound on his forehead. Several more men in black uniforms, guns drawn, rushed in behind him.

"Hauptsturmführer!" the wounded man called.

Kleist swirled around as the man sank to his knees. "Yes sergeant, what is it?" Then seeing that the man's scalp had been cut to the bone, Kleist snapped, "Where is the ambulance, Herr Doktor Winkel is, I am afraid, out of his depth with this."

The White Raven

Braham and Krol found the wounded man a chair and helped him to it. Then, with a trembling voice, the sergeant told of how, after the shots were fired, he was running toward the house near the gazebo when a man came at him from the darkness and hit him with a shovel. He went down, but then saw the man run off toward the edge of the woods, and he was dragging a woman behind him, she appeared to be bound." That was the last he said before passing out.

Coffee in the Library

Albrecht Theurer was not above hitting a woman, especially if she was not behaving as he instructed. Now, the Countess von Teischen lay at his feet, blood trickling from the side of her head where he had struck her with his fist. He was not, he thought, a misogynist. He liked women, but as he thought about it, mostly as receptacles for his penis. Perhaps that was why he had never seen fit to marry any of the women he had bedded over the years. Once the passion of the moment was over, they held little interest for him. God forbid that he would ever have to curry the favor of one of the mothers of his conquests. No, he was better off alone. Gisela von Teischen, despite her obvious sex appeal, would not have been someone for whom he could care, however briefly. She was too independent. He had been forced to give her a sharp knock to the side of her head when she tried to run from him on the way to the truck. She was quiet now, sleeping from the shot of pentothal that he gave her. She would be out for a few hours, enough time for him to get her to the airfield and wait for Braham and the others. If he could get them to see reason and let him fly away, it did not matter about Himmler and the rest, if not, well, he had time enough to think that through. All of them were damned anyway. He would just help them on their way to hell.

The White Raven

It had been an inspiration to steal the catering truck earlier that day. None of the SS oafs had bothered to check to see if it was the same caterer who was handling the affair; they were looking for a potential terrorist, not *paté foie gras*. All he had to do was drive onto the grounds and park it behind the gardener's shed. He had seen the white 540 cabriolet sweep up the drive from his observation post inside the shed. The simultaneous arrival of the airplane confused him at first, but its use as a prop for the evening's festivities reassured him that his plans would work.

Theurer congratulated himself on his planning. With all the commotion after the shots were fired, it was simple enough to fade away, while the guards ran in the opposite direction. Still, he had to be careful; soon enough even the Gestapo would be looking for anything remotely connected to the party. A caterer's van would be easy enough to spot on these narrow country roads. Entering the Grunewald he pulled off the road and into a small clearing where a black Audi Type 3 was parked. He pulled the truck alongside and opened the car's bulbous trunk. Hefting the countess from the rear of the truck, he placed her inside the car's trunk, making sure she was still breathing. Although the night was not cold, he covered her with a blanket and closed the lid. With luck, by the time the police found the truck, he would be airborne and out of the country.

At the von Teischen home the efficiency of the SD had begun to take hold. Two ambulances had arrived. A squad of medics bearing stretchers and medical supplies had relieved the weary Doktor Winkel. Kleist was going to have to own up to the shooting of an important Nazi supporter, he would have to call Heydrich of course. Both the head of the SD and the SS were meeting in Nuremburg in preparation for the annual Party rally, which was two weeks away. If he was artful in how he described the killing, he might just get away with a slap on the wrist.

By two a.m. Kleist had been given a curt rebuff from Heydrich, who was more interested in the whereabouts of Theurer than the loss of von Teischen. "You have permission to kill Theurer on sight when you locate him." Then, changing to a wistful tone, Heydrich said, "You know Kleist, I have always liked that house, especially the grounds. I understand the lawn is long enough for one to land a plane. Yes, perhaps, once you dispose of the count's killer, his lovely wife might be induced to sell the place to me."

Kleist turned out all the men he could command. It was clear from the note that, once Theurer called, the action would move to an airfield nearby.

"Captain Braham, just where did you leave your airplane?"

Braham looked at Stiffler, "I left it in the care of the German air force at Templehof." Turning to point at Reinhardt, he continued, "Since it is officially a US Government aircraft, Colonel Stiffler has it under guard there, along with the other planes that will fly off tomorrow morning."

Kleist paced the room for a few moments and then realized that he had been duped. He had to wait for Theurer's call to verify that, indeed, he would release the countess in exchange for safe passage, but there would be more than one airplane flying away from Templehof in the morning. In fact, there would be more than ninety, German, Polish, French, Italian aircraft and even this American's airplane departing into the skies at the same time. Theurer could be aboard any of them. He would have to move fast. Stepping to the phone, he called his office again and requested that a team of SS marksmen be assembled and ready to meet him at Templehof at dawn. Now they all just had to wait. "Let us hope that this can be settled before the Führer's arrival at the airfield," Kleist mused. "In the meantime," he pointed at Braham and the others," All of you will remain here. If we can locate any of the kitchen staff, I will have coffee brought to us. That will make the waiting more endurable."

Jerzy Krol coughed and arched an eyebrow at this suggestion, and then, as if on command, the men looked at the body, the bloodstains on the floor, and then at one another. Kleist looked around and beckoned one of the SS troopers standing guard. "Please have the count removed and his body taken to a mortuary. Call the duty office in Albrechtstrasse, they will know which one to use, ask them to send a hearse immediately. Meanwhile, gentlemen, I think we will be more comfortable in the library. Shall we?"

Kleist knew the house and pointed the way. At a nod from him, one of the armed troopers stepped quickly ahead, opened the door to the library and swept the room with the barrel of his weapon. As he did so the sound of heavy snoring was evident. The trooper, sure that he had cornered another assassin, shouted, and two more troopers rushed past Kleist and the others to bring their weapons to bear.

"*Wer ist da?*" They shouted in unison. Then they spotted the bulk of a man in evening dress, sprawled on a couch at the far side of the room. Getting no response but a gurgle and snort from their first entreaty, they tried again. This time the figure moved and, half sitting, blinked his eyes at them.

"Arndt, Arndt Dietrich, what the hell are you doing here?" asked Stiffler, and turning to Kleist said, "Tell your men to drop their weapons, this is Arndt Dietrich. He is one of the Air Olympiad pilots."

Kleist gave Stiffler a wary glance but told the troopers to stand down. Stepping forward he looked at the man on the couch, who was rubbing sleep and drink out of his eyes. Two empty champagne bottles toppled from the couch as Dietrich tried to stand up.

"Who the hell are you?" the flier growled in confusion. "Reinhardt, what's going on? I was trying to get some sleep, what is all this? Hey, Jerzy, Harry, good to see you."

Kleist spun around and looked at Krol and Braham, "Do you know this man?"

"Certainly," Braham replied, "We are old comrades from the fighting outside Warsaw a dozen years ago. That's where we beat those Bolsheviks, didn't we Arndt?"

Dietrich nodded coming fully awake, "You can say that again. We sent those bastards straight to hell. What the hell is the SS doing here? I thought this was a party for us fliers."

"Herr Dietrich," Kleist asked, "Did you not hear the shooting some while ago?"

"Shooting? Who was shot?"

"It was our host, the Count von Teischen. You didn't hear the shots?" asked Stiffler.

"Must not have, I came in here with these," Dietrich pointed at the bottles, "and took a nap. I have got to fly that 108 out there in the morning so the Führer can give us his blessing. What the hell time is it?"

Kleist winced at Dietrich's blasphemy but chose to let it go, the man was obviously drunk and not worth his time.

"Nearly two, Arndt," Braham said, and then slowly asked, "Will you be able to fly in the morning?" Braham was looking intently at the man upon which so much would depend in a few hours time.

"Harry, you know me. I fly better with a little booze in me."

"It's an important flight, you know. Do you have enough fuel?" Braham asked this question offhandedly, but it registered with Dietrich who was sober now.

"*Jawohl*, Harry."

"Well," Kleist stated, "Since our pilot has availed himself of the couch, I suggest that we make ourselves as comfortable as possible. I am certain that Herr Dietrich will not mind waiting with us, do you?"

Dietrich was about to protest but a glance from Stiffler silenced him. Twenty minutes later one of the troopers returned with one of the von Teischen maids. Clearly a country girl, the maid had been found hiding in the butler's pantry. Scared and aware only that something dreadful had happened in the house, she had been convinced to make coffee for, as the trooper put it to her, "the gentlemen in the library." Now she entered the room pushing a teacart laden with a coffee pot, cups, and a plate of cakes that were to be served to the evening's guests as dessert.

"Thank you, *fräulein*." Kleist smiled at her. The girl gave a little curtsey and, stifling a sob, ran from the room. "Gentlemen, help yourselves," he added. At four-thirty, the jangling of the telephone roused them into action.

Kleist took the call, "*Ja*," was all he said, and then Theurer gave him instructions. Theurer had already hung up when Kleist attempted a rebuttal.

"Templehof in two hours. If he sees any troops or police, he will kill the countess. Now, Captain Braham, let us see how skillful you are in effecting the safe release of the Countess von Teischen."

Man on Fire

Blood red, the rising August sun seared its way into the morning sky. Above, the sky was clear, dotted only here and there with twists of night clouds. Everything in the atmosphere promised to make it a torrid day. It was the kind of day that made you beg for an afternoon thunderstorm, just to wash away the gritty feeling from the dense air. Braham harkened to the sailor's omen of red sky at morning and remembered so many other mornings when he had launched into the heavy summer air to engage in battle. This morning there was no horde of Cossacks charging out of the east, just a man with a gun and a woman who needed his help. They had come to the back gate to the airfield. In the distance, past the cluster of hangars and the broad sweep of grass that marked the landing area, beyond the rows of neatly parked airplanes with each country's national insignia on their sides, a phalanx of flags fluttered around a platform, a fence of microphones at its fore. All it needed was the bombast and vitriol of the day's featured speaker as he sent his team of fliers off to show the world that German aviators were the best.

Braham's brightly painted Mailwing was parked along the flight line fifty yards from the other planes. Nearby were a pair of tarred-roofed hangars against which sections of assorted wings and

339

fuselage parts had been stacked. Weeds grew among empty fuel drums, which stood like rusty pilings in a sea of grass. From what little Kleist had conveyed to him after he received Theurer's call, the countess and her captor were in one of these hangar's waiting for him. Theurer said that once he was sure Braham was alone, then he would set the Gisela free and Braham would fly him to safety. Braham did not believe a word of it.

The gate at the rear entrance to the field was, in fact, a long wooden telegraph pole painted white and black. Its tip was chained to a stanchion set in concrete on the far side. At the butt end a counterweight was attached that extended beyond a simple fulcrum. In order to admit vehicles to the field, a guard had to unchain the tip and then, using his arms, push up on the tip until the counterweight took over and raised the bar. There was a candy-striped guard hut to the right of the gate. Inside, a pair of armed sentries, already sweating in their heavy field gray uniforms, watched as several cars approached and then stop a hundred yards up the road. For a moment, they just stared at the long black cars. Neither man knew what to do. They had been assigned to the post the previous evening. They were told they would be relieved at dawn, and then they could get something to eat. They had no instructions about letting anyone through, and, anyway, were not sentries supposed to challenge everyone coming toward the gate? But these cars were just sitting there. They did not have a telephone on which to call someone if trouble did arrive. But then again, who were they to call? A crusty old sergeant, named Kurtz, drove them out in a truck around midnight and dropped them at the guard post. Their NCO was an arrogant piece of work, a veteran of the war, and he would never let you forget it either. Finally, after staring at the men by the cars for a while, the pair decided they'd best take up a position on either side of the road, just behind the locked gate. They were clearly outnumbered and could not put up any real resistance if these men wanted to come in, but then that swine Kurtz could not accuse them of failing to do their duty.

Braham sat in the front of Krol's car as it idled just outside the gate to the airfield. Stiffler was in the rear seat. All three were smoking and watching as Otto Kleist and a pair of troopers stepped from the lead car and walk with slow determination toward the guards.

"Harry, take this, you may need it," said Krol and from under the front seat produced a Walther PPK. "It is small enough to tuck into your trousers, in the middle of your back. I don't like you going in to that place with empty hands."

Braham looked back at his friend and at Krol. "He's right Harry. There is no telling what might happen. Especially if the SS here get trigger-happy." Krol smiled.

"What are you going to do when you see Theurer?" Stiffler asked.

Braham shrugged, "I have no idea. Just get her the hell out of here before one of those black-shirted goons gets trigger happy." Then he tucked the gun into his waistband and looked up. Kleist had come to a stop a yard from the barrier. As the Hauptsturmführer came up to them, the hapless guards snapped to attention. A moment later, nervously fumbling with the lock on the chain, they were able to free the barrier. As if they had accomplished the most difficult of maneuvers, the guards proudly swung the barrier up, and Kleist's Mercedes rolled past. Knowing that time was critical, Kleist impatiently beckoned Krol to drive forward.

The White Raven

Braham and his companions stepped from their car and walked to where Kleist and his squad of troopers had taken a position behind his car. Below them, in the hangar nearest to Braham's Mailwing, Theurer was waiting.

Kleist looked at Braham with renewed hatred. He did not like being in the position of having to trust the American. Whether he liked it or not the deaths of both the Count and Countess von Teischen while he was in charge would not go down well in the exalted regions of the Albrechtstrasse, nor, he thought, at Berchtesgaden. He was also sure that if something befell Braham, the repercussions would be severe. Still, he had few options. As long as Theurer had the countess, Kleist would have to play along. Finally, he said, "Theurer said he would deal with only you before releasing the countess."

"Then what are they for?" Braham asked, pointing to a pair of Jaegers dressed in green and carrying hunting rifles with telescopic sights. The pair had joined the caravan of cars from their headquarters at Zossen. Marksmen and mountain troopers, the Jaegers were Kleist's insurance that Theurer would never step into Braham's plane.

"They are my fall back. If we were to storm the building, Theurer would kill the countess and, likely, you as well. But I cannot allow him to fly away with you. Not now." Kleist patted his tunic pocket. Braham was sure the documents that Krol had provided were tucked away there. He was just as certain that Kleist would use them to justify any outcome of the morning's events.

"Just as long as they don't shoot the Countess von Teischen, or me, by mistake. So just what do you want me to do?"

"Captain Braham, the Führer himself will be here in a few hours to address the participants in the Olympiad. I want this situation over and done with before he reaches Berlin. Go down there and get Theurer to show himself. The Jaegers will do the rest. Or, kill him yourself, you are not above that are you? It would certainly save us all a lot of trouble. I can assure you that German justice would find the killing justified."

"Sure, and I'm the next Kaiser. Look, Otto, I am going down there to get the Countess von Teischen and bring her out safely. What happens to Theurer is of no interest to me. As far as I am concerned, you can shove a bone up Theurer's ass and let the dogs drag him away. Meanwhile, in order for this charade to not turn into a massacre, I am going to act like I am playing along with Theurer. If those Jaeger boys can get a shot at him so be it, but if they miss and hit me or the lady, Reinhart over there is going to put a nine-gram slug in your head. Understand?"

Kleist looked over to Krol and Stiffler and saw that they both held automatic pistols in their hands. With a wry smile Stiffler raised the barrel of his to the visor of his uniform cap and saluted the Hauptsturmführer.

"You see Otto, this is what we call in my country a Mexican standoff. You or your boys over there may get a shot at me, but if they do, you will certainly be dead. You might get one of us, but one of them will certainly get you. Now I'll go down and see about the countess, *nicht war?*" With nothing else to discuss, Braham stepped around the car and walked down the sloping grass toward his parked airplane. That he had no real plan gnawed at him. The feeling of the Walther in the small of his back gave him little comfort. He might need it, but he knew his limitations, he was no quick draw artist. Besides, once the shooting started, anything could happen.

Braham thought it best to approach the Mailwing and go about the normal steps of a pre-flight check—the normal things a flier would do before a flight. He would walk around the plane and check the control surfaces and movements of rudder, elevator and ailerons. If Theurer were watching him from inside the hangar, all would look normal. Maybe that would lessen the man's anxiety a bit. As Braham stepped around the parked plane, he saw movement at the door of the hangar on his left. Theurer appeared in a doorway, half hidden from Braham's position and totally out of the line of sight of Kleist's marksmen.

"Captain Braham!" Theurer hissed. Theurer's voice was raised, but not loud enough to carry to where the others were waiting and watching. Braham kept about what he was doing, and Theurer shouted again, louder this time.

Braham turned to look at the man. Theurer was dressed in a waiter's jacket and trousers, the same costume that allowed him to move freely through the von Teischen home the previous night. "Captain Braham, what are you doing? Where is the Russian?"

Near the cars, the Jaegers, with their rifles resting on sandbags laid across the hood of Kleist's car, watched through their telescopic sights. "Can you see what he is doing?" Kleist asked.

"He is standing by the airplane. He seems to be speaking to someone in the hangar just beyond it. Yes, Hauptsturmführer, he seems to be walking in that direction." As the sharpshooters followed Braham with their weapons, Stiffler and Krol moved further apart, just in case.

Although the appearance of Ryshkov could not have helped his predicament, Theurer still held onto a thread of hope that he could pull off his minor *coup d'état*. Braham looked back up the slope to the barricade of cars and then toward Theurer. "He's dead," Braham lied. "The NKVD found him in Paris, before we could get him out of there. I am afraid it is just the three of us now. There is room in the front seat for the two of you. Where is the countess?"

"She is in here. Please, put your hands up and see for yourself."

Braham walked around the plane and over to where Theurer stood holding a large caliber revolver pointed toward him. Probably, thought Braham, a souvenir of the last war.

Theurer stepped back to allow Braham to enter the hangar. With its large doors rolled closed, the cavernous space was in darkness, except for a few shafts of sunlight that shone down from gaps in the structure's roof. Several planes were parked inside along with a half dozen partially assembled engines of various sizes. The workbenches were covered with metal parts, wrenches, taps and die sets, and the assorted other tools that were used to maintain airplanes. Several batteries lay there awaiting service, and a hydrometer, a long tube with a bulbous rubber head, like a turkey baster, that is for testing acid levels in batteries, had been left in the top of one by some absent-minded mechanic. Along the top of one bench there was a shallow metal tray in which grimy parts soaked in pools of gasoline, waiting for a good wire brushing to make them gleam again. There was no difference between this and any aircraft hangar anywhere in the world, except that at the center of this array was a chair to which Gisela von Teischen had been bound.

Braham started toward her, stepping over a pair of wing struts that lay on the cement floor, but Theurer stepped into his path and raised the revolver, "Not so fast Captain Braham." Then with his free hand, Theurer patted Braham down along his chest and hips. Finding nothing, he took a pace back and waved him on with the barrel of the gun. "You may lower your hands, but don't make any fast moves. I don't wish to shoot either of you, but I will have no hesitancy, of course I will shoot the countess as well if you try anything."

Gisela's evening dress lay on the floor, soaking up oil from the puddles there. She was dressed in a pair of mechanic's overalls, which were as grease stained as the floor. A long red welt ran down her left cheek, and there was bruising under her eye.

"What the hell did you do to her?" Braham shouted and spun around to face Theurer. But he stayed beyond his reach and kept the pistol leveled at him.

"Now, now Captain Braham no theatrics. She became uncooperative, didn't you my dear?"

Gisela's eyes flashed at Theurer and then turned toward Braham, as if imploring him to do something. Above them, the low droning of an approaching airplane could be heard.

At the cars, the men turned to see the silver shape of Arndt Dietrich's Me-108 slide down out of the sky and touch down with a soft whishing sound on the grass. Kleist turned to Stiffler who said, "That should be Dietrich." Then the men returned their gaze to hangar. "Can you see anyone down there?" Kleist asked impatiently.

"No, sir," came the sharpshooter's reply.

Braham heard Dietrich's plane land and then the increased roar of its engine as he maneuvered the plane close to where the Mailwing was parked.

The sound of the plane's engine ceased. Braham looked at Theurer and then at Gisela. He had made his decision.

"There is something particularly despicable about a man who hits a woman," said Braham. "So what is your plan Doktor? Is the countess going to be your shield until we get into the plane?"

As he spoke, Braham moved away from Gisela over to the workbench.

"What are you doing?" Theurer was growing impatient.

"Well, Doktor, I don't know how much you know about aircraft engines, but that plane of mine," he said, casually using one of the hydrometers to point toward the Mailwing. "The problem with leaving airplanes parked overnight is that condensation occurs in the fuel system, and that means water in the gas. I do not suppose you would be too happy if we were to fall out of the sky because I had not drained the fuel sump before we take off. The three of us could end up scattered over the countryside. I need to borrow one of these to check." Braham moved the hydrometer over the open cell of the battery and squeezed the device's bulbous head filling the tube with battery acid. "I will need to use this to check the levels and then the three of us can go."

Braham smiled and then stepped to within eight feet of Theurer, the hydrometer in hand.

Theurer looked at the American and then moved the aim of his weapon from him to Gisela. "You keep talking about the three of us leaving," Theurer replied. "I do not really think that it is necessary to subject the countess to the rigors of such a journey." Theurer pulled back the hammer of the revolver with his thumb and pointed it at Gisela. Braham did not hesitate. He pointed the end of the hydrometer at Theurer's face and squeezed its bulbous head. A long stream of sulphuric acid leaped forward, striking Theurer in the right eye. Theurer turned toward Braham, screaming as the acid burned his face. The pistol clattered to the floor and discharged, its muzzle flash igniting the wad of cloth that had been Gisela's evening gown. Theurer, in agony, dropped to his knees his hands scrabbling to wipe at the burning acid as it ate into his skin.

Braham stepped around Theurer and began to untie Gisela. Flames were already racing over the oil soaked floor. Braham knew that everything in the hangar was flammable; they needed to get away. Theurer blinded and in agony, stumbled against the bench that held the long metal parts pans. As they tipped over onto the floor, gasoline splattered ran across Theurer's shoes and trousers. Still screaming in agony, he teetered back and forth until his feet became entangled with the debris on the floor. Theurer tumbled forward into the flames. As he did a bluish flash shot up from the floor followed by another loud whoosh and Theurer became a human torch, staggering in his death throes as fire spread through the hangar.

Gisela sat frozen in the chair. The shock of what she was seeing rooting her in place. Braham pulled her up and hoisted her over one shoulder, in a fireman's carry, and ran away from the flames toward the far side of the hangar. There was a door held in place by an iron hasp. Braham tried to kick at the door, but it would not budge. He tried again, then again. Behind him the flames were reaching to the rafters as waves of fire swept toward the parked airplanes. When the fire reached them, the dope that was used to tighten the fabric that covered the airframes would ignite, and it would only be a moment before the gas tanks inside them exploded. Braham tried the door again. He thought about setting Gisela down, so he could find something else with which to batter the door, but the fire was too close. Suddenly, there was a splintering sound, and the door swung open. Arndt Dietrich stood on the other side holding a length of pipe.

"What the hell is going on Harry? You said to wait for you, but I heard the shot, saw those SS boys near the gate, and thought you needed some help."

"Thanks Arndt, help me get her to your plane. You've got to get her out of here, like we planned."

Dietrich dropped the pipe and ran ahead to the Messerschmitt.

Kleist heard the discharge of Theurer's gun and looked toward where Braham had gone in to the hangar. Stiffler and Krol edged forward, weapons in hand. All of them remained frozen in place for a moment, and then they heard the screams from inside the hangar. They then set off at a run toward the sounds.

"Arndt, you need to go, just as we planned. When you land in Switzerland, you will be met. Karl Lieberman will be there to meet you and take care of the countess. As I promised, Miss Bliss from the US embassy will be there. She will have your passports and travel documents. With luck you will be with your Gracja in Havana in a few weeks."

"Gracja, at last. Harry, I can't thank you enough."

"Arndt, there's time for that later. Get out of here, while I try to deal with Kleist."

Braham reached into the cockpit and kissed Gisela on the cheek. She looked at him with quiet resignation. "Arndt will get you to safety," he whispered. Then Dietrich kicked the plane's engine to life and taxied away from the burning hangar, past the on-rushing fire engines. A moment later he and Gisela were but a speck in the morning sky.

Explanations

Braham had no time to think, only to act. Kleist would be there any moment, and whatever he told the bastard would have to stick. From across the field came the clang of fire engines racing toward the column of black smoke that was pouring into the sky. Braham ran around to the flight-line side of the hangar just as the fire reached the fuel tank of one of the airplanes parked inside. A loud bang was followed by a column of flame shooting out from a gaping hole in the roof. As debris began to rain down, Braham ran to the Mailwing and pulled free the knots that held the wings to the tie downs and kicked away the wheel chocks. He could see Kleist and his troopers about twenty yards away. With all the smoke and the arrival of the fire brigade the Hauptsturmführer hadn't seen him run from the far side of the hangar. Kleist rushed about and shouted to his frightened men to surround the fully engulfed structure.

Braham raced to save the biplane it was his means of exit. He turned away and, by grabbing one of the handles under the Mailwing's tail, he raised the tailwheel and dragged the plane out and away from the conflagration. The plane was heavy, and once he got it rolling over, the smooth grass he found it hard to stop. Over his shoulder he heard shouting.

"Harry!"

Braham turned to see Krol and Stiffler running toward him, their pistols still in their hands.

"Harry," panted Stiffler. "Harry, what the hell happened? Where's the countess? Where is the guy who took her?"

Braham lowered the tail of the plane to the grass and caught his breath.

"You look like shit, you know." Krol added and holstered his pistol. "You are covered with soot and bits of tar."

Braham grimaced. "As for the countess, she wasn't in there."

"She wasn't there?" Stiffler and Krol asked bewildered. "What do you mean she wasn't in there? Was Theurer in there?"

The three of them looked over at the wreckage of the hangar. Flames were leaping along wooden girders and over the bent frameworks that a few moments before had been airplanes.

"Reinhart, Jerzy look at me. She was not inside that building, understand?" The two looked at him, understanding beginning to dawn on them. Then Stiffler asked, "And Arndt? Where is Arndt? We saw him land a few minutes ago."

Braham shook his head. "I don't know anything about him. Last I saw he was in the library back at the von Teischen's house. You say he flew here?"

Krol looked toward where he had last seen the silver Messerschmitt. A large fire truck now occupied the space with a nozzle on its roof from which a helmeted fireman was playing a stream of water into the interior of the wrecked hangar.

"So what happened in there?" Krol asked. But it was Kleist who got the answer. He came up to Braham and asked, "Where is Theurer?" Braham looked at the SD officer and then at the smoking mess of wood and steel behind him and simply nodded his head toward it.

"He's in there, or what is left of him is. Unfortunately, he is a little overdone right now." Braham smiled and waited. He resisted the temptation to embellish but decided to be smart and not answer any unasked question.

It turned out to be a long morning. While the Templehof fire brigade did their best to ensure that the Führer would not notice the smoking wreck of the hangar when he arrived, Kleist along with Stiffler and Krol accompanied Braham back to the Adlon. For the next two hours Braham told the story of how Theurer told him that the Countess von Teischen would be released once Braham flew him out of the country, and then he and then he and Theurer had come to blows. During the struggle Theurer's gun went off, igniting some oily rags. Braham got out, Theurer did not, end of story.

Finally, Stiffler spoke up, "Hauptsturmführer, the man you were seeking is dead. What more do you need to know? Captain Braham is a guest of our government; he is in Berlin on a diplomatic mission. By his action this morning, he is deserving of our congratulations for ridding the Reich of a dangerous man and not to be subjected to an interrogation. If you please Captain Braham, Colonel Krol and I are expected for the ceremonies at Templehof."

Kleist had to acknowledge that there was nothing more that Braham could add. He would have enough to tell Heydrich and perhaps the American did not have to figure into his version at all. Standing to leave, a thought crossed his mind. "But what about the Countess, where is she?"

It was Krol's turn to chime in. "Hauptsturmführer, with all the power of the SD and Gestapo at your command, I am sure that it will be only a matter of time before she is found. After all you only have to search the routes from Wansee to Templehof. *Auf wiedersehen, Hauptsturmführer.*"

"You know, Harry," said Stiffler; "it would probably be a good idea if you simply skipped the ceremony. I don't think our leader would mind if you just hopped in your plane and went back to France this afternoon."

"Sounds like good advice to me too, Harry," Krol added.

Last Acts

Police the world over have been known to be slow to react to reports of missing persons. They have found that most often the "missing" person wanted to vanish. A bad debt, a rotten marriage, a love affair gone wrong, there was a laundry list of reasons people decide that they will drop out of sight. For the most part, they show up in a couple of days, contrite and embarrassed for the commotion their disappearance caused. The desk sergeant at the police station in barrio Nuevo Paris, one of Montevideo's working-class neighborhoods, was inclined not to take much notice of Senora Rigoni's complaints about her new tenant. Sergeant Caprone was Italian, like the lady standing in front of his desk, both had been born in the city, the children of immigrants who flooded Uruguay at the turn of the century. He wanted to help her, he really did. After all, she was a *paisan,* or close to it, in any event.

The sergeant rolled his eyes, but she just wouldn't stop yammering about her damned tenant. Then there was the smell coming from the apartment, what about the smell? She must be aware that this was the area of town that was home to the tanneries. Their smell never left you nostrils. Fat rendering, hides being tanned—the stench was awful throughout the barrio. Nuevo Paris, bah! Sergeant Caprone was certain that the old Paris didn't stink like this place. All right, all right, he would send some men by to check. Yes, they would come that very day. *Adios Senora Rigoni.*

It was nearly three o'clock when the pair of cops arrived. Late winter in Uruguay and the air was just warming up. Soon the heat would settle in and everyone would be making for the seafront just to get some fresh air from the Rio de la Plata. Senora Rigoni met the men as their car pulled up in front of the small hotel, Casa Azul, which provided her a living.

"Casa Azul? The white paint is peeling off. I don't see anything blue, do you?" Inspector León sat in the front passenger seat of the '32 Ford. Grimacing, he looked at the ramshackle building, nodded his head and shot a wad of tobacco-stained saliva out on to the curb. Detective Villegas, León's younger and very-much-on-probation partner sat behind the wheel waiting for instructions.

"Follow me detective. We shall talk to the complainant and take a look at this man's room. Did you bring your notepad? Yes? Good, the lesson begins now." And with that Inspector Reynaldo León hoisted his bulk out of the car and stood in front of Senora Rigoni.

The story was as she had told the desk sergeant. The man was a new tenant. He was Greek, or so his passport said, a Senor Heraclitus. He had been there about a month. No, he did not socialize with anyone. In truth, Senora Rigoni said, one never saw the man. He had given her a month in advance when he arrived.

No, she told the policemen, he did not get any mail at the hotel but then most of her guests seldom did, except for the Englishman on the top floor. That Mr. Kent received letters nearly every day. Well, who knows? He said he was a professor. Oh, yes, the Greek gentleman. Yes, she last saw him about a week ago. He had left the building in a hurry. It had been raining the night she saw him leave, and he was running down the street. After that she had not seen or heard him coming or going.

Senora Rigoni, once started, was impossible to shut up. As she reported at the station, the other guests began to complain to her about a peculiar smell. Inspector León was not surprised. Smells in that fleabag were nothing new. If she could, the proprietress would charge extra for fresh air, or what passed for it went the wind blew the stench of the tanneries away.

"Please let us see the room," the inspector asked.

Senora Rigoni nodded and fished out a key from a large ring that she had in her apron and led them up a narrow stair to the third floor. If it was not the stink from the sewers or the garbage rotting in the cans in the alley as they simmered in the growing heat, this odor was different. León knew before they reached the door what they would find. "Senora, perhaps you should let me unlock the door."

The woman looked at him and then, understanding, a look of terror crossed her face. "Certainly, senor."

It was hot up there in the hallway, and they could smell the odor, knowing that only one thing smelled that way. León supposed that even Villegas knew what was on the other side of the flimsy door. León signaled for quiet and put his ear to the door. From the other side came a dull humming. Taking the key, he unlocked the door and pushed it in. Then he stepped back as the humming of flies rose to a roar.

Squadrons of flies rose from the body. On the bed they found a man, naked, and tied to its iron frame with electrical cord. An old sock had been shoved into his mouth to stop his screaming, and a second mouth had been carved across his throat. There was nothing to identify the dead man, and they could only use the name under which he had registered, Aristides Heraclitus.

"Is this the man Senora?" León turned to look for the landlady. She was standing by the door, her fist in her mouth, trying to stifle a scream. All she could do was nod.

"Appears to be dead about a week," León said, but his partner was looking at a stack of books on a chair in the corner.

"Does he look Greek to you, sir?" asked Villegas.

"Hard to tell, detective, what with the decomposition and bloating. Maybe, why?"

"Well, for a Greek, he had an odd interest in Russian and German. There are two dictionaries here. Maybe that will give us something."

León looked over at the books his partner was holding. "You think so? That may be, but for the time being we will stick with his being Greek. Complications give me a headache. Besides, I have a feeling this will be just another one we will mark unsolved. In any case it is time for some refreshment. There is a café down near the seafront. They have the loveliest waitresses there."

———

Arndt Dietrich had stood at the rail of the battered freighter since sunrise. As the necklace of shore lights began to wink out as dawn swept over the land to the south he strained his eyes to catch a glimpse of Morro Castle at the entrance to Havana harbor. Everything up to this point had gone as Braham had told him. The woman from the American embassy had been at the airfield outside Zurich with travel papers and money.

The White Raven

His passenger had been in rough shape by the time he brought the plane into land. When Braham had brought her out of the burning hangar Dietrich could see blood on her face and clothes and shortly after taking off from Berlin the countess slumped over and remained that way until the bumping of the Messerschmitt's landing gear on the grass runway at their destination woke her. He hoped that the people who led her away would take care of her.

Two days of train travel and he was in Marseilles where he boarded the *Valparaiso*, a rust bucket tramp steamer bound for Havana with a mixed cargo picked up in a half dozen ports along the Mediterranean. Nine days later and he was only hours from Havana. Gracja was supposed to be there already. The nice lady from the embassy said she would be. Still, he could not leave the rail of the ship until he was sure.

As the *Valparaiso* inched its way up to the wharf Dietrich scanned the crowd on the pier. How would he find her in all these crowds? Surely she would not be allowed outside the customs office. And yet, there she was. A yellow dress and white hat, the image of the tropics, somehow she had made it there and nothing would keep them apart again.

———

Arriving in Moscow Mikhail Andropov found that there had been a number of changes. His boss, the vile General Petrenko had been replaced. Petrenko had of course as a fascist spy going back to the 1920s. Now he was lounging in a damp cell in the basement of the Lubyanka waiting for his nine-gram dose of lead. Who could have guessed? Well apparently someone had. Apparently the lovely Oksana was not the blushing ingénue that she appeared to be and had provided ample evidence, contrived to be sure to the NKVD collegium to rid the directorate of the man. She had been sent vis-à-vis Leningrad to root out traitors in the bosom of Moscow Center—so she did.

Oksana Malinina had made her choice for a man and as long as Mikhail treated her as she felt that she deserved, then she would see that his career would prosper. Yet as she romped through the bedroom with him on the night of his return from France he could not fully enjoy the experience. With Oksana's nakedness wrapped around his sleep would not come. He waited for the pounding on the door and his imminent arrest. Then a day went by, but nothing happened. Then another day went by and it was business as usual, no suspicious looks from others a Moscow Center, no mysterious coincidences, until after two weeks of sleepless nights he began to sense they weren't coming for him. Still, he remained wary.

The report of the death of Ryshkov from the Montevideo station could be taken either way, either he had succeeded in closing the case or as the boss said, "Death solves all problems. No man, no problem." Andropov knew that he could be blamed and taken to task. It was Oskar who saved Andropov's skin, with the assistance of Oksana. She was now his personal assistant, with the full knowledge of her superiors. Now she was working with him on the management of Oskar. His reports from Berlin of the intrigues between Heydrich and Himmler and the Abwehr were terse, but the crafty Oksana saw how with a little editing here and there her man would seem to the collegium to be the spy master of spy masters, at least until the next round of paranoia gripped the service.

———

The White Raven

Summer was a distant memory and the gusts of wind off the Mediterranean were damp with autumn rains. Braham followed the path up the brown hillside toward the low, stone house overlooking the slate blue sea. He had brought flowers; he could not remember what she liked, so he had a large bouquet made up by the hotel florist. Karl had said she would be there, waiting. Karl said she never left the place other than to ramble about the stony paths that led to the olive trees and the summer garden.

It was the crone Mathilde who saw him first. She was standing by a battered table under one of the sloping eaves that formed a galleria on the north face of the house. As he came forward she fixed her hard black eyes on him, warily watching each step he took. Like a mountain lion guarding its den, she was the protector of her charge. The place was bigger than Lieberman had first described. Zaharoff must have had made improvements; it was no longer just a few simple rooms, fit for an old man. There was now a long balcony that jutted out toward the sea, and there were new rooms with furnishings fit for a woman of means. Sir Basil was her patron, even though she had money of her own. Heydrich's machinations to seize her property in Germany had not prevented her from using funds in her several Swiss banks accounts.

Lieberman had filled him in on what had happened since that day in Berlin. He said that she seldom spoke. With Mathilde she had developed a kind of telepathy so that the servant almost always anticipated her wants and needs. The Countess von Teischen now lived a simple life. She retained her beauty, but something had happened to her in those last days in Germany. When Dietrich got her to Zurich, Lieberman whisked her away to a safe location. He could see she was injured and exhausted. One of Zaharoff's doctors from Bern came to examine her. He advised just a little rest, the bruises on her face would fade. He had treated the wound on her head that Theurer had given her, but she soon complained of headaches. At Zaharoff's request Lieberman took her to see another of his doctors. The physicians were perplexed; perhaps the effects of Theurer's blow were not simply superficial. She spent the winter of 1935 in a Swiss clinic overlooking the Thungersee. But there she began waking in the night to nightmares about a burning man who set the world on fire. At one point she shouted that she had strangled her friend. The nurses in the clinic gave her sedatives. When Lieberman came to see her, the doctors advised him that she required continued and indefinite rest under their care. But Zaharoff, sensing that they were more concerned about maintaining the steady stream of their fees, had the house in Provence made over for her. And here, watched over by Mathilde and with occasional visits by Zaharoff's personal physician, Gisela began to put the White Raven behind her.

"Yes, monsieur?" Mathilde said, as he reached the end of the path and stepped on to the flagged veranda.

"My name is Braham. I have come to see the Countess von Teischen."

"We have been expecting you. Please wait, and I will tell her you are here." Mathilde turned toward the door, but then turned back to him. "Monsieur, I must tell you that she has forgotten that name and title. She prefers to be called Gisela, please do not remind her of the past. Monsieur Lieberman has told me that you are of that time in Germany. Please, monsieur she has forgotten about Berlin and whatever happened to her there."

"I understand."

Mathilde went into the house and returned a few moments later. "She is on the veranda, I will take you to her."

Braham followed her into the house and through a long stone hallway into a much larger and newer room with two sets of tall French doors, were open to the view of the sea beyond. There on a wicker chaise sat Gisela, dressed all in white, looking out toward the dark line of the horizon.

Braham stepped forward toward her. She turned at the sound of his step, and he saw the smile that he remembered slowly spread over her face.

"Hello, Gisela."

THE END

Author's Notes

This story is based upon several historical facts. I have chosen to interweave them into a story of what might have been.

There was indeed an Air Olympiad that took place in the late summer of 1934. Called the *Challenge International de Tourisme 1934*, teams were recruited from Poland, France, Fascist Italy, Nazi Germany, and Czechoslovakia. The idea was that various national teams would fly around Europe to promote air tourism as well as to compete in areas of speed, fuel management and endurance. The 1934 event was the last in a series of such events. The teams in the 1934 race flew mainly low-winged monoplanes. The German team used both the Messerschmitt Bf-108 and the Fieseler Fi-97. Surviving Br-108s have been used by Hollywood as stand-ins for their more lethal descendent the Bf-109; they can be seen flying in movies such as *The Longest Day.*

The Nuremberg Nazi Party rally went ahead unimpeded on September 5, 1934. The young filmmaker Leni Riefenstahl became infamous for her film of the event, *Triumph of the Will.* Film clips of this unabashed paean to Adolf Hitler and his evil rule can often be seen on cable TV in the never-ending Second World War histories that certain channels run around the clock. Her second film, extolling the virtues of Aryan supremacy, was about the 1936

Olympics, during which Jesse Owens quite clearly debunked the myth of the Nazi superman.

From 1934 through 1945 Messerschmitt and its licensees built over 34,000 Bf-109 single-engine fighter airplanes. Clearly the most numerous of the Luftwaffe's front line fighter aircraft, it saw service from Russia to North Africa. The Spanish air force retired its last Bf-109 in 1965. (As a personal note, the author's father had four confirmed Bf-109 kills.)

During the period of this story, Vyacheslav Menzhinsky, Felix Dzerzhinsky's successor, ran the NKVD. Menzhinsky ran his vast operation from the comfort of his office couch. The comfort was short-lived. He, like many of his successors, ended up a victim of the service he helped to create.

The Intermarium was an often touted and discussed concept during the rise of Nazism. Like every such international body, its creation was plagued by national hubris and suspicion on the part of its proponents. One can only wonder what might have happened if the countries of Europe's bloodlands had forged a viable alliance.

Flanders, NJ
June 2015

Made in the USA
Columbia, SC
17 December 2018